AEONS

INFINITY ENGINES BOOK IV

ANDREW HASTIE

To Nanna Wyn, the oldest time traveller I know, one hundred and one and still going...

Other books in the Infinity Engines universe.

The Infinity Engines

Infinity Engines Origins

Infinity Engines Missions

1

THE KILLING

The silver blades of the weapon were buried deep into his back, a crimson stain spreading across Josh's white shirt like a red flower.

Caitlin sat huddled in the corner of the room, her eyes wild and filled with tears, screaming. 'It's not him. It's not him.'

Armed men came out of the walls; out of the bookshelves, out of mirrors, emerging from every vestige in the room. They wore the uniform of his Praetorian Guard, each one sworn to protect him, none of them believing that she could take his life.

He was their messiah, their founder, an immortal and yet there he lay, pallid and lifeless on the floor of the royal bedchamber, his existence extinguished with a many-bladed knife, ended by the woman who loved him the most.

'It's not him,' Caitlin screamed manically as they fought to restrain her. 'They've taken him.'

Swords were drawn in anger, every fibre of the guards' being was aching to exact revenge for their failure. Only their years of training prevented them from killing her where she stood.

Dragging her away, she pleaded with them. 'He's not in there. They've taken him.'

Lyra woke from the nightmare, her bedsheets soaked with sweat.

She shivered, not from the cold night air that moved the curtains of her open window, but at the memory of her dream.

2

CAITLIN

[The Great Library]

Caitlin was sitting in her office, hidden behind a fortress of books piled high on her desk. She should have been enjoying the latent energies of the dusty tomes, excited by the opportunity to explore the centuries of uncharted timelines contained within them, but she couldn't concentrate. Something else was bothering her.

There was nothing specific that she could put her finger on, but the irritability had grown over the last few days now, like a scratch she couldn't itch.

And it was getting worse.

Caitlin had been feeling out of sorts all that morning and when Penwynn, her new assistant, burst in with the news of a new discovery in Knossos, she had bitten the woman's head off for entering without knocking. The look of shock on her happy little face was still painful to recall. Caitlin apologised later, but it was inexcusable and totally out of character.

She found stupid little things really annoying: the order

of the books stacked on her shelves, the way the morning sun made patterns on her desk, the overpowering smell of Penwynn's perfume from the outer office.

So she decided it was time to reorganise.

It was usual practice for the newly-appointed Head of the Library to insist on changes. Every curator began their term of office by imposing their personality on the collection, some with radical and wide-ranging consequences. Caitlin hadn't gone so far as to initiate a dreaded re-indexing of the stacks, but that wasn't off the table, once she had got her own space in good order.

Taking one book from the top of the pile, she read the title.

'La Chanson de Saisnes by Jean Bodel.'

She closed her eyes, feeling the worn leather of the twelfth-century binding, letting its chronology slip through her fingers. The centuries rolled back as she wove into its timeline. The epic poems of Charlemagne, written at the time of the First Crusades, unwound temptingly, reminding her how much she loved medieval France and how she and Josh could really do with a holiday.

It would be their four-year anniversary next month and she wanted to do something special. Something that would distract Josh from his relentless search for a way to cure his mother.

'Hey,' Sim's voice broke Caitlin's reverie. 'You off somewhere?'

Her eyes snapped open. 'No,' she replied, putting down the book. 'Well, yes, maybe. I was thinking about taking Josh away somewhere, just for the weekend.'

Her stepbrother smiled, sliding a stack of books aside so he could sit on the desk.

'Ah, yes. Four years of marital bliss.'

She scowled at him. 'Don't start that again.'

'Well, it's about time he made an honest woman of you!'

'What does that even mean?'

Sim shrugged. 'No idea. I'm guessing it's something to do with the Victorians.'

'I don't need a ring on my finger. What I do need is someone to sort all of this out!' She waved at the piles of books scattered around the room. 'Master Dorrowkind's cataloguing of the indices was eccentric to put it mildly.'

'Pressures of the new job getting to you already?'

She laughed, pointing to the enormous diary open on the desk. 'Do you know how many meetings I've had in the last week? There are at least four department heads trying to resign over my appointment; a whole sub-guild of classicists threatening to go on strike and that's before we get to the fact that every librarian and his grandmother seem to think they have a better idea of how to re-index the collection than I do.'

As she spoke, a list of new messages appeared across the pages. Inscribing themselves across the smooth vellum in fluid copperplate, as if being written by an invisible hand.

Sim watched the notes move down the page.

'I heard there was a minor altercation last week.'

'Minor altercation! Master Ellerton tried to set fire to the lost scrolls of Herculaneum. Honestly it's like managing a bunch of school children, not respectable senior academics.'

He folded his arms. 'Well, if anyone can get them under control it's you. Your grandfather would be very proud of you. Youngest librarian to ever wear the chains,' he said, nodding to the heavy necklace of thin safety chains hanging on the back of her door.

She rubbed her neck, remembering the weight of them

during the investiture ceremony. 'They're purely ceremonial. No one could ever actually use those on the stacks.'

'Which brings me to the reason for my visit,' he said, his eyes glinting as he took out his almanac. 'My graduation is less than two weeks away and you've been avoiding my messages.'

'I've been a little busy,' she replied.

'Are you and Josh coming?'

Caitlin reached for her diary. 'I'm pretty sure I can,' she said, flicking through the pages. 'Josh might be harder to pin down. You're probably seeing more of him than I do.'

'Not me. He spends all of his time with Eddington. There are rumours he's close to finishing the engine.'

She sighed. 'He's been saying that for nearly a year.'

'Are you two okay?'

Caitlin found it impossible to lie to Sim, he knew her too well. There were no secrets between them and he used to joke that it was probably best she became a librarian because he could read her like a book.

'We would be, if we ever saw each other for more than ten minutes. He comes in to bed in the middle of the night and leaves before breakfast. Sometimes I don't think he even notices that I am there.'

'Well in his defence, the infinity engine is an important project.'

'So are people!' she snapped. 'All he seems to bloody care about is the Napoleon test!' There were tears gathering in the corners of her eyes.

'And the future of humanity,' Sim reminded her.

'I know, sorry. It's just that sometimes the Order seems to take all of him and there's nothing left for me.'

Sim put his almanac away and held out his hand. 'Cat, why don't you come and stay at the house for a couple of days? Lyra would love to see you and Mum has an entire pod of Spinosaurus in the baths. They make the most amazing symphonies at feeding time.'

Caitlin wiped the tears away with her sleeve like a ten-year-old.

'Does your father still cook the boar every Wednesday?'

'And most other nights. Mum and Lyra have persuaded him to go meat-free on Mondays.'

She stood up and closed her diary. 'Fine, let's go. I'm starving.'

3

NAPOLEON TEST

[Map Room, Copernicus Hall]

Shimmering ribbons of energy flared out from the small brass sphere, painting the walls of the chamber with lines of light. As the layers of the holographic model expanded and stabilised, tiny clusters of symbols flickered across Josh's vision. The complex algorithm of the engine was processing infinite quantities of data to plot the course of the last twelve thousand years.

'Temporal precision at ninety-four per cent,' intoned the voice of Professor Eddington.

Not good enough.

Josh heard the words form in his mind, the thoughts of the founder surfacing like a whale from the sea of his subconscious.

At first, it had been difficult to retain his identity. Keeping his father's consciousness from merging with his own was a constant challenge. The man's mind was vast and sometimes it felt as though he was drowning in a bottomless ocean of alien memories. There were so many lives, so much information, that it became difficult to see where he started and the founder finished.

It's only six percent. Josh replied.

The ghost of the old man appeared, as solid as the professor beside him. Josh learned not to stare, he knew it was nothing more than his mind playing tricks.

Six percent of twelve thousand years is seven-hundred and twenty, that's ten lifetimes. Tell Eddington he needs to recalibrate the Seldon Coefficient.

Caitlin insisted he see a psychologist who thought he was bi-polar, warning him that he would find it difficult to maintain a clear perception of reality without medication. Josh refused, he needed the old man — his knowledge was the key to finishing the engine.

'Try checking the Seldon Coefficient.'

Eddington frowned over his spectacles, his hands moving deftly through the layers of illuminated formulae until he found the relevant equation.

Josh was glad that they'd managed to recover the professor. The founder insisted that he was the only man for the job; his innate talent for temporal mechanics had been essential in refining the algorithm.

Dalton Eckhart had done such terrible things to the man, saving him from that ordeal was just one of the many secret adjustments Josh had made during the last four years.

'Seldon Coefficient optimised,' reported Eddington in his dull monotone. 'Temporal precision now at ninety-eight per cent.'

The blueprint for the engine was embedded inside Josh's mind, hidden among the thousand years of collected memories of a man he hardly knew.

When Josh explained to the High Council how he could build a temporal model of the last twelve thousand years, they laughed. Konstantine, the Grandmaster of the Antiquarians, scoffed at the idea, saying: 'Such a device would be nothing short of magic,' and he was right. Designed by a civilisation far more technologically advanced than their own, it did seem impossible to imagine.

Professor Eddington wore his usual stoic expression throughout the entire session, but approached Josh once the others had left and questioned him further on the finer details of the temporal equations. It was all there, stored away in the memories of the founder, like a treasure chest waiting to be unlocked.

'Expanding linear regression,' remarked the professor, his hands a blur as they moved over the ever-expanding cloud of algebra.

The engine was the missing piece of the puzzle. After countless reboots and minor adjustments he'd finally managed to build a timeline that was as close to the original without the Nihil. Four years had passed in his linear age, but for him it was more like twenty. This was timeline 421 and for the most part it was a success, the Order was stable, Caitlin was alive, and there had been no global catastrophes, although climate change was beginning to worry him.

Focus on the task at hand, interrupted the ghost, pointing at the vortex of timelines which had begun to settle into a distinct pattern.

'Stabilising,' reported Eddington.

. . .

And suddenly there it was.

A perfect model of every event and interaction of the past twelve thousand years.

In the founder's original design, it was never possible to focus on the life of an individual, but using Eddington's brilliant mind they were able to improve the algorithm. The professor and a select group of his actuaries spent over eighteen months refining the formulae so that Josh could trace the effect of a single man.

The professor looked over to Josh, gesturing as if inviting him to try it for himself.

Josh raised his hand, letting the lines flow around his fingers, feeling the familiar frisson as the power caressed his skin.

Moving through the lines of temporal flux, he located a nexus and enlarged it with a tiny movement of his finger and thumb.

'Seventeen sixty-eight,' the professor read the symbols that expanded around it. 'Corsica.'

Josh nodded, twisting the cluster until he found what he was looking for.

'Target acquired: Napoleon Bonaparte.'

They watched the central timeline of the man's life expand as thousands of other lines branched away from it. The Napoleonic test had always failed up until now. His influence on nineteenth century Europe had been too complex for the most advanced Copernican calculus.

'Amazing,' said Eddington, staring in awe at the beauty of the structure.

Josh felt the relief wash over him.

'I may still need to make some small refinements,' he lied. It was perfect, but he needed an excuse to come back. 'To the Von Neumann stability matrix.'

'Of course,' agreed Eddington. 'I will instruct the guards.'

4

NIGHT GARDENS

[Chapter House. Date: 1880]

Dinner was served in the Viking longhouse as usual. There were over forty guests sitting on both sides of the fifty-foot solid oak table that Eric the Red had allegedly cut from a single tree. Sim's father, Methuselah, had attached the building to the Chapter House as a temporary dining hall when Caitlin was ten. Twelve years later it was still hosting the evening meal for the De Freis family and all of their guests. She'd missed the homely atmosphere, it had always been one of her favourite places when she was growing up. A rose-tinted memory, filled with the aromas of exotic food, palatial bedrooms and enthralling tales from travellers who roamed across thousands of years.

Except this time the scent of roasting boar was making Caitlin feel nauseous. She hid it well, smiling and chatting with Alixia, Sim's mother, while pushing the meat around her plate and taking small bites of vegetables.

Sitting opposite her, Sim was in deep conversation with his brother, Phileas. He was the eldest of the De Freis siblings, a dark-haired man who followed in the footsteps of his father as a temporal architect, and who generally disagreed with nearly everything Sim said.

Lyra was nowhere to be seen.

'They have the most dynamic of ranges,' Alixia continued, 'at least four octaves.'

Caitlin was only half listening. Alixia had a passion for prehistoric creatures and could talk for hours on her research. She was a xenobiologyst and an extinction curator, one who liked to bring her work home, and who usually took over the baths, a vast flooded Byzantine chamber connected to the basement, which was currently home to a pod of previously extinct aquatic dinosaurs.

'How's the new job?' asked Alixia, pouring a large glass of red wine and handing it to Caitlin.

'Fine,' she replied, taking a sip and grimacing at the strange taste.

Alixia looked concerned and took the glass. 'Is it corked?' she said, sniffing the wine and sampling it herself. 'No.'

Caitlin shrugged. 'Something wrong with my tastebuds I guess.'

Alixia felt her forehead. 'Are you sickening for something?'

'I'm just tired, they've been keeping me busy and Josh —'

'Should be taking care of you, not burning the candle at both ends trying to build that infernal machine!'

Alixia's eyes darkened and there was fire in her cheeks. 'Sim's been telling me what he's been up to. Grandmaster Konstantine is making all sorts of complaints to the Council. The Antiquarians are very unhappy about its development, but Eddington insists that it's vitally important to the future of the Order.'

Caitlin felt an uncontrollable surge of emotion, her cheeks burned hot and she fought to hold back the tears. 'He's just trying to save his mother.'

'But at what cost?' Alixia snapped.

Lyra walked into the dining hall.

Her stepsister looked pale, with large baleful eyes and wet, tangled hair. She came directly to Caitlin and hugged her tightly like a lost child. Her skin was cold and Caitlin felt Lyra shivering in her arms.

'Where have you been?' Her mother asked, running her hands through Lyra's wet hair.

'Swimming,' Lyra replied, releasing her grip on Caitlin.

Alixia frowned. 'The baths are off-limits.'

Lyra shrugged, picking up the meat that lay untouched on Caitlin's plate. 'I like their songs. They soothe me.'

Caitlin noticed there were fresh scars on Lyra's bare arms.

Her stepsister was a seer, a rare talent within the Order. Born with the ability to read the timelines of people in a similar way that Caitlin could use artefacts, but unlike her ability to travel back in time, seers could look into potential futures, the ways not yet taken.

It drove many of them to madness and eventually suicide. Lyra had sailed very close to the edge on a number of occasions.

'I had a dream about you,' she said in her childlike voice, twirling a strand of her damp hair around her finger. 'It was full of tears.'

'Let her finish her meal,' her mother insisted, but Caitlin pushed the plate away, she really wasn't that hungry.

'It's okay,' said Caitlin, taking Lyra's hand. 'Tell me in the garden.'

The Chapter House was the nearest place Caitlin had ever had to a home. Her parents had disappeared during an expedition when she was ten, leaving her in the care of Alixia and Methuselah De Freis. It was a staging post and boarding house for time travellers, built using various rooms borrowed from the last seven hundred years. Disparate sections of old palaces were connected together behind what seemed, from the outside, to be a respectable three-storey Georgian townhouse, but within it was an eclectic mansion; hundreds of rooms that could be expanded to accommodate an unlimited number of guests.

The night garden was another of Caitlin's favourite places. Lyra's father had created it especially for his daughter. Trapping a perfectly still, cloudless midnight in a permanent moonlit loop. They walked barefoot on the dewy grass, letting the cold drops wash over their feet and made their way down to the small pond to watch the dragonflies.

Lyra hummed to herself as they walked, reminding Caitlin of the day she first met the troubled five-year-old.

When her parents went missing, Rufius Westinghouse had taken Caitlin to the Chapter House and left her in the care of Alixia De Freis and her young family. Lyra was the only other girl and they instantly bonded. Caitlin became the older sister that Lyra never had. Back then, it was obvious that she had a unique talent. There had always been a certain 'other-worldliness' about Lyra, even after she stopped believing in fairies and unicorns.

Until she tried to kill herself.

Seers were fragile souls, susceptible to psychosis and addictions. Lyra's early teenage years were more traumatic than most. Struggling to deal with the raging hormones and an overactive sex drive, she also carried the burden of being an empath and when she discovered reaving everything went quickly downhill.

Reaving was forbidden, and so it attracted the rebellious and curious alike. It involved reading the timeline of the dying, in a quest to understand the afterlife. Reavers became obsessed with death and the dead, dressing in black and hanging out around graveyards and battlefields. They were generally shunned by the rest of their guild, seen as heretics by some and mad by most.

In extreme cases, some would even practise on themselves. Lyra's arms were a testament to her experiments.

When Lyra was fourteen, Caitlin found her lying on the cool grass of the night garden, her blood turned black in the silver light of the moon.

They stood by the pool, the statue of the dragon reflected in the still pool, its two koi carp floating near the surface, waiting for food.

'When you first met Josh did you know?' asked Lyra, sitting down by the water's edge.

'Know what?'

'That he was the one.'

Caitlin thought back to the first time she saw him in the library. She knew that someone would come, the Copernicans had already predicted it, but had no idea who it would be. There was no hiding the fact that she was pleased to find the handsome boy wandering around in the Second World War section.

'Not at first, no. There was something dangerous about him. Like Rufius, you could never tell what he was going to do next.'

Lyra dipped her toes into the pool of still water.

'Not like a Copernican then?'

'No.' Caitlin watched the ripples move across the pool, disturbing the tapestry of reflected stars and wondered how different her life might have been if she'd never met him.

'Does he make you happy?'

Lyra always asked direct questions, it was an innate ability to see right to the heart of the matter and it was really annoying.

She sat down beside her. 'He used to. Things are different now, more complicated.'

'How are they different?'

Caitlin sighed. 'We have responsibilities. Other things that get in the way. We have to make sacrifices for the good of the Order.'

Lyra walked into the pool, the hem of her dress spreading out into the water. 'Would you like to hear about my dream?'

'Yes,' replied Caitlin, relieved to be changing the subject.

'It's not a very nice one.'

'I don't care. It's only a dream, it can't hurt you.'

'Well, that's not strictly true. Seers' dreams are different. There's always a chance that ours may come to pass. Like fatecasting.'

Lyra stood perfectly still, letting the pond settle, until she seemed to be standing in the middle of the stars.

'I saw Josh die.'

'Really? How?'

Lyra paused, biting her lip as if unsure of what to say next. 'You killed him. Stuck a knife into his back.' She made a violent stabbing motion with her hand.

Caitlin laughed. 'I think I'd probably use a gun.'

Lyra pouted. 'It's not funny.'

'I'm sorry sis, but it's just a dream — it just means you're worried about us, and you're right there is something that needs to be fixed, but that's what relationships are about: dealing with the tough times as well as the good ones.'

'So you're not going to kill him?'

'Annoying as he can be, no I don't think it would ever come to that.'

'Good.' Lyra clapped her hands together and leapt out of the pool. 'I don't think it would be nice for the baby to grow up without a father.'

'What?'

'You're pregnant,' Lyra cooed, stroking Caitlin's belly. 'It's a boy.'

5

LINEAR A

[Knossos, Crete. Date: May 20, 1941]

The low drone of the Luftwaffe's Junkers Ju52s rumbled over the Psiloritis mountains. Rufius ducked out of sight beneath the shade of a tamarisk tree. It was hot, perhaps nearing forty degrees in the midday sun, and he felt the sweat run under the collar of the paratrooper's uniform. He took a long cool drink of water from his flask and waited for the planes to pass.

Looking down into the stony valley through a pair of modified German field glasses, he could make out the ruins of the Minoan palace. The Antiquarian lenses accentuated every detail, annotating historical data onto the magnified remains of the ancient building.

'Looks like we're too late,' Rufius said to Rollins, handing him the field glasses.

George Rollins was a short, sturdy man, with close-cropped hair and sharp eyes. He raised the binoculars to his face and studied the excavation below.

Billowing clouds of dust and smoke marked the arrival

of the German tank division. They heard the crack of gunfire as the locals tried to defend their homes, scattering into the fields as two Panzers roared into their village, followed by a column of Nazi paratroopers.

'What are you going to do?' asked Rollins, adjusting the focus.

It was a reasonable question, and in any other situation Rufius would have dignified it with a sensible answer, but today was turning out to be something of an unusual day. It had begun with a flurry of messages from the Copernican monitoring station in 1953, who thought they had detected a temporal anomaly right in the middle of his least favourite war. The powers-that-be then decided, in their infinite wisdom, to send an overseer, Rollins, to ensure that Rufius didn't create an adverse event while investigating the issue.

He hated ride-alongs. What he did was not for the faint-hearted, changing the past was a subtle art and not something that could be learned from a manual, and it certainly wasn't a spectator sport.

Rufius worked alone.

Rollins handed him back the glasses. Then, taking out his notebook and pencil from inside his jacket, he waited for Rufius's response.

The mission briefing had given Rufius the background on the excavation: discovered by Arthur Evans in 1900, the archaeologist and his team worked for five years to uncover the remains of the palace and a civilisation which he named 'Minoan' after their King Minos. It was a neolithic site which developed into an advanced cultural centre by 2000 BC with a population of over one hundred thousand.

Previously, a Draconian survey team classified the

Minoans at level seven: no temporal significance. This completely overlooked the fact that during the excavation, Evans discovered three thousand or more clay tablets which were written in a hieroglyphic language that no one had ever seen.

There were two distinct forms, known as 'Linear A' and 'B', both of which confounded numerous Scriptorian researchers for years, driving some of them to madness. Finally, fifty years after they were unearthed and much to the dismay of the bookworms, a young Antiquarian by the name of Ventris deciphered the archaic syntax of Linear B and unlocked five hundred years of early Greek history.

No one had the first idea as to why the Führer would suddenly become interested in the site or its archaic language. The temporal implications of the Third Reich's activities were being mapped out in ever-changing formulae across the pages of Rollins's almanac as an entire Copernican department tried to predict what Hitler was going to do next.

But there were too many unknowns, too many gaps in their model and when that happens, they call in a Watchman.

'Whatever they've found, it's brought them to the palace,' said Rufius, putting the binoculars back into their leather case. 'We need to get closer.'

Rollins nodded, making a series of notes in a cryptic shorthand. 'In time or space?'

'Both,' replied Rufius, taking out his tachyon. The casing was heavily scratched, worn from constant use. 'But first we need to get out of these uniforms and into something less likely to get us shot.'

They were both dressed as *Fallschirmjäger,* German paratroopers, who had been deployed for the first time in the Second World War, but it hadn't gone well. The local resistance had fought back hard and the Germans had suffered heavy casualties before they could establish a base of operations at Knossos.

6

NAPLEON OF NEUROSES

[Map Room, Copernicus Hall]

It was the middle of the night, and the map room was empty. Eddington's team had gone to celebrate the success of the Napoleon test.

Josh rolled his hand gently over the smooth surface of the Infinity Engine, feeling the metal warm to his touch.

He hesitated before opening the model. It had taken so long to reach this moment, hiding the real motive from everybody, even Caitlin. Although it seemed to take little more than a year in linear time to build the engine, it was far longer in elapsed time. Spending thousands of hours in alternate versions of this timeline, Josh studied the eventualities of every minor change, perfecting the algorithm that was dancing around inside his head, trying to improve the chances for his mother.

But nothing seemed to change the outcome.

In fact, in most cases it made it worse — his mother was still dying.

He was becoming desperate. Frustrated by the power to change the past and future of the human race, yet unable to change the fate of one woman.

All that was left was finding a cure for his mother's condition and the engine was his last hope.

Caitlin complained that it was becoming an obsession, spending every waking hour in the map room with Eddington working on the device. And perhaps it was; somehow Josh found it easier to focus on trying to fix his mother than confess to Caitlin that there was a ghost rattling around in his head.

No one within the Order had any idea of the founder. Josh carefully rebuilt the entire organisation without the knowledge of the original architect. Preferring to leave its governance in the hands of the High Council, he took a back seat, following in the footsteps of the Colonel and joining the Watchmen. It was a job that allowed him to move about in the past without raising any concerns and allowing him to make the adjustments to improve his mother's chances.

He opened the timeline at 1868.

'Jean-Martin Charcot,' he said to himself, singling out the man's chronology as a branching line of red amongst the gold threads.

From his research into the early pioneers of neurology, Josh learned that Charcot was a professor of anatomical pathology at Pitié-Salpêtrière Hospital in Paris and one of the first physicians to identify multiple sclerosis. His plan involved sharing enough knowledge with Charcot to accelerate the treatment of the disease in the present day. It was a trick he learned from Fermi, and it was a misuse of their power.

To adapt the timeline for their own ends went against everything for which the Order stood. It was a rule that Josh had instilled in them from the very beginning.

Josh studied Charcot's timeline and those of his students, watching the web of individual lives that spread out from the one man, following the development of the science through the next one hundred and fifty years.

'Risk of change?' he asked, realising too late that he had spoken it aloud.

No significant threat, said the ghost.

The founder walked over to join him, squinting at the formulae surrounding the lines Josh selected. *Although there is always an underlying risk when adjusting the timeline, none of those affected can be classified as significant actors.*

Taking knowledge into the past always came with risk; Caitlin used to say it was like giving a nuclear weapon to a five-year-old, but Josh had tried everything else and this was his last, best hope of finding a cure.

Posing as a visiting English doctor interested in Charcot's research, Josh went to the Salpêtrière Hospital in Paris 1882, and joined one of his lectures. It was a long, detailed medical monologue in French. The founder translated the most interesting parts, but Josh found it hard to follow, science never being his strong point.

Afterwards, the doctor invited him to observe one of his hysterical demonstrations.

In a room packed with sombrely dressed medical students, Josh watched as a female patient known as 'Blanche' was wheeled into the room in a semi-catatonic state.

He knew the look only too well, his mother suffered similar seizures. Like a grand mal, the muscles of Blanche's face were twisted in spasm and her arms made sharp, jerking motions, prompting the assistants to strap the patient to the chair.

Charcot hypnotised her in a matter of minutes, bringing her out of her mania and proceeded to ask her a series of questions that she was able to answer like any other sane human being.

He was not the kind of neurologist that Josh expected. The aptly named 'Napoleon of Neuroses' was something of a tyrant, and Josh soon realised that passing on the knowledge to such a man was going to prove more difficult than he thought. The learned doctor was not about to take the word of a complete stranger on a subject that hardly anyone else was taking seriously.

The colonel warned him many times of the inherent problems with trying to manipulate the past. 'It's never just a case of whom to adjust, but also how,' the Watchman told him in his usual gruff way. 'The more influential the individual, the less likely they were to be open to the ideas of others, especially if it challenges their theories.'

So it was with Charcot when Josh approached him after the demonstration.

'Non Monsieur,' said the doctor, shaking an angry finger at Josh. 'These so-called "new developments" are nothing but fantasy. I have spent years studying the workings of the mind and you, a mere boy come to me with this!'

The doctor tore up Josh's notes and threw them on the floor.

Josh realised then that Charcot was never going to listen and that he was going to have to try a more radical approach.

7

KONSTANTINE

[British Museum]

Grandmaster Konstantine pored over the plans of the new tachyon, scrutinising the intricate details with a large magnifying lens. His engineers had been slaving over the Mk VI refinements for five years and his chief artificer, Magnus Bailey, stood on the other side of the desk like a nervous schoolboy awaiting punishment.

The tachyon was a highly complex piece of temporal engineering. Originally developed to act like a temporal compass, it quickly became the most important item of equipment in the field.

The Antiquarians were very proud of their creation. Its ability to bring operatives back from distant times with the click of a button or rewind the last two minutes had saved countless lives.

'You've integrated a radio receiver?' he asked, hardly masking the sarcasm from his voice.

'Two-way communications,' the chief corrected him.

'The Copernicans will argue that is the purpose of the almanac.'

Bailey took a deep breath and delivered the line that he had been rehearsing for months. 'This is instantaneous. You can speak to anyone, in any time period, instantly.'

'And how exactly do I do that?' asked Konstantine, holding it up to his ear.

The engineer took out his own model and pressed the third button on the side of the casing.

'Call Grandmaster Konstantine,' he said, walking towards the outer office.

A light flashed on the side of the Grandmaster's tachyon as Bailey closed the door behind him.

'We've established a listening post in the eleventh century, the operators can route your request in under six seconds.' His voice came out of a small speaker on the side of the Mk VI.

Konstantine looked impressed.

'And what do we do if we're unable to answer?' he said, holding down the talk button.

'There's an answering service, which transcribes the message and sends it to their almanac.'

'Very good. How long before we can get these into production?'

'A matter of weeks. The production facility has already started on the tooling.'

'There's one other function I wanted to propose.'

The chief engineer opened the door and stepped back into the office. 'Which is?'

'Remote detonation.'

Bailey looked concerned.

Konstantine held up the prototype. 'To ensure that this never falls into the wrong hands.'

'I'm not sure other members of the Council would agree.'

The Grandmaster stamped the blueprint with his official seal and handed it back to the chief.

'Let's keep it to ourselves shall we.'

After Bailey left, Konstantine rose from his chair and walked over to the window. His office looked out over the Great Courtyard of the British Museum. This was the heart of the Antiquarian guild, filled with artefacts from thousands of years of dead civilisations. A mere two percent were on display for the general public while millions more sat below in the vaults.

The museum was a terminus for the Order. Thousands of time travellers used its artefacts every day to take them to the furthest corners of history.

His guild kept history alive, guarding its most precious treasures and ensuring the safety of those that used them.

And none of them knew about his secret. He smiled inwardly at how easy it had been to infiltrate them, they were blinded by their arrogance.

All except for the mysterious Joshua Jones. His engine could expose everything, thousands of years of careful planning could be ruined if he wasn't stopped.

'Sir, excuse the intrusion, but we've had a rather cryptic message from Special Acquisitions,' his assistant said, waving a piece of paper as he came through the door.

'What is it Cummings?' Konstantine snapped. The man knew better than to enter without knocking, so it was obviously important.

Cummings's hand was shaking when he handed over the note. It had all the usual official Antiquarian codings to prove its authenticity, followed by two words:

KNOSSOS 1941.

'Get me Kellerman.'

8

LYRA

The Grand Seer sat hunched over his desk studying the wing of a butterfly through an array of glass lenses. It shimmered iridescently under the lamplight while Kelly compared the colours against jars of chemical compounds.

'With love's light wings did I o'er-perch these walls, for stony limits cannot hold love out,' he recited to himself, picking up a fine sable brush and adjusting his lenses. He dipped the brush into the first of the compounds and applied it to the wing of a mechanical model.

It was a delicate thing, with a tiny golden thorax no thicker than the wick of a candle. As he breathed, the fine silver wings trembled, causing him to hold his breath until he laid down the first of the colours.

Lyra stepped out from a long, dark mirror which stood at the far end of his study.

'What have I told you about using the shadow paths?' Kelly mumbled without taking his eyes from his work.

She laughed, pulling a cobweb out of her hair. 'That they're full of dust and forgotten ways?'

He raised a single finger, warning her not to approach.

'Do you know what befalls a pixie who strays from the moonlit way?' he asked, cleaning the brush in a glass of water and dipping it into another compound.

'Forever to walk on the graves of men and ne'er the sun shall touch the fay,' Lyra finished the poem.

Kelly turned slightly, his cloak of black feathers rustling like the wind through autumn leaves, and placed the butterfly carefully back onto the leaf of a wild orchid.

'There are worse things than the fay in the shadow realm.'

Lyra dropped a small curtsy. 'Indeed master, and you have yet to teach me their names.'

'Names are powerful things, they must be given their due,' he said, applying the second colour to the wing. The two compounds matched the original pattern exactly.

'So what brings you here at such an hour?' asked Kelly, waving at a large grandfather clock ticking morosely in the corner.

Lyra thought it looked rather uncomfortable, wedged between two grand bookcases and possessing only the hour hand, it was hard to tell how far past two o'clock in the morning it was.

'My troublous dreams this night doth make me sad,' quoted Lyra, collapsing into one of the old leather armchairs.

Kelly stroked his long beard. 'Dreams is it? Of bloody deeds and death?'

She nodded and went on to tell him about the murder of Josh.

He listened intently, stopping her only to describe the

blade in more detail, then handed Lyra a piece of paper and a pencil so that she could draw the many-bladed dagger.

Lyra finished the sketch and handed it to him. There were tears drying on her cheeks, but she couldn't remember when she started crying.

'Dreams should always be taken with a pinch of snuff. I dream of my own demise at least once a week, yet here I stand,' he said, scratching a series of symbols onto her drawing with his quill. 'But this blade intrigues me. You've never seen it before?'

She shook her head as he handed back the paper.

'Go to Cuvier in Paris and show him. He may know what kind of weapon it was.'

Lyra thanked him and walked towards the mirror.

'Use the door,' he reminded her, picking up his brush once more.

9

FATHERHOOD

[Rothes Glen House, Banffshire, Scotland. Date: Present day]

Caitlin lay in bed listening to the storm winds shake the trees. Going to the house to be alone had seemed like a good idea, but pulling the blankets a little higher, she was beginning to wish she'd stayed at the Chapter House with Sim and Lyra.

It was a Scottish baronial mansion that came with the position of Head of Library. An eleven-bedroom house with a square central turret of four storeys, the top floor of which she'd converted into a bedroom.

Opening her almanac, Caitlin checked for any messages from Josh, but as usual there were none.

Rain lashed the windows and she gave up trying to sleep and went to sit by the fire with a stack of reports on Knossos, trying to distract herself from the conversation she was rehearsing in her head.

After five minutes of agonisingly boring indexing schedules, she changed her mind and scribbled a note to Josh.

Come home soon.
Then, crossing out *soon*, she wrote *now*.

Josh was working alone in the map room when he got the message. His almanac shuddered in his pocket as if some part of her anger had been transferred along with the note.

He looked at the slant of her handwriting as it flowed across the page. Caitlin had a beautiful, old-fashioned style that made his own look like something an illiterate five-year-old would do.

When she crossed out the soon, he knew it was serious.
Time to go home.

Although he could step back to any part of their life and pretend he'd never been away, Josh found life was simpler between them if he lived it in a linear way. Trying to remember what had happened last week when you'd spent the previous month in another timeline was hard, and generally led to deep meaningful silences and sarcastic remarks.

Over the last four years, as Josh learned to control the founder's memories, their relationship had failed more than once. His father's thoughts would surface like a drunk uncle at a wedding, random facts would appear unannounced, disrupting whatever he was doing. Various versions of Caitlin had noticed he would speak differently, using new words or read books in languages of which even she'd never heard.

Once, she even thought that he was showing signs of a mental breakdown and insisted he see a psychologist.

Doctor Falret was an eminent French psychiatrist

studying 'circular insanity' in Paris in the 1850s. He was Director of the Pitié-Salpêtrière Hospital, thirty years before Charcot. Josh hated hospitals after the countless visits to his mother's bedside and this one had once been a prison for the prostitutes of Paris.

Falret examined Josh, subjecting him to the most random examinations and treatments, including an early form of electro-convulsive therapy, that had left Josh paralysed for three hours.

The doctor told them he suspected it was the early symptoms of bipolar disorder, whose effects would only grow worse over time. He proposed a course of lithium salts and a less stressful lifestyle.

Josh ignored the advice, reset the timeline and found his own way to deal with the ghost in his head.

With practice, he managed to create a mental construct that he called 'The Archives'. The entire collection of the founder's memories were organised into a virtual museum inside his head.

Hiding the fact that he was hosting another mind from Caitlin still came with consequences. It created a distance between them, as if she could sense that something was wrong and slowly a tension formed like scar tissue around the things that were not said.

'We need to talk,' Caitlin whispered into the darkness.

'It's one o'clock in the morning,' replied Josh, sliding under the blankets and snuggling up to her back. 'Can't it wait?'

'No,' she snapped, moving his hand away from her breast. 'You're never here when I wake up.'

He sighed into her neck and she felt the hairs rise. The

heat from his body was warm and comforting and he smelled good, but the last thing she wanted right now was sex.

Caitlin spent most of the day thinking of how she was going to break it to Josh. Wondering how he would take it. They hadn't really discussed starting a family, and with her new job the timing could have been better. She thought about not telling him and seeing if he noticed, but he was so preoccupied with his work, he probably wouldn't.

'I'm pregnant. We're going to have a son.'

The words still felt strange in her mouth, even after she rehearsed them in front of the bathroom mirror. The idea that there was another life growing inside her hadn't really sunk in. In fact, nothing felt quite right, it was as if they'd crossed into some alternate timeline. No amount of books on the subject could prepare her for the way she was feeling.

So she opted for the simple approach — just put it out there and see what happened.

Josh's breathing seemed to stop and so did time while she waited for his response.

'How?' he asked, sitting up.

Caitlin turned towards him. 'How do you think?'

'No, I mean when?'

'About ten weeks ago, I think. That night we got drunk celebrating my new job.'

She was glad it was dark. So that she couldn't see the look on his face. From the way he was reacting there was a good chance she would have punched it by now.

'Wow.'

Better, she thought, beginning to relax a little.

'Are you sure?'

Not so good.

'Yes, I saw Doctor Crooke yesterday. Are you going to ask me how I feel?'

There was an awkward pause.

'It's just a bit of a shock.'

'A good one?'

Again there was a long pause. She could feel her pulse quickening.

'Josh? Say something, you're worrying me.'

She felt his hand touch her shoulder and then pull her close.

He kissed her. 'I never thought I'd be a dad.'

'And?'

'And it's weird to think that there's a baby in there,' he whispered, his hand stroking her belly.

'Tell me about it.'

'Have you told your parents?'

'Not yet.'

She cannot stay in this timeline, the child will be at risk. The founder's voice echoed Josh's own concerns.

'I have some news too.'

'This is my moment,' she said, laying down on her stomach and pulling down the blankets. 'You can start by massaging my back.'

'Does it ache?'

'No, but you need the practice.'

10

SPECIAL ACQUISITIONS

[Knossos, Crete. Date: May 28, 1941]

The German army were moving off to the South in pursuit of the retreating Allied forces, leaving a small contingent of walking wounded to guard the scientists who were encamped at Knossos.

Rufius and Rollins exchanged their paratrooper uniforms for peasant clothes, only to find that the area around the site was deemed off-limits to the locals. Everyone was being treated as partisan resistance, and some had even been shot.

The Copernicans had infiltrated ULTRA, the signals intelligence division at Bletchley Park, who were intercepting Enigma encrypted messages being sent to Nazi High Command. Amongst the thousands of military communiques they discovered a series of reports on Knossos. These were allegedly from Ahnenerbe, a research division of the Nazi Science Directorate under Heinrich Himmler. They spoke of finding something of 'incredible archaeological value', but remained vague about what exactly it was.

Based on the type of heavy machinery being off-loaded from the trucks, it was clear that they were planning on re-opening the excavation.

'I think we should inform headquarters,' Rollins said nervously. It was obvious he wasn't comfortable being this close to reality.

Rufius ignored him and started towards the barbed-wire fence that was being hastily erected around the perimeter.

Two guards were taking a break from setting the wire, sitting on an embankment smoking Turkish cigarettes, whilst dark patches of sweat seeped through their shirts, their jackets and helmets hanging on a nearby tree.

One of them spotted Rufius coming across the field and picked up his rifle.

It was unbearably hot out of the shade and Rufius could tell by their red faces how unaccustomed they were to the southern climate. He held the wineskin aloft as he walked towards them, knowing that no one ever got shot for bringing a thirsty man a drink.

'Both hands! Up!' ordered the guard in passable Greek, shouldering his weapon and sighting it at Rufius's head.

He did as he was told, revealing that his other hand held a loaf of bread.

The man's eyes widened. Rufius had guessed that their rations would be running low. The supply ships were being held off the coast by the British Navy and the locals had run off into the mountains with all the provisions.

'Lunch!' said Rufius, in a thick Greek accent, repeating it in German.

The man lowered his gun and waved him forward.

As he reached the fence, a German officer appeared in full uniform and time slowed.

. . .

'What are you doing here Westinghouse?' the man asked, tapping a cigarette against a silver case.

Rufius didn't recognise him, but the fact he was inside a temporal distortion field and speaking in perfect English was enough to identify him as another member of the Order.

'Copernicans sent me.'

'Did they now?' the officer said, looking over at Rollins. 'Must be some kind of mix up back at HQ. We're in charge of this site now, so you can stand down.'

'And who are you exactly?'

The man's eyes narrowed slightly, unsure as to whether Rufius needed to know.

'Kellerman, Special Acquisitions,' he said, pulling back his sleeve to show the Ouroboros tattoo.

'And what does the Antiquarian Guild want with this site?'

The officer shrugged. 'Grandmaster Konstantine's orders.'

'I was sent here to investigate a temporal anomaly.'

'That's all in hand now. I think you'll find your orders have changed.'

The man snapped his fingers and time returned to normal.

As Rufius walked back to Rollins he could hear Kellerman berating the guards for leaving their posts.

'We've been recalled,' said Rollins with a sigh of relief.

'So I hear,' replied Rufius, taking out his almanac. 'When did Evans find the tablets?'

'1900.'

'I'll meet you back at base.'

And with that he disappeared.

11

MOTHER

'Doctor Crooke has made your mother as comfortable as possible,' the nurse explained while walking beside Josh through the cloisters of Bedlam.

Crooke's clinic was based in the seventeenth century and had none of the benefits of modern medicine. They had something better: Crooke's potions could harness time. Josh had no idea how he did it, but the foul smelling concoctions could accelerate healing or slow down the progression of a debilitating disease like MS.

His mother suffered with relapsing, remitting multiple sclerosis for most of his teenage years, but now she'd developed the secondary-progressive stage with all the other complications that came with it.

MS was the demon that Josh spent most of his life trying to defeat. Of all the monsters he encountered since discovering the Order, it was the only one he never managed to beat. It clung to his mother like a shadow, a terrible curse that nothing seemed to be able to lift.

The stasis chamber that Crooke constructed for his mother reminded Josh of the *Nautilus*. She was resting inside a large brass cylinder which, the doctor explained, was the temporal equivalent of a hyperbaric chamber; the kind that divers used when coming up from the deep. Crooke was using it to gradually reduce the effect of time on the body, slowing down the ageing process.

It was a temporary fix, holding her back from the brink of death.

Caitlin's parents offered to take her with them into the Maelstrom, where time would have little effect, but Josh turned them down. He sheltered his mother from the world of the Order and there were still too many unknowns beyond the borders of the continuum. The effects of the chaotic realm would probably have driven his mother insane.

Josh peered through the small glass porthole at the sleeping form inside.

'Does she ever wake up?'

'Rarely,' said the doctor, 'and not for long. We're keeping her on a very low temporal loop.'

Josh placed his hand on the cold glass. 'I need to talk to her.'

'Of course,' agreed Crooke, taking down the speaking tube. 'You can leave a message on this. It will take a few hours to synchronise but she'll be able to hear you.'

Josh shook his head. 'In person.'

It took three hours to bring his mother's time into sync with standard. Josh could tell that the doctor was unhappy about the procedure, making various remarks about the dangers of bringing her back, but Josh insisted, he had to speak to her face to face — to tell her about the baby.

'Hi mum,' whispered Josh as she slowly opened her eyes.

She smiled. 'Hello love.'

Sitting on the side of her bed, he took her small frail hand in his.

'Have you been away?'

'Paris. Just for a couple of days.'

'Sounds romantic. Did you take Caitlin?'

He gripped her hand a little tighter. Sometimes she would forget that Cat even existed. 'No, it was a work thing.'

'You're still working for Mr Westinghouse?'

Josh laughed, she was the only one who insisted on calling the colonel by that name. 'No mum, he works for me now. He's gone to Crete, to look at a new site.'

'Crete. I've always wanted to go to Greece.'

'Maybe when you're better we can take a trip?'

'Yeah, that would be nice.' She looked around at the room. 'Where am I? This doesn't look like Barts.'

Her isolation in the stasis chamber meant that she was still remembering their original timeline. Josh had to be careful of what version of events he used when talking to her.

'Got you a private room Mum, all to yourself.'

'Did you love? Well, don't go spending all your money on me. You need to be looking after that beautiful girl of yours.'

Josh nodded. She was right, the pregnancy was going to affect his plans unless he could find a way to keep her safe.

'So I've got some news,' he began.

'Are you in some kind of trouble?' she asked, letting go of his hand.

He laughed. 'No, well, not me, but Caitlin's going to have a baby.'

Her smile was so wide it shone out of her eyes, which quickly filled with tears.

They sat for an hour talking about the old days, before she got ill. Good times, that he was too young to remember clearly. What a handful he was.

'You were always so headstrong. You never would listen to anyone, not even me.'

'I'm sorry Mum. I know I made it hard for you.'

She shook her finger at him. 'Never, you never talk like that. You were my boy, my life. All those times they brought you back in a squad car, they meant nothing in the grand scheme of things.'

Her voice was growing weaker.

'You just hadn't found your place in the world. A square peg, your Nanna used to call you. Look at you now, all grown up and having a family of your own. I knew it would turn out all right.'

There were so many things he wanted to tell her. About how hard he'd worked to try and fix everything.

'What if they found a way to fix you? Say like in twenty years.'

Doctor Crooke came in to check her, and gave Josh the look that said his time was nearly up.

His mother chuckled. 'I don't think it would do me any good love. I don't think I'll be around long enough to see it.'

'There might be a way, but it means breaking a few rules.'

'That never stopped you before. Is there a new treatment?'

Josh shook his head. 'Not exactly, it involves some difficult decisions.'

He knew that any other changes to the timeline could jeopardise Caitlin's pregnancy and the only way to ensure she stayed safe was to put her outside the continuum for a while, which was not going to be an easy conversation.

His mother mulled it over for a few seconds, her tongue working across the edge of her lip.

'Well, I would like to see my grandchild. Will it give me enough time for that?'

Josh kissed her on the cheek. 'Yes mum.'

12

KONSTANTINE

Grandmaster Konstantine reviewed the intelligence report from Kellerman, letting his eyes drift over the words for a third time.

>>THE SITE HAS BEEN SECURED AND THE EXCAVATION RESTARTED STOP ALLIED FORCES HAVE BEEN DRIVEN OUT OF THE REGION STOP WESTINGHOUSE SHOWED UP TODAY STOP<<

The presence of a Watchman meant that the Copernicans were interested in the site too. The chances were that they had picked up some kind of temporal anomaly, which meant his instinct had been correct. There was something unusual buried down there.

'Have we made any progress on Linear A?' he asked his assistant who was hovering at the door.

'No, Master, the cryptographers have made little progress.'

'So what did the Führer find so interesting that he

invaded the island?' Konstantine said to himself, filing the report away in a drawer.

'The Copernicans have deployed an agent into Bletchley Park. She's sending data from ULTRA, but so far there is no clear indication of their intentions.'

Konstantine closed his eyes and took a deep breath.

'Inform the Council that we have designated the site as special significance, make sure that Eddington keeps his watchdogs on a tight leash, and fetch Ventis. I want your best man on this, we need to crack that damned code before the bloody Copernicans.'

When the assistant closed the door, Konstantine activated a secret drawer in his desk and took out a small metal statue.

Holding it in both hands, he closed his eyes and whispered. 'When are you?'

'1814,' came the answer.

'I won't be able to keep them from Knossos forever, are you any closer to finding the one?'

'The lines are converging.'

'Time is of the essence.'

'Time is an illusion.'

13

GENETICS

[Map room, Copernicus Hall]

Over the next few days, Josh spent every spare moment with the engine, looking for another way to change the timeline without affecting Caitlin. Before he'd known about the pregnancy he'd already decided on a different approach: if he couldn't accelerate the identification and treatment of the disease, then he would look into gene modification.

Genetics was a difficult area to influence. The study of the building blocks of life required a significant level of technology: X-ray crystallography, computers, electron microscopes, all of which would alter the continuum drastically if they were introduced too early. So many of the engine's potential scenarios ended in some form of global disaster.

Josh was careful to hide his research, working out of hours when Eddington's team had finished their shifts. It was important that no one else knew what he was attempting, that he was breaking the prime directive.

During a quiet moment, whilst the engine was recompiling yet another scenario, Josh went over his options with the ghost.

Caitlin has to leave the continuum. There is no other safe option.

And go where?

The Maelstrom. Her mother has a timeship.

I can't just send her away, she's having our baby.

Then your mother dies.

What if —

There is no scenario where both objectives can be met. To change the state of genetic research requires a significant advancement in too many technologies. The adjustment would seriously threaten the pregnancy's existence.

He suddenly realised how much he missed the counsel of the colonel. Weeks had passed since he'd seen the old man. Their last meeting didn't end well, their conversation rapidly escalating into an argument.

'Altering the timeline to such an extent would lead to disaster. We're not called the Oblivion Order for nothing,' the colonel warned after Josh told him about Charcot.

'But if the model can prove it can be done,' Josh protested. 'The Infinity Engine will show us the best way to do it.'

'Statistics,' the colonel spat the word like a curse. 'Never trusted them. There are too many variables. Even if your so-called engine can do as you say — it's a facsimile, a simulation, not even the Copernicans will ever say with any certainty whether something will happen or not. They talk in percentages, whereas the real world is far more clear cut.'

He's wrong, whispered the founder. The pattern of human interaction is finite. When viewed through the lens of history we can determine a clear causality at scale.

Josh ignored the ghost.

'I'm not going to change the world. One man won't make any difference to the fate of humanity.'

The colonel shook his head, and Josh could still see the look of disappointment on his face.

The colonel resumed his field duties the next day.

The engine sprang to life, fine lines twisting out like petals unfolding from a flower. Within the complex web of moments it identified a Swiss chemist, Friedrich Miescher, working at a laboratory at the University of Tübingen in Germany, 1869.

His research focused on tissue chemistry, and he was investigating the composition of white blood cells, trying to isolate the phosphate-rich chemicals stored within the nucleus.

The algorithm predicted it would take another hundred years before the discovery would reach a critical milestone, the discovery of DNA, but watching the scenarios run through the engine, Josh could see how such a small adjustment could have a significant effect on the science of genetics.

But the chemist was struggling to extract the cells from lymph glands and needed a new source of material.

All that was needed was for Miescher to realise there were vast quantities to be found in the pus soaked bandages of the local hospital and he would have enough to perfect his purification processes and make the first step to identifying nucleic acid.

Josh closed down the scenario and gathered his things.

Before he could take the next step, he had to convince Caitlin to go.

14

LEAVING

[Rothes Glen House, Banffshire, Scotland. Date: Present day]

Caitlin was asleep when he stepped back into their house.

It didn't feel like home. Josh was so focused on the engine that he'd hardly spent any time there. Most of his clothes were still in the old apartment that Methuselah attached to the Chapter House three years ago.

She had left a plate of food in the oven and he sat at the table and ate quietly, reading over his notes and listening to the sound of the storm outside. It was winter here, and soon there would be snow. Caitlin wanted everyone to come up here for Christmas. There were enough rooms to house them all and she was already making plans about the decorations.

And now he was going to ruin it all.

After the war with the Nihil, he had tried many ways to fix the timeline. Most, if not all, involved rebuilding the Order in some form. Their influence had a positive effect on the future of humanity and he quickly learned that without them, things tended toward chaos and disaster.

There were always three constants in every timeline, his mother, Caitlin and the colonel. They were his cornerstones, the things that gave his life a purpose and meaning.

Yet now he was in danger of losing all three.

'Morning sleepy head,' he said, putting a steaming cup of tea on her bedside table.

Caitlin groaned, half-opening one eye like a waking dragon.

'I need to tell you my news,' he said, sitting down on the bed.

'Asleep,' was all she could manage.

He looked at the clock, it was after eight in the morning. Caitlin was usually an early riser, obviously the baby was changing her routines.

He shook her gently. 'I need you to listen. It's important.'

'Go away,' she pulled the bedclothes over her head.

'Cat. Please. I need you to pack a bag.'

She sat bolt upright. Something in his tone had penetrated her dozing brain.

'What?'

'I've finished the engine, it passed the Napoleon test.'

She looked confused. 'So we're going somewhere?'

'You are, it showed me something last night. We need to get you somewhere safe. Just until I know it's okay.'

'Where?'

'The Nautilus. I need you to go into the Maelstrom.'

Still only half-awake, she looked like a frightened little girl.

'Are you serious?'

'I know what I'm doing Cat. There's no risk to you or the baby. I've got it all worked out.'

Caitlin got out of bed and started to get dressed.

'What did it show you?'

He thought about lying to her, telling her there was some other external threat, but she deserved to know the truth.

'There's a chance I can save my mum, but it could change the timeline dramatically and I don't want to put you or the baby at risk.'

'Your mother? What?'

He explained about the genetic scenario, about what he needed to do to advance it enough to save her.

'But I thought Crooke was keeping her in stasis?'

He tried to be strong, to put a brave face on it, but she could see that it wasn't good news. 'It's not working. She's not going to last much longer.'

She pulled a leather bag out of the wardrobe and began to stuff clothes into it.

'I get that you're trying to save her Josh, but are you sure screwing around with the timeline is a good idea? What if Mallaron finds out?'

Nathanial Mallaron was the Chief Inquisitor, the leader of the Protectorate, and he would show him no mercy if he found out.

She turned towards the door.

'He won't.' Josh got up from the bed and wrapped his arms around her. 'I just need to fix this. I want her to meet our baby.'

Caitlin pushed him off.

'You're sending us away, don't expect me to agree with you!'

'I need you to —'

She held up her hand to stop him. 'You need to get your head out of the past and realise some things are just meant to be. Why does it always have to be Josh versus the rest of the universe?'

He pulled Solomon's ring from his finger and held it out to her. 'Take this.'

Caitlin sneered at it. 'It's a bit late for a marriage proposal don't you think?'

Josh could still remember the first time he'd worn it, like stepping into a deep, gushing river. The full force of history was overwhelming.

'It's a talisman. It allows you to travel without a vestige.'

She took it, her eyes widening as she felt its power. 'They're forbidden. Where did you get it from?'

'It's a long story. Just promise me you'll keep it safe.'

'What do you want me to do with it?'

He shrugged. 'You might need it in an emergency.'

Caitlin laughed and took the ring, threading it onto her dragon necklace. 'You're sending me into the chaos realm so you can fix your mum, what could possibly go wrong?'

Josh grimaced. 'I can't just let her die.'

'Everybody dies,' she said, picking up her bag and walking out of the door.

15

THE UNCERTAINTY RATIO

[Copernicus Hall]

Striding through the Department of Differential Equations, Rufius stared straight ahead, trying not to look at walls which were in constant motion. Formed from the machinery of the enormous calculating engine that was the building around him, the movement of the gear wheels, calibers and pinions was known to induce motion sickness in the uninitiated, and the last thing he wanted to do now was throw up over Eddington's shoes.

The sounds of a hundred thousand differential equations made it impossible for normal speech so Rufius resorted to sign language when he reached the entrance to central processing.

'I need to see Professor Eddington,' he demanded, using forceful gestures to convey a sense of urgency.

'Do you have an appointment?' the receptionist responded politely, consulting a large diary that lay open on a brass stand in front of her.

'No, tell him Rufius Westinghouse requests one immediately.'

His name seemed to have the desired effect. The woman
typed out a note on a tiny typewriter and placed it into a
pneumatic tube, sending it off with a satisfying hiss.

Rufius followed the progress of the note as it joined
hundreds of others flying back and forth across the ceiling
and into the machinery. He wondered how long it would
take to get an answer.

Five minutes later a message arrived.

'He will see you,' she signed, turning to open the intricate lock on the door.

Eddington's office was an oasis of calm and tranquility, the
walls were heavily sound-proofed from the clattering
cacophony outside. For a moment Rufius wondered if he'd
gone deaf.

It was a tall, marble-floored chamber with high bookcases lining every wall. In the centre, rising out from a
perfectly cut circular hole was an analytical engine. Over
twenty feet high, its stacks were constructed from hundreds
of brass wheels, each inscribed with their own set of
symbols.

It was known as the "Output", the results of every calcu-
lation in the entire building were flowing into its constantly
moving wheels.

The professor was studying one of the columns of
numbers as they slowly turned, once a second, like the
ticking of an enormous clock.

'The fourth partial derivative of the stochastic requires a
further reduction,' he said to one of his assistants who was

taking notes. 'And have Chief MacKenzie increase the Maclaurin series by two-point-seven per cent.'

Rufius was in no mood to be made to wait. 'Professor?'

Eddington looked up from the mechanism. 'Westing-house, you're as impatient as ever I see.'

'I've just returned from Crete.'

'Rollins has informed me.'

'Did you know that Konstantine's men have claimed the site?'

'I did not. The Antiquarians are being somewhat obtuse about their interest in the excavation.'

'And we're going to let them get away with it?'

The professor looked at the shifting dials. 'The Antiquarians were the first to decipher the B script, they have asserted their right to investigate the site further and the Council have agreed.'

'And the Nazis?'

'That is something of a mystery. We are still calculating the potential outcomes from their involvement. There is a high probability that they have made progress in deciphering Linear A.'

Rufius made no attempt to hide his dissatisfaction with Eddington's answer. 'So why send me there in the first place?'

'Your report has helped to reduce the uncertainty ratio.'

'Has it indeed?'

Eddington ignored him, walking away from the engine and his assistants, gesturing for Rufius to accompany him.

'There is another matter I wish to discuss with you,' said the professor, lowering his voice. 'Have you spoken to Joshua lately?'

'Not since I returned, no.'

'Then I would suggest you do so urgently. There is a

high probability that he is about to make a terrible error of judgement and there are some within the Council that will use it against him. His new engine has divided them, not everyone welcomes the changes it will bring.'

Rufius could see the genuine concern in the usually stoic face of Eddington. He knew that the Copernican was never one for politics.

'Where is he now?'

'1869.'

16

MIESCHER

[University of Tübingen, Germany. Date: 1869]

Josh tried not to gag as he pushed a basket filled with foul-smelling bandages along the corridor of the local hospital in Tübingen. He had already delivered a letter requesting Miescher's attendance at the clinic, now all he had to do was make sure the chemist turned up.

Miescher was a shy man, keeping his eyes to the floor as he walked towards Josh. The basket was filled to the brim with pus-soaked rags and as they passed each other it took little more than a flick of the wrist for Josh to turn the contents of the cart over on the man's shoes.

'My apologies, Herr Doctor,' Josh mumbled in German, kneeling to gather the bandages back into the basket — the rancid smell made him gag.

'No need,' replied Miescher, stepping back and dragging some of the cloths with him.

Josh gathered as many as he could while the chemist untangled himself.

'What are you going to do with these?' the chemist

asked, wiping the mess from his highly polished shoes with his handkerchief.

'Burn them. They're infected, from wounds and sores.'

Josh watched the man's mind processing the information waiting for the small glimmer of an idea.

'How many do you have of these?' he asked.

'Hundreds.'

'A week?'

'A day.'

Miescher smiled.

There it was, thought Josh. The future of genetics, glinting in the eye of a twenty-five year old, half-deaf doctor.

17

CIRQUE D'HISTOIRE

[Exposition Universelle, Paris. Date: 1889]

Lyra walked between the arches of the newly erected Eiffel Tower, pausing to look up through the iron latticework. She spotted the tiny metal cages packed with tourists travelling slowly upwards through the legs of the structure, wondering what on earth would possess someone to want to get into such a confined space.

Beyond the tower, spread over the field of Les Champs de Mars, was the Exposition Universelle — the 'World's Fair'. The temporary town had been built to house over sixty-thousand exhibitors. Glass and iron galleries rose up on both sides of the central avenue, the grand Palaces of Liberal and Fine arts, and at the far end past the Coutan Fountain: the golden dome of the Gallerie des Machines.

Following the flow of visitors along the esplanade, Lyra wandered past the exotic pavilions of the foreign nations: Finnish and Javanese villages stood alongside African huts, complete with natives dressed in traditional costumes.

Egypt had recreated an entire street from Cairo with market stalls, belly dancers and musicians.

The exposition celebrated the hundredth anniversary of the Storming of the Bastille and the beginning of the French Revolution. Which meant that most of the countries still ruled by a monarchy declined to participate, but that didn't stop them coming to visit all the same.

Her parents had brought Lyra here many times. Since virtually every nation attended in some form, the multinational factions of the Order could meet without drawing too much suspicion. It was a popular destination for Antiquarians looking for rare artefacts and Draconians in search of new maps.

Hidden amongst the thousands of exhibitors were traders from the more shady and eccentric parts of the Order, ones that the general public would never know existed. There were merchants selling grave goods from the tombs of forgotten kings, fossil hawkers with eggs of undiscovered dinosaurs and mapmakers selling routes into parts of the past few had dared to explore.

The exposition was an unregulated event, even the Protectorate turned a blind eye to what went on under its glass roofs, creating a marketplace for all manner of dark and interesting trades.

One particular attraction that Lyra never grew tired of visiting was the *Cirque D'Histoire*. A magical show involving creatures from pre-historic times created by Georges Cuvier. Her mother took a reluctant Lyra to see the circus when she was very young and she became fascinated by the strange and dangerous creatures. Uncle Georges was a flamboyant Ringmaster, who would make his entrance on the back of a woolly mammoth while sabre-tooth cats would prowl around the outer edges of the ring.

The circus was housed in a tented pavilion hidden behind the Gallery of the Machines, a vast hall dedicated to the greatest engineering feats of the age.

Lyra loved the way the sun's rays glinted off the highly polished housings of the steam engines. The air was warm and filled with the tang of grease and oil. Lyra passed a large crowd gathered to listen to Edison's phonographic wonder; recording their voices and laughing as they were played back on black, lacquered cylinders.

She turned left past a sleek locomotive as a spokesman regaled his audience with stories of how it could reach the unimaginable speed of one-hundred-and-twenty-five miles per hour.

The circus was the brain child of Uncle Georges, a xeno-biologyst who was responsible for many discoveries in French natural science and was commonly known as the 'founding father of palaeontology'.

The entrance to the circus was a deceptively small, bell-shaped tent made of a rich scarlet Arabian silk. Above the door hung a hand-painted sign which read, 'Cirque d'Histoire' in the decorative lettering of a carnival sideshow. It was guarded by an extremely tall man wearing a turban, gold waistcoat and striped pantaloons. When she was younger, Lyra used to imagine he was a genie, with his plaited black beard and his thick muscular arms. His name was Abbas and he was a gentle-spoken giant.

'Mistress,' he said, bowing until his beard touched the ground. 'It is good to see you.'

His smile was filled with the glint of gold and gemstones, his teeth were like a cave of treasures.

'Abbas, I have come to see Master Cuvier.'

'Of course my lady,' he replied, holding back the tent flap. 'Enter.'

The interior of the tent was lit by ornate lanterns, each candle burning with a cobalt blue flame. Ever the showman, Cuvier's attention to detail was meticulous and quite brilliant. A small crimson baize card table stood in the centre of the space on which stood a singular exhibit. Behind it hung a tapestry showing a scene from the Pliocene, filled with intricately woven images of dinosaurs towering among Pliocene jungles. To the enquiring passer-by it was intentionally underwhelming, meant to dissuade anyone from spending too long inside.

Beneath the glass bell jar stood the skeleton of a tiny dinosaur known as *Compsognathus*. It had been posed as if rearing up on its hind legs to greet the visitor. Small articulated rods were connected to a clockwork mechanism in the base so that its jaws would open and close while the small arms clawed at the air.

It was some of Cuvier's finest work, the automaton moved with a natural grace that would have been lost on most. His mechanical reconstructions of long-dead creatures began as a way to understand the anatomy of the prehistoric bones he discovered, but they had become an obsession, and this 'toy' was nothing more than precursor to what awaited beyond.

The exhibit was more than a perfect miniature of his art, it was a vestige, an entry point for the more discerning visitor; all Lyra had to do was touch the key inserted into its base.

A timeline unwound around her fingers, a fine ribbon of history unfurled from the brass fob and she followed the threads into another point in time: one single moment separated from the millions of seconds that had passed since the exposition had opened.

The entrance to the Cirque d'Histoire appeared in the fabric of the tapestry.

The Circus was a vast marquee, dwarfing the Gallery of the Machines. Its roof stood over a hundred feet high, supported by an internal metal framework of armatures that reminded Lyra of a giant umbrella.

Beneath it was housed the entire Cuvier collection. She walked through the maze of wheeled display cabinets, each one containing an animated extinct species placed into their own diorama. A magnificent sabre-tooth cat lay regally on a rock studying Lyra with glassy eyes, its head turning as she passed; the enormous *Helicoprion* shark that swam leisurely around its tank in a never-ending loop and of course Cuvier's pièce de résistance: the mammoth, complete with eight foot long tusks that he famously unearthed from the permafrost in Siberia, losing a finger to frostbite in the process.

Cuvier was working on the wing of an archaeopteryx when Lyra finally found his office. It was a large Romany caravan which had a tendency to move around the tent under its own steam.

He was smoking a pipe, dressed in an ornate silk *robe de chambre* and wore a fez. The man had become something of a convert to the ways of Araby since a visit to Marrakesh in 1810. Lyra liked his eccentricity; there was something of the mystic East about the whole ensemble.

'My dear Lyra, how lovely to see you,' he greeted her in French, getting to his feet.

'Uncle Georges,' she replied, allowing him to take her hand and kiss it. He wasn't really an uncle but her mother always referred to him as such.

'What brings you to my humble circus? My, haven't you grown! It seems like only yesterday since you were here with your mother.'

'It probably was,' said Lyra with a chuckle. 'You know how it is.'

'Indeed. How is she?'

'Very well. She's rearing Spinosaurus.'

Cuvier looked impressed. 'Have you heard them sing?'

She grimaced. 'Yes, it's not exactly Bizet. I have a favour to ask of you.'

'In that case we shall need tea, and some of Madam Cuvier's galettes.'

While Uncle Georges boiled the water and pottered around making the tea, Lyra told him about the dream.

'How many blades exactly?' he asked, stirring the leaves in the old metal tea pot.

'Five I think,' said Lyra, catching the crumbs from one of the cakes as she bit into it.

Amongst his other talents, Georges was something of an expert on ancient hunting weapons.

'Sounds like the dangerous end of an African hunting spear. Was the central blade larger than the other four?' He moved his hands apart to indicate length.

Lyra nodded, grimacing as the thought of it brought back a vivid memory of the scene.

'Grandmaster Kelly thought you might know what it

was,' she said, taking out the sketch of the dagger and handing it to him.

The old man scratched his head as he studied it, tilting the fez. 'That old fraud wouldn't know the difference between a Hawkbill and a Gut Hook. This looks to me like a ceremonial weapon, used to ward off legendary monsters, like the Grootslang.'

Georges gave her back the sketch and sat down on the chaise longue.

'Grootslang,' asked Lyra. 'What's that?'

He handed her a cup, delicately balanced on its ornate saucer and poured the tea. 'It's an Afrikaans word meaning "Great Snake." A monstrous hybrid of snake and elephant, supposed to be in excess of sixty feet long. Its cave was called a 'Wonder Hole' and was supposed to be filled with diamonds. It sounds quite ridiculous when you say it out loud.'

'One of my students, Benoir Cousineau, has just returned from studying Paranthodon in the South African Richtersveld, he may have come across something like your spearhead.'

Lyra looked confused. 'Paranthodon?'

Georges shook his head. 'A stegosaurian from the Early Cretaceous. Benoir's a promising zoologist studying the mating habits of the mastodon at the National Museum.' Cuvier got up from his seat. 'In fact he's exactly the person you need to talk to. Come with me.' He disappeared through the curtains at the back of the caravan.

She followed Cuvier through the folds of fabric and into another world.

Her mother had told Lyra about his conservation work.

They were both extinction curators of sorts, although Alixia didn't agree with some of Cuvier's techniques, believing that the study of prehistoric creatures should be in situ rather than behind bars. He would always argue that the Pleistocene was far too dangerous a place for any research team to spend time getting to know the mating habits of a mammoth.

The roar of a sabre-tooth announced their entrance, making Lyra jump in the process.

Benoir Cousineau was in the middle of a large circular cage with two big cats sitting to each side of him. He was kneeling down examining the belly of a third that was lying on its back.

'The female is pregnant,' Georges whispered.

They were in another section of the enormous tent, hidden even from the members of the Order. It had five ringed metal enclosures, each one containing a prehistoric creature. Lyra counted two elephant-like mastodons, three woolly rhinoceroses and an enormous cave bear. Attendants wearing metal ringed shirts were feeding them through the bars using long poles.

'We usually only bring them here for observation and measurement. Benoir has raised those three from cubs, their mother was killed by a steppe bison.'

Lyra tentatively moved closer to the bars. The cats were magnificent, proud animals who watched the strangers with a wary eye. Benoir stood up and brushed off his trousers. He was a tall, handsome young man, with dark hair that fell over his eyes. She thought he could be no more than twenty.

The tigers nuzzled his legs as he made his way to the inner gate.

'Ajani! Enough,' he barked at one of them, taking a handful of biscuits out of his pocket and throwing them across the ring. The pride leapt away, chasing their prize across the sawdust.

While they were preoccupied, Benoir slipped out of the outer gate and locked it. There was a sign in French that reminded the attendants to ensure that both gates were secured. He hung the keys on a hook beside the plaque.

'Benoir!' said Cuvier, raising a hand. 'Come here. There's someone I want you to meet.'

'I'm busy,' he replied, then turning towards them, he saw Lyra and blushed a little as he bowed.

'My apologies mademoiselle, one of the mastodons has a bad tooth.' He pointed towards the elephant rubbing his cheek against the bars of the next cage. 'And he must be returned today before he becomes too acclimatised.'

'Lyra,' she said, offering her hand. She wanted to touch him, to read his bloodline.

He held up his gloved hands as if surrendering. 'Excuse me if I don't.'

She smiled. 'Of course, you're busy. I can wait.'

'Would you like to accompany me? The tooth should only take a few minutes.'

Lyra nodded.

Cuvier had a wry smile as he made his excuses before going to oversee the feeding of the sabre-tooths.

18

PREGNANCY

The *Nautilus* slid into the air above her without a sound. Caitlin felt a subtle tingling sensation as the hairs on the back of her neck reacted to the magnetic waves of the breaching field. It was a magnificent ship, one of which Captain Nemo would have been proud. With a sleek brass hull shaped like a sword and a Gothic conning tower rising out of the upper deck it looked more like a Victorian spaceship than a time machine.

She waited impatiently while the gantry was cranked up to the hatch and the technicians gave her the thumbs up to go aboard.

By the time she reached the pressure door her mother was already waiting.

'This is an unexpected surprise,' she said, wrapping her arms around her daughter. Then spotting the bag at Caitlin's feet. 'Has something happened?'

Caitlin managed a half-smile. 'I could really do with a cup of tea.'

. . .

The galley of the timeship doubled as the map room. Its walls and tabletops were inscribed with various charts of the Maelstrom: the chaotic realm that sat beyond the borders of the continuum. Her parents were Nautonniers, part of the exploration division of the Draconians, and spent most of their lives in the timeless expanse, which meant they appeared to be only a few years older than Caitlin.

With his usual aplomb, her father appeared carrying a large pot of tea and an impressive tin of biscuits; he was always prepared for an impromptu tea break.

'I thought you should be the first to know,' Caitlin began, picking up a Jammie Dodger and dunking it into her Earl Grey.

'Oh my gosh!' her mother squealed.

'What?' asked her father, his face a picture of bewilderment.

'She's pregnant!'

'Are you?'

Caitlin nodded, putting the entire biscuit into her mouth and taking another.

'Well, I never.' He sighed, sitting down heavily and rubbing his chin. 'I'm going to be a grandfather.'

'Suits you,' said her mother.

'How long?'

'I don't know, I think it could only be a couple of months at the most.'

'And what does Josh think?'

Caitlin bit her lip, trying not to cry for the third time that day. 'He sent me here.'

'What!' bellowed her father.

'Thomas, go and make a fresh pot,' her mother said, her

expression imploring him to go away and leave her to deal with it. Which he dutifully did.

She turned back to Caitlin. 'Start at the beginning.'

Caitlin still wasn't quite sure how she felt about being pregnant, it had all been rather chaotic since Lyra's revelation. She told her mother how she visited Doctor Crooke and he confirmed the initial diagnosis. The foetus was at least ten weeks old and was perfectly healthy.

'So, why send you away?'

'Because staying was going to have consequences.'

'Babies generally do,' her mother agreed.

'He's planning to do something to the timeline. I can't say exactly what, because it might implicate you.'

'Does it have something to do with that engine he's been building with Eddington?'

Caitlin nodded. 'It's become an obsession, he's a different man.'

Her mother frowned. 'That device will bring nothing but trouble, mark my words.'

'He says it's safer if I leave the continuum.'

Her mother folded her arms. 'Well, it probably is, if he makes the wrong adjustment you could lose the baby.'

Her father returned with another pot of tea and rounds of toast thickly-coated in strawberry jam.

'Sounds like we should have a word with that young man,' he said.

Caitlin shook her head. 'No, I think he needs to sort this out himself.'

Her mother smiled and took her hand. 'Whatever you think is best. I realise we haven't been the best of parents to you. God knows I would do that differently if I could, but you're right, he has to make a decision about what is more important. This is about your future.'

Caitlin felt the tears welling up and tried to hold them back, but they came all the same. She hated the way her emotions were becoming so uncontrollable, the last thing she wanted to be was an emotional wreck in front of her parents. She wanted to be strong, she needed to be strong. Caitlin knew deep down that nothing she could say to Josh would change what he was going to do. Saving his mother was not something she could ask him to give up. But the idea of her never knowing about the baby, worried her more than anything.

'So can I come and stay with you?'

Her mother gathered Caitlin up in her arms. 'Of course, my love. We'll protect you. The *Nautilus* will keep you safe, no matter what he does to the timeline.'

19

MEDICAL

[Bedlam. Date: 1660]

Doctor Crooke's hands were a painful testament to his profession. His joints were swollen by arthritis, the skin stained with the salts of a thousand compounds. The years as a physician had left their mark on him. Josh watched the old man deftly remove the needle from his vein, pressing a compress of cobwebs against the flow of blood.

Stoppering the vial, Crooke sealed the cork with wax and held it up to the light. His dark beady eyes squinted at the crimson liquid like a connoisseur examining a fine wine.

'When will you know?' asked Josh, rolling down his sleeve.

The old doctor grunted. 'I'll need to send it up to the xenobiologysts. Their electron microscope is far more likely to detect an anomaly than my old Janssen lenses.' He nodded towards a large brass microscope sitting on his desk amongst detailed illustrations of human anatomy. 'Quite honestly I don't know why you didn't go directly to them.'

Josh got up from the bench. 'I'm staying away from the frontier. The present is too chaotic.'

Crooke nodded in agreement. Many of the elder members of the Order preferred to live in the sixteenth and seventeenth centuries, finding the pre-industrialised period more conducive to their experiments — electricity had a tendency to destabilise the sensitive temporal dynamics of their work.

'If I've got it, what are the chances that I might pass it on to my children?' asked Josh, glancing over at his mother's stasis chamber.

Crooke placed the vial of Josh's blood into a brass cylinder and wrote a date on the side in a fluid copperplate.

'Multiple sclerosis has a genetic component, but there are many other factors. I would hazard the chances of you inheriting it from your mother are quite low — less than three per cent. It's higher in women, up to three times more likely, no one knows why, but I understand your concerns. Caitlin came to see me a few days ago. I take it she's well?'

Josh shrugged, there was no point in hiding the fact that she had left. By now most of the Order probably knew. 'She's gone to stay with her parents.'

'Has she now,' said Crooke, raising an eyebrow.

Josh walked over to the stasis cylinder and looked through the porthole at his sleeping mother.

'Is she getting any worse?'

Crooke sighed. 'I can keep her in there indefinitely, but that's not what you're asking. After your last visit we had to take her time down further than I would have liked, her body does not respond well to temporal decompression.'

Everyone dies, Caitlin's parting words came back to Josh.

It was something he knew only too well. His early attempts to recreate the timeline had ended with someone he loved dying or never existing. Unlike everyone else, he remembered every one of them.

'Professor Eddington tells me your engine has succeeded in the Napoleon test,' said Crooke, snapping Josh out of his reverie.

'Yeah, I don't think I've ever seen him smile like that before.'

The old doctor chuckled. 'The Professor is a hard man to please, you must be very satisfied. This is a significant step for the Order. One might say a marvel of ingenuity.'

'I'm not sure the High Council would agree.'

Crooke tutted and waved a bony finger. 'They're not all like Grandmaster Konstantine. He despises change and your engine represents the greatest technological advancement since the tachyon. I suspect the man is more than a little jealous.'

'How do you figure that?'

'For the longest time, the tachyon was the single most important piece of equipment in the Order, placing the Antiquarian guild in a powerful position. They've dominated the council for years, but now the Copernicans have the engine, the balance of power will change.'

20

BENOIR

[Cirque d'Histoire, Exposition Universelle, Paris. Date: 1889]

The mastodon must have weighed over five tons. Lyra could see the strain in the men's faces as they hoisted the massive beast into the air. Heaving at the block and tackle, they lifted the animal a few feet off the ground in a thick leather harness.

'We find that it is easier to operate on them when they are suspended,' explained Benoir while his team carefully rotated the animal until it was upside down. The creature groaned as its head came level with theirs.

'She sounds as if she's in a great deal of pain,' Lyra observed, her empathy catching the waves of agony emanating from the mastodon.

'There is no saving it,' replied the handsome zoologist, taking a long pair of blacksmith's tongs from a bucket and a lantern from one of the assistants.

'Would you mind?' he asked, handing Lyra the lamp.

She took it and pointed the light into the mouth of the slowly swaying creature.

'Hold her steady!' barked Benoir, stepping between its long tusks.

Placing the metal tongs into the open mouth, Benoir manoeuvred them around the swollen tooth.

The creature kicked at the air, screaming in pain as he gripped the instrument tightly and began to pull on it.

Lyra could smell the sweat on him as he worked, it was strong and sweet, and she found herself moving a little closer.

The mastodon was clearly in agony, its legs began to thrash the air. Benoir worked the molar far enough out of its gum to place a cord around the tooth, but it shook his head at him every time he attempted to bind it.

'Don't you have any anaesthetic?'

Benoir shook his head. 'They're too heavy, the pressure on their lungs would be too great if they lay down.'

Lyra sighed, putting down the lamp and kneeling beside its head. 'Let me.'

She stroked its upturned cheek, allowing her mind to weave into the timeline of the animal. Suddenly she was standing on the grassy plains of the Pleistocene, a vast savannah stretching out towards the horizon. Surrounded by a herd that had been grazing the same lands for millennia, it was a simple, tranquil existence and Lyra brought the calm feeling back to the creature.

'Just a little longer,' whispered Benoir, working inside its mouth.

Seconds later it was over, the rotting tooth came loose and swung in the air beside them.

'Good work!' he said, helping her up from the floor.

They stepped out of the cage as the men lowered the creature to the floor.

'Will she go back now?'

Benoir nodded. 'In a day or so. When the gum has had time to heal. They'll let her chew guava leaves to reduce the swelling.'

'How did you bring her here?' Lyra asked, watching the enormous creature get back to its feet and take a long drink from the water barrel.

'I can bring them with me.'

'Really?' said Lyra, trying not to sound too impressed. 'I've never heard of anyone doing that. Is it hard?'

He shrugged. 'I've always been able to do it.'

'But all that way, how far is it?'

'From the end of the Pleistocene, twelve thousand years or so.'

'Wow. I've never been back further than the ninth,' Lyra lied. Her mother had taken her back much further than that, but she didn't want to ruin the moment.

Benoir took off his leather gauntlets. 'Georges mentioned that you wanted to ask me something?'

'Oh yes. He told me you might know what this is?'

She took out the drawing of the dagger and handed it to him.

One of Benoir's eyebrows arched slightly. 'That's not the question I was expecting.'

Lyra's eyes widened, sensing he liked to play games. 'Really? What were you expecting?'

The young man blushed a little. 'This isn't the first time Georges has tried to set me up with one of his female relatives.'

She looked over at the old man who was talking to one of the keepers. 'Cunning old fox.'

'So what do you want to know about this blade?' he asked, studying the sketch.

'He said you were in Africa recently, that you might have come across one?'

'To kill a Grootslang by any chance?'

Lyra laughed. 'Yes, he mentioned that too.'

'He has a penchant for mythical creatures, as if these weren't bad enough!' Benoir added, hanging his gloves beside the cage door.

'So, do you know what it is?'

Benoir frowned, his lips pursing in an all too cute way that made Lyra want to kiss them.

'The blades are similar to that of a Xhosa assegai, a tribal spear, but I've never seen them clustered in such a way. Where did you see this?'

'In a dream,' said Lyra, wondering about how he would react if she told him she was a seer.

'A dream?'

'I have visions, ones that tend to come true,' she added coyly.

He couldn't hide the look of surprise. 'You're a seer?'

She nodded.

'And you saw this?'

'Embedded in the back of one of my friends.'

21

WATSON & CRICK

[King's College, London. Date: January, 1953]

Rosalind Franklin felt exhausted. Leaning back in her chair, she rubbed her shoulders, soothing the tension from hours bent over a microscope studying the results of her latest diffraction experiment. The light in her tiny basement laboratory was inadequate. In any other institution her lab would have been classified as a storage cupboard, but somehow she managed to fit the cumbersome equipment of the X-ray tube and hydrogen cylinders into the space.

Photo 51, she wrote in her daybook. *Exhibits signs of a helical structure, there are ten bases on each turn of the helix.*

She checked her wristwatch, it was quarter to six, time for her to clock off.

Standing in the corridor outside, Josh opened his almanac and watched the various lines moving towards the convergence. He could see Watson was less than an hour away, but Wilkins's line was wavering erratically.

Franklin had done pioneering work on X-ray diffraction photography at King's for the last three years. Together with Maurice Wilkins and Raymond Gosling at the Biophysics unit, she had identified two kinds of DNA and concluded they were some form of helical structure. It was no easy task; problems with the crude equipment meant long laborious hours to create the most basic of images.

Thanks to the Infinity Engine, Josh had identified a second team of scientists, James Watson and Francis Crick at the Cavendish Laboratory in Cambridge. They were close to building a molecular model of the B form of DNA and were on the brink of making the discovery that would unlock the secret of life.

The problem was that Franklin was unwilling to share her findings until she had verified her data and today was the day that Watson was going to fail to persuade her to collaborate.

All Josh had to do was ensure that Watson saw a copy of photo fifty-one.

He heard the scrape of her desk drawer as Rosalind put her notes away and gathered her coat and scarf. Then the metallic click of her desk lamp being switched off, followed by the tap of footsteps as she made her way to the door.

Josh moved back into the shadows, watching her lock her office and stride towards the exit. When she reached the stairs, Rosalind looked back as if forgetting something, and for a moment Josh saw the fierce intellect in her eyes. She was a strong, assertive woman, with whom the painfully shy Wilkins found it difficult to work.

Franklin was leaving King's, transferring to Birkbeck College in March and her boss had insisted that all her research stay behind, so there was a short window of opportunity to act.

Rosalind had less than five years before the ovarian cancer would end her life. There was little Josh could do to change that outcome. They explored the possibility of prolonging her life, but the engine predicted that an earlier diagnosis of the cancer would have led to a change in her career, leading her away from X-ray crystallography altogether.

It was a terrible decision to have to make, one that would lead to others taking the credit for her work, but it was a necessary one.

After she left, Josh broke into her office and collected the diffraction plates from her desk. Making sure that number fifty-one was clearly visible, he took the box of research to Wilkins's office.

The bespectacled biologist was hunched over his desk reading an American scientific journal. The British scientific community were reeling from the publication of Linus Pauling's research on DNA and his theory of the triple helix.

Wilkins knew it was wrong, Watson and Crick had made the same mistake, and he was determined to secure the discovery for King's before Pauling realised his error.

Wearing the dull brown overcoat of a porter was like a cloak of invisibility in the college and the scientist hardly acknowledged Josh's existence when he walked in.

'Doctor Franklin asked me to deliver these sir,' he mumbled in his best subservient cockney.

'Did she indeed,' replied Wilkins, his tone edged with

surprise. It was well-known that the two of them didn't get on, but Eddington was confident that the man's ambition would get the better of him. 'What are they?'

'Photographs.'

'Diffraction plates.' corrected Wilkins, taking a glass slide from the box and holding it up to his lamp.

His telephone rang.

'Put them down over there,' he said bluntly, picking up the receiver. 'Wilkins. Yes. He's here? Good, I'll be up in a moment.'

Josh did as he was told and left. Taking out his almanac, he watched the timelines of Watson and Wilkins converge and the future of genetics was formed.

Rufius sheltered from the rain on the opposite side of the street to King's College. He watched the unassuming figure of James Watson, struggling under a slightly broken umbrella, make his way through the steady flow of students into the college entrance.

He was waiting for Josh to appear, but his interest was piqued by the two Protectorate officers who were following the scientist along the Strand. They were good, but Rufius was better, his keen eye noticing the subtle mistakes they made as they tried to remain inconspicuous.

Josh appeared from beneath the arch looking very pleased with himself. Pulling the collar of his brown coat up against the rain, he glanced along the Strand, unaware of the two men watching him from Somerset House, then moved off in the other direction.

Eddington hadn't given Rufius any details on what Josh was planning, but it was clear from the actors involved that it was to do with DNA, and it didn't take a rocket scientist to work out he was trying to advance genetic research.

Rufius had warned him countless times about changing the timelines for his own benefit. The Protectorate had been created to stop exactly this kind of behaviour. Now they were investigating him, which meant the Chief Inquisitor was involved, and that would only lead to trouble.

22

ENDINGS

[Bedlam. 1660]

Removing his mother from the stasis chamber seemed to be taking forever.

Bringing her back to relative time was always a delicate process, the doctor reminded him, if they were to ensure that she didn't suffer any dilation effects.

Josh checked his tachyon for the tenth time, it was taking longer than usual to acclimatise her.

All he needed to do now was move her to the present. Genetic scientists had already identified twelve mutations that could trigger the immune system to send white blood cells against its own central nervous system, destroying the myelin sheath around the nerve fibres. They were working on a gene therapy that could be used to repair them.

There were other consequences of his adjustment, all of which seemed to be positive. In 2017 they had made break-throughs using gene therapy on sickle cell, haemophilia and certain types of rare cancers.

'How much longer?' he asked Doctor Crooke.

The doctor looked concerned. 'Another hour, perhaps less,' he said, checking the dials on the side of the chamber.

Josh looked through the porthole, his mother's face was grey.

'Is something wrong?'

'She doesn't appear to be responding as well as I'd hoped.' He took another reading and consulted a journal.

'You said her condition wouldn't change while she was in there?'

'It hasn't, but as she comes out of stasis there is always a certain amount of slippage.'

'Slippage?'

'The dynamics of a temporal field have to be carefully balanced, when they are not we lose a few minutes, sometimes hours.'

'How much time has she lost?'

The doctor made some calculations in his notebook with a pencil.

'Three months.'

'What?'

He looked up from his notes. 'If we continue, she may lose more.'

'Bring her out now!'

Crooke grimaced. 'I would advise against any hasty decisions.'

Josh reached for the door of the chamber. 'You've already done enough damage.'

Her hands were cold.

'Mum?'

Her eyes fluttered open. 'Hello love.'

Josh smiled, ignoring the doctor and his nurses who were frantically trying to treat her.

'You looked tired,' she said, stroking his cheek. 'Working too hard?'

There was a wheezing as she breathed, and there was a blue tinge to her skin.

'I've found a new doctor,' he said, leaning over her to whisper in her ear. 'One that can fix you.'

She shook her head. 'Had enough of doctors.'

Josh gripped her hand tightly, fighting back the urge to shout at her. He'd forgotten how stubborn she could be. 'But Mum, it's taken ages.'

Her breathing was shallow and she closed her eyes.

'So tired Joshua, don't want to be any bother.'

'You're not. I can have us there in the blink of an eye,' he said, suddenly regretting that he'd given Solomon's ring to Caitlin.

Holding a large brass syringe, Crooke traced his finger across her forearm searching for a suitable vein, they shone out through her papery skin like a map of tiny rivers.

'Maybe later,' she said with a sigh.

Josh tried another approach. 'Do you remember I told you that you were going to be a granny?'

The injection roused her a little, her thin lips twisting into a smile.

'Grandma,' she corrected him. 'Never liked granny.'

'So I'm going to need you to help out. You know with babysitting and nappies.'

There was a twinkle in her eye. 'Boy or girl?'

'Boy.'

She coughed and one of the nurses gave her a sip of water. 'Boys are more trouble.'

He laughed. 'He might not turn out like me.'

'My beautiful boy,' she gripped his hand tightly. 'I've never regretted a single moment.'

He felt the tears rising. 'Can we go now?'

She nodded.

Crooke looked up at something behind Josh and before he could turn around, he felt hands on his shoulders.

'Joshua Jones you're under arrest.'

He struggled as they bound his arms behind his back.

Dragging him away from her, Josh could see the look of fear on her face.

'It's okay Mum. Just a misunderstanding. I'll be back.'

They were the last words he would ever say to her.

23

THE COUNCIL

[Star Chamber]

Chief Prosecutor Mallaron was known to most as 'The Raven'. His long black hair, sharp nose and dark, piercing eyes were feared throughout the Order. It was a face that was perfectly suited for his position as the head of the Protectorate. He was a cold, efficient man with an encyclopaedic knowledge of their laws and the best alternative to Ravana Eckhart Josh could have wished for. Although, when the founder had suggested him, Josh had hardly envisaged that he would ever be standing before him.

'Master Jones, you stand accused of manipulating the continuum for your own ends,' the prosecutor's monotone resounded off the walls of the Star Chamber. 'How do you plead?'

Josh stood chained to two Protectorate guards. His face was expressionless, staring blankly at the members of the High Council who were sitting behind a crescent shaped desk, each one wearing a more grave expression than the last.

'I was trying to save her,' he said through gritted teeth, 'and now she's dead!'

My mother is dead. He still couldn't bring himself to accept the fact. It was less than a week since they had arrested him. She died soon after. Crooke came to visit him in prison, along with a sorry-looking colonel. It was the news that he'd been dreading, having spent so long and sacrificed so much to keep her alive.

'This is the most serious of crimes, the prime directive has been broken,' the prosecutor continued, ignoring Josh's outburst.

I know I wrote it, the founder's thoughts intruded on his own. It was the first law, written on the day that he formed the Order.

Piss off. Josh said to the ghost who was now standing beside the Chief Prosecutor.

Ravana would never have let it come to trial. The founder continued. *She would have killed you, then pleaded self-defence.*

The fate of the Eckharts was one of the adjustments Josh had little conscience about changing. The root of Ravana's problems lay in her husband, Valtin, and the curse that he spent his life trying to hide. The founder's memories contained a number of alternative suitors for Ravana, and it only took two attempts to ensure that she would never meet the psychopath. In this life she was happy and content, nothing like the monster that she could have become, nor did she create the twisted son, Dalton, who nearly ended the human race.

. . .

The Star Chamber was in closed session, the tiered benches of its auditorium were empty except for a line of witnesses for the prosecution who had been summoned to attend.

'Master Donaldson,' the Raven began as his first witness, the head of the Outliers Division, took to the stand. 'Would you say that the defendant's actions could have had a significant impact on the technological advancement of the human race?'

Donaldson was a middle-aged man with thinning hair that was combed over to hide his baldness. Wearing a grey, pin-striped suit rather than the formal robes of a Copernican, Josh thought he looked more like a bank manager or an accountant, hardly someone who spent his days calculating the fate of the world.

'I would,' Donaldson agreed solemnly. 'There is an eighty-seven per cent probability that genetic engineering will have a catastrophic effect on human development.'

'How so?'

'The eradication of diseases such as cancer would extend the average lifespan. Eugenics would result in a more resilient population. Our calculations predict that the pressure on global resources from the increased population density would precipitate a third world war within four generations.'

'And has your department been able to develop a suitable resolution to this situation?'

Donaldson shook his head. 'We are still considering the options.'

'Thank you, you may step down. I call upon my second witness: Doctor Helkiah Crooke.'

The hunch-backed physician rose slowly from his seat and shuffled over to the stand.

'Doctor Crooke. Is it true that Master Jones has recently

consulted you over his concerns about a potentially debilitating medical condition?'

He's going to try and have you committed for mental instability. The founder suggested.

'That is a private matter,' Crooke replied gruffly.

'Not if it concerns the safety of the Order. Section four, paragraph three of the third amendment states that: "If by his actions, an officer should bring the continuum into jeopardy, said individual will lose all personal rights and privileges until the High Council or its representatives have determined the cause and resolution of the aforesaid act.'

That damn third amendment. We should have never agreed to that.

Crooke grimaced, his knuckles whitening as he gripped the sides of the stand.

'The defendant was concerned about contracting the same affliction as his mother. He came to me to be tested.'

'For multiple sclerosis?'

The old doctor nodded.

'And the symptoms of this disease?'

'Vision problems, fatigue, muscle spasms, weakness of the limbs.'

'And mental faculties?' the Raven prompted.

Crooke sighed deeply. 'And mental acuity yes.'

Mallaron folded his arms. 'And what were the results of your tests?'

Crooke looked directly at Josh. 'He shows no signs of having the disease.'

Josh felt a wave of relief flow over him and smiled weakly at the doctor who was already turning to leave the podium.

'One last thing Doctor,' added the prosecutor, raising a

long, bony finger. 'In your medical opinion, how would you classify Master Jones's current mental state?'

The doctor looked back at Josh. 'He's showing signs of anxiety and stress, which is to be expected in someone who is dealing with the death of a family member.'

Grandmaster Konstantine suddenly spoke up from his seat on the council: 'And what are the usual symptoms associated with chronic stress?'

This is all his doing, thought the founder.

'Stress can manifest itself in many ways: poor thought patterns, negative attitudes, frustration and anger,' replied Crooke.

'Thank you Doctor,' said Mallaron, dismissing him with a cursory wave of his hand. 'I call on Professor Eddington to testify.'

Eddington stood up and walked to the stand. In his dark robes he looked like a priest going to offer the last rites to a condemned man.

'Professor Eddington, you've been working on this Infinity Engine with the accused have you not?'

The professor placed his arms behind his back. 'I have.'

Mallaron copied Eddington, walking around the circular chamber as he continued. 'An engine that he used to calculate the exact changes that led to the advancement of DNA research by thirty years?'

Eddington's expression hardly changed. 'I wasn't aware of that. No.'

'Because you allowed him unfettered access to the Copernican facilities?'

'Because it was his creation.'

'Yes, so I hear.'

'And remind me what is the penalty for manipulation of the timeline for personal gain.'

The professor turned towards Josh, the look of disappointment in his eyes was slight but Josh saw it all the same. 'Excision.'

'Excision. His timeline expunged, his family adjusted,' repeated Mallaron.

'She's dead!' screamed Josh.

'The accused will remain silent!' the clerk reprimanded him.

The prosecutor turned to address the council members. 'I see no other option than to recommend that the accused be excised.'

Grandmaster Derado, the Head of the Draconian Guild stood up. 'I object! This is an outrageous farce based on nothing more than his speculation!' He pointed at Donaldson.

Some of the other council members nodded in agreement.

Konstantine scoffed. 'Of course Grandmaster, the Draconians have never endangered the continuum. I'm sure there was a perfectly valid reason for the breach of the second dynasty.'

Derado's face turned a dark shade of purple. 'That was out of our control,' he said through gritted teeth.

'I merely state the penalty as it was set down,' Mallaron interrupted, perhaps sensing he was losing control of the court and opting for a compromise. 'Those in favour of committing the accused to Bedlam while an excision review is undertaken. Raise your hands.'

He won the motion by four to three.

'And the engine to be handed over to the Antiquarian Guild,' proposed Konstantine.

'I object!' protested Eddington. 'The engine requires a

highly trained actuary, it could be easily damaged in the wrong hands.'

Derado abstained, getting to his feet and walking out with his lieutenants.

The others were split on the motion and Konstantine left in disgust.

24

REAVERS

[Bedlam]

Tomorrow I bury my mother, Josh thought, sitting in his cell listening to the rantings of the other inmates. An insane chorus of cries echoed down the empty corridors; some pleading their innocence, others howling out into the darkness to an unnamed god. Many were in languages that neither he nor the founder could recognise, but he could definitely sympathise with the sentiment.

This was the Seers Sanatorium. The wing of Bedlam set aside for the care of the gifted, the ones driven insane by the things they'd witnessed, whose fragile minds were unable to cope with the infinite futures.

We should leave. The founder's voice rose out of his subconscious. *Before they excise us.*

Maybe we belong here? Josh replied. *Maybe they can cure me of you.*

He closed his eyes and let his mind enter the archives.

It had taken time and a great deal of training before the

founder's memories finally settled into a construct that Josh could navigate. The building resembled the inside of an old museum, one with infinite halls and reading rooms. Shelves of books filled with memories lined the walls. Organised in such a way that only the founder could navigate, he acted as the curator, librarian and index. It was a mental model that gave them some common ground, an interface into the over-whelming collection of accumulated knowledge of his father.

In the main hall was a virtual version of the Infinity Engine. Floating like a sun in the air above their heads, its surface was in constant flux as millions of calculations inscribed themselves across its golden shell.

Standing beneath the sphere was the founder, just as Josh remembered him. His long grey beard and scarlet robes making him look like some kind of temporal wizard.

His eyes were dark and voice solemn as he spoke. 'Do you know what an excision entails?'

Josh shrugged. 'They wipe me out, I never exist.'

'Not just you, everyone you've ever known, everything you've ever done.'

'Caitlin would lose the baby?'

The old man nodded.

'So what do we do?'

The image of the founder flickered for a moment, reminding Josh that he was nothing more than a collection of memories. When he stabilised, his robes seemed to have darkened to a midnight black.

'We need to find your mother.'

'But she's dead.'

The shelves of books that lined the walls around them shifted, thousands of leather-bound volumes reordered themselves like sliding puzzle pieces until the relevant documents surfaced.

'Excision is a delicate process that requires a skilful seer. Since they cannot trace your father, they will target your mother, and as she has passed, it will complicate matters. If we can reach her in the afterlife, we may be able disrupt the entire process.'

The founder raised his hand and a book glided gently down to land in Josh's palms.

'Reaving?' exclaimed Josh, reading the cover.

'No seer would dare touch your timeline if it has crossed over.'

Most seers experimented with death, either with their own lives or those of others. This practice was known as reaving, but no one had ever managed to go beyond the veil.

The night guard ambled across the hospital courtyard towards the outer gate, a large ring of keys jangling from his belt. He was a short, round man with a head that seemed to be connected directly to his chest, the jowls of his chin hiding any sign of a neck.

'Master Bellamir,' Rufius greeted him through the bars.

'Master Westinghouse. What brings you here at such a late hour?'

'I wish to speak with Joshua Jones.'

Bellamir sucked air in through the last of his crooked teeth. 'I'm not sure that's allowed. The Raven gave strict instructions.'

'Not even for an old friend,' said Rufius, holding up a bottle of rum.

Bellamir rubbed his hands together. 'Now that squire, is an entirely different matter.'

. . .

The asylum was a terrible place at the best of times, but by night it became a true madhouse. Rufius followed the guard along the corridors of barred cells, inmates' hands springing out like pale flowers as they passed. Their sallow fingers clawed at the air and Rufius shuddered at the sight of the hollow faces caught in Bellamir's lamp. These were stark reminders of the dangerous game they played with fate. He knew too many people for whom the ever-changing past had become too much, whose minds had simply broken under the strain.

One of the founder's books contained the memory of Nathaniel Mallory, an English alchemist who studied under Kelly during the reign of Elizabeth I. Doctor Mallory's reputation for healing the sick during the Great Plague of 1665 brought him to the attention of the Grand Seer. His talents as a seer had only manifested as a keen instinct to diagnose an illness, and Kelly had recognised his potential.

Mallory's abilities developed rapidly under Kelly's mentorship, quickly becoming one of the Grand Seer's most promising students — until he began to experiment with the dead.

He became a murderer. His fascination with reaving grew into a fatal obsession, an irresistible hunger for dark knowledge. Unable to wait for his patients to die of natural causes, he simply took their lives. When he was finally arrested, the Protectorate discovered a macabre laboratory of corpses. Some of his less fortunate victims were repeatedly killed and resurrected as the madman tried to unlock the secrets of the afterlife.

Mallory had come closer than anyone to breaking the

barriers between life and death, and he was imprisoned in the same wing as Josh.

The cells of Bedlam were carefully constructed to ensure that nothing could ever be used as a vestige. Imprisoning someone who could use the history of an object to move through time was not a simple task. The door, desk, bed even the bars on the windows were specially treated to 'lose' time, but Josh had the memory of its creator floating around in his head, and like any good jailer there was always an escape route, just in case the lunatics ever took over the asylum. There was one bolt in the door, hardly distinguishable from the others, but with a little work could be loosened and there, soldered to the end of it, was a key. No larger than his fingertip, it could take him to any other door in the hospital.

By the time they reached Josh's cell, Bellamir had already managed to drink half of the bottle.

His fat fingers fumbled through the keys, calling off their names as if they were his children. There was no obvious system to it, not alphabetical or grouped in any particular way, but he eventually came to the right one.

'Here he is,' he announced, handing Rufius the key. 'You've got ten minutes while I take a turn around C wing.' He winked and wandered off with a drunken swagger.

Rufius waited until he disappeared around the corner before turning the key in the old lock. His plan was a simple one: give Josh his spare tachyon and keep the guard busy long enough for Josh to escape. It was all going to plan until he opened the door.

Josh had vanished.

Standing in Mallory's cell, Josh's eyes took a moment to adjust to the dim light. The walls were covered in runic symbols, scratched into the stone like a child chalking the pavement, written in a language that even the founder's memories couldn't decipher.

Mallory crouched on his bed, his knees drawn up to his chest beneath a stained linen night shirt. Matted ringlets of hair curtained his face, hiding his eyes. He scratched at the wall with a shard of bone, muttering something under his breath too quietly for Josh to hear.

'Doctor Mallory?'

The man ignored him.

Josh came closer until he could hear what Mallory was saying.

'The everliving have no place among us, they feed off our souls.'

The man repeated the phrase over and over, carving tiny runes into the darkened stone.

'Doctor Mallory, I have something for you,' said Josh, taking out the small parcel of liquorice from his gown and unwrapping it. The founder remembered that Mallory used them when poisoning his patients. The strong taste hid the bitterness of the arsenic. He even had a theory that they were part of some childhood experience that Mallory was reliving. The guards kept them in a storeroom for when they needed to bathe the madman.

Mallory looked up, his nose twitching at the scent. 'You have brought cakes?'

'Pontefract cakes, yes,' Josh said, placing the open paper on the floor and stepping back.

The doctor swept the hair away from his face, revealing his wild, haunted eyes. Like a feral cat he leaped from the bed and snatched up the present, taking it back to his straw-filled mattress and shoving three small black discs into his toothless mouth.

'What manner of man are you?'

'My name is Josh. I have come to ask you about the world of the dead.'

The man laughed, waving at the walls. 'You wish to know of Hades? Read on, everything is there for those with the eyes to see.'

Josh looked around the room at the thousands of lines of illegible text.

'You want to know if there is something beyond this life?' asked Mallory, picking out another piece of liquorice.

'I want to know if they can be reached.'

The doctor frowned, his voice becoming less manic. 'I'm afraid I've had rather limited success with summoning. It requires the most delicate balance of circumstances.'

'But it's possible?'

He smiled, and for a second there was a glimmer of sanity. 'Indeed it is. I have been shown to the gates of hell and communed with their spirits.'

Josh held out his hand. 'Can you show me?'

Mallory shook his head and shrank away, his eyes becoming wild once more. 'No, no. They will know. They will come for me in the darkening.'

'Who will?'

The madman tapped on the wall beside his bed. 'The Lazarus Brotherhood. They're the only ones to have broken the veil. The alchemists don't take kindly to my meddling.'

'So where can I find them?'

The man got up from his bed and walked around his

cell, his finger running over the lines of text like a blind man reading braille.

'In the castle of the Winter King.'

25

FUNERAL

R ain fell in cold grey sheets, lashing against the
windows of the horse-drawn hearse and the procession of mourners that passed slowly through the gates of the
cemetery.

Josh walked behind his mother's carriage like a
condemned man. His head bowed, shuffling his feet in
measured steps with the guards that escorted him.

He felt numb. There was a yawning void where the
memory of his mother should have been. All his attempts to
keep her alive had amounted to nothing, and worst of all, he
was probably responsible for her death. Crooke said it was
unavoidable, that nothing would have changed the
outcome, but Josh knew better. If Caitlin hadn't become
pregnant he could have saved her.

After returning to his cell, he found the colonel waiting for
him. The old man wanted to help him escape, but Josh

refused, he wanted to attend her funeral. He had to say goodbye.

They sat in the cell and drank rum, talking about his mother until dawn.

And although he trusted the man with his life, Josh kept what he'd learned from Doctor Mallory to himself.

When the horses could go no further, her coffin was removed and hoisted onto the shoulders of six Protectorate officers, each wearing temporal armour beneath their black cloaks.

Mallaron was leaving nothing to chance. His men surrounded every access point in and out of the cemetery, both physically and chronologically.

The colonel took the lead and the entourage followed him through the narrow streets of Victorian tombs. Josh remembered the first time Caitlin brought him to Highgate. It was after a gig in The Flask, their first ever date — his first ever Caitlin. Nothing he could do would ever bring that timeline back, he came close with this version, but there were still subtle differences.

There was no way to reach her while she was travelling in the Maelstrom. No way to tell her how sorry he was, or how much he needed her right now. He was glad it was raining, it helped to hide the tears that were running down his face.

The mausoleum was dark and cold. Josh shivered as he was escorted inside. It was a true house of the dead: carved angels looked down from the ceiling with sightless eyes, their wings creating arches that spread across the ceiling. It smelled of dust and stone, and it was the last place he wanted to think about her body being left: his mother would have preferred to have her ashes scattered on a rose garden on a sunny day, not some dark, gloomy tomb in the middle of a Victorian graveyard.

But he hadn't the strength to argue, she was gone, Caitlin was gone and their baby would never know its grandmother.

'Do you wish to say something?' the colonel asked while the Dreadnoughts slid her coffin silently into a dark hole in the wall.

Josh shook his head. 'She wasn't religious.'

The colonel patted Josh on the shoulder and ordered the men to seal up the tomb.

Taking out a hip flask and raising it into the air. 'She was a fine woman, with a kind heart,' he said, before taking a long drink and handing it to Josh.

'All she wanted was a garden.'

The guards bowed their heads and left.

'Will you take this now?' insisted the colonel, taking back the flask and handing Josh a battered old watch. 'It's only a Mark II, nothing special, but you know, just in case you wanted to leave that dreadful place.'

Josh felt the weight in his hand before flicking open the case with his thumb. 'Thank you,' he said, admiring the ornate brass dials that span in rings beneath. 'Won't you get into trouble for this?'

The colonel scoffed. 'When has that ever stopped me? Konstantine's got it in for you boy. I suggest you make a sharp exit whilst the others are too busy consoling each other.'

'No, I need to say goodbye.'

. . .

Outside, the mourners were waiting to pay their respects. The De Freis family, Professor Eddington and the grandmasters of some of the guilds waited patiently amongst the crypts of forgotten artists and engineers.

'My deepest condolences,' said Alixia, taking his hand. 'You are always welcome in our home.'

Before Josh could thank her, Lyra had her arms around his neck sobbing into his shoulder.

Sim stood behind her, his face set in grim determination trying not to cry, slightly embarrassed by his hysterical sister who continued to hold Josh tightly.

'I dreamed you died,' blurted Lyra between sobs. 'Caitlin stabbed you in the back. When I told her she said she would probably use a gun, not a knife and now there's the baby. God, I wish she was here.'

Josh tried not to look too confused. 'Me too.'

Alixia placed her hand on her daughter's shoulder. 'Come now dear, leave the poor man in peace.'

They separated and Lyra wiped the tears away with the sleeve of her dress.

Sim stepped forward. 'We're going to get you out of that awful place,' he assured Josh as the guards came to stand on either side of him.

'It's okay,' said Josh, glancing back to the colonel. 'I have time.'

Sim looked confused for a moment and then the realisation slowly dawned on him.

'Good, well,' he leaned forward for an awkward hug. 'Take care of yourself.'

Josh tried to smile and failed. 'Tell Cat to keep the ring safe, she'll know what it means.'

26

LETTER

[Nautilus, Day 1]

To my little one,
    I'm starting this journal for you, so that you would know how your life began.

At this moment, you're nothing but a flutter of tiny wings inside my belly as I sit on the observation deck of your grandmother's timeship watching it leave the continuum.

In real time it has been days since I last saw your father, but you will soon learn that time is a rather fluid concept for us, one that I hope you will learn to master.

His name is Joshua Jones and I want you to know him. To know the kind of man he was, because others may choose to remember him differently when we return to linear time.

In fact, I have no idea what the timeline will be like when we come back.

My hope is that when you read this we will all be safe and well, but I'm no seer and the chances are that the future will hold something quite different.

.   .   .

As I write this, your grandmother is piloting us into the chaotic realm, whilst your grandfather is hard at work in the kitchen singing to himself while he makes his speciality, a lamb stew, although with the distinct lack of sheep on board I have the sneaking suspicion it might be some form of rodent — I haven't the heart to tell him that I stopped eating meat.

They've spent the last ten years roaming the maelstrom, and for eight of those I thought they were dead, that's not something I would ever wish for you. I want you to know who your parents are. I want to watch you grow up — they had their reasons, but that my darling, is another story.

Your other grandmother is very ill and your father is doing everything he can to save her, which is highly commendable but also the reason I had to leave. We have the power to change the past, and as such we have a duty to protect it. Your father has taken it upon himself to use his abilities to cure her no matter what the consequences. We couldn't let those adjustments affect you, which left us with no other choice but to take you somewhere safe.

Perhaps when he realises what he's missing he will come and find us, until then I will be eating pizza, getting fat and exploring the dark realm with your crazy grandparents.

Beware the lamb stew,

xxx

27

GRAND SEER

[Oxford, England. Date: 1669]

The Grand Seer held the vial of blood up to the lamplight, tapping the glass with one of his long fingernails. 'A paradox you say?'

'That's what the xenobiologysts are calling it,' said Crooke, shifting uncomfortably in his seat. 'Their tests showed temporal anomalies — multiple displacements and timelines. They believe he didn't originate from this continuum.'

Rufius stood beside the fireplace, stirring the coals with a poker. 'They say that about most things. They've spent too long in the Maelstrom for my liking. Damned monster hunters.' He threw another log into the grate, sending a shower of sparks spiralling up the chimney. 'Do you think you can use it to find him?'

Kelly unstoppered the bottle and waved it under his sharp, aquiline nose. 'Why do you have his blood in the first place?'

The doctor paused, as if unsure whether he was

breaching a patient's confidence and then changed his mind. 'He thought he may be carrying the same defect as his mother.'

'And that he would pass it on to his child,' added the colonel.

Kelly took off his cap and dipped his forefinger into the blood. 'A reasonable concern to be sure, and now he's gone missing?'

'Konstantine is livid,' said Crooke, grinding his teeth. 'He's demanding my resignation.'

'Wasn't your fault old man,' Rufius reassured the doctor, patting him on the shoulder. 'Someone must have slipped him a tachyon at the funeral.'

Crooke's mouth twisted into an awkward smile. 'He'll have the Raven's men looking for him.'

'If I know that boy, he knows how to stay lost. They'll not find him.'

Kelly rubbed the blood against his thumb. 'Is that why you wish me to unravel this?'

'As only you can,' said Rufius, crossing his arms over his chest.

'Very well.'

Kelly pressed his thumbs together and then placed them on his temples. His head lolled as his eyes rolled back into his head.

'What, will the line stretch out to the crack of doom?' he said in a deep, booming baritone.

The colonel glanced at Crooke who simply shrugged. Both were used to Kelly's theatrical performances, although neither had witnessed him go into such a state of trance.

. . .

The blank-eyed seer drew a series of quick breaths and then sighed deeply.

'He's travelled many paths, some on this world, but there are others.'

He raised his hands into the air, fingers teasing out invisible knots.

'The lines are hard to weave. They lay over each other like the threads of a thousand carpets.'

Kelly shook his head and his eyes began to clear. 'Never have I seen such a timeline. There seems to be more than one, he carries a shadow of another's past like a curse.'

'Did you see where he is?'

The seer took a long drink of wine. Rufius noted the tremor in his hand as he picked up the glass.

'No, I can hardly tell you where he's been.'

Rufius cursed under his breath. 'Then he is truly lost.'

Kelly put his cap back onto his head. 'Not necessarily, I suggest we speak to Father Cappella.'

28

HOME

[London, England. Date: 2017]

Josh never thought he would ever be glad to see the Bevan Estate again.

It was hardly a welcoming place. Fourteen grey tenement buildings towered over him like tombstones as he walked through the communal garden towards their old flat. He'd experienced so many versions of his past, but somehow the original one still shone out among them, one that reminded him of his beginnings and he relied on it to keep him from forgetting who he was.

The usual patrol of BMX riders circled outside the fence like hooded vultures, watching him cross the grass, trying to decide if he would be an easy target.

Josh knew most of them by first name. In another time, he would have been a roadman, a member of the Ghost Squad, but 'Crash' didn't exist, not in this reality — nor for that matter did Lenin.

His numerous alterations resulted in a very different life for his mother at least. She'd lived well, lottery wins and various windfalls keeping her comfortable without growing suspicious, but Josh was cursed with a faultless memory — no matter how many times he adjusted their past, he would always remember his first life - trapped inside a dingy flat on the fifth floor, sometimes for weeks on end, while she recovered from yet another episode. It was a miserable childhood, but it was still the closest thing he ever had to a home, and where some of his oldest friends still lived.

For some reason, he always came back to the same point, like taking out an old shoe box of photographs, they were a living memento of his old life.

In the middle of the kids' playground, Shags and Gossy were sitting on the roundabout drinking cheap vodka and smoking weed. The dominance of their gang on the estate had shifted in their favour thanks to Josh. After this day, he'd tried various ways to improve their chances. Making subtle changes that would give them a better life. Gossy, Lilz and Dennis found good jobs and moved out of the Bevan, but the others preferred to stay put and get into trouble — some people just couldn't be helped.

'Hey,' Josh greeted them, leaning against what was left of the seesaw.

'Joshy,' Gossy said with a nod. 'Where you been bro?'

'Mum died.'

'Shit,' said Shags, throwing the joint away and stopping the roundabout's spin.

'Sorry man,' added Gossy, getting up and handing him the bottle. 'Take a pew.'

. . .

They talked about the old times for hours. Although some of their stories weren't quite the same as the ones Josh remembered, he enjoyed them all the same. It was the closest to normal he'd felt since the war with the Nihil.

'You ever wondered what it would've been like if your mum hadn't got sick?' asked Gossy, his words slurring slightly.

Josh took another swig from the bottle. 'Many times.'

The vodka was cheap but effective. He could feel the wall of ice that was holding back his grief slowly beginning to melt.

A BMW X5 announced its arrival with a deep booming bass as it pulled up on the kerb beside them.

'Sweet ride,' said Josh as Coz stepped out of the car.

'Business is good,' his friend replied with a smile. 'Wanna take it for a ride?'

'Oh yeah.'

Cars were always Josh's favourite form of escape. Driving fast through London's empty streets in the early hours of the morning had become something of an addiction when he was younger. Sneaking out after his mother fell asleep, he would use his abilities to break into any car, disabling the alarm and immobiliser with a touch of his hand. At twelve he was borrowing cars from the estate for fun, by thirteen he was stealing them to order.

The steering wheel felt good in his hands.

It was years since Josh had driven. In all of his adventures through history nothing ever came close to this kind of machine. The colonel had a similar passion for flying — they both loved the feeling of speed.

He drove the X5 onto the main A-road out of town. Gossy rode shotgun in the passenger seat and Coz and Shags lit up another joint in the back. Josh squeezed the accelerator and cranked up the stereo, slipping effortlessly between the afternoon traffic as he headed towards the motorway.

Ten minutes later, they reached the site of the accident. Josh's palms grew clammy as he approached the underpass. The others were too busy singing along to some random tune to notice he was slowing down.

Josh felt the memory surface like a shark.

Gossy died right there. He relived the moment his twelve-year-old friend lost control of the car and spun end-over-end into oncoming traffic.

He dropped into fourth and pulled out into the fast lane.

'Woah dude!' shouted Gossy as he was thrown back into the seat. 'Careful, you'll stack it.'

The others were laughing in the back.

He swerved around a lorry, accelerating past the place where Gossy crashed.

His friend sat beside him, watching the world speed past in a blur, blindly unaware of the gift that Josh had given him.

When the founder gifted his knowledge, Josh learned that small changes to individual lives made little or no difference to the overall destiny of the human race. It was depressing to realise that their lives were so insignificant, but it felt good to know that he'd saved someone at least.

29

BALTHAZAR'S EMPORIUM

[Exposition Universelle, Paris. Date: 1889]

Benoir took Lyra to the African pavilion on a miniature railway that had been built around the park. They sat opposite each other while the locomotive gently steamed along the three kilometre route. The carriage was filled with other visitors dressed in their 'Sunday best'. Men wore three-piece suits and the women beautiful dresses trimmed with lace. Many of them were obviously young couples using the anonymity of the crowds to spend some time together without the need for a chaperone.

Lyra pretended to look out of the window, but she couldn't stop glancing over at Benoir. There was an energy radiating from the zoologist that she was drawn to. He must have been in his early twenties, but his eyes were wise, filled with an unassuming confidence of a man who has seen the world. His hands were strong, as were the muscles that pulled the arms of his suit jacket taut.

'Have you been here before?' he asked.

She nodded. 'My mother would bring us to the circus every year. For the eggs.'

He smiled. 'Your mother is something of a legend.'

'You know her?'

He shook his head. 'No, but Georges speaks her name in hushed tones. I believe he is scared of her.'

Lyra laughed at the idea of the old man hiding from her mother. 'She does have that effect on some people.'

The train crossed over the Seine.

'But have you ever been to the Trocadero?' asked Benoir, pointing at the many-arched Byzantine palace that looked across at the Eiffel Tower from the hill of Chaillot. 'The American soprano Sybil Sanderson is singing in *Esclarmonde*.' He blushed slightly, realising that it sounded as though he were asking her on a date.

Lyra shook her head. 'We hardly ever spent any time mixing with the linears, and *never* had any time for opera. What's it about?'

Benoir smiled. 'A love story between Esclarmonde, an empress of Byzantium and a French knight. She's also a sorceress who visits him every night, wearing a veil as a disguise.'

'Is there a magic ring?'

He laughed. 'A magic sword, which the knight, whose name is Roland, uses to defeat the Saracens who threaten her land.'

'And, don't tell me.' She held up her hand. 'The sorceress dies before revealing her identity!'

'No. For vanquishing their enemy, the King of France offers him the hand of his daughter, but the knight refuses and his affair with the sorceress is revealed.'

'So he dies?'

Benoir sighed and the old lady next to Lyra chuckled behind her fan.

'If I tell you, you won't want to see it!'

Lyra leaned forwards. 'If you don't tell me I definitely won't come.'

'So the sorceress curses the knight and is told by her father, the emperor, to renounce him or have her powers revoked. He organises a tournament to find a suitable suitor for her, and the black knight who wins her hand is revealed to be none other than Roland, her lover.'

The train came to a halt as Lyra frowned. 'So no one dies?'

'No. This is our stop.'

The pavilion of Africa wasn't quite as grand as that of India or Argentina. There were elephants giving rides to children around the reconstructed mud huts of a village where a troupe of Maasai warriors were performing a traditional dance.

Taking Lyra by the hand, Benoir ignored the main attractions and led her into an unassuming wooden shack with a roof made of palm leaves.

Beyond the beaded curtain, the interior was a vast warehouse filled with African masks, shields and spears. Lyra spotted a number of Antiquarians perusing idols carved from ivory — this was obviously a black market dealer, one that traded in forbidden artefacts.

'Cousineau!' someone shouted from across the hall. It was a tall dark-skinned man wearing a long white linen shift gathered in the middle with a crimson sash and a curved sword, a scimitar.

'Balthazar, what on earth are you wearing?' asked Benoir in French.

The man spread his arms wide and grinned. 'I'm a Saracen, what do you think?' He turned around showing off a beautiful turquoise cloak.

'I thought you were from Tunisia.'

'Ha! You white people can't tell if I'm from Botswana or the Barbary Coast. This is all part of the act. How have you been my friend, I haven't seen you since — '

'Since I pulled you out of that dig site in the Olduvai Gorge.'

The man's eyes lit up. 'Ah yes, Tanzania. I still have a couple of quartzite hand axes if you're interested?'

Benoir shook his head, reverting to English. 'We've come to ask you about an artefact.'

'Have you now? And who is this fair maiden?' asked Balthazar, bowing slightly to Lyra.

'Lyra De Freis,' she replied.

'Welcome to my humble bazaar Miss De Freis — ' The merchant froze mid-sentence. 'No relation to Alixia De Freis?' he asked, his tone slightly higher than before. 'My apologies for the presumption, but it is such an unusual name.'

'She's my mother.'

'Ah. Well, would you excuse me for a moment?' He looked around anxiously, as if expecting Alixia to enter at any moment.

'She's not with me, I came alone.'

He looked relieved. 'Did you now? How very progressive of you. I've always believed young women should have freedom to explore the world.' He took a breath. 'So, Miss De Freis, how may I be of service?'

Lyra took out the sketch of the spear-head and showed it to Balthazar.

'Have you ever seen such a thing?' asked Benoir.

The merchant studied the drawing closely, his eyes narrowing as if needing reading glasses.

'Looks a little like something I sold a few years ago. Not African though, much older, the metal was like nothing I'd ever seen, very unusual timeline.'

'What kind of unusual?' asked Lyra.

The man's eye widened. 'Old, antediluvian.'

'Like a talisman?'

He waved his hands as if warding off a demon. 'My friend, I am an honourable man, I would never sell such a thing, that would be illegal.' There was a glint in his eye that suggested to Lyra that he was being less than honest.

'So who did you sell it to?' continued Benoir, ignoring his protests.

Balthazar sucked air in through his teeth. 'Well, that is confidential information,' he said, rubbing his hands together. 'I have my reputation to think about.'

Benoir took something out of his jacket pocket. 'You're a pirate and a bandit who would sell his own grandmother for the right price. I assume this will be sufficient,' he said, handing him a small leather package.

The merchant unwrapped it carefully. 'Mastodon tooth. Very nice. The Japanese go wild for ground tooth says it improves their —' He went to make a gesture with his arm and then thought better of it.

'So the buyer?' insisted Benoir.

'Was a linear. I do some business through a shop on the rue des Rosiers here in Paris. The man paid a very good price for it.'

'What was his name?'

Balthazar's eyes flickered as he tried to recall the name. 'Rothstein, I believe he said.'

'When exactly was this?'

'A decade ago maybe more. You know I don't go much on paperwork.'

Benoir shrugged and began to look around the room for something.

'Anything else I can do for you?'

'Do you still trade in gravestones?'

The merchant feigned a look of horror. 'What do you take me for? A reaver?'

Benoir sighed. 'You sell famous graves to rich collectors. There is a book in your office with the location of every notable grave within three hundred years.'

Balthazar shrugged. 'I'm just servicing a need. If it wasn't me then there are twenty others that would do it in my place. The dead are hardly going to notice.'

'I need a local one.'

'Fine. Where do you want to start?'

'Père Lachaise Cemetery.'

30

WELLINGTON'S GOLD

Eddington's scowl deepened as he read the report for the third time.

'Are you quite sure about this?' he asked, looking up at Sim, whom he considered to be one of his most promising actuaries.

The young man, unfazed by the questioning of his master, began manipulating a series of levers and dials until the ten years leading up to June 1815 settled into a web of fine lines in the space around them.

Eddington was impressed, although he didn't show it. Sim had taken little more than a day to master the workings of the Infinity Engine.

'These are all of Napoleon's military campaigns,' his student explained, making fine adjustments to the controls until certain date nodes on the paths glowed red. 'The key turning points were his capture after the Battle of Leipzig, the retreat from Russia and finally his defeat at Waterloo against the Seventh Coalition, known as the Hundred Days War.'

Eddington studied the subtly shifting nexus of lines that made up the event. Temporal glyphs hovered around it, symbolic equations showing the probability of each outcome.

'It appears that someone has adjusted the outcome of that particular moment,' he observed, pointing at a branching line.

Sim nodded and walked into the centre of the model. 'My calculations show that the coalition forces should have won the battle and deposed the Emperor of France.'

'By what percentage?'

'Fifty-two-point-five,' replied Sim without hesitation.

Eddington studied the point closely. 'But instead Napoleon's empire flourishes and Louis XVIII never takes his rightful place on the throne.'

'The Anglo-Prussian army were narrowly defeated by the French. One of the main contributing factors was the high levels of desertion they suffered during the weeks leading up to the conflict.' He pointed to thousands of fine lines that split away from the main timeline like a fraying rope. 'Many of them were mercenaries and there seems to have been an issue with their pay. A large shipment of gold bullion had been stolen and morale suffered as a result.'

'Stolen?'

His assistant nodded and shifted the focus of the model. 'I believe that it was taken in transit somewhere between leaving England and Wellington's headquarters in Brussels.'

'Do we know by whom?'

'We don't. There isn't enough data to determine who might be responsible.'

'And so you're recommending that we send a watchman?'

Sim nodded. 'I am.'

Eddington turned to the final page of the report. 'Your estimates for correction have been verified?'

'They are within one standard deviation.'

'Then I approve your plan, but on one condition.'

Sim already knew what it would be. 'That I accompany the agent.'

The professor smiled. 'I believe you're ready for your first active engagement. Now all we need to do is find West-inghouse.'

31

THE WINTER KING

[Prague, Bohemia. Date: 1620]

J osh woke up under a bridge.

Rain cascaded down from the high stone arch, sending a cold stream of water across the cobbles, under his back and into the river beside him. His head was pounding. Whatever his friends had persuaded him to drink after they finished the drive had been lethal.

A breeze swept along the embankment, bringing with it the aroma of rotting cabbage and human excrement. He felt his stomach heave at the smell and turned over to find people huddling together in the shadows, it was too dark to see if they were sleeping or dead.

Welcome back, the founder greeted him.

Where are we? asked Josh, looking up at the arches that stretched across the wide river.

Prague 1620, beneath the Charles Bridge.

Josh closed his eyes, primarily to stop the world from spinning, but also so he could enter the founder's archives.

'This is the time of the Winter King, Frederick V,'

explained the ghost of the founder, sitting beside an imaginary fire.

Josh was confused. 'And you brought me here why?'

'You were incapacitated and I calculated that there was an eighty per cent probability that Mallaron's men would have recaptured you if we had stayed there any longer.'

'But why here?' asked Josh, ignoring the worrying fact that the founder could take control of his body when he was asleep.

The old man rose and pulled a memory from his shelf. 'This Lazarus brotherhood interests me. Nathaniel Mallory gave us a temporal location, a specific point in history to work from. Somewhere in this period there are men who might have the answer, someone who could help you reach your mother.'

Josh's body shivered, reminding him that the fire wasn't real and that right now he was still lying in a puddle of something awful on the bank of a river.

'So where do we start?'

'With a lesson,' said the founder, opening the book. The history of Frederick V of Bohemia flooded into Josh's mind.

Standing on the bridge, Josh watched the black waters of the River Vltava flow silently beneath his feet. It was still night and the streets were dark. Light from the windows of the Royal Palace shone out over the roofs of the surrounding houses. It stood over Prague like an ancient sentry, the thick walls a testament to a turbulent history. The Winter King's rule would be no exception, the founder's memories told Josh that it would end in little over a year from his coronation.

.   .   .

Alchemy had been practised in Prague since the reign of Rudolf II, a king whose fascination with the occult sciences brought many renowned astrologers and scientists to his court, including Edward Kelly, the Grand Seer himself.

Which raised the question of why Mallory had sent him to his castle nine years after Rudolf ceded the crown to his brother? A man who had no interest in alchemy and moved his court to Vienna.

This was what intrigued the founder. Whoever the Lazarus Brotherhood were, they had survived the loss of their patron. It was a gap in his knowledge, a period of history that drew a blank from the old man's memories.

Josh pulled his travelling cloak tighter around him and walked over the bridge towards the castle. Whoever they were, Mallory thought they could reach into the afterlife and that was all he needed, the rest was waiting behind the walls of the fortress.

'Oi ty! Zůstaň kde jsi!' a man shouted, walking out of the shadows at the far end of the bridge. Dressed in a long leather coat, he carried a lantern and a heavy-looking wooden cudgel.

In the time it took the nightwatchman to utter those first words, the founder recognised and installed the language into Josh's conscious mind. *Stay where you are.*

'State your business,' he ordered, holding the light up so Josh could see his lumpy, potato-shaped face and unruly beard.

The man's nose was bright red, and Josh could smell the alcohol from a few feet away, which was doing nothing for his own hangover. He considered rewinding and taking another route. His fingers feeling the weight of the tachyon in the pocket of his cloak.

'I'm Jaromír, a merchant,' replied Josh in what he hoped was a convincing local Czech dialect.

'Not from round these parts then?' the guard noted, looking at Josh's boots as if he were sizing them up for himself.

'No, a bookseller — I travel widely,' lied Josh, hoping that the man wouldn't notice he wasn't carrying any books.

'Hah!' The man spat. 'I've no time for any book but one. Where are you staying?'

Josh noticed the wooden crucifix hanging from around the man's neck.

'At the Brabantskeho Tavern,' came the answer before Josh had time to think. The founder hijacking his mouth.

The man looked back over his shoulder towards the castle. 'You're on the wrong side of town.'

'I had business in the Klementinum,' the founder spoke through Josh again, a map appeared in his mind that put the library directly behind him.

'At one o'clock in the morning?'

Josh shrugged. 'Librarians keep long hours.'

The man didn't look convinced. 'The library's been closed since the curfew was imposed.' He lifted the cudgel onto his shoulder. 'This is no time to be out on the streets. I think you should accompany me to Daliborka — the Captain of the Guard will be interested in hearing why you're out after dark.'

Before Josh had a chance to reply the guard swung his staff, hitting Josh in the temple and knocking him to the ground.

32

FATHER CAPELLA

[Cerebrium]

For over five hundred years the greatest minds of the Order had been carefully removed and stored in the Cerebrium. Each one sealed inside a glass bell jar and preserved for eternity in specially prepared stasis fluids. Members were allowed to access and transfer these precious memories through a process known as 'Intuiting'.

Doctor Crooke made some excuse of having other matters to attend to and left the others to converse with the old monk.

Kelly refused to go alone. To the sensitive nature of the seer, it was a place of ghosts and echoes, which he would generally refer to as the 'house of the half-dead,' or 'pickled madness'.

While others required the physical contact of the copper electrodes to connect with the dormant minds, Kelly's abilities were so finely tuned that merely being in the same room was like standing in the centre of a debating chamber with everyone clamouring to get his attention.

.   .   .

Walking along the long corridor, its walls stacked high with jars, Kelly bowed to the various grey matters as though he were meeting old friends at a party. It was made more comical by the fact he was wearing a knight's jousting helmet, insisting that its metal insulated him from the worst of the mental wittering.

Rufius followed the Grand Seer as he wandered from side to side like a chess piece trying to avoid stepping on the white squares of the tiled floor.

'Would you mind telling me why we're here?' asked Rufius.

Kelly pirouetted around on one foot to face him. 'There is only one way to walk between the timelines in the way that young Joshua has.'

Taking a ring from his finger, he rolled it over the back of his knuckles like a magician. 'I believe he possesses a talisman — perhaps even the fabled Ring of Solomon. There is one here who knows of such forbidden things. '

Father Joaquin Cappella was generally regarded as a maverick among the guild of Antiquarians. A Capuchin monk, he spent most of his long life curating the archives of the Medici family, which were stored deep below the Vatican in 1540.

Cappella was the director of the collection for nearly three hundred years and learned more about its artefacts and manuscripts than any other curator. He was also something of an expert in a contentious field of research that was often ridiculed by other archivists — the study of the talismans.

Talismanic objects were the stuff of legend. Many academics believed they were nothing more than wish-fulfilment, created to bring a sense of mystery to the otherwise banal life of an Antiquarian. These were the so-called 'Holy Grail' of artefacts, passed down from the gods, ones that would imbue the owner with supernatural powers.

The term 'Grail hunter' became synonymous with certain factions of the Antiquarian guild, those who sought out such mythical objects, and there were many from which to choose. Various versions of Excalibur, the Spear of Destiny and the Turin Shroud were gathering dust in the Antiquarian's special repository in the Vatican. It was given the name of 'Medici' in an effort to lend it some credibility, but the Order's scholars scoffed at the idea of any truth to the myths.

But Capella was a single-minded individual with the entire collection of the Vatican at his disposal, and he spent most of his adult life in a quest to find the truth.

Dying at the grand old age of ninety-eight, he bequeathed his brain and its accumulated knowledge to the Order.

He was stored in a small alcove amongst the less distinguished Antiquarians. Obviously misfiled, as if someone was intentionally making it difficult to find him.

Kelly sang to himself as Rufius struggled to put the net of copper wires over his mass of red hair. Capella floated in a bell jar on the table and the seer tapped the glass, watching the bubbles begin to form across the surface of the grey matter.

WHO? WHAT? - Came the usual initial response from the awakening mind.

'Ask him about talismans,' Kelly whispered, rubbing his temples with his fingers.

I AM WESTINGHOUSE. I COME SEEKING KNOWLEDGE.

Rufius thought in response.

Memories of the Vatican vaults flooded into his head. Thousands of images of books and artefacts unfolded inside his mind like a Chinese puzzle box, creating a complex four dimensional model of the entire collection throughout Capella's entire career.

SUBJECT?

Came the response from the old monk, reminding Rufius that this was nothing more than a biological machine, its tone devoid of all personality.

TALISMAN.

The model shifted, reconfiguring itself and removing irrelevant exhibits until only a few items remained. They were like random playing cards connected by a single line of red thread.

TALSIMAN> ANCIENT CIVILISATION > Anunnaki.

Following the line, which was clearly the old monk's train of thought, Rufius was taken on a journey through a medieval treatise on Solomon's dynasty, the monk noting some obscure reference to powerful beings in the illustrated marginalia; then to the Lingyin Temple in Hangzhou showing god-like beings carved into the walls and lastly to a temple in Babylon, where the priests seem to worship winged men with glowing weapons.

Gradually Rufius began to see the pattern. The old priest had managed to piece together the strangest jigsaw puzzle of tiny fragments, like finding the bones of some mythical creature scattered across millennia.

What Capella discovered was undeniable. The fleeting remnants of a group of beings with god-like powers, ones that had been lost in time, the talismans the only proof of their existence.

Suddenly the connection was interrupted. Rufius's eyes snapped open to find Kelly holding the broken wires between his fingers, his jousting helmet covering the glass jar.

The Grand Seer was staring at something over Rufius's shoulder and before he could turn around to see what it is, Kelly spoke.

'Simeon, what a pleasant surprise.'

'Master Westinghouse,' Sim said nervously. 'The Professor requests your assistance on an urgent mission.'

33

DALIBORKA

[Prague Castle. Date: 1620]

Daliborka was a prison.

Josh was still unconscious when the guard brought him into the tower and stripped off his clothes. He woke to find he'd been lowered through a trapdoor into a cold, dark dungeon.

Shivering beneath the small disc of light in the ceiling, he watched as the chains were winched back up through the hole into the floor above.

'Well, we're in the castle,' he said to himself.

The founder failed to respond.

'Welcome to hell,' said a stranger's voice.

Josh stepped back out of the light, allowing his eyes to adjust. 'Who are you?'

'An unfortunate man,' replied the silhouette.

Josh heard the skittering of claws on the stone floor and the shuffling of feet amongst the straw.

'One that couldn't pay his debts.'

Trying to keep the voice in front of him, Josh moved backwards until he felt the rough stone wall at his back.

'How long have you been here?'

There was a long sigh. 'What year is it?'

'Sixteen twenty.'

The man groaned. 'Two years.'

'How much do you owe?'

He coughed, a hollow sound that was tinged with a sickening rattle. 'That depends on your point of view,' he began. 'The doctor who sold me the potion says I owe him ten ducats, but since it failed to save my daughter's life, I tend to disagree.'

'So they threw you in here?'

'No, he did far worse — he accused me of divination and consorting with Lucifer. I'm cursed in the eyes of the church, they would burn me if they could.'

'What's your name?'

'Thaddeus.'

He stepped into the beam of light as they closed the grate above them. In the fading light, Josh glimpsed the skeletal form of a half-starved man, his ribs protruded from his chest like a deeply ploughed field and sores covered his withered legs. Most of his face was hidden behind a large bushy beard and long unwashed hair. The smell of the man was overpowering.

'Well, Thaddeus, how would you like to prove them right?'

'I don't understand?'

'How would you like to disappear?'

. . .

Twelve hours earlier, and they were standing in the grounds of the castle. The good people of Prague were making their way home across the Charles Bridge while the water of the River Vltava turned gold in the dying rays of the sun. Thaddeus could hardly stand on his feet. He leaned against Josh sheltering his eyes and staring in wonder across at the city like a man seeing it for the first time.

'How?'

Josh could have explained how he'd used the timeline of the broken jug the guard threw at him when he wouldn't stop singing rap tunes, going back to the moment when the serving girl from the local tavern brought it into the castle, but somehow that felt too boring.

'I've read a few books. I know a little magic.'

Thaddeus's eyes widened and he stepped away from Josh. 'You're an alchemist?'

'Of sorts.'

Thaddeus's mouth widened into a broken-toothed smile. 'Then you may be able to help me lift this damned curse.' He looked around nervously. 'But first we must visit my wife.'

'First, we need to find some clothes,' Josh reminded him as they set off.

34

DIRECTORY OF THE DEAD

[Père Lachaise Cemetery, Paris. Date: 1880]

Benoir was a druid, Lyra realised as they appeared inside the crypt of Rossini. It was a nickname members of the Order used for those who could navigate the timelines of natural substances like rock and wood. He could do it well, she had hardly felt the shift when they left Balthazar's Bazaar.

Stone was a particularly difficult material to weave. Many believed it was too dangerous to even attempt; the epoch-spanning length of its timeline and the fractal nature of its geological structure made it virtually impossible to read. There were very few members with the skill, but it did explain how Benoir could travel back to the Palaeolithic without a man-made object.

They stepped out of the composer's crypt and into an avenue of tombs. The sky was dark and the moonlight silvered the mausoleums lining both sides of the path.

'Why here?' she asked in a hushed voice, fearing that she would wake the dead.

'If you're trying to find a linear, easier to start with their ancestors,' said Benoir, taking her by the hand.

He's weird, but kind of interesting, she thought to herself.

After the crowds of the exposition, Lyra found walking through the necropolis together strangely romantic. Large moths gathered nectar from the lilac bushes that hung overhead, their wings nothing but a silver blur in the semi-darkness. Somewhere in the distance, she could hear the haunting strings of a violin, reminding her that beyond the walls of the garden cemetery was the 20th arrondissement.

Benoir was quiet and brooding, his free hand touching the passing crypts like a farmer walking through a field of corn. Lyra could feel his lifeline shifting beneath her fingers, but resisted the temptation to read him. She wanted to get to know him the old-fashioned way. So many of her previous relationships had been ruined by the "seer's curse", by her ability to look into their future.

He should have been honoured at that level of restraint she was showing. She smiled inwardly at the thought of kissing him, which of course she would do before long, you didn't need to be a seer to know that.

'Here,' he said, stopping at an ornate Gothic tomb.

The door to the vault was a large piece of polished granite inscribed with the names and dates of the dead, but it was too dark to read the details.

'How do you know?' asked Lyra.

'The stone talks,' he replied, striking a match against a sculpted angel wing. 'These are members of the Rothstein family. Four generations are buried here.'

'So which one is our buyer?'

Benoir ran his fingers over their names: Nathaniel, Jacob, Gustav and Alphonse.

Lyra watched him work, calculating their ages as she went. 'There's something odd about them.'

'What?'

'They all died at seventy. Look at the dates.' She pointed to the golden numbers inscribed into the dark marble.

'Strange indeed.' He blew out the match and placed his hand on the door. 'Shall we?'

She nodded, taking his hand once more.

Inside the crypt it was cold and dark. Lyra shivered as Benoir took down a small lamp and lit it. Their breath froze in the air between them, lingering like unspoken words in the pale light. She didn't like tombs, they smelled of emptiness and despair, of bone and dust.

There were four shelves inside the chamber, each one containing a dusty coffin shrouded in a curtain of cobwebs.

He put the lamp on a shelf and took off his jacket, placing it over her shoulders.

Cracking open the lid of the nearest coffin with his bare hands, Benoir looked inside. 'It's okay, there's no one here.'

'Other than the dead you mean,' said Lyra, unconsciously stroking the scars on her arm. The dead were a dangerous obsession for seers. Too many of her kind had gone mad in search of the afterlife.

'No, look.'

Nervously she peered inside, the box was empty.

'So someone stole the bodies? Resurrectionists perhaps?'

Benoir shrugged and opened a second coffin, again it was empty.

'Why would they bother interring four empty coffins,' he asked himself when he'd checked all of them.

'Perhaps they died at sea? And their bodies were never recovered,' suggested Lyra, sitting down on a small altar that had been carved into the opposite wall.

'They would have to be a particularly unlucky family to have lost four generations in the same way.'

Lyra's eyes lit up. 'Maybe they're vampires, faking their own deaths to stop arousing suspicion.'

His expression changed, as if he were seriously considering the idea.

'That was a joke by the way.'

'Maybe, but there have been reports of attacks here in Paris. The police barred all the gates to the catacombs because they believe the murderer is using them to move under the city.'

Lyra laughed. 'It's more likely this Rothstein is one of us pretending to be a linear, one of my uncles did that for three hundred years.'

Sitting down beside her, Benoir didn't look convinced. 'Doesn't explain why he bought your dagger.'

'No, but it's a good start.' She nuzzled into him, for warmth as well as comfort. 'Will you help me?' she added, titling her head up towards his.

'Of course.'

She let her lips part a little, feeling his warm breath on her neck.

'Good.'

His arms went around her and she felt his mouth on hers.

35

GOLEM

[Prague. Date: 1620]

Thaddeus took Josh to a small town house on Boršov, a street not far from the bridge on the opposite side of the river from the castle. Walking along the embankment, he explained how he was once a physician to King Rudolf II, but lost favour with the court after Rudolf died.

'The king was obsessed with the occult. Sendivogius brought alchemists from all corners of the world to help his majesty find the philosopher's stone.'

'Sendivogius?' asked Josh, when the founder's memories were not forthcoming.

'A Polish alchemist and metallurgist, one of Rudolf's favourites,' Thaddeus replied bitterly. 'When Rudolf died, he ingratiated himself with his brother Matthias, who had little interest in the sciences and removed us all from court.'

Thaddeus's wife was so pleased to see him when she opened the door that she wept for over an hour. She treated Josh with suspicion until her husband explained how he helped him, carefully avoiding the magical details of their escape.

'These are troubled times,' she apologised, shaking his hand for the third time. 'Men of science are being punished.' She nodded to her husband who was playing with their children.

'Why?' Josh asked.

'The Golem,' she whispered, as if the word alone might summon the creature. 'It walks the streets at night and takes the wicked and innocent alike.'

The founder's memories shared the origins of the Golem. *A Jewish mythical creature formed from clay that was supposed to be able to summon the spirits of the dead.*

Thaddeus disentangled himself from the younger of his children and came to join them at the table. 'The legend has it that the Maharal created the Golem to protect the Jews from Rudolf, but that he forgot to immobilise it before the Sabbath and it went on a murderous rampage.'

The Maharal was a Jewish scholar, mystic and philosopher who served as a leading rabbi in the cities of Mikulov in Moravia and Prague in Bohemia. Died 1609.

His wife gripped her husband's hand, wiping her eyes with her apron. 'Many men and women have disappeared in the last two years. The City Guard arrest anyone who has any links with Kabbalah or breaks the curfew. They will come looking for you soon, my love.'

Josh could see they clearly believed there was something stalking the streets.

Hardly likely to be a monster created from river clay. The founder's logic interjected, *but there must be some element of truth to the story.*

'That was ten years ago. Why do you think the Golem has returned?'

Thaddeus looked nervously at his wife, who nodded and went off to the stove to tend to the dinner.

'After Rudolph's death, Sendivogius formed a secret brotherhood of alchemists, one that continues to study the ancient texts. I met one of them while I was in the tower. He said they knew of the Golem maker. That they have found all the pieces of the original clay and put it back together. He believed that these are the men that have been taking the people, using them to feed the creature.'

'Did he tell you where they meet?'

The physician shook his head. 'There are many places to hide below the streets. Old parts of the city that have been forgotten.'

His wife returned with two steaming bowls of pork and dumplings. 'Enough talk. Now we eat.' She fetched a bottle of brandy from a high shelf. 'And work out how to get you out of the city.'

36

WATERLOO

[Waterloo, Belgium. Date: June 18, 1815]

'After the battle at Quatre Bras, Wellington's army withdraws to a defensive position on the low ridge of Mont-Saint-Jean, south of the village of Waterloo,' explained Sim, standing beside Rufius while they studied the battlefield from beneath the eaves of a windmill.

Through the fog of war, they caught glimpses of Napoleon's Imperial Army marching in regimented squares across the ground towards the escarpment. The sound of fifty thousand infantry and fourteen thousand cavalry thundering across the fields towards the allied position was deafening.

'This is not my first Waterloo,' Rufius reminded Sim, patting him on the shoulder. 'You never forget your first battle, try not to soil your breeches.'

Sim smiled awkwardly, unsure whether the old man was joking. They were both dressed as Prussian officers, pretending to be part of General Bülow's IV Corps.

Opening his almanac, Sim scribbled a note onto a blank

page and watched as messages and battle plans began to appear around it. Somewhere, back in the Copernican headquarters, an entire department was working on the best approach to this problem. The notebook was sympathetically linked to a twin, using a form of quantum entanglement, allowing the Copernicans to communicate with their field agents throughout time.

'Nineteen hundred hours,' noted Sim, checking his tachyon. 'Napoleon will bring his Imperial Guard to bear on Wellington's centre in the next thirty minutes.'

The sound of the artillery boomed across the grey sky like thunder.

'And the Thirtieth Foot will break, leaving it to the Prince of Orange to hold the second line,' added Rufius, taking out his sabre and removing his hat. He was a tall, broad-shouldered man with a thick neck. Sim was sure that he would be more than capable of defending himself in the conflict, in fact he seemed quite eager to join the fray.

'We're supposed to be following the gold shipment,' Sim reminded him, watching the man prime his flintlocks. 'You can't change the outcome of this, there are over a hundred-thousand men down there.'

Rufius chuckled to himself. 'I wasn't intending to.' Tucking the pistols into his belt. 'But, I'm not going to stand by and watch a whole regiment get slaughtered. We need to find a vestige and they need assistance, I think that leaves only one course of action.'

With that he grabbed hold of one of the arms of the slowly-turning windmill and slid down the sail.

Watching the man disappear into the fog below, Sim froze, he wasn't a fighting man and the carnage unfolding on the fields below was sickening. It had rained hard the night before, turning the ground into a deadly quagmire, men and horses were dying in the cloying mud.

This was exactly why Professor Eddington sent him: to experience the grim reality of war, to understand what went on behind the millions of calculations of their algorithm. 'Death is unavoidable,' the professor reminded him while they formulated a plan for this mission. 'The purpose of our work is to minimise it.'

'Are you coming?' Rufius called up from the ground, like a child asking if he wanted to come out to play.

Sim waved and went back into the windmill to use the stairs.

'Study the environmental factors, follow the watchman closely,' the words of his mother came back to him as he descended. 'Stay close to Rufius, he'll know what to do,' she added, fussing over him like it was his first day at school.

The 'watchmen' were field agents. What Sim's department would call the 'Executors of Change'. Their job was to apply the adjustment. Thousands of hours of work would lead to that one decisive moment that would change history. Secondary to that were the investigations, when no amount of statistical modelling could explain the course of action. They would be sent in to follow the timeline back to find the anomaly and to ensure a suitable vestige was recovered — one that could be connected to the specific event that would need a subsequent repair.

A vestige could be any object connected to the scene, preferably one whose timeline could be followed back to the inciting incident.

Reaching the ground, Sim took a deep breath and stepped out into the battle.

37

ROTHSTEIN

[Cirque D'Histoire, Paris. Date: 1889]

'So Rothstein bought your spear and now you think he's Nosferatu?' asked Cuvier, struggling to hide his disbelief.

Benoir ignored his tone and continued. 'There were no bodies. The man calling himself Alphonse has simply changed his name.'

'Four times?'

'At least.'

'They're one of the richest families in Europe,' said Cuvier, taking a gold twenty-franc coin from his pocket. 'During the depression, Alphonse was awarded the Grand Cross of the Légion d'Honneur for his support through the economic crisis.'

'It's the same man,' Lyra assured Cuvier. 'We checked.'

After the night in the cemetery, Lyra explained how they followed the trail of the elusive banker back through time.

'Jacob Mayer Rothstein came to Paris in 1812 and changed his name to James. Five years later he formally created the *de Rothstein Frères* bank with four of his brothers. Highly successful investors, they became bankers to Leopold I of Belgium and earned the hereditary title of Baron from the Emperor of Austria by 1822. There were rumours that Louis Philippe owed his rise to power after the July Revolution in no small part to James's loans.'

They went back further, to Frankfurt, where they found the man going under the name of Mayer Amschel Rothstein, who was acting as principal international banker to Wilhelm IX and was handling payments of German mercenaries for Britain.

'He was said to be buried in Frankfurt cemetery,' said Benoir. 'The casket was empty too.'

'There are five main branches of Rothsteins: Frankfurt, Paris, Vienna, London and Naples. We have been to every one of them, the so-called brothers are all the same man.'

Cuvier looked surprised. 'How has he managed to live this long?'

Benoir shrugged. 'Maybe he's one of us?'

'No, the Copernicans would never let one of our own have so much power.'

'Maybe he's immortal?' suggested Lyra. 'Not like Dracula, but something else. There are other animals that can live longer than humans.'

'Like tortoises,' joked Cuvier, 'or whales?'

'Or something from the Maelstrom,' she replied.

'Well, in that case you will need to speak to an expert, and for that you need a permit.'

38

FINDING THE THIEF

[Waterloo, Belgium. Date: June 18, 1815]

Sim followed Rufius as he skirted around the edge of the battlefield. It was slow going, the ground was soft and littered with injured and dying men. Through the smoke he caught glimpses of Wellington's forces on the ridge, preparing to engage the Imperial Guard.

The French were moving their artillery forward and hammering the allied lines with cannon fire. Sim didn't need to consult his almanac to know the chances of victory for Wellington were low; his men were outnumbered by at least two-to-one and there was no sign of the Prussians.

Although most of Napoleon's army were focused on attacking the centre of the enemy position, there were some soldiers who'd either lost their unit or had enough of the cloying mud and were making their way to drier land.

Rufius was swift and brutal when these desperate men came at them out of the fog. His pistols took down the first two in quick succession and the sabre another four. By the time they reached Hougoumont Farm an hour had passed and at least six other men had died by his hand.

The chateau lay in ruins. Its thick stone walls had crumbled, its gates decimated by artillery fire and the garrison abandoned. Piles of corpses were scattered inside the compound, most bearing the insignia of the 2nd battalion of the Coldstream Guards.

Rufius searched the dead until he found their commanding officer, Lieutenant-Colonel Wyndham, his body sitting propped against the wall of a well in the middle of the courtyard. A musket shot had taken away half of his face.

Dropping his sword, Rufius picked up Wyndham's sabre, feeling the weight of it in his hand and opening its timeline. Scenes from the attack filled his mind. In a ghostly replay he watched the French breach the gates and Wyndham's men trying desperately to repel them, but their numbers had been too great and the farm had fallen.

'Wait here,' he said to Sim.

Weaving back to the moments before the gate was lost, Rufius moved back seven hours.

12:30

It was chaos.

A French lieutenant wielding an axe broke through the North gate with the 1st Light Infantry following behind him. What was left of the British garrison were doing their best to force them back in the confined space of the courtyard, but it was a gruelling melee of hand-to-hand combat.

Rufius grabbed the arm of an ensign. 'What's your name son?'

'Gooch sir,' said the young man, recognising Rufius's rank. He was wearing the epaulets of a captain.

'We need to get those gates closed.' He pointed at the splintered wooden doors that were half hanging off their twisted hinges. 'Find me three men and follow me.'

An officer standing nearby overheard them.

'Corporal James Graham,' he introduced himself with a strong Irish accent. 'Lead the way!'

Rufius drew his pistol and shot the axe-wielding Frenchman through the heart before taking out Wyndham's sabre and carving a path towards the gates.

The four of them put their backs to the wooden doors, straining against the oncoming tide of soldiers, thrusting at any man that tried to squeeze through the rapidly closing gap.

Corporal Graham found the bar and between them they managed to force it into place.

Thirty French soldiers were trapped inside the courtyard and the British made short work of them, only sparing the life of a young drummer boy who found himself on the wrong side of the wall.

While the others were congratulated for their bravery, Rufius walked over to an ammunition wagon that was being unloaded into one of the barns. The insignia on the driver's uniform told him that he was a member of the Royal Wagon Train.

'Did you come through the French lines?'

The man snapped to attention. 'Yes, sir, those Frenchies are no match for Bess and me.' He patted one of the horses on the rump.

'Where were you stationed?'

'Mont St Jean, but the main company is quartered in Brussels.'

'I heard Wellington is running low on supplies.'

The man nodded grimly. 'Ever since we lost the gold, sir. Sergeant Greeves says it will lose us the war.'

Sim appeared from the barn. Rufius had never seen a more ill-prepared looking soldier.

'Yes, the gold,' echoed Sim, giving Rufius the 'I told you so' look and tapping his watch.

'They're saying it was us that lost it, but I know the boys who were in charge of that shipment. Never a more solid bunch could you hope to meet. They swear blind that they watched it put onto the boat, but when it arrived at Ostend — nothing!'

Rufius nodded to Sim. 'What's the name of this friend of yours?'

39

THE GOLEM

[Prague. Date: 1620]

J osh followed Thaddeus through the dark labyrinth of abandoned cellars and vaults that ran beneath the streets. This was the forgotten city, buried as Prague prospered, building upon its older self.

I know how it feels, thought Josh. The memories of every timeline he'd experienced were stored away in the recesses of his mind like old maps gathering dust, layers upon layers of alternate realities had brought him to this one. There were hundreds of them, he used to give each one a number and sometimes even a name, but he lost track over time, pushing them down into his subconscious.

Thaddeus held the small lamp ahead of them, its weak candlelight illuminating the damp stone walls and scattering the rats in their path.

He paused at an archway, holding the lantern up to show Josh a skull that had been cemented into the keystone.

'When we were children, our mothers would threaten to send us down here if we misbehaved. The guards believe that the Golem uses these tunnels, they're too afraid to come down and search them.'

He spoke in a hoarse whisper. His eyes were still red from saying goodbye to his wife, who had to prise the children from his legs as they left. She was a wise woman, who had survived the last two years on her wits. She knew it was only a matter of time before they realised their prisoner was missing. They could hear the hob-nailed boots of the City Guard marching down Boršov as they descended into the basement of the shop across the street.

They walked for hours. Thaddeus dousing the light every time they heard the sounds of patrols echoing down through the iron grates above them.

'Will they arrest her?' asked Josh.

'They may try, but her sister is married to a magistrate and he will have her out by morning.'

'What are you going to do?'

'The Brotherhood of Lazarus includes some of the most influential men in the city. Your talents will be welcomed and by association my status elevated. Sendivogius has the power to have the charges quashed and perhaps the Golem might even be persuaded to visit my accuser.'

Josh could see the years in Daliborka had taken their toll on the man's mind, spending far too long considering the ways in which he would exact his revenge.

They came to a half-submerged tunnel. Water leaked through the old brick roof where the river ran above it.

'One of Rudolf's secret escape routes,' explained Thaddeus. 'After the Bocskai uprising, he wanted to make sure he could leave the castle without being seen.'

Wading waist-deep through the cold water, Josh could feel the chill leeching all the heat from his legs. He let his mind wander away from the thought of the thousands of gallons of water flowing over his head.

Bocskai uprising?

The founder's voice echoed inside his head. *A Hungarian nobleman who organised a revolt against Rudolf II.*

Sounds like the king had quite a few enemies.

The long war against the Ottoman Empire created a great deal of animosity amongst the local aristocracies of the Holy Roman Empire. It created terrible poverty and famine in Hungary, Transylvania and Slovakia.

The alchemist's laboratory was hidden away in the lower levels of the castle. This fact made Josh smile, considering that the guards were scouring the city for them.

Climbing the stairs, the air was heavy with the scent of chemicals. It smelled of fire and iron, like a blacksmith's workshop. *The heating of gold, used in the preparation of philosophic mercury.*

It was a tall circular chamber and glass jars lined the high walls, each one containing a pale specimen of some freakish creature.

Standing inside a chalk circle in the centre of the room was Sendivogius. The leader of the Lazarus Brotherhood was dressed in richly embroidered robes, with a pentagram hanging on a gold chain around his neck. The palms of his outstretched hands were burning with a cold blue flame.

'What brings you here?' the old man asked.

Two men appeared from behind them and Josh felt the cold edge of a blade against his neck.

'We seek enlightenment,' the founder spoke through Josh's mouth.

The alchemist nodded. 'And which three elements will lead you to such a revelation?'

Thaddeus looked to Josh for the answer, who tried to hide the fact that he had no idea.

'Sulphur, salt and quicksilver,' came the involuntary response, the founder using the old name for mercury.

Sendivogius's eyes darkened with suspicion.

'And tell me, what is the Alkahest?'

Josh made a sign with his hands. 'The universal solvent.'

The final answer seemed to satisfy Sendivogius, who brushed the flames from his hands and motioned for them to come forward.

'Welcome.'

As they came into the light, the old man seemed to recognise Thaddeus.

'Nemicus is that you?'

Thaddeus bowed his head. 'I wondered if you would remember me.'

The alchemist looked pained. 'What has happened to you?'

'Daliborka,' he replied, as if that one word was explanation enough.

Others stepped out of the shadows, forming a circle around them. They were all old men, many whom bore scars and burns.

Sendivogius sighed and placed his hand benevolently on Thaddeus's shoulder. 'Science has become a dangerous occupation. What brings you here?'

Josh could see Thaddeus was shaking, trying to control his emotions.

'I asked him to bring me to you.'

'And what is it that you seek?' Sendivogius asked, turning to face Josh.

Josh stepped forward. 'Golem.'

The alchemist laughed. 'Only the brave and the foolish would knowingly seek the Golem. Which one are you?'

'He is a time lord,' interjected Thaddeus.

Sendivogius's eyes widened slightly. 'We all follow the arrow forward through time. It's one of the universal constants.'

'I can travel backwards through time.' The words felt strange in Josh's mouth, he'd never spoken them aloud before.

There was a sharp in-take of breath from some of those that surrounded them.

'Can you indeed?' the alchemist asked, his tone remaining neutral. 'And would you be able to prove such a claim?'

How am I going to do it? Thought Josh, realising that his tachyon was still locked in the prison, if one of the guards hadn't sold it already.

'I need something personal, an object,' he said, sounding like a cheap stage magician.

Sendivogius smiled at his colleagues and removed one of his gold rings. 'This was given to me by his Highness.'

Josh held it up for a moment, allowing the others to see, while secretly weaving back through its timeline until he found the goldsmith that made it.

Nothing up my sleeves, he said to himself, returning in less than the blink of an eye.

'Please read the inscription,' he said, handing it back to Sendivogius.

The bemused alchemist inspected the inner side of the ring.

'It's written in Latin,' he said, squinting at the tiny characters etched into the metal. 'My name is Joshua Jones and I am from the future.'

Thaddeus clapped his hands in delight and the others gathered around their leader, taking it in turns to inspect the inscription.

Sendivogius was clearly impressed.

'What brings you here?'

'I was told you've travelled into the realm of the dead.'

'And yet here I stand,' he said, placing the ring back onto his finger. 'I believe we may both be able to benefit from each other's talents. Who is it you really seek?'

'My mother.'

'Has she recently passed?'

Josh nodded.

'And you have unfinished business?'

'Can you show me how to reach her?'

Sendivogius's lips twisted into a thin smile, his tongue brushing across his teeth. 'I must admit it is an intriguing proposal, the Golem has never known a willing sacrifice.'

40

NAUTILUS

[Nautilus. Maelstrom]

Caitlin lay on the old sofa watching time flash past the Oculus, a huge, lens-like window that her mother had installed on the observation deck to watch the Maelstrom. The chaotic void was mostly empty except for the odd disconnected moment that floated by like a soap bubble in a tornado. Every so often they would gather into clusters, scudding past the ship giving fleeting flashbacks of the past.

There was no perceivable pattern to them and she found its randomness mesmerising, a welcome break from the Knossos texts she was studying. Caitlin's notes were scattered over the cushions, the floor and the low table, hiding a number of plates that needed clearing.

There was a growing pile of crumpled balls collecting around the over-flowing bin too. Symbols of her frustration and failure to come even close to unravelling the cryptic puzzle.

. . .

Her mother appeared through the hatch carrying a tray of tea and toast.

'Thought you might want something to eat,' she said, putting down the tray.

'I'll be the size of a house at this rate,' complained Caitlin, moving some of her notes to make space on the table. 'This is the third meal I've had today and it's not even lunchtime!'

Sitting down beside Caitlin, her mother placed a hand on her daughter's belly. 'Well, excuse me for being an over-protective grandmother! Anyway, you need a bit of feeding up,' she added, pinching her waist. 'There's hardly anything of you.'

Caitlin grunted and took a piece of toast, slathering it with strawberry jam. 'You won't be saying that in a couple of months when I can't get up off this sofa.'

Her mother's eyes misted over. 'You were such a good baby, never gave me any trouble.'

'Not now mum, please. I've got work to do.'

Her mother sighed at the mess spread over the floor and began to retrieve the dirty plates from beneath the notes.

'You should be resting, not bothering yourself with all this nonsense,' she added, looking at the symbols scrawled onto the paper.

Caitlin scowled. 'It's not nonsense, just indecipherable. Our cryptography department have been working on it for months and got nowhere. Anyway, I need something to do on here before I go crazy.'

Her mother tutted. 'You're just like your father, can't relax.'

'I need to keep busy. It stops me thinking about what Josh is doing.'

The emotions welled up in her like a sandstorm on a

sunny day: fear, anger, love overwhelmed her and she felt hot tears on her cheeks once more.

'Why didn't he listen?'

Her mother's arms gathered her in. 'Because he's a man, they're terrible at it.'

41

SOCIÉTÉ DES ANTIQUAIRES

[Bibliothèque Mazarine, Paris. Date: 1812]

The headquarters of the French Order was based in Bibliothèque Mazarine. It was overseen by Abbé Gaspard Michel, a Scriptorian Grandmaster who most called 'Leblond'.

Lyra followed Benoir through a maze of book-lined corridors until they reached a small door marked with the symbol of the Ouroboros. He produced an ornate brass key from his pocket and inserted it into the old lock, turning it first one way and then the other before opening it.

Her father had shown Lyra the technique when she was a small child. Back then it had seemed like magic, but in reality it was a displacement key, a safety measure to ensure that any inquisitive members of the public who followed them would find themselves in a broom cupboard or a toilet.

And not the grand entrance hall of the *Société des Antiquaires.*

The atrium was an impressive feat of temporal architecture, borrowing from various French palaces such as Château de Fontainebleau and Versailles.

Lyra had visited the *Société* only once before. Her father was one of the architects who designed the headquarters and he had brought her along on one of his site visits. At the time, she'd been too young to appreciate the grandeur of his vision. It was a far more elegant and ornate creation than anything she had seen in England.

'Welcome to the Société,' said Benoir, as they walked down the steps of the Palais Garnier and onto the chequered marble floor of the Grand Trianon from the Palace of Versailles.

There were hundreds of floors sheltering beneath the domed ceiling. The glass roof was so high that it appeared to have its own weather system coalescing beneath a seemingly permanent blue sky.

Candy-striped hot-air balloons were ascending and descending between the levels, slowing to take on passengers as they went.

The atrium was crowded with men and women dressed in travelling robes or period clothes. Benoir acknowledged some of them and actively ignored others. Lyra smiled politely at those who stared at her for a little too long. She was used to the strange looks; her mother called it the 'Lyra effect', there was something about a seer that made others nervous, as if they gave off some kind of distortion field. Lyra had given up caring what others thought a long time ago.

'Before we can travel, I need to get a permit,' he explained. 'There is an embargo on where we need to go.'

'How far back are you thinking of going?'

He looked up at the balloons. 'Not back, forward. To the frontier.'

. . .

The present was usually referred to as the 'frontier' by members of the Order. It was generally considered to be a terrible place to visit due to the temporal flux and uncertainty that surrounded the point where the future became a reality.

Lyra was pleasantly surprised to discover that the 'Department for the Frontier' was situated on the three-hundredth floor and so got to take her first ever hot-air balloon ride.

'Why the present?' she asked, holding on to Benoir's arm as the old aeronaut opened the valves on the burners and the basket began to lift.

'For its technology.'

Lyra was intrigued. The other reason that no one from their Order went so close to the frontier was because of electricity. The twenty-first century was polluted with millions of electrical devices that interfered with their abilities. Many Copernicans refused to go any further than the late seventeenth-century, believing the Industrial Age, and electromagnetic fields in particular, were detrimental to their sensitive instruments.

'Obviously, I meant why are we going there?'

Benoir nodded. 'There's a doctor working at a xenobiology research station that may have some answers.'

Lyra knew about Xenobiologysts, they were an ultra-secretive group of Draconian scientists who studied the creatures of the Maelstrom like Monads and Strzyga: memory vampires who could breach the continuum in search of prey. Xenos were one of the only departments that actually argued for having the most highly advanced technology available in pursuit of their research. They built a containment facility for the most unusual monsters directly under Regent's Park Zoo in present-day London.

'Madame Gaucher, may I present Lyra De Freis,' said Benoir, bowing slightly to the stern woman behind the baroquely carved desk of the Frontiers Department. She was older, perhaps in her mid-fifties, with silver hair tied in a tight bun and dressed in a suit, which Lyra recognised immediately as Chanel. Her face was austere, but her eyes smiled at the young man.

'Benoir Cousineau,' intoned the older woman in a deep, husky voice that spoke of years of smoking unfiltered cigarettes. 'How can we be of service?'

Behind Madame Gaucher stretched avenues of cabinets each lined with hundreds of small index drawers. Assistants in dark uniforms were busily flying between the indexes on wires that stretched up to metal rails in the high ceiling.

'We require permits for the Frontier.'

She raised one eyebrow ever so slightly and picked up a silver fountain pen.

'For how long?'

'Twenty-four hours should be sufficient.'

Madame Gaucher put on a pair of horn-rimmed glasses and made a note in the large register that lay open before her. 'Geographic location?'

'London.'

Her handwriting was smooth and artistic. 'And the purpose of your visit?'

He glanced towards Lyra. 'Pleasure.'

Lyra giggled, she was quite enjoying playing the part of his girlfriend.

The old woman's eyebrow arched a little further as she pursed her lips. 'I see from the register that you are due for a vacation.'

A thin metal ticket appeared from a slot in the desk and she handed it to him. 'I have approved seventy-two.'

'Thank you Madame.'

She produced two small leather boxes and placed them in front of the couple.

In each one was a brand new Tachyon Mk VI.

'They have been configured to return you here as soon as the permit expires. You are expected in the costume department, for appropriate clothing.' She handed them two cloakroom tickets. 'Try to blend in Benoir, and take care, the frontier is a wild and dangerous place.'

42

THE BOAT

[Ostend, Belgium. Date: May 1815]

It was night and the boat rocked gently against the quay, its lines straining against their moorings.

Rufius stood on the foredeck looking out to sea through a leather-barrelled telescope while Sim was studying something in his almanac under the light of a storm lantern.

'There's nothing to suggest the gold ever left England,' said Sim, tapping on a page of animating symbols.

Rufius inhaled deeply, letting the salt air fill his lungs. He missed the sea, it had been a long while since he'd sailed; the last mission involved sinking an out-of-place artefact off the coast of Crete, which hadn't exactly gone to plan.

He collapsed the telescope and put it away in one of his coat's many pockets.

'I think it did,' he said, taking hold of the ship's wheel. 'I think someone took it off this boat.'

'But it's a heavily guarded man o' war! How would someone be able to come aboard, make off with over a ton of gold bullion and no one notice?'

Rufius could feel the timeline of the ship moving under his fingers. 'That my dear Simeon is exactly what we are about to find out.'

The seas were rough when they appeared two days earlier. Towering grey waves crashed into the hull and washed the deck clear of anything that wasn't tied down. The crew were busily bringing in the sails while the boat lurched violently from one side to the other. The captain was wrestling with the wheel while the bosun barked his orders over the high winds to the men in the rigging.

Amongst the frantic activity it was easy for Sim and Rufius to slip unnoticed below decks. Their Royal Marine uniforms granting them access without question as they moved through the crew's quarters towards the hold.

Two men stood guard at the entrance, its doors barred with heavy iron locks.

'You're relieved,' Rufius said, producing a written order.

He knew it was unlikely that either of them could read, and they seemed only too happy to relinquish their duties. The ship was pitching violently and both of them had turned a distinct shade of greyish-green.

Sim knelt down and inspected one of the locks. 'Barron's double-acting tumbler. Five levers.'

Rufius tapped on the door. 'And a nice solid bit of English oak.'

'You still think it was stolen at sea?' Sim said, standing up.

'It's where I would do it. No one expects it.'

'For good reason.'

The boat rocked violently, throwing Sim against the

door, his hands grasping one of the metal bars to steady himself. His eyes widened as he touched the iron.

'It's on another ship?'

Rufius smiled knowingly. 'Indeed it is. Someone has very carefully connected this door to another just like it. When the men loaded the gold at Ramsgate, they assumed they were walking into the hold of this ship.'

'But they were storing on another.'

'Classic portal enclosure,' he said, inspecting the door frame. 'Your father couldn't have done it any better. Now let's see if we can get this thing open and find out who's been tampering with our timeline.'

Rufius produced a small set of tools from an inside pocket and picked the two locks in a matter of minutes. If Sim hadn't been so concerned about finding out what was behind the door he would have been impressed.

Elba. Date: February 23, 1815

'Where are we?' Sim asked, standing at the bottom of the ladder while Rufius poked his head through the hatch.

'Looks like the Mediterranean.'

'Why here?'

The colonel stepped back down and took out his tachyon. The dials were spinning slowly and he squinted, reading the small numbers in the dim light. 'February twenty-third, eighteen-fifteen. Ring any bells?'

Sim shook his head.

Rufius looked up through the open hatch. 'Check your dates. This brig is a three-hundred ton warship. French, but she's flying English colours, and she's fully stocked for a voyage.'

Sim consulted his almanac, the realisation dawning on his face as he studied the dates scrolling across the page. 'You think this is the *Inconstant*?'

'Aye lad, I believe we're on Napoleon's escape ship.'

'But he's not supposed to leave Elba until the twenty-sixth?'

Rufius smiled, putting away his tachyon. 'If I remember rightly, HMS *Partridge* was patrolling the coast, he's probably sent the ship out to avoid suspicion.'

'Someone stole Wellington's gold to help Napoleon?'

'It has a certain sense of irony doesn't it? The Emperor was in need of funds, he still had a guard of seven hundred men to pay and there were rumours that the French were going to crown the Duke of Orleans as King.'

Sim turned the page of his book, the lines of consequence branched out like a tree across the paper. 'There's a seventy-seven per cent probability that he'll take Paris by March and defeat the Seventh Coalition at Waterloo. Most of the army are still loyal to him. He will go on to found one of the longest Empires in Western Europe.'

Rufius scratched his beard. 'So you have to ask yourself who would benefit most from that?'

'Not the House of Bourbon that's for sure. Napoleon effectively ends a line of French rule that stretched back nearly six hundred years.'

Footsteps walked over the deck and they shrank back into the shadows.

'So basically we've got an anti-royalist funding his campaign by stealing from his enemies,' Rufius whispered stroking one of the wooden beams. 'Someone who knows how to build a portal.'

Sim went over to one of the strong boxes. 'Should we take the gold?'

Rufius shook his head. 'No, let's move forward to March and see who shows up in Paris.'

43

THE STAR

[Prague. Date: 1620]

The brotherhood blindfolded Josh and led him through a maze of secret passages beneath the castle. He could hear Sendivogius somewhere ahead, repeating a Latin verse:

'Verum sine mendacio, certum, et verissimum.

Quod est inferius, est sicut quod est superius.

Et quod est superius, est sicut quod est inferius, ad perpetranda miracula rei unius.'

The founder quickly translated.

Tis true without lying, certain and most true.
That which is below is like that which is above
and that which is above is like that which is below
to do the miracle of one only thing.

The first part of the Tabula Smaragdina — the Emerald Tablet.

. . .

When they finally came up out of the cold, damp underworld, Josh had lost all sense of direction. He could tell they were in a building from the sound of their footsteps on wooden floors and the honeyed aroma of beeswax candles.

When the blindfold was removed, Josh found himself in the attic of a townhouse.

The Golem was laid out on a table like an effigy on a tomb. Its pale body was over seven feet long and covered in hieroglyphic symbols pressed into the clay.

Sendivogius lit the oil lamps by its head, the light throwing shadows over its eyeless face and mouth.

'Leave us,' he commanded, waving his hand at the other men.

They filed out of the room in silence, taking Thaddeus with them. He looked like a bewildered child as he was escorted out of the room.

Josh waited for the founder's memories to decipher the script on the Golem, but nothing came. They looked vaguely Egyptian, like the Book of the Dead and he wondered if they were some kind of ancient spells.

'Belief is a powerful thing,' said Sendivogius from somewhere in the flickering shadows. 'The human imagination is without doubt their greatest asset and yet their greatest weakness. Better that they think a thing of clay can come to life than a mortal man could live forever.'

'You've been killing them?'

'My experiments require living subjects. It is a necessary evil.'

'Because you want immortality?'

Sendivogius laughed. 'I have no need of the Philosopher's Stone. What I seek now is the power to travel through time.'

'What are you?'

Moving into the light, Josh saw that Sendivogius had removed his robe. His skin was smooth and hairless and much younger than his face would have implied.

'I am death,' he said, his long fingers stroking the head of the clay effigy. 'You came here seeking a way to cross over. I have been there many times, like Charon, I can take you across the river to Hades, but beware, the ferryman charges a heavy price.'

He opened his mouth slightly and Josh saw something flicker inside his throat.

'Whatever it takes,' Josh replied.

The alchemist's eyes darkened and his jaw began to distort as if it were dislocating. There was a rough, slithering noise coming from deep inside his chest like something was working its way out. Josh tensed as he felt the sting of tiny needle-like teeth bite into his neck.

Paralysed, he felt the poison enter his body as it began to feed. Blood was a powerful binding agent, seers would use it to read a person's timeline. Whatever kind of toxin Sendivogius was using, it moved through his body like a virus. Josh felt his breathing weaken, his pulse race and he began to lose consciousness.

A dark wave enveloped him. His conscious mind separated from his physical self and he felt himself falling.

He travelled down a tunnel of light, his lives branching out on each side like roots, weaving off into the void. Somewhere above, Josh thought he heard the voice of the founder, calling to him but he was too far away to hear what he was saying.

The memories were slipping by quickly as he descended, snatches of old conversations playing out like broken records.

'Joshua?' his mother said, her voice calm and gentle.

He turned towards the sound, but there was no one there. 'Mum?'

This wasn't death, this was something else, as though he were being dragged back through his oldest memories.

The falling slowed, the sounds and sights were becoming alien now, from a time before he could recall. He was younger, a child of no more than five or six, a time before his mother became ill.

'What are you doing?' Her question sounded as if she found him doing something naughty.

'I came to save you.'

'Joshua. Be a good boy.'

He couldn't be sure if she was listening or these were just random moments misfiring in his brain.

'Can you hear me?'

She came in close, her hair was long and curly, and she was smiling. The room was unfamiliar and he realised they were in the house, the one that she had to give up when she got ill.

'You shouldn't be here.'

He knew if he had eyes, they would be filled with tears. 'I came to save you.'

The room changed, he was still moving backwards, the years slipping by as she grew ever younger.

What happens when I reach the day I was born? He thought, *do I cease to exist?*

'I love you,' she said, looking down into his cot. 'You're my little star.'

'I love you too Mum.'

But it was pointless, he realised. She couldn't hear him. He was overwhelmed by the intense sense of loss, it was like being under a thick, soft duvet on a cold night. Josh could feel himself letting go, all of the pain and anxiety of the last ten years ebbing away.

For most of his life, Josh had felt like a ship lost at sea with no map or compass. His mother was the only constant until he met Caitlin. She was the star that guided him back to safety — the centre of his universe for so long that it was difficult to remember a time when he hadn't taken care of her. These final few memories of her changed that, made him realise that she had a life before him, that there had been good times too, it was a gift of sorts, just not the one that he had hoped for.

Wake up! commanded the founder.

What?

Something — is coming. There was another word but it was garbled, as if the founder was having trouble communicating.

What is it?

Unknown. Was all he sent, along with a whole series of pain responses.

Suddenly Josh could feel his heart beating once more. The air in his lungs rising and falling as his consciousness returned to his body.

· · ·

The pain in his neck was intense and his hand instinctively went to the wound. The bite had sealed, leaving a bruise but no sign of blood.

On the floor behind him lay the body of Sendivogius, his half-naked corpse shrivelled and wisened, like one of the mummies in the British Museum.

Josh's head swam, he assumed from the lack of blood. Whatever creature was living inside of the alchemist had drained them both. He searched the room, but found no trace of it.

It was time to leave, the words of his father echoing in his head as he made his way down the narrow stairs and onto the street. 'Something unknown is coming.'

44

XENOS

[Regent's Park Zoo, London. Date: Present Day]

For reasons that were best known to themselves, the Xenobiology department located its facility deep below the Zoological Gardens in Regent's Park. The metal ticket included a timeline that brought them to a disused platform in Great Portland Street underground station. Five minutes later they were walking in through the park on a balmy summer's day.

'Why didn't you mention the Xenos to her?' Lyra asked, walking beside him and wondering if he was going to try and hold her hand.

'The Société isn't on speaking terms with the British. We've had issues with them over certain events that have led to something of a diplomatic impasse.'

'I didn't realise the Order could be so political.'

He scoffed. 'When the Société is involved it's always political. Sometimes it's better not to ask permission, but apologise afterwards.'

They reached the gates of the zoo where a long line of families and tourists snaked back from the ticket office.

'Do we have to queue?' asked Lyra.

'No, I worked here a couple of years ago. We can use the staff gate.'

The entrance to the Xeno facility was hidden halfway along the East Tunnel. Lyra followed Benoir through a nondescript door and down a winding iron staircase. Descending deep below the park, the smell that rose to meet them reminded her of a stagnant pond. It hadn't improved since the last time she'd come with her mother.

Back then, Lyra couldn't have imagined the myriad collection of nightmarish creatures they studied. Captured outside of the chronosphere by scientists who used themselves as bait, losing limbs and even their lives in the pursuit of science.

They came to a door that looked as though it belonged in a bank vault. Constructed from a set of heavy, circular brass discs with locking bolts every thirty degrees, the centre was a series of concentric circles, similar to those on a tachyon, except these rings were engraved with symbols of different species of animals.

Benoir took out his almanac and began to move the dials based on his notes.

Lyra shivered, as if suddenly something had walked over her grave. The level of malevolence waiting behind the door was disorientating, like stepping off a merry-go-round before it had stopped.

. . .

The Xeno laboratory was built inside a vast circular shaft with curved iron stairs that wound around and up the centre of the metal tube like a helix. Gantries branched off at certain points leading to riveted pressure doors built into the walls — the kind they used on submarines.

Scientists lumbered around in heavily shielded suits, their faces obscured behind toughened glass visors. A group passed them carrying large specimen jars filled with billowing luminous gases, while others followed behind with lethal-looking weapons. The whole scene reminded Lyra of something from a nuclear power station rather than a biology department.

A small figure approached them, accompanied by a large sabre-tooth cat.

'Good to see you Benoir and welcome back Lyra,' she said, pulling off her headgear. 'How is your mother?'

Lyra bowed slightly. 'Very well, Doctor Shika, thank you.'

The cat nuzzled into Lyra's leg and she tickled its ear.

Benoir looked slightly puzzled and Lyra shrugged her expression conveying something along the lines of: 'You never asked.'

'We need your help,' said Benoir, filling the awkward silence.

'Let me get out of this suit and we can talk.'

They passed another team of scientists who were cautiously manoeuvring a glass tube into place above a bigger tank filled with a putrid liquid. Lyra could see translucent eel-like creatures swimming inside.

'Lampreys,' explained Kaori Shika. 'We're trying to understand how they're able to fold spacetime.'

The tube was gently submerged and the creatures swam out into the green soup. One attached itself to the glass near Lyra, and she could see the hundreds of rows of teeth in concentric rings.

'They're petromyzontiformes,' explained Benoir. 'From an ancient line of jawless fish.'

'And they can warp space?' asked Lyra, leaning over the safety barrier to study the creature more closely. Benoir instinctively reached out to stop her.

Kaori laughed. 'Don't worry they are mostly harmless. They tend to prefer the Paleozoic. Trilobytes are one of their favourite foods.'

They followed Doctor Shika into a decontamination chamber where she removed the rest of her hazmat suit and hung it alongside six other suits.

One for every day, thought Lyra, admiring the Einstein-like organisation of the Japanese doctor.

'So, how can I help?' Kaori asked, ushering them through the opposite door and into her office. 'Your message mentioned something about an unusual lifespan?'

'Yes,' said Benoir, taking out his almanac and handing it to her. 'We have discovered a particularly unusual specimen, which seems to have a longevity in excess of five hundred years.'

Kaori took the notebook eagerly and began to read his notes, lines forming on her forehead as she processed the information. 'But these are human names.'

'As I said, this specimen has lived far longer than it should.'

The Japanese doctor seemed concerned. 'What evidence do you have for this?'

Benoir told her what they had discovered on the Rothsteins. Kaori listened intently, nodding as he described the historical details of the growth of the banking empire.

'So you believe there's a human-like species that live among us with hyper-extended life expectancy?'

Benoir shook his head. 'I don't know. Whatever it is, it has amassed a vast fortune and is now financing half of nineteenth-century Europe's royal houses.'

'And it's collecting talismans,' added Lyra.

Kaori took a key from her desk drawer and opened a small door at the back of her office. 'Let me show you something.'

The elevator descended quickly into the sub-basements of the laboratory, only slowing as they reached minus four hundred and finally stopping at four-hundred and forty-five.

'We first encountered this species during a Protectorate investigation. Someone was experimenting on prostitutes in the East End of London in 1888,' explained Kaori, holding her palm against the security pad of the darkened storage facility while a laser scanned her retina.

The doors slid apart, and ceiling panels flickered on to reveal a man's body frozen upright inside a containment cell.

'This is Henry Knox. A Victorian doctor who was identified by a Protectorate Inspector as the man behind the crimes of Jack the Ripper.'

Lyra stared at the man's motionless body. He looked serene, as if dreaming, she thought. 'He looks less than forty.'

Doctor Shika tapped lightly on the glass and an animating three-dimensional scan of his body appeared.

'He is, but we believe the parasite is over five-thousand years old. It seems able to extend the life of the host as well as move to a new one when necessary.'

She expanded an area of the screen and they could see a worm-like creature wrapped around his brain stem. 'It's controlling his major motor functions and there are signs that it has integrated with the cerebral cortex.'

'What do you call it?' Lyra asked, coming closer to the glass.

'Aeon.'

45

NAUTILUS

[Nautilus, Maelstrom]

Caitlin woke with a start, and for a moment she could still see the images of her nightmare. Terrible haunting spectres ghosted across her vision, armies of bloated monsters like decaying jellyfish tethered to gaunt-faced men whose bones punctured their blackened skin, looking as if they had been turned inside out.

They had a name, one that she had never heard before: Nihil.

Whether it was the chaotic influence of the Maelstrom or the hormones from her pregnancy, something was causing her to have the most bizarre dreams.

She'd fallen asleep on the sofa. Someone, probably her mother, had covered her with a soft blanket that smelled of lavender. It reminded her of childhood, a memory of waking in the bedroom of her grandmother's house in the late seventeenth century. She rubbed the blanket against her cheek and let it ease the sense of despair that the Nihil had created.

. . .

During her troubled sleep, she'd kicked her notes on the Knossos tablets off the table. They lay scattered across the floor, any sense of order lost. She sighed at the thought of having to reorganise them and sat up. A wave of nausea overwhelming her as she moved. Caitlin only just made it to the toilet before throwing up.

'Cat, are you okay?' her father asked through the door.

'Yeah,' she replied, wiping her mouth. 'It's just morning sickness.'

'Ah, yes, your mother suffered quite badly with that too.'

'Great.' She got to her feet and looked at herself in the mirror. There were dark circles under her eyes and her hair looked as if she had slept in a wind tunnel.

'She used to swear by Garibaldis. We used to call them squashed-fly biscuits.'

The thought of it made Caitlin gag. 'Don't talk about food!'

'Sorry. Do you want a cup of tea?'

'Yes, please.'

When he returned, Caitlin was sitting on the sofa once more. The colour was slowly returning to her cheeks.

She took the tea with two hands and breathed in the soothing steam. Earl Grey had always been her favourite, ever since she was small, even before they disappeared.

When she was ten years old, her parents were assigned to a top-secret mission. They were both members of the Nautonniers, the navigational division of the Draconians, whose job it was to explore the gaps in the historical records.

It took a few weeks before they were officially reported as missing-in-action. The mission had developed complications and their entire team had disappeared into the timeless wasteland that was the Maelstrom.

It was nearly eight years before she saw them again.

'Where are we going?' asked Caitlin, staring out through the Oculus. A cluster of time was flowing past the window like pages from an old picture book.

Her father smiled, his eyes gleaming like a boy with a new bike. There was no way for him to hide his emotions, which made him easy to read and terrible at poker.

'Your mother thought we should visit Tycho Station. It's in a rather stable cluster of sixteenth-century Sweden.'

'Why?'

He began picking up some of the cushions that she'd kicked off in the night. 'Well, you can't spend the next seven months stuck on this ship. The station has better living quarters for starters and a decent kitchen, not to mention an astronomical observatory and a rather interesting library.'

Their timeship, the *Nautilus* was a beautiful piece of temporal engineering. Her mother was a first-class engineer who had somehow managed to build the sleek submarine from random pieces of old copper and brass they had found in the forgotten junkyards of the void.

But he was right, Caitlin would go crazy if she spent another seven days in the confined space let alone seven months.

'Do you need any help?' her father asked, looking at the notes scattered over the rug.

Caitlin put down her tea and picked up the nearest sheet

of paper. 'That depends on how much you know about ancient ideograms?'

He shrugged and sat down beside her. 'Not a thing, although I did learn a little about cryptography when we were helping Alan Turing with the German Lorenz cipher.'

'You were at Bletchley Park?'

'I was seconded to the Target Intelligence Committee. At the end of the war we were sent in with the front line troops to capture documents and technology before the Nazis could destroy them. I was tasked with smuggling the information back to Signals Intelligence a few years earlier.'

'You were a time spy?'

He winked. 'Don't tell your mother.' He took the sheet from her. 'So what do we have here?'

'It's a writing system devised by the Minoans at around 8,200.'

Her father looked at her blankly.

Caitlin sighed. '1800 BCE. I still don't understand how you never managed to get your head around the Holocene calendar.'

'I'm just old-fashioned I guess.'

'Anyway, it was discovered during an excavation in Crete. An archaeologist called Arthur Evans unearthed a bunch of clay tablets with them on. The Scriptorians have managed to identify two distinct scripts, which they're calling Linear A and B.'

'And you're trying to work out what they say?'

'They've deciphered Linear B. This is A.'

'Why not just send someone back to find out?'

Caitlin frowned, her nose wrinkling. 'We're not allowed. The Special Antiquities division have set up an exclusion zone around the site and its history. Rufius only just managed to get these inscriptions out before Grandmaster

Konstantine closed it all down. No one knows what the threat is and the Antiquarians aren't sharing.'

'And you think this text will hold the answer?'

'These are the only documents we have from the period. Whatever Konstantine's lot are up to it has something to do with this.'

Her father picked up a blank sheet of paper and pencil. 'So, where do you want to start? Dates or names of rulers?'

Caitlin smiled. 'Tried both of those, and pattern matching against other contemporary languages at the time. This is like nothing I've ever seen. It may not even be a language.'

46

JANUARY

[Paris, France. Date: March 20, 1815]

Napoleon entered Paris on 20th March 1815, accompanied by the fifth regiment of Marshall Ney — who was originally sent to capture him before he entered the city.

The streets around the Tuileries Palace were filled with spectators, young and old, all come to see the return of their emperor. There was a fervour about the crowd that bordered on hysteria. They sang revolutionary songs and waved the tricolor. Many of them seemed to be ex-soldiers and Sim wondered if this was how it felt in the days leading up to the storming of the Bastille over two decades before.

Rufius wasn't happy with the situation.

'Too bloody dangerous,' he grumbled, leading Sim through a series of alleyways until they reached a safe house on rue des Rosiers.

The house was run by the *Société des Antiquaires*, the rather idiosyncratic French arm of the Order. Its entrance was through a decrepit bookshop whose owner hardly blinked when they entered. The man looked older than any of his books, tired and wrinkled with a fine layer of dandruff on each shoulder.

'Gaspar.' Rufius nodded towards the back of the shop. 'Still under Caesar?'

'Non,' replied the shopkeeper. 'Voltaire.'

The shop was a warren of badly stacked shelves, with no obvious sign of an indexing system. *Caitlin would have a fit*, thought Sim trying to keep up with Rufius, who was making random course changes through the maze.

'Rodin, Shakespeare, Tiberius...'

Sim realised that Rufius wasn't interested in the books at all, concentrating instead on the busts of famous historical figures that sat above the stacks.

'Voltaire!'

Only one spine amongst the leather-bound volumes carried the symbol of the Ouroboros, its timeline was a simple one that led directly to the entrance of the Chapter House. With his usual heavy-handedness Rufius rapped on the large double doors.

It was opened by a doorman who looked nearly as ancient as Arcadin.

'Grenier!' he declared, grabbing the old man by the hand before he had time to respond.

'No, English!' the doorman protested, trying to close the door, but Rufius was already halfway through.

'How is Madame Flaubert?'

Grenier threw his hands in the air and said something that made Sim blush as he made his apologies and quickly followed in behind.

· · ·

The Chapter House was nothing like the one Sim had grown up in. His father had extended their home over the years with architecture borrowed from many different centuries. He called it 'eclectic' which was another word for 'unplanned,' according to his mother. There was a certain charm to the juxtaposition of styles, and for a child it was an Aladdin's Cave of adventure.

The interior of this house was more elegant, as if constructed from the work of one architect. It was still vast, with a staircase that seemed to climb ever upward, whilst the decor looked as if it had been borrowed from the seventeenth-century.

'François Mansart,' said Rufius, before Sim could ask.

Grenier rang a bell, announcing the arrival of new guests and seconds later two stern-looking musketeers appeared from the porter's office and blocked their way.

'No, English!' one of the men repeated in a heavy accent, his hand resting on the hilt of his sword.

Rufius bowed to the guards, who looked slightly bemused, but reciprocated nonetheless.

'Gentlemen, I appreciate our superiors have yet to reach an agreement on the impasse, but surely we're old friends. Armand, who was it that helped you with the Duchess of Lauraguais? And as for you Isaac, you should know better than to greet me without a bottle of Petrus in your hand.'

Their expressions softened, a smile breaking out on the face of the larger man until he laughed.

'Westinghouse you old dog, you think I've forgotten?' He produced a bottle of wine from behind his back and pulled the cork out with his teeth.

. . .

The dining hall was modelled on the banqueting hall of Château de Chambord, its long oak table laid out with trays of succulent roasted meats on silver platters. Travellers from the past five hundred years were sitting on benches along both sides. One group looked as if they hadn't eaten in weeks, tearing at the food like starving men.

'Siege of Paris,' said Isaac, sitting down beside Sim. 'Terrible time to be a dog.'

'Or a cat,' added Rufius, tearing off a haunch of roast chicken.

'I heard they emptied the zoo,' added Armand.

Suddenly, Sim didn't feel that hungry.

As the others ate, he learned that the men were the original inspiration for Alexander Dumas's book. Isaac de Porthau, the larger of the two, was a member of the Black Musketeers, the guards charged with protecting the Sun King, Louis XIV. His cousin Armand d'Athos was a slighter build, but held himself like a fighter, Sim could tell from the way he used his knife that he would be equally deadly with a sword.

While Rufius and Isaac traded stories, Sim took out his almanac and reviewed the latest predictions on the Napoleonic period. The lines weaving across the page, constantly rewriting themselves as a hundred actuaries on the nineteenth floor of Copernicus Hall updated their calculations.

Sim missed the sound of the analytics department, the clacking of the difference engines as they processed millions of possibilities. He spent two years sitting at a desk with his slide rule and log tables, learning the differential equations that make up the Prime Radiant, the algorithm that his guild developed to model the future. Then, everything changed when Josh created the Infinity Engine.

'So Copernican, what brings you to Paris?' asked Armand, peeling an apple in one continuous spiral.

'Napoleon,' answered Sim, closing his book.

The musketeer sneered. 'Le petit caporal, what an earth would you want with that tyrant?'

Sim wasn't sure how much information to share with the stranger. Although he bore the mark of the Order on his forearm which meant he could be trusted, Sim was taught to be cautious when discussing uncertain scenarios.

'He's stealing Wellington's gold!' interrupted Rufius, who had already finished the first bottle of wine with Armand and had started on the second. 'You have to give him credit for his audacity.'

'It's changing the outcome of a major period in European history,' complained Sim, trying not to imagine what Professor Eddington would say.

Armand waved a gloved finger at Sim like a parent disciplining a child. 'French history to be exact. You bean counters always like to generalise!'

Sim ground his teeth, holding back the hundred ways he could have countered the argument, letting the emotion drain out of him, he repeated the mantra of the Copernicans in his head.

It is by the power of logic that time will be kept in motion.
It is with purity of thought that I balance the equation.
The equation becomes the future, the future takes form.

Actuaries were trained from an early age to think in probabilities. To consider all of the risk factors and determine the best course of action, while men like Armand and Isaac would be the ones left to execute their strategies. It was a delicate balance between the theoretical and the practical, like oil and water, the two did not mix well. Sim was beginning to realise why Professor Eddington had sent him on this mission; to remind him of the consequences of their work. Turning their formulas and equations into reality. These were men of action, the only thing he needed to do was appeal to their loyalty.

'Someone is helping the Emperor. One who is trying to end the Ancien Régime. The right of kings.'

Armand drove his dagger into the table, causing the other diners to stop their conversations. 'So how are we going to find this *agent provocateur*?'

Isaac swayed a little as he got up, his bulbous nose was now a deep shade of purple.

'How can we help?'

'We need to talk to January,' said Rufius.

The grandmaster of the French Antiquarians, Antide Janvier, lived in the clock tower of the Collège Mazarin, one of the oldest universities in Paris. It was an impressive feat of clockwork construction, each floor housing multiple gearing systems for what was the most complicated astronomical clock ever designed.

'Janvier!' bellowed Rufius, climbing the last of the many stairs. 'When are you going to invent the elevator!'

A white-haired old man leaned over the railings above him and laughed. 'Westinghouse you old fool! Why hasn't anybody killed you yet?'

The two greeted each other with open arms, like old comrades. Sim never ceased to be surprised at the number of people Rufius could call friend.

Grandmaster Janvier was a thin-faced man with kind eyes. Dressed in a dark silk kimono and smoking a long pipe, he was nearly as tall as Rufius but willowy, his pale skin was translucent like a fragile old vase.

His office was housed in the upper most storey of the tower where the elaborate clock faces on east and west walls acted like enormous stained glass windows.

'I take it you are not here for a casual chat?' the old man said, nodding towards the two musketeers.

'Afraid not old friend, I'm in need of an auspice.'

Janvier put down his pipe and folded his arms into the sleeves of his robes until they seemed to disappear.

'An auspice you say? Haven't used one of those in a month of Sundays. It's not something many know exist, let alone ask to borrow.'

'It's important.'

The grandmaster sighed. 'It always is with you.'

The gearing around them was in continuous motion, marking out the time. As it reached the quarter hour the grandmaster placed his fingers in his ears.

There was a sudden cascade of bells as the clock chimed the quarter. Sim was too slow and the sound left him dizzy and quite deaf for a few minutes afterwards.

Rufius seemed to be unaffected, he was following Janvier to the back of his office where a pair of old wooden cabinets were pushed against the wall.

The grandmaster took a key from around his neck and opened one of the doors. By the time Sim was steady enough on his feet to join them, the old Antiquarian was already holding what Sim could only assume was an auspice.

It was a odd-looking device, a kind of pocket-sized orrery with five metallic spheres rotating around a larger one like planets in a solar system. The central orb was inscribed with intricate temporal symbols.

'This has been in my family for fifteen generations.'

'What does it do?' asked Sim, watching the hypnotic motion of the spheres.

'Tells the time,' the grandmaster said with a chuckle.

'Tells your time,' added Rufius, taking the device from Janvier and pointing it at Sim. The spheres' pattern changed and Sim could see small glyphs lighting up across its surface.

'11.860,' Rufius read the Holocene date aloud.

'So you can tell when I was from?'

The grandmaster nodded. 'Exactly, in the right hands, an auspice can be used to date anyone to within an hour of their birth.'

'It's also quite useful for detecting when you're not following linear time.'

'Are you taking it out of this century?' asked Janvier, looking nervously over at the Musketeers who were stuffing wadding in their ears in preparation for the approaching strike of the hour.

'No, we're staying local.'

'Good. It takes an expert to reset the internal calibrations if you move too far. And I'm too old to want to go gallivanting around in the past any more.'

Two hours later, Isaac and Armand were leading them through the old quarry catacombs that burrowed under Paris. Walking through the maze of pillared tunnels, their walls made entirely from skulls, Sim found it difficult not to think of the six million people that were buried down here. The ossuary had been built after cemeteries like the Holy Innocents, could no longer deal with the increasing volumes of dead. Their bones had been exhumed and dropped down a mine shaft into the tunnels below.

The catacombs were one of the quickest ways to move unseen across the city. The air was dry and smelled of dust and decay. The musketeers used scented lanterns infused with incense to mask the miasma as they navigated without a map through the labyrinth.

They were heading for the Champs Des Mars; a park in the centre of Paris that was used for Bastille Day festivals during the revolution and later for the Exposition of 1889. The Copernican team had proposed a list of potential times and dates for a safe interaction with Napoleon and Rufius chose June 1, when the Emperor celebrated the ceremony of Champ de Mai.

Climbing out from a grate on the south-west corner of the École Militaire, Rufius took the lead. He was dressed in the blue and white uniform of a captain of the Imperial guard while the others were junior officers.

It was just before ten in the morning and the day was already warm and humid. As the sun broke through the cloud, they crossed the courtyard and were met with the sight of a hundred thousand soldiers massed on the field before them. Following the steady stream of gold epaulets and red plumed bearskins, they made their way into the canopied amphitheatre, taking their seats before a raised dais. Standing upon it was Napoleon's throne. A golden chair with a purple circular back embroidered with his initial 'N' at its centre. Sim stared at the empty seat, hardly able to contemplate the fact that in a few minutes, the greatest military strategist of the age would be sitting in it.

. . .

Outside, the roar of the crowd marked the arrival of the emperor's imperial coach from the Tuileries Palace.

Everyone rose to their feet and in the ensuing commotion Rufius took the auspice out of his hat and pointed it towards the general staff and senior officers who were lining up beside the throne.

Isaac and Armand began to clap and cheer with the others, hiding Rufius from enquiring eyes. He shook his head at Sim when the glyphs returned their dates.

Napoleon entered from behind the throne with an entourage of his closest marshalls.

The emperor was dressed in ceremonial robes, wearing a black cap festooned with white feathers. The man looked unwell, thought Sim. His face paunched, and his skin pale and liverish.

After the Archbishop of Tours said mass, the master of ceremonies invited the central assembly to witness the signing of the latest constitutional charter.

Then, as Napoleon gave his speech, Rufius scanned his inner circle.

'As emperor, consul, soldier, I owe everything to the people,' Bonaparte began. 'In prosperity, in adversity, on the battlefield, in counsel, enthroned, in exile, France has been the sole and constant object of my thoughts and actions. Like the King of Athens, I sacrificed myself for my people in the hope of seeing fulfilled the promise to preserve for France her natural integrity, honour and rights.'

Sim studied the crowd, looking for anyone that seemed out of place. The entire audience were on their feet, fifteen thousand officers clamouring for their emperor.

'Got him,' Rufius whispered in his ear, pointing towards

a dark-haired soldier standing nonchalantly to the right of Napoleon.

'He's come from 1799, literally in the last day or so.'

Rufius turned to Isaac and whispered something in his ear. The musketeer nodded and disappeared into the crowd.

'What are you going to do?' asked Sim.

'Small diversion, just need to get close enough to trace him.'

As the ceremony drew to a close, Isaac returned wearing a mischievous smile and rolling a ball of wadding around in his hands. He placed one piece into each ear before handing the rest to Sim and motioning him to do the same.

'My own glory, honour and happiness are indistinguishable from those of France,' Napoleon's final words carried over the silent audience.

Members of his general staff rose as one to lead the cheer and as the entire congregation began to applaud, Isaac checked his tachyon and nodded to Rufius. Seconds later, a thunderous noise filled the air above their heads like a hundred cannons going off at once.

Guards leapt to defend their leader, assuming that it was some kind of attack. The fireworks continued to explode in bursts of bright colour across the sky. As the ceremony degenerated into chaos, Rufius took his chance and moved closer to the dark-haired officer.

It took less than a second to attach the tracker onto his jacket. It was a small golden pin that looked much like the other buttons on his uniform. Connected to a sympathetic twin in the Copernican headquarters, it would allow them to single out his timeline and trace his movements throughout history.

Sim opened his almanac and watched as the lines of data started to flow across the page. The man had a simple, linear life until 1799 when everything seemed to change.

'They've located the bifurcation,' he shouted to Rufius over the barrage of explosions.

Having recovered from the shock, Napoleon ordered his guards to find out what was going on. Armand bid them adieu and followed Isaac out of the tent and onto the Champs de Mars.

Rufius and Sim took out their tachyons and disappeared into thin air.

47

ELETHIUM CONDENSATE

[Xenobiology Department, Regent's Park Zoo, London. Date: Present day]

'Is there any way to extract it?' asked Lyra.

Doctor Shika shook her head, zooming in still further on the holographic display to show the man's brain. 'Our scans show that its dendrons are too tightly entangled with those of the host for a physical extraction. It would cause too much damage.'

'So how do they live so long?' asked Benoir.

'Blood flukes can survive for decades in humans by regenerating their organs. I assume these have a similar capability.'

Lyra placed her hand on the glass, but felt nothing but the cold.

'He's in stasis,' explained Kaori. 'You won't be able to reach him.'

'Take him out then,' demanded Lyra, drawing a series of symbols on the icy surface with her fingernail. 'Let me read this thing.'

Doctor Shika crossed her arms, her expression hardening. 'Why on earth would I want to do that?'

'Because there's more than one of these things out there.' Lyra pointed to Benoir. 'And he thinks they may have infected one of the richest families of the nineteenth century.'

Kaori shook her head. 'It's too dangerous. People died capturing this one. We know nothing of its origins nor what it's really capable of.'

'And you never will if you keep it locked in a freezer! I thought you were supposed to be scientists not zoo keepers. I'm a seer, all I need to do is touch it.'

Lyra couldn't explain why she felt the compulsion to read its timeline, only that she knew it was somehow linked to what was going to happen to Josh.

'Perhaps if we use Elethium Condensate?' Benoir suggested diplomatically.

Kaori's eyes widened. 'And where did you hear about that?'

Benoir smiled. 'I read your paper.'

'What's Elethium Condensate?' asked Lyra.

'It's experimental,' said Kaori, unfolding her arms. 'We're using it to study the non-corporeals.'

'They usually have to work at near-zero Kelvin,' added Benoir.

'How cold is that?'

'Close to absolute zero, heat death of the universe kind of cold — as cold as it gets.'

Entering the hall of the non-corporeals required wearing several layers of heated undergarments as well as huge Inuit-like parkas with face masks and breathing gear.

Everything inside the hall glistened with a diamond-coating of ice. The creatures trapped inside the cases looked as if they had been sculpted from glass.

'We've documented over two-hundred species,' Kaori explained through the radio built into their masks.

Benoir looked around in wonder at the collection of translucent monsters. It was just as Lyra remembered from her last visit, they were still some of the strangest creatures she had ever seen, especially the giant nethershark that hung in the air above their heads.

'If we're going to use the condensate you need to be aware of the dangers,' continued Kaori. 'It's a superfluid in a quantum state, you will find that time will become less stable. We have created a dampening field around the chamber but as Benoir says, it's still experimental.'

They followed a team of engineers who brought Knox's body up in a temporary stasis chamber. It floated like an ice coffin between the four men, the gases venting from it leaving a trail of small white butterflies in its wake.

'Gynaephora. We believe they are distantly related to the arctic moth,' the doctor said, waving her hand through them. 'Their wings are weighed down by the ice crystals.'

Lyra caught one of the tiny creatures in the palm of her mitten and watched the thing disappear as the warmth of her glove melted the ice.

At the far end of the hall was a sign above a door with the words: 'Hazardous Materials' stencilled onto it.

Benoir looked back at Lyra, his breath condensing on his face plate. 'You sure you want to do this?' he asked.

She nodded, taking his gloved hand and walking towards the door.

. . .

The body of the Victorian explorer was lowered into position, held in place by an elaborate set of steel clamps. Doctor Shika typed a series of commands into a screen bolted to the wall and an opaque shield shimmered into place around the frozen man.

'I'm going to bring him out of temporal stasis,' she said to her assistant as a series of temperature gauges appeared on the display. Then turning to Lyra: 'When he reaches zero degrees, you should be able to take your glove off.'

They watched the dials moving slowly up from minus two-hundred and seventy degrees celsius.

'Releasing the Elethium Condensate,' said Kaori, watching the silver liquid drain away from the chamber in transparent tubes and flow into a series of heavy metallic spheres.

Taking off her glove, Lyra immediately felt the presence of the Aeon. Her fingertips went numb, the temperature in the room was only just above freezing, but she could feel the aura surrounding the body, it slipped over her fingers like oil on water.

She reached through the shimmering field and took hold of the man's hand.

There was always a specific moment when Lyra initiated a connection with another's timeline that was difficult to describe to a non-seer. Without years of training it would have led to instant madness, and the cells of Bedlam were a testament to that. Immersing herself in the vast ocean of a person's life was overwhelming, drowning in their sea of experiences was more than many could bear.

But not with Henry Knox — his life was empty, a void, a nothingness.

Lifelines were usually like finely-threaded maps that wove through the years, creating a tapestry that could be unpicked by a skilful seer, and Lyra was one of the best.

This man was nothing but an empty shell, a vessel for the parasite that it was hosting.

She took her hand back and rubbed the life back into it.

Benoir caught her look of concern. 'What is it?'

'There's nothing left. It's like his life was erased.'

Doctor Shika tapped something into the screen sewn onto the sleeve of her parka. 'Interesting, it may be that the Aeon has been sustaining itself using his past. I have wondered whether it would be able to survive in a temporal vacuum.'

Lifting off her face mask, Lyra bit into her thumb, letting the blood flow freely over her fingers.

'What are you doing?' asked Benoir.

'If that thing has eaten his memories then I need to find another way into its timeline, blood creates a stronger bond.'

She placed her hand on his once more.

Closing her eyes, she focused on her breathing, allowing her mind to settle. The warmth of the blood on her fingers was comforting as she submerged herself into the dark void of his past.

It was like standing on the surface of a dead moon at the edge of some distant universe. Far off in the distance she could see the glimmer of a fading star, a tiny pinprick of light.

'I see it,' she whispered.

The star grew gradually brighter, as if sensing her presence, until a glowing sphere hovered before her.

The orb was pulsing hypnotically like the heartbeat of a foetus. Now that Lyra was closer, she could see that it was made up of tiny veins, like a ball of thread spun together. She reached out with her mind and entered the cocoon of light.

48

CHAMPOLLION

[Grenoble, France. Date: September, 1822]

Jean-François Champollion sat back from the desk, rubbing his aching shoulders and admiring his masterpiece. The translation tables were laid out before him in simple rows of phonetics, each symbol matched to a Greek letter or demotic homophone and tested against the greatest cartouches of their age: Cleopatra, Rameses and Ptolemy. There, on the pages before him, was the solution to a puzzle that had frustrated Egyptian scholars for decades — after years of careful research, he had finally deciphered the hieroglyphs.

'Je tiens mon affaire,' he whispered to himself. 'I've done it.'

He had spent the last two years on the inscriptions of the Rosetta stone. A granodiorite stele inscribed with three versions of a decree by Ptolemy V. It was discovered by Pierre-François Bouchard, a French Lieutenant in

Napoleon's expeditionary force, who unearthed it whilst surveying the defences of a fort a few miles north-east of the Egyptian town of Rosetta.

General Bonaparte invaded Egypt as part of his campaign against the Ottoman Empire. Unusually, his army included a large corps of *savants*: scientific experts, artists and engineers who were supposedly helping with the mapping of roads and the opening of the Suez Canal. These scholars went far beyond their remit, finding and cataloguing thousands of ancient objects, but none more important than the Rosetta Stone.

Unfortunately for him and many other French academics, most of the antiquities were seized by the British Navy when Napoleon was defeated at the Battle of Alexandria, leaving Jean-François with nothing more than a lithographic print taken before the stone was shipped to the British Museum.

Heavily damaged in places, the stele held three versions of the same decree. Issued in Memphis by King Ptolemy V Epiphanes in 196 BC, the first two texts were Ancient Egyptian in both heiroglyphic and demotic scripts, and the third was in Ancient Greek.

The Greek section had been translated by Hubert-Pascal Ameilhon, a French librarian in 1803 and Antoine-Isaac Silvestre de Sacy had made progress on the demotic, but no one attempted to decipher the heiroglyphs, or so he thought. It was only in 1814 when Jean-François discovered that Thomas Young, the foreign secretary of the Royal Society in London, was studying the hieroglyphic and realised he had a rival.

As the years passed, Young made some progress on deciphering the names of kings, but no one had managed to decrypt the entire text.

Until now.

Jean-François had finally unlocked the language of the pharaohs.

'Monsieur Champollion?' asked a man's voice.

Jean-François turned, unaware of anyone entering the room, the door was still closed as was the window.

The stranger lingered in the shadows.

Fearing that this was an assassin sent by the royalists, Jean-François reached for his letter opener.

'No, there is no need to be afraid. I am here to ask for your help.' The man's tone was direct and disciplined, one that was used to giving orders.

Still unsure as to how he'd entered the room without him knowing, Jean-François picked up the knife.

'Who are you?'

'I am Captain Pierre-François Bouchard,' he said, stepping into the light and standing to attention. His face was sharp and angular and there was heavy scarring around his right eye. Beneath his cloak Jean-François could make out the uniform of the Imperial Guard. 'I have come directly from the Emperor. He requires your assistance with an important historical matter.'

Jean-François's hand shook as he held up the thin metal blade. 'Napoleon died in exile a year ago. What kind of royalist trick is this?'

'My apologies,' said Bouchard, taking off his cloak and sitting down on a stool by the fire. 'I know you have just completed the translation of my stone. I have much to tell you and little time to do it. Do you have some brandy?'

. . .

Jean-François reluctantly took down the bottle of Cognac he had been saving and poured them both a large glass. Bouchard toasted the Emperor and drank the first in one go, wiping his mouth with his sleeve he held his glass out for another.

After the second, the captain relaxed a little.

'Not long after I discovered the stone, we lost the fort of El-Arish. General Cazals and I were sent as envoys to the Grand Vizir who imprisoned us in Damascus for forty-two days. It was a terrible place, the heat and the cockroaches were enough to drive a man insane. I kept a broken fragment of the stele and as I studied the letters I began to see things. Parts of its past opened up to me like a vision, over time I found that I could visit them with my mind.'

'Sounds as if you were hallucinating.'

'No,' he said gravely. 'I have travelled here from 1799, following the timeline of the stone. The moment that I touched it, I knew that you would be the one who would unlock its secrets.'

Jean-François scoffed. 'You're drunk man!'

'I don't have time for this.' The army officer scowled, grabbing the man by the wrist and twisting it until the knife fell from his hand. 'Your emperor needs you. Come with me.'

With that the room darkened and the world twisted away.

49

ROSETTA

[Rosetta, Egypt. Date: July 15, 1799]

It was close to midday and the heat was intense. Rufius watched the excavation through the distorted lens of his telescope. The shimmering haze over the River Nile twisted the men into candle flames as they worked below the wall of the dilapidated old fort on the opposite bank.

'Is he there?' asked Sim, swatting at the cloud of biting flies that were swarming around him.

'I think so,' said Rufius, handing him the spyglass. 'To the right, near the west wall.'

There was a group of French grenadiers stripped down to their waists clearing away rock and rubble from the base of one of the walls. Blinking back the sweat that ran into his eyes, Sim could just make out the figure of an officer standing over the men while they hauled a large piece of black granite out of a hole. The man knelt down beside it and began brushing away the dirt from the surface.

'He's found it.'

'How long before he knows what it does?' asked Rufius, taking back the telescope.

Sim opened his almanac and flicked through the pages until he found Bouchard's animating timeline.

'Between ten and twelve days after he gets captured by the Turks.'

He paused, checking the calculations on a pocket slide rule.

'There's something else. The tracker shows him visiting Jean-François Champollion.'

'Who's he?'

Sim held his finger down on one of the floating notes on the page until a series of details began to appear around it. 'Apparently, he's the man credited with deciphering the hieroglyphics on the stone.'

Rufius slapped his neck, scraping the mosquito off his palm and flicking it away. 'And how exactly does that help Bonaparte?'

Sim shrugged. 'Hard to say, although I think you'll be interested in the location.'

'Show me,' grunted Rufius, taking the book from Sim. 'What the devil is he doing in Crete?'

'Knossos to be precise. There's an eighty-nine percent probability that he will take Champollion with him.'

50

DECODING THE STONE

[Second Palace, Knossos. Date: 1799]

Holding up the oil lamp, Jean-François carefully brushed the dust away from the surface of the clay tablet. His eyes were having trouble focusing on the unusual symbols, whatever Bouchard had done to bring him to this place had affected his vision and his stomach in equal measures.

There was no rational explanation for what had happened. One moment they were in his study and the next in some ancient temple of a forgotten civilisation.

From the crude style of the hieroglyphics, he deduced it was a civilisation that was never conquered by the pharaohs. The symbols were strange and intriguing, not like any writing system he had ever seen before.

Holding the lamp made his arm ache and he put it down. Bouchard was nowhere to be seen, he had wandered further into the tomb.

'I need to take this back to my study,' said Jean-François,

his voice echoing along the stone walls. 'It will be easier to work with my reference books.'

'Nothing can leave this place,' replied Bouchard from the shadows. 'Everything must remain here.'

'Then we will need ink and paper, so that I can copy them down.'

'Look in my pack.'

Jean-François tutted and went over to the bag. The dust was irritating his asthma and the collapsed roof above them was doing nothing for his claustrophobia.

Bouchard's backpack was military issue, made from cowhide, and it had seen a lot of wear. Jean-François recognised the captain's uniform the moment he removed his cloak. It was that of the *Armée d'Orient*, the expeditionary force that Napoleon had taken into Egypt in 1798. He was in no doubt that this really was the man who had discovered the Rosetta Stone, but that didn't explain why or how on earth the officer had brought him here.

Opening the bag, Jean-François took out a leather bound journal, pen and ink and set about copying down the symbols.

Bouchard was fascinated by the walls of the tomb. Each sandstone block was carved with intricate reliefs of battle scenes: winged warriors skewering monsters with multi-bladed spears. The creatures' bodies were masses of tentacles.

It was a motif that he had seen in the tombs of Egyptian kings.

· · ·

Napoleon had obtained many fine pieces of art during his Italian campaign. The walls of the Tuileries Palace were adorned in the works of Correggio, Raphael and Rubens; spoils of war from the Dukes of Parma and Modena.

But amongst his general's most precious possessions were his books. On the fourteen-week voyage to Alexandria, Napoleon insisted on bringing a small library of one hundred and twenty-five volumes; histories of Rome and Greece, Heroditus and Plutarch, which he encouraged his officers to read. The General knew many of them by heart and quoted from them like others would use the bible.

There was, however, one book that he favoured more than the others.

One that he discovered on his conquest of Venice.

When the Doge abdicated in 1797, it was the end of a republic that had lasted over nine hundred years. While the French army plundered the city, looting the palazzi and churches for their gold and artworks, Napoleon was in the Bessarion Library of the Biblioteca Marciana.

Cardinal Bessarion had a passion for Ancient Greek history and had collected many rare and unique manuscripts, one of which was Ptolemy's *Almagest*.

Amongst the astronomical, mathematical treatises on the movement of the heavens was a reference to a forgotten civilisation, one whose fabled riches had never been equalled. Pharaohs who were buried with their fortunes in tombs below the desert, ones who had reigned for hundreds if not thousands of years.

Napoleon's conquest of Egypt was no ordinary campaign. Creating a corps of savants: engineers, artists, chemists, geologists and antiquarians that were seconded to the army with specific orders to collect and document the antiquities of the pharaohs, a long-dead civilisation that at the time, Bouchard never knew existed.

Bonaparte was fascinated by the tales of King Solomon and his treasures, and since the government had refused to fund the campaign, he was forced to borrow from other sources, ones who had been promised a share of the treasure and more particularly access to the secret knowledge of the pyramids.

Egypt was a harsh, arid place, unwilling to surrender its secrets easily. The remnants of the once great civilisations lay hidden, submerged in the shifting sands of the desert.

Bouchard was ordered to locate them. Using his special abilities to survey the landscape at various points in time until he found the entrances.

He quickly learned the limitations of his power. He could travel a few hundred years back in a single 'leap,' and the further back he went the harder it became.

Unfortunately, the tombs that he did manage to locate were usually empty. Tomb robbers had ransacked and stripped them of anything valuable. All that was left behind were the cryptic writings in a language that no one, not even the local guides, seemed to be able to read.

There were frescoes painted on to the stone walls of the oldest tombs, of images of creatures just like the ones in the temple in which he stood. The savants concluded that the depictions were mythic, illustrating old legends of ancient gods fighting evil to create a better world.

But now Bouchard was seeing them for the second time,

carved by a civilisation that existed outside of the dominion of the pharaohs and he was less convinced it was a work of fiction.

Two separate cultures dreaming up the same monsters was very unlikely and he didn't believe in coincidences.

51

LETTER

To my little one,
It's been nearly two weeks since I left your father. Although in the time vacuum of the Maelstrom, days are only marked by the clock that your grandmother made to remind us when to go to sleep.

I dreamt of him last night. It was a strange one, like a life I've lived but never remembered.

We were in a cave, back in the early Mesolithic. He was young and inexperienced. Still learning about his range; no one should be able to travel back that far in one jump, but just as with everything else, your father didn't play by the rules.

The earth was still in the grips of the last Ice Age and I still shiver at the thought of how cold it was. He was the one who went out and found the wood for a fire. I was useless, curled up in furs waiting for the Draconians to find us. We would have died in that dark hole if it hadn't been for him.

Your grandfather had taken me back to the Neolithic many

times as a child, so I knew how to survive, how to forage for food – live off the land, but I was so sure they would come.

After a few weeks, Josh convinced me that we should move further south, to a warmer climate.

At that time there was a land bridge between England and Europe, the geologists later named it Doggerland and it meant that we could cross into France without getting our feet wet.

Doggerland was to the East, and once we crossed over it, our plan was to head for Amsterdam, or at least where the city would be in twenty-thousand years, and then turn south for the Mediterranean.

We didn't realise how large a settlement we'd find when we arrived there. It took us nearly three weeks to walk to it. They were magical days, travelling through a landscape untouched by man. We saw herds of woolly mammoths wandering over the hills of Kent and ice sheets glistening in the early sun as we stood on what would one day be the English Channel.

The villagers were wary of us at first, treating us like outsiders. They marvelled at Josh's blond hair and blue eyes. Most of them were dark and less than five feet tall. He was like a giant among them, the children took to him quickly, following him around like baby ducks.

There were few men when we arrived, and although we couldn't speak their language it was clear that they were away hunting. Skins of the enormous beasts were stretched out on the roofs of their huts or staked on wooden frames to dry in the sun. Josh shared some of the food we had caught during our journey and they reciprocated, we reached a measured peace, at least until the hunting party returned two days later.

These men were less welcoming. The first group that arrived bore the wounds of a savage attack, terrible rents in their arms and chests made by vicious claws. It was obvious from the reactions of the women that there should have been more of them. Their wailing carried on long into the night.

We did what we could. I helped the medicine woman to treat the worst of them. We saved a few but without antibiotics some of the weaker ones couldn't be helped.

The second group were in better shape and their leader was obviously the chief of the clan.

He was a massive brute of a man, bigger even than Uncle Rufius. With sharp bones forced through his nose and ears. His men put down the carcass of the large bison they had been carrying between two poles and the women fell upon it with their flint knives, butchering it like skilled chefs.

The chief seemed to ignore us at first, he was obviously concerned with the well-being of the other group and disappeared with the old medicine woman.

Your father was taken by them in the middle of the night. It was the most scary thing I've ever experienced. I followed them as they dragged him down into the village. There was an enormous fire and everyone was eating. The chief was sitting on the stump of tree talking to one of his men.

I was in no doubt that they would have killed him if the medicine woman hadn't intervened. I have no idea what she said to the man, but he listened intently to her protestations and when she finished, ordered his men to release him.

She woke us at dawn the next day and sent us on our way with enough supplies for two weeks.

52

INFERNAL MACHINE

[Paris, France. Date: December 24, 1800]

Josh had no idea how he came to be standing in the rue Saint-Nicaise on a cold winter's evening in the middle of Paris. The last thing he could remember was waking up next to the Golem in Prague, 1620.

He tried to access the founder's archives, wondering if the old man had moved him like the last time, but there was nothing, no grand museum of memories and no sign of him.

The sky was darkening, heavy clouds hung overhead threatening snow and there was an icy tinge to his breath. He was on the corner of a busy junction, a steady stream of horse-drawn carts made their way along Rue du Faubourg Saint-Honoré on their way home from market.

Scanning the street and the faces of the passers-by, he searched for something that might jog his memory. People avoided his gaze, keeping their eyes down as they passed him and when he caught his reflection in a shop window, he realised why: he was dressed in the uniform of a French Consular Guard.

Gripping the hilt of the sword, he felt the timelines flow under his fingers.

It had been given to the original owner of the uniform by General Lannes, Commandant of the Guard and the man responsible for the protection of the first consul himself, Napoleon. The memory was hazy and Josh found it hard to focus on the timeline.

His reverie was broken by the clatter of hooves as an escort of light cavalry rounded the corner from the Tuileries Palace. Between them came two ornate coaches pulled by six black horses. High ranking officers flanked the coaches whose windows were dark, obscuring the occupants.

'Vive mon general!' shouted an old soldier waving his hat as they passed. Others took up the call as the coach passed by.

As the entourage turned the corner onto rue Saint-Nicaise, there was a massive explosion, Josh watched Napoleon's carriage shatter like matchwood. The blast sent horses and their riders into the air, shredding them with shrapnel and shattering every window along the street.

Josh was knocked to the ground by the shockwave and, for a moment, time seemed to stop. No one moved and he wondered if the Protectorate were about to intercede. Then slowly, his ears still ringing from the percussion, he heard the screams of the injured like distant children calling for their mothers.

Josh got unsteadily to his feet. There were bodies strewn across the street, like discarded toys, their limbs folded at odd angles, necks twisted or heads missing. He stumbled towards the carnage, using his sword like a cane to keep himself from falling over.

There was nothing left of Napoleon's guard, his carriage was lying on its side, the entire upper half having been ripped away from the undercarriage. Wild-eyed horses flailed around on the ground, trapped by their yokes. Josh cut them free and watched them gallop along the street.

People came out of shops and cafes, their initial shock replaced with anger and fear as they helped the wounded or searched for their relatives and friends.

The blast had scorched the cobble stones, leaving long black lines that led back to the source, to the carcass of a burned-out wagon and the remnants of a large barrel.

It was still burning as Josh walked towards the cart, as was the horse that had been left harnessed to it. The heat was too intense to get any closer, but he found what he was looking for, a piece of iron hoop from the wagon lay steaming in a pool of blood.

Reaching into its timeline he saw the events that led to the explosion, found the dilapidated warehouse on the Rue Paradis where it had been prepared and moved into the moment.

It was late evening and the dimming light made it easy for Josh to move unseen to the rear of the building, finding a grimy window to watch what was going on inside.

The wagon sat in the light of a ring of bullseye lamps.

Two thick-set men were working on the cart with hammers, securing a large wine barrel to the back with thick iron hoops. Another man was packing the inside of the barrel with smaller kegs and bags of nails. A well-dressed man watched them from the shadows, reading aloud from a letter. It was hard to hear what he was saying, but it was clear from the reaction of the others that it was good news.

The gentleman patted one of the men on the shoulder, before handing over a small bag of coins, and leaving.

Josh followed the gentleman.

The tap of his cane echoed down the cobbled street of Rue Paradis, making it easy to follow at a distance. He was a brave man to walk the back streets of Paris at night alone. They were no different to those of London, filled with drunks and prostitutes, pestering passers-by with fetid, sour breath and rotten teeth.

There was something else too, Josh could see it in their eyes, a madness, an ever-present sense of danger, a lingering undercurrent of revolution.

The gentleman turned left and onto the well-lit street of Rue Sainte-Anne.

Josh thought it looked familiar, in one of his previous lives he'd visited this place with the colonel, and knew instantly that the man was heading for the Palais Royale.

53

___

KNOSSOS

[Second Palace. Knossos. Date: 1799]

Something had bitten Bouchard. It came out of one of the mummified bodies that he'd found in a burial chamber at the far end of the passageway.

At first, he thought it was a rat. But the toxins that were racing around his body felt more like that of a spider. He was finding it hard to concentrate and his legs and arms were growing numb.

He sat down beside one of the sarcophagi and took a long drink of water, but Bouchard couldn't shake the overwhelming sense of fatigue. His eyelids were becoming heavy, and he poured the rest of the waterskin over his head, *I must stay awake*, he told himself. He couldn't die in this tomb, his mission was not complete.

When Bouchard was released from Damascus and returned to his garrison, he decided to keep his new-found ability a secret. Concerned that his fellow officers would think him insane, he did his best to lead a normal life.

But it wasn't to last. When General Kléber was assassinated by an Arab Syrian student in the garden of the palace of Alfi bika in Cairo, he felt duty bound to save him.

It was a simple jump, as he called it, stepping back a few minutes before the murder and intercepting the student before he reached the General.

Kléber was head of the army at that time and when Napoleon was told of Bouchard's heroic act, he demanded that Bouchard be brought to him in France.

'How did you know that the beggar had a knife?' Napoleon asked him over dinner in Paris.

Bouchard could have lied, made up some story about seeing the attacker's blade, but there was something about Bonaparte that demanded the truth.

'I can move through time.'

The words felt strange coming out of his mouth, even Bouchard thought he sounded like a crazy man.

Napoleon's reaction was slight, a small twist of the lip, nothing more. He was an enlightened man and a scholar of the Classics, modelling himself on historical conquerors such as Julius Caesar and Alexander the Great.

'Can you prove this?'

'I can. All I need is a name, something I would not guess.'

'Plutarch.'

Bouchard nodded, it was a simple exercise. He jumped back a few hours and wrote a line on a small piece of paper and placed it under the cushion of the chair that Napoleon would be sitting on later.

All of this happened in the blink of an eye.

'Please, my general, look beneath your seat.'

Napoleon unfolded the note and read aloud. 'The mind is not a vessel to be filled but a fire to be kindled.' He smiled. 'One of my favourite quotes.'

Bouchard was given a new role and re-assigned to the Imperial Guard. His missions were carefully planned and subtle, ones that gave Napoleon a tactical advantage without making it too obvious. Primarily, Bonaparte's campaigns needed financing and his time-travelling captain was the perfect agent for acquiring it.

'My thief of time,' he began to call him, convincing Bouchard that it was his destiny to help France become the most powerful empire in Europe.

After nearly drowning while recovering gold from the *L'Orient* during the Battle of the Nile, it became clear that Napoleon would need more than just money to achieve his aim.

The general became obsessed with learning more about his enemies: the Royal Houses of Europe that were commanding the Austrian, Prussian, Dutch and Spanish armies and in particular Francis II and the Habsburgs.

The Habsburgs ruled over Europe for the last three hundred years. Their descendants intermarried with other houses, creating what became known as the Holy Roman Empire. They were violently opposed to the revolutionary government after the overthrow of the French monarchy, creating a coalition of allies to challenge Napoleon's Grand Army.

Fighting their combined forces was draining him of both men and money, but with his new secret weapon he was hoping to destroy or at least weaken the Hapsburg lineage.

His general was a master strategist, who understood the consequences of changing the past too radically. He favoured small tactical assassinations, hoping that its effect would jeopardise the coalition. But the houses were too strong, removing one head of state seemed to do nothing but create a viable replacement. Napoleon likened them to the Greek legend of the Hydra of Lerna, referring to himself as Heracles and Bouchard his Iolas.

Bouchard became his assassin. Killing various members of the royal houses and royalist supporters before they became a threat, and yet no matter what he did, fate seemed to work against him, there seemed to be no end to the Hydra.

'No amount of flaming swords can seem to end this,' he wrote to his wife, Josephine, in one of his letters. 'I am plagued by the spawn of the Habsburgs.'

Now as he lay in the dust, feeling his breath weaken, he wondered if he had done the right thing.

It was a lonely, thankless task wandering through time. Changing the past was something only he remembered, every time he returned to the emperor the man would have no memory of the adjustment they'd planned together. Bouchard was beginning to believe that the universe was somehow working against him, repairing the damage, as if fate could not be changed and that Napoleon was always destined to fail.

54

EMERGENCY

[Chapter House. Date: 1880]

'What happened?' asked Alixia as Benoir laid Lyra's limp body on the kitchen table.

'She tried to read an Aeon,' Benoir explained.

Alixia gently stroked the hair away from her daughter's neck and felt for a pulse. 'A what?'

'A xenomorphic parasite, the one we captured in 1888,' explained Kaori.

'The one you thought was responsible for the Ripper murders?'

Kaori nodded.

Lyra's face was pale and her eyes stared blankly at the ceiling. Her dry lips moved as if whispering a silent prayer, while her fingers worried frantically at something invisible to them.

Alixia's eyes hardened as she assessed her condition. This was not the first time she had seen Lyra in such a terrible state. Being a mother to such a powerful seer was a thankless task, and there had been more than one occasion where she'd brought Lyra back from the brink of death. The fine scars on her daughter's arms were testament to her skills as a seamstress.

She turned to Benoir. 'Fetch the Grand Seer and Doctor Crooke.'

Benoir's face went ashen as he nodded solemnly before disappearing.

The old seer appeared seconds later, dressed in his usual cloak of black feathers and carrying a piece of obsidian glass in a golden frame.

'Alixia,' said Kelly, placing the mirror under Lyra's chin and kneeling down to look up at her reflection. 'How long has she been like this?'

'Two hours,' replied Kaori, checking her tachyon. 'We had to stabilise the chamber before we could leave.'

'The stars shine darkly in her eyes,' noted Kelly, shifting the position of the mirror.

Benoir appeared at the back of the room with the hunchbacked doctor.

'Crooke,' acknowledged the Grand Seer. 'Bring forth Morpheus and apply his tears, whilst I unwind this prison of time.'

The doctor produced a small vial of white powder from inside his cloak and tipped it into a glass of water, turning it a luminescent green.

'Get her to drink this,' he instructed, handing the glass to Alixia.

They lifted her head and she sipped at the water whilst still muttering to herself.

Kelly took off his feathered cloak and rolled up his long white cuffs. Benoir noted the old scars on the man's arms, they were long and parallel like the claw marks of a tiger. The Grand Seer removed his hat and pulled a small knife from his boot.

He cut a long fine line along his left forearm and handed the knife to Alixia. Taking a quill from his hat he dipped the nib into his blood and drew a crimson symbol on Lyra's forehead.

The glyph seemed to boil on her skin and quickly evaporated.

Kelly grimaced and drew two new symbols in its place. This time they were absorbed into the skin. 'Better,' he murmured.

He wrote a string of characters on his own arm and watched them fade away.

'Something wicked this way comes,' he warned them, picking up the obsidian mirror once more and drawing a series of symbols onto its surface before holding it up for all to see.

They watched as tendrils of smoke were drawn out of Lyra's body, the dark mass coalescing into the head of a tentacled creature before being absorbed into the blackened glass.

As soon as it had completely disappeared, Kelly wiped the marks from the surface of the mirror and smashed it violently on the floor. Grinding the shards with the heel of his boot and cursing. 'Out! Out! Thou dost infect my eyes.'

The colour was returning to Lyra's cheeks. Alixia gathered her up as if she were a doll and smothered her with kisses.

Crooke examined her and recommended a few days of bed rest and one of his more noxious tonics.

Benoir helped Kelly back into his cloak, noting that the cut on his forearm had already begun to heal.

'Thank you, boy,' the Grand Seer said, picking up his hat and pushing the feather back into it. 'When she is recovered, bring her to me.'

Kelly bowed to Alixia and disappeared.

55

TYCHO STATION

[Tycho Station, Maelstrom]

A shudder ran through the hull of the *Nautilus* and the pitch of the engines changed ever so slightly, a sure sign that her mother was bringing the ship in to land.

Caitlin tried to ignore it. She was re-reading Ventris's notes on the deciphering of Linear B. His grid of characters and ideograms was spread across the table, mapping out over eighty symbols and one hundred ideograms. He correctly identified it as an early form of Greek using a syllabic system where the characters represented sounds. She tried speaking the words of a long dead language aloud, knowing that no one had uttered them for over three thousand years.

Some of the ideograms were simple representations of the object in question: a horse, jug, spear and wheel, whereas other symbols were grouped in threes, with common roots and different endings. Most of the scripts were obviously inventories of grain and livestock, so Ventris was able to identify words for 'Total' and a basic numbering system.

None of it was any help with Linear A.

Linear A was written by the devil for all she knew.

Her father appeared through one of the hatches.

'Hey KitKat, we're about to dock. Do you want to come and see?'

Caitlin resented the interruption. The sofa was comfortable and warm. Her mother had begun to call it her 'nest', since she'd hardly moved from it in the last three weeks. But her eyes were beginning to ache and she needed to stretch her legs.

'Yeah, why not.'

She followed him up a spiral staircase inside the conning tower and out onto an observation platform. It was heavily shielded, protecting them from the worst of the Maelstrom's chaos energy.

Her mother was piloting the ship using a series of levers and hand cranks built into a chair that sprouted from the deck like a mechanical sunflower. She smiled as Caitlin came up out of the hatch.

'Hi,' she said, frantically adjusting the downward planes. 'Nice to see you out of your nest.'

Caitlin poked out her tongue and stretched her arms above her head. The sky above them was a swirling mass of anomalies, large bubbles of time clustered together like frog spawn, each looping through their own tiny slice of history.

Her parents had charted thousands of similar clusters in

the Maelstrom, although they had no idea how they came to be there. Her father called them 'offcuts' or 'remnants', branches of time that had somehow become separated from the main trunk of the continuum, left to repeat their moments ad infinitum in the eternal void.

They discovered a number of stable areas in the otherwise chaotic realm where two or three remnants had collided, creating a strange hybrid of different periods, with some interesting and potentially disastrous results.

Tycho station was the underground observatory of Tycho Brahe, a Danish astronomer, who had built the research facility on an island called Hven off the coast of Sweden.

'The castle of the stars,' said her mother, bringing the ship to rest gracefully a thousand yards from the observatory.

It was a strange building. Above ground all they could see were a series of turret roofs, making it appear as if the rest of the castle had sunk into the ground. Beside it stood the remains of Uraniborg, the fairy-tale palace that Brahe had originally constructed as the research facility for his astronomical studies, but whose towers had proved too unsteady in the winds. As was usual with the Maelstrom, parts of the palace were in better condition than others.

They disembarked and made their way over the windswept fields towards the entrance. An icy wind reminded Caitlin that the island was once situated in the sea that separated Denmark from Sweden. She pulled her coat tighter around her, wondering how the farmers survived the winter.

Her father went ahead and opened the heavy door that led down into the subterranean basement, inside which Caitlin could see the flickering glow of a fire.

'How long does it last?' Caitlin shouted over the howling wind.

'The loop runs for nearly a year,' her mother replied. 'The winds will drop in a few days. Summer here is lovely.'

'Is anyone trapped here?'

Her mother nodded. 'Five families and the caretaker. We do our best for them, but once the loop resets they forget we were ever here.' She pulled the heavy iron door shut and bolted it from the inside, silencing the storm outside.

'And Tycho?' Caitlin spoke too loudly, her ears still ringing from the wind.

Her mother shook her head. 'This is 1599, he's in exile, working as the Imperial Astronomer for Rudolf II in Prague.'

The observatory was a series of interconnecting circular chambers, each one with a view up into the heavens. The roofs of the turrets that Caitlin had seen from the outside could be rotated and opened by a series of pulleys and chains, giving a view out into the sky over sixteenth century Sweden or the Maelstrom, depending which direction you looked.

A large collection of the astronomer's instruments were still stored in the laboratory, including an enormous quadrant that curved down from one wall with divisions of degrees marked along its arc.

'This was before telescopes,' her mother noted. 'All of his observations were done with the naked eye.'

Caitlin caught the scent of something hot and spicy and her mouth began to water at the smell.

Her father was busy in what she assumed was the alchemical laboratory. It had been transformed into a kitchen. A black cauldron was hanging over the fireplace, and he was busy chopping vegetables and depositing them into the stew.

'What's for dinner?'

He pulled a swede out of a sack. 'Vegetable stew. There's no meat, but the caretaker keeps a very well stocked garden. After his master left the laboratory, this place became something of a storehouse.'

Caitlin sat on a small wooden chair and kicked off her boots. Her ankles were swollen and she rubbed them to ease the pain.

'How are you doing?'

'Okay, I guess. Better than sitting at home wondering what Josh's going to do next.'

'How's his mother?'

'Stable. Last time I saw her, Doctor Crooke had put her in stasis. Josh was talking about some kind of gene therapy.'

'Crooke's a good man, if anyone can find a cure it would be him.'

Caitlin picked up a knife and began to peel the swede. Her parents hadn't mentioned Josh up until now. They knew that she would need some time. It was the elephant in the room and it needed to be discussed.

'Do you think I should have stayed?'

Her father chuckled. 'I think you're just like your mother. You know instinctively what is right, and even if it isn't — you have to do it your way.'

Caitlin tried to remember exactly why she'd agreed to leave. She missed Josh, but there was a darkness inside him that had grown over the last four years. He brooded over his mother, to the point where nothing else seemed to matter. Trying to find a cure for her had become an obsession, it consumed him, and perhaps it was partly that feeling of abandonment that Caitlin resented, that and the fact he was breaking the Order's primary directive trying to fix her.

She consoled herself with the fact that he had wanted to protect her and the baby.

The realisation suddenly struck her.

There was another human being growing inside her.

Tears rolled down her face at the thought. This wasn't about fate or pride, it was nothing more than a mother protecting her child, a primeval instinct to keep it safe.

'He's a good lad,' her father said, trying to sound reassuring. 'Whatever happens, never forget who he is.'

Caitlin bit her bottom lip. 'I know.'

He wrapped his arms around her and she buried her head into his chest and cried.

Before dinner, her mother came into the kitchen carrying a small round table whose top was divided into many sections, like a compass. At its centre was a small vertical pole, on which sat a series of lenses on a moveable arm.

'Look what I found.'

Caitlin was ladling the stew into bowls. 'What is it?'

'A cosmolabe, or pantocosm. It's a rare sixteenth century astronomical instrument.'

'And what does it do?'

Her mother suppressed a smile. 'Measures the angles between celestial bodies, but it can also be used for predictions.'

Caitlin sneered. 'You're not going to do my horoscope are you?'

'Not yours no, your grandmother did yours before you were born. It's a tradition of sorts.'

'And how did that turn out?'

'Well, okay. There were complications, I'll admit it's by no means an exact science. But since we're stuck here for the foreseeable future, I thought we'd have a little fun.'

Caitlin turned to her father. 'What do you think?'

He held his hands up as if surrendering. 'Don't get me involved in this. Your grandmother was the fiercest woman I ever met, second only to your mother of course.'

The lens arm spun on a central axis, like a roulette wheel, as her mother shuffled a deck of Tarot cards while watching it slowly come to land on the first astrological symbol.

'Mars,' her mother said.

'The God of War?' asked Caitlin, folding her arms.

'Not just war, but passion and willpower! It is a powerful ruling planet,' she read from the back of the respective Tarot card. 'The tower — a fire sign.'

She laid the card on the table and spun it again.

'And destruction,' added Caitlin sourly.

'Jupiter,' said her mother, putting the Wheel of Fortune card next to the Tower. 'Now that represents someone who will be naturally fortunate — who's been blessed by the gods.'

Caitlin sighed and pulled a face at her father.

'Last one,' her mother said.

'Moon.'

'That's not really a planet is it?'

She laid down the high priestess card. 'The moon represents psychic abilities and emotions.'

'Great, so I'm having a psychic baby with anger issues and potential gambling problems.'

'Or a strong leader with special abilities,' suggested her father.

'Can we eat now?'

56

PARASITE

[Chapter House. Date: 1880]

Lyra woke three days later, much to her mother's relief. She was weak and visibly drained. Alixia managed to get her to drink half a cup of Crooke's restorative tonic before her senses returned completely.

'It smells like a badger died in it,' Lyra complained, pushing it away.

'It's good for you. I'll put some honey in it.'

She got up to leave, meeting Benoir at the door.

'I'm not sure she's ready for visitors,' her mother warned him, blocking the doorway.

'It's okay Mum,' croaked Lyra, shifting the pillows so she could sit up.

'Just five minutes,' said Alixia, raising a stern finger to the man who was nearly two feet taller than her.

He brought flowers. A large bunch of Michaelmas daisies, the kind that you find growing wild on embankments. He had obviously picked them himself. Her mother raised one eyebrow as she left. Lyra ignored her and thanked him all the same.

'How are you feeling?' he asked, sitting on the end of the bed.

'Like a mastodon sat on my head.'

He tried to laugh, but failed. Lyra took his hand and cautiously read the last few days of his timeline.

'You stayed with me the whole time?'

Benoir blushed as he nodded. 'It's all my fault.'

'No, you shouldn't blame yourself. My mother will tell you that no one has ever stopped me from doing something, once I've set my mind to it.'

'But it nearly killed you!'

She winced as she shifted herself into a more upright position. 'I think it actually did. But it's not the first time, I've been there before.'

Benoir didn't know what to say.

'More importantly I know what it is now,' she continued, letting go of his hand and picking up her almanac and tearing out a page. 'You need to find my brother Sim, he's on a mission with Rufius Westinghouse.'

'Westinghouse?'

'Have you heard of him?' Lyra scribbled a note on the paper.

Benoir nodded. 'The watchman.'

She folded the note and held it out to him. 'Well, find them and bring them here, and the Grand Seer, I'm sure he will want to hear this too.'

Benoir took the note and turned to leave.

'But before you go, one last thing.'

'Yes?'

'A kiss, s'il vous plait.'

57

MISSING

[Palace of Knossos, Date: 1799]

'Are you sure this is the place?' asked Rufius, shading his eyes from the sun as he studied the rock-strewn site. It was the same location that he'd been sent to in 1944, the one that Kellerman and the Antiquarians had mysteriously quarantined.

Sim opened his almanac and held it out to him. 'See for yourself. Bouchard's tracer stops right here. It hasn't moved in over two days.'

Rufius squinted at the map that was floating in the middle of the page. 'What's so important about this place? Why would Bonaparte send him here?'

'Napoleon stayed at Ierapetra on the south coast of Crete after the Battle of the Pyramids. Perhaps the locals told him of the legends of Knossos.'

'And which legend would that be?' asked Rufius, looking at the faded frescoes on the walls.

'There will be excavations here in 1900 by an archaeologist called Arthur Evans. Apparently, the layout of the palace reminded him of the mythical labyrinth of King Minos and he named the civilisation Minoan.'

Rufius groaned. 'Not a bloody minotaur.'

'More likely they were worshippers of the bull-god.'

Striding towards the stone doorway, Rufius pulled out a long sabre from its scabbard. 'I think it's time we find out what Hitler and Bonaparte thought was so important about this place.'

'Hitler?' asked Sim, putting his book away and running after him.

'He invaded Crete and sent an army of scientists and engineers here. I was investigating why when Konstantine's Antiquarians showed up and shut the whole place down.'

A squad of Dreadnoughts in full temporal armour shimmered into existence in front of the entrance. In silence they moved swiftly over the rubble taking a defensive position on each side of Sim and Rufius.

Their commander came towards them, drawing his weapon as he approached.

Rufius nodded at the Dreadnought commander who signalled his men to move inside.

'Commander,' said Rufius.

'Watchman. This is a quarantined zone, by what authority are you here?'

'Professor Eddington,' said Sim, before Rufius could think of a reasonable lie.

The man glanced sideways at Sim, as if seeing him for the first time. 'And you are?'

'Simeon De Freis. First Actuary of the Copernican.'

'As far as I was aware,' interrupted Rufius. 'This site is

under Antiquarian jurisdiction. What brings a team of the Draconians' elite guard here?'

The commander's eyes returned to Rufius, his knuckles whitened as he gripped his sword a little tighter. 'We've detected abnormal temporal activity.'

'Like a breach?'

'I'm not at liberty to say. I know of you Westinghouse. You're a trouble-maker.'

'And you are?'

'MacKenzie.'

'Well, Commander MacKenzie, it seems neither of us is supposed to be here. Which seems a little serendipitous don't you think? Shall we crack on before the Antiquarians realise what we're up to? Unless of course you like standing around in this heat?'

The Dreadnoughts moved silently through the semi-darkness, their armour making them almost invisible, only the glints on their blades giving any hint of their position.

Talk of a breach had made Sim regret not taking a weapon. Although he'd never really been very good with a sword, preferring a bow, the idea that they were about to face something from the Maelstrom was making him more than a little nervous.

Compared to the searing temperatures outside, the interior of the complex was cool and still. The palace was a series of interconnecting rooms linked by long stoned-paved corridors. The columns that supported the tiled ceiling and the floors above were crumbling. Rubble from weakened sections lay piled up in places, making it hard for them to navigate.

Ahead of them, rats and beetles scurried across the drifts of sand and broken crockery. While spiders wove webs along the ceiling, lacing old twisted vines had broken through the plaster with skeins of grey — nature was slowly reclaiming its own.

There was an odd smell permeating the palace; a mixture of soured milk and rotting meat. Sim tried breathing through his mouth, but the dust caught in his throat and made him cough.

Rufius turned and glared at him. 'Are you quite sure you wouldn't rather wait outside?' he asked in a rough whisper.

Sim shook his head and walked on. This was his first ever field mission and he wasn't about to bail out. Copernicans were already thought of by most as theorists who didn't like getting their hands dirty. This would be his one and only assignment, he wanted to make sure he gave a good account of himself — Professor Eddington would expect nothing less.

He checked his almanac for the last location of Bouchard's tracer. The perspective shifted on the illustration showing the location was somewhere beneath their feet.

'There must be some kind of basement below this,' he said, turning the book around to orientate it with the room.

'More likely to be a dungeon,' said Rufius.

'How far down?' asked the commander.

'It's not like a GPS,' Sim reminded him. 'I would say approximately one hundred and fifty feet.'

The Dreadnoughts went ahead, scouting for a way into the lower levels. Sim watched them sweep each room with military efficiency. They always kept a watchful eye for any unexpected guests; tomb robbers were a constant threat and the Draconians lost some of the best teams to unexpected attacks from local bandits. It was one of the key reasons the Dreadnoughts were formed. They were the martial arm of the Draconians, tasked with ensuring the safety of their expeditions as well as performing search and rescue when someone inevitably went missing.

They were also the main defence against the creatures of the Maelstrom.

Their survival rate was generally less than five years.

Commander MacKenzie signalled it was safe to proceed and they moved out into a sun-scorched courtyard.

'We've found an entrance,' he reported.

'Good job! Lead the way,' said Rufius.

'One problem,' said the commander, holding up his gloved hand. 'I sent two of my men in and they've not returned.'

Rufius's brow furrowed. 'How long have they been down there?'

'Elapsed time, ten minutes, but their trackers are showing some erratic time fluctuations.'

'How much?' asked Sim.

The man tapped a series of dials strapped to his forearm. 'Between one hundred and two thousand years.'

Sim knew this was a bad sign, there was only one reason for such a wide discrepancy. Rufius said it before he could.

'So there's a breach.'

'I need to inform command,' the commander said, taking out his almanac.

'Hold that thought soldier,' said Rufius, gripping the man's arm. 'If you call it in, it'll alert the Antiquarians and Konstantine will have us thrown in the brig. Give me five minutes down there and I may be able to save them.'

The officer went to protest but changed his mind.

'Sim, you wait with Commander Mackenzie, while I investigate.'

Sim nodded taking out his tachyon and handing it to Rufius.

'It's a Mark VI. We can talk to each other. I have a spare.'

Rufius looked at the third button and smiled. 'What will they think of next?'

58

<hr>

WIRELESS

[Tycho Station, Maelstrom]

'I thought you might like this,' her father said, depositing an antique Bakelite radio onto her desk.

Caitlin looked up from her notes. 'Where did you find that?'

He stroked the brown tortoiseshell case with pride. 'Isn't she a beauty? The *USS Helena* drifted into Tycho space yesterday, your mother and I spent most of the day salvaging it for parts.

'Doesn't it need electricity?'

He shook his head and turned one of the dials on the front. The valves shone through the mesh grille and lit up the tuner. Caitlin smelled the dust burning off the coils inside.

'It's hardly going to find a radio signal though is it?' she said as the speaker crackled.

'Ah, now that's what I thought originally.' He began to move the tuner along the frequencies, and Caitlin heard snippets of something other than static.

'This is 1939,' he said as the haunting notes of 'Moonlight Serenade' filled the room.

'The year or the frequency?'

'The year. Now, if you give me a second. He shifted the dial once more and classical music poured out of the speaker. 'The Last Night of the Proms from 1969.'

'How?' asked Caitlin.

'Radio waves get trapped in the Maelstrom as easily as time it seems.'

He twisted the dial, and the music changed again.

'Spandau Ballet?' He said, shifting his feet to the music.

Caitlin was not a big fan of eighties music or her father's dancing. 'I think I prefer the classics.'

'Suit yourself. I think there are a couple more batteries in the others that I can scavenge.'

59

INFINITY ENGINE

[Map room, Copernican Headquarters]

Professor Eddington was surrounded by an ever moving cloud of equations as the Infinity Engine projected complex sequences of possibilities in streams of light around him.

'Eddington, playing with your new toy I see.'

The voice of Konstantine echoed around the chamber.

'Grandmaster this is an unexpected surprise.'

The man appeared from the shadows, walking through the formulas and waving his hands at them as if swatting flies.

'It never ceases to amaze me how you Copernicans can get anything from this jumble of nonsense.'

Eddington dropped his arms and the ribbons of light retreated back into the small clockwork globe.

'We do our best. It is by no means an exact science.'

The Antiquarian put his hands behind his back and leaned over to study the inactive sphere.

'They say Jones built this without any plans.'

'Indeed.'

'Don't you find that a little odd? Even the simplest tachyon has to be machined. Something so intricate and unique. I would have expected at least a series of prototypes. To come out with this masterpiece on his first attempt seems rather unusual. Don't you think?'

Eddington positioned himself on the other side of the engine.

'Is there something I can help you with Grandmaster?'

'A demonstration perhaps,' he said, crossing his arms across his chest. 'Can this device of yours tell me where Jones is now?'

Eddington nodded. 'It has the capability to trace individuals, yes.'

'So would you be so kind as to show me?'

60

MAZE

[Knossos Palace, Date: 1799]

The light from Sim's Mark VI was infinitely more powerful than his own. The beam of the torch lit up the walls of the labyrinth revealing faded frescoes of warriors fighting and dying at the feet of a bull-headed giant. Rufius ignored them, he'd spent long enough in antiquity to know how such myths could be used to pacify a superstitious population. A wise king could use them to keep his illiterate peasants in check without having to resort to the expense of a police force.

There were no such things as monsters, not in this realm at least. Beyond the borders of the chronosphere it was an entirely different matter.

The tiled floor was covered in a layer of sand and he quickly found a trail of recent footprints.

No cloven hooves, he noted, *but no sign of Mackenzie's men.*

'Testing, testing. Are you receiving me? Over?' Sim's voice crackled out of the watch.

'Loud and clear,' replied Rufius.

'You have to press the button to talk,' said Sim.

'Roger,' said Rufius, depressing the button. 'Keep the channel open.'

The underground maze was just as complex as the legend described and Rufius wondered if King Minos constructed the labyrinth as a form of prison. He imagined the poor, frightened villagers wandering around the darkened corridors listening for the sound of the beast, dying of hunger or thirst when they lost all sense of direction.

At every junction, Rufius carved a series of notches into the wall with his blade. Something he could find in the dark, just like Theseus and his ball of twine.

Moving deeper, Rufius noticed the temperature was beginning to drop. He also realised that the floor was on a steady decline. The footsteps of Mackenzie's men were becoming harder to read as the sand thinned, but he continued nonetheless. If they were following Bouchard, then perhaps he had some way to navigate the maze. They clearly knew where he was going, having hardly double-backed on themselves more than once or twice.

'You're following a map aren't you?' he said to himself, standing at a junction between two passageways. 'But which way did you go?'

'Sorry?' said Sim.

'Just trying to work out which way to go.'

There was a long pause before Sim responded. 'There'll be some kind of clue, the guards would have been illiterate so they would need a visual sign.'

Rufius studied the paintings on the walls.

There was nothing obvious at first, but as he looked closely, he noticed the direction that the warriors were facing when they fought the beast. On one wall they looked towards a particular entrance, and on the other they faced away. It was such a simple motif that could easily be missed, but once you knew it, the maze was solved.

At the centre of the maze, Rufius found a small circular chamber. Its walls were covered in depictions of bulls, much like a shrine to Taurus. In the middle of the floor was a hole. The stone plinth that used to cover it had been pushed aside and Rufius could see a set of spiral stairs winding down into darkness.

Stale, fetid air rose up from the depths as Rufius descended. The unmistakable miasma of a tomb recently opened, releasing the scent of things that had been sealed for centuries.

'Bouchard,' Rufius called into the darkness. 'I know you're down there.'

His voice echoed off the walls, but there was no reply.

The stairs descended for over a hundred feet into the rock. Rufius ran his hand along the inner wall, feeling the rough marks of the chisels on the stone, catching glimpses of the hundreds of slaves who had been used to carve out the route. There were no frescoes here, whatever this led to was not part of the myth of the minotaur.

But the king had hidden something down here, in the centre of his maze, a secret protected by a legend. Rufius was beginning to have new found respect for the old king.

Reaching the bottom of the shaft, Rufius entered a vast tomb, or at least a storehouse of the dead. Mummified remains were laid to rest on shelves carved into the rock.

Tunnels spread out from the stairs like the spokes of a wheel, each filled with bodies. Obviously used by generations of Minoans to preserve their ancestors, some were carefully stored in wooden sarcophagi while others were just tightly bound parcels, painted with ancient hieroglyphs.

The tracks of the Dreadnoughts were easy to follow here, and Rufius could clearly see the difference between their boots and that of the leather soles of the man they were following.

Walking through the corridors of the dead, Rufius noted the same pattern of glyphs on the bodies. It was nothing more than a series of strokes, which he thought might have been a date at first, until he realised it must be something else, unless everyone had died on the same day.

Taking out his almanac, he sketched the glyph and tagged it for Sim's attention.

Champollion was lying unconscious on the floor. Stripped of clothes, his body was half-wrapped in what Rufius mistakenly thought was linen. Kneeling down beside him, he realised that it was more like fine silk threads, as if he were being cocooned.

Rufius shook him roughly, trying to rouse him, but the translator hardly stirred. His pupils were dilated, hardly responding to the light of the tachyon. He'd been drugged. Rufius found a puncture wound on his neck, a ring of tiny marks outlined the wound like a bite.

Rufius tried to saw through the binding with the edge of his sword, but it was slow going; the fibres were sticky and tough, clinging to the blade like candy floss.

Once Champollion was free, Rufius dragged his body to

the stairwell and then went back to look for the two Dread-noughts.

Searching the rest of the cave, he found them already fully cocooned. The webbing that enshrouded them had hardened into a casing that his sword was unable to penetrate.

Yet they were still breathing, and so he carried each of them back to Champollion.

Something stirred deep within one of the tunnels. The skittering of claws on stone made Rufius pause and assess his options. There was no way to protect the men and himself.

'I'm on my way up,' he said into his tachyon.

He threw Champollion over his shoulder and grabbed the Dreadnoughts by the feet.

61

NEPHILIM

[Tycho Station, Maelstrom]

Time passed slowly over the next few weeks on Tycho station. Caitlin's father helped her create a study in one of the observatories, allowing her to work under a canopy of stars every night. The wireless kept her company, and she quickly mastered the tuning, finding her favourite years amongst the scattered frequencies. Her days fell into a pattern: while her mother spent most of the day repairing the *Nautilus*, her father tried to organise the books into some kind of order.

'Pointless really,' he said, holding a stack of thick volumes. 'In six months time they will revert back to their original positions.'

Caitlin was becoming obsessed with deciphering Linear A. It was not going well, everything she tried failed.

Frustrated with the printed versions, Caitlin turned to the physical tablet itself. Stored in the cargo hold of the *Nautilus*, it took all three of them to bring it back to the station.

. . .

The surface was smooth, each glyph had been etched into the clay while it was still wet.

Closing her eyes, she explored the indentations with her fingertips.

Weaving with stone was virtually impossible. In the Order's history, there had only been a few who could traverse the timeline of rock and although this was in essence a man-made object, it still retained the characteristics of its original elements. Its timeline was a fragmented, non-linear mess that could leave her trapped in some early geological epoch if she was not careful.

She pulled her mind out of the weave and opened her eyes.

One of the symbols caught her attention.

'Where did you put those tarot cards?' Caitlin asked her mother when she returned that evening.

Her mother looked confused. 'I thought you didn't believe in divination systems?' she said, taking off her heavy tool belt.

Caitlin started rooting around in the wooden cupboards. 'I don't, but there was a symbol on one of them that I wanted to check.'

'I think your father was playing patience with them yesterday. I'm not sure what he did with them.'

Caitlin found the game half-finished on a table in the 'chess room', so named because of the impressive chequerboard floor.

She scattered the deck, flicking through the picture cards. There were the usual illustrated cards of the major arcana, elegantly coloured woodblock prints of The Magician, The High Priestess, The Lovers, The Hermit and Death, which she couldn't help but turn face down. Then she reached the card she was looking for and held it up to the lamp.

There it was — in the corner of the card, the same symbol as she'd seen in Linear A.

At that moment, her father walked in. 'Hey, I wasn't finished!'

She ignored him. 'Do you know what this is?' She tapped her finger on the symbol.

'The Devil.'

'No, the glyph above it.'

He took the card and squinted at the details. 'Reminds me of something from the Kabbalah. Hold on, there's a book on that in Tycho's collection.'

Her father went over to the shelves that lined one side of the room. Running his finger along the gilded spines, he read aloud the names of the various mathematical and astrological treatises.

'Here we go,' he said, pulling one from the shelf in a cloud of dust. The bindings creaked stiffly as if they hadn't been opened in a century.

'That's the symbol for Astaroth, the Grand Duke of Hell,' he said after a few minutes of flicking back and forth through the yellowing pages.

Caitlin turned the book towards her and examined the text. It was written in Hebrew in a black Gothic script. 'Who are all these?' she asked, pointing at a long list of names.

He looked over her shoulder. 'Fallen Angels.'

She found another symbol from Linear A. 'How old is this?'

'This book was probably written in the Middle Ages

around the twelfth century, but some believe the Kabbalah was based on an ancient oral tradition that goes back to the time of Moses, around 1300 BC.'

Caitlin sat back in the chair and absent-mindedly played with the golden ring hanging on the chain around her neck.

'How is that useful?'

'I'm not sure. I'm trying to work out what possible reason the Minoans would have for using the same symbols on a clay tablet two thousand years before.'

62

CONSPIRATORS

[Paris, France. Date: 1800]

Josh awoke to find himself standing in a luxurious drawing room surrounded by the bodies of dead gentlemen. The gilded furniture and patterned satin cushions were decorated with their blood.

He rubbed his temples, trying to ease the throbbing in his skull and wishing he was in an era with basic pain medicine — paracetamol was something of a luxury item for a time traveller.

Once again there was a gap in his memory. The last thing he could recall was following the gentleman towards the Palais Royale and then nothing. The back of his head felt as if someone had coshed him from behind.

Instinctively, he reached for his tachyon, but it was gone, as was the uniform of the Consulate Guard. He was no longer dressed as a soldier, instead he wore a well-tailored jacket, waistcoat and silk breeches.

The clothes of the dead men told him that he was still in

the same era, but as far as he could see, the man he'd been following was not among the dead.

Josh looked down at his blood-stained hands, and realising that none of the blood was his, he went to the nearest of the bodies. Turning the heavy man over, Josh found he was still clutching a flintlock pistol. A musket shot had taken part of his face, disfiguring him beyond recognition.

Checking the other corpses, Josh discovered that they were all killed in a similar way, shot through the head.

Some of the men were obviously military, their uniforms adorned with medals and ribbons from Napoleonic campaigns. Two of them wore the white star of the Legion d'Honneur.

Josh's throat was dry and although the room had been completely ransacked, he managed to find an unbroken bottle of wine. Sitting down in the cleanest seat he could find, he took a long drink, letting the warm red liquid slide over the ache in his throat.

Studying the way the bodies were lying, it was obvious that the attack was unexpected. They had been running away, no one had time to draw a weapon, let alone defend themselves. Someone killed these men and from the amount of blood on him, Josh had been there when it happened.

Are you there? He asked the ghost. *Did you see it?*

The founder's silence disturbed Josh more as much as the carnage around him. They had been together for four long years and many lifetimes. He couldn't remember the last time he felt so alone.

. . .

There were voices from the corridor; the deep, hushed voices of men obviously debating whether it was wise to break down the door.

Not wanting to have to explain how he had survived the massacre, Josh went to the balcony. He could tell from the position of Notre Dame that he was nowhere near the Palais Royale. The way the silvered towers looked West into the moonlight put him on the wrong side of the Seine. They were also three floors up with no obvious way to climb down.

Somebody tried the door handle, but it was locked.

Josh realised he'd probably been left there to take the blame.

He went back into the room and knelt beside one of the victims. Taking hold of his pistol, he felt its time unwind around his fingers.

Watching the entire scene unfold in reverse, Josh saw the men rise to their feet, ribbons of blood flowing back into their heads as shards of bone fell into place in their skulls. He witnessed the musket ball leaving their heads, sealing up the hole it made and fly back towards the gun.

The man holding the pistol looked directly at Josh, smiling as he fired the same shot seven times in as many seconds.

Josh let the timeline reverse until he reached the beginning of the meeting.

'You're late,' said a wiry man with a thin moustache, standing by the fireplace.

His eyes were small and beady, sitting close on each side of a long, aquiline nose that reminded Josh of a weasel.

He pulled at the cuffs of his coat, which were fraying and a little too short for his arms, as if he was wearing another man's jacket.

Josh lowered his head submissively, waiting for the man to ask another question, hoping that it would give him some idea of why he was here.

Before the weasel could continue, the door opened and two more gentlemen entered.

'Saint-Régent,' greeted the taller of the two men, bowing to the host.

'Monsieur Coster.'

'Who is he?' said the other, spotting Josh, his hand instinctively going to his sword.

Saint-Régent unfolded a letter and handed it to Coster. 'A messenger from General Cadoudal.'

The shorter man eyed Josh suspiciously, while his friend read the letter.

'Where's Limoëlan?' asked Saint-Régent.

The man shrugged. 'Helping Carbon with the Machine Infernale.'

'Cadoudal says the attack is to be on the third nivôse!' said Coster, using the French Republican calendar.

'Ten days? That hardly gives us much time to prepare!' the other man complained.

There was a large, hand-drawn map laid out on the table, showing the Tuileries Palace and the surrounding streets.

'He says there is to be a performance of *La Création* at the Opera. Josephine will insist that the First Consul attend. Napoleon will leave the Tuileries at seven with an escort of cavalry from the Consular Guard and his ministers,' explained Saint-Régent, turning the map towards them.

'Where are we to leave the bomb?' asked Coster, leaning on the table.

Saint-Régent tapped on the map. 'North, on the rue Saint-Nicaise. Limoëlan will be stationed at the Place du Carrousel where he can signal to me to light the fuse.'

'Will it be ready?' asked Coster.

'Carbon won't let us down,' replied another man from the doorway. It was the gentleman that Josh had been following from the warehouse.

Coster looked cautiously out of the window. 'Limoëlan. Were you followed?'

The man scoffed. 'Fouché's men couldn't find their arses with their elbows.'

Saint-Régent handed out small glasses of brandy and they looked at each other with grim determination. 'So finally we shall be rid of this tyrant! Vive le Roi!'

The others echoed his sentiments.

Saint-Régent wrote a quick note on the back of the letter and handed it back to Josh. 'Tell the General we will not fail him.'

Coster tore up the map and threw it onto the fire.

'And how is his Majesty?' asked Limoëlan.

Saint-Régent smiled and poured them all another glass. 'He is well. He awaits word of our victory at the Jelgava Palace.'

There was a knock at the door and another man entered. He carried himself like a military man, his shoulders were broad, and beneath the brim of his hat Josh could see scarring down one side of his face.

It was the gunman.

'Saint-Hilaire, what are you doing here?'

The man seemed not to hear the question, his hand slid inside his coat and pulled out a flintlock.

'It's not Saint-Hilaire,' growled the shorter man, reaching for his own gun.

Before he could take aim, the stranger shot him through the head. Saint-Régent screamed and rushed towards a door at the back of the room.

Without seeming to reload, the gunman shot him in the back of the head.

Coster had time to raise his own weapon, in the few seconds that followed the gunman fired two more rounds, the first bullet struck Coster in the shoulder, the second took off the side of his face.

Josh froze, he stood against the wall watching the massacre as if it were a movie.

The man turned his gun on him, his dark eyes narrowing, hesitating as if unsure of why he was there.

Opening the chronology of the letter from the General, Josh moved inside its timeline.

63

COLONEL

[Knossos Palace, Crete. Date: 1799]

Reaching the top of the stairs, Rufius collapsed onto the floor.

Sim and the rest of the Dreadnoughts were waiting for him.

'Are you hurt?' asked Sim, offering him a wineskin.

'Seal it up,' Rufius said to the commander, who was inspecting the bodies of his men.

Two of the Dreadnoughts began shifting the stone plinth into place over the hole.

'I'm getting too old for this shit,' said Rufius, taking the skin from Sim and drinking deeply.

'What happened?'

'He's been bitten by something.' Rufius pointed at Champollion. 'There's a mark on his neck. When I found him he was wrapped up like a fly in a cobweb. Got the others too.' He pointed to the men who Mackenzie was trying to extract from their cocoons. 'The catacombs are like some kind of giant spider's web.'

'Not a Minotaur then?'

Mackenzie was trying to cut through the binding with his knife. 'No spider web that I've ever seen. It's like steel.'

Champollion stirred, his eyes snapping openly suddenly. 'Where is he?'

Sim turned to the Frenchman. 'Who?'

'Bouchard,' said Champollion, one hand touching his throat. 'He bit me.'

'I don't think it was him,' said Rufius, struggling to his feet.

'You have to find him!' the Frenchman insisted. 'He's infected.'

'Infected with what?'

Champollion's eyelids fluttered and his breathing shallowed. Rufius took his pulse and sighed. 'He's not going to make it.'

Commander Mackenzie walked over to join them, a dark shadow seemed to pass over his face. 'I've called the Xenos.' Holding his hand up to stop Rufius before he could protest. 'Two of my men are dead and it looks like this man is not long for this world. Whatever this is, I've requested a specialist team down here immediately.'

As he spoke, a team of six xenobiologysts appeared out of thin air, wearing the equivalent of a temporal hazmat suit and carrying large boxes of equipment.

They surrounded the two cocooned officers and began to work on the bindings with hand-cranked cutting equipment.

'You have to find Bouchard!' gasped Champollion.

'What's he babbling on about?' snapped Mackenzie.

Sim tried to get Champollion to drink something.

'There's someone else down there. A French soldier by the name of Bouchard.'

Mackenzie swore under his breath. 'We can't go back in, not until the Xenos have a better idea of what it is.'

One of the scientists came over and began to examine Champollion. The others stepped away to let the medic work.

'We need to find him,' Sim whispered to Rufius. 'If he's got out of the catacombs it could be very serious.'

'Where's his tracker now?'

Sim consulted his almanac, his face a mask of concentration. 'It's here,' he said pointing at Champollion. 'Right there.'

Rufius pushed one of the Xenos aside and searched the man's body.

The metal stud had been pushed into his arm.

'What do you think you're doing?' a scientist asked, standing over him.

'Doctor Kaori Shika?' said Rufius, staring into the glass visor of her leather helmet. 'Is that you?'

'Westinghouse! I should have known,' the doctor said, putting her gloved hands on her hips. 'What the hell are you doing here?'

Sim had never seen Rufius look so humble, the big man bowed his head before the tiny scientist. 'I was following this man.'

'Into a tomb that had been designated a site of special interest by the Antiquarians.'

'I had backup.'

64

HOUSE OF BOURBON

[Jelgava Palace, Courland, Latvia. Date: 1799]

'The audacity of the man! The Bourbons have ruled France since 1589!' screamed the king, reading the latest letter from Napoleon while servants struggled to dress him.

Josh stood amongst the members of Louis exiled court, trying to work out exactly what series of events could have brought him to the palace.

He seemed to be travelling backwards, jumping through random parts of someone else's life. Someone who was trying to kill Napoleon.

He was tired, and the ache in his head was getting worse. The last thing he could remember clearly was opening the timeline of the letter for General Cadoudal and the gunman with the scar. *Six shots in three seconds,* he thought, *with a flintlock — he had to be one of us.*

'The Tsar will protect you,' one man assured the king.

Josh recognised him as the Count of Artois, although he had another name, an older one.

'At least until Cadoudal can unseat the Corsican imposter.'

'There is talk of making him an emperor,' added the Count of Avaray, 'and that France will never return to the *Ancien Regime*.'

'We've reigned for over a thousand years, brother. This isn't the first threat we've faced and it won't be the last,' said Artois.

There was a sharp pain and Josh felt something moving inside his head, another mind swimming below his consciousness, trying to break through the surface.

Founder?

'What do the others say?' asked Louis.

'Austria is struggling to hold back his armies in Italy. The Russians have driven him back over the Alps, but in truth we need the British.'

Louis dismissed his valets.

'Is George no better?' he asked, once the last of the servants had left.

Avaray shook his head. 'The host is too strong-willed. His mind refuses to meld and it's broken him. The government believe he's gone mad.'

'I knew it! We should have replaced him after he lost the American Colonies.'

'The regent's powers have been severely limited by the Prime Minister, William Pitt. We have an agent in the House of Commons, but it's clear that the power no longer sits with the king.'

'This host is also proving to be troublesome,' said Josh. The words coming out of his mouth were in an alien language.

Louis turned towards him. 'Azazel, is that you?' he

replied in the same tongue. 'We thought you were with Rudolf II.'

'I was until he died, then I used his physician until I met this one. He has brought me back through time.'

'Backward, how is that possible?' said Count Avaray, unable to hide his disbelief.

'He has a unique ability, but I cannot control him completely. Even now I struggle to master him, he's like a wild horse.'

Louis moved closer, studying Josh's face. 'We have always wondered if there would be others. Can't you access his memories and learn the secret of his talents for yourself?'

Josh shook his head. It was as though he were sitting in a room inside his mind, watching someone else driving his body.

'There is something else here. Another presence that is protecting him. I cannot reach the central cortex, but I have made some progress on the one that guards it.'

The king's fat fingers stroked Josh's cheek, his eyes growing distant. 'How far back in time can he travel?'

'I've no idea.'

'Could we use him to find the Hegemon?'

'That's over five thousand years.'

'Don't remind us,' said Artois.

'If I can break through his defences, perhaps. It may take some time; this is a most unusual being.'

Avaray dismissed the comment with a wave of his hand. 'We have waited this long.'

'Until then we must focus on Bonaparte's assassination,' insisted Artois.

'Someone killed Cadoudal's lieutenants in Paris,' said Josh.

The king looked confused. 'When was this?'

'December 1800. They were massacred by a gunman. Probably one of Fouché's men. All of the conspirators were killed.'

'There will be others who can take their place. You should go back and ensure that the work is finished. Find new royalists, I'm sure there are more than a few disgruntled aristocrats willing to help you restore the House of Bourbon.'

'Leave it to me.'

65

XENOS

Doctor Shika put them all into quarantine.

Sim never imagined his first visit to the Xenobiology lab would be as a patient. It was one of the most secret departments in the Order, and he'd grown up listening to his mother's stories about their unusual menagerie of monsters.

They separated the group the moment they arrived, holding each of them in an isolation chamber while scientists in hazmat suits proceeded to take copious amounts of blood samples.

'We've escalated our biohazard security protocols,' explained Doctor Shika through the intercom on her suit helmet. 'After the incident with your sister.'

Sim winced as the medic withdrew the needle. 'Lyra? Is she all right?'

'She is now. We're still trying to ascertain what the Aeon parasite is capable of.'

'Aeon parasite?'

The technician inserted the blood sample into a small handheld device and handed it to Kaori. Sim marvelled at the technology, it was so advanced as to be almost magical to someone who spent most of his time in the steam age. He could see the display in the reflection on her visor as she swiped through a series of diagnostic charts and graphs.

'Results are normal. You're clear,' she said, handing it back and pulling off her helmet. 'Come with me.'

Sim followed Kaori into a boardroom. Its walls were made of semi-transparent screens that were displaying data on all the active missions. Rufius, the Grand Seer and Professor Eddington were sitting on opposite sides of the long black table.

Floating in the space above the table was a holographic display of a worm-like creature. The professor fidgeted uncomfortably, obviously disturbed by the presence of so much technology. Kelly on the other hand was like a child with a new toy, fascinated by the image, as he rotated the model around with a swipe of his hand.

'Gentleman,' said Kaori as she entered. 'I believe we may have a serious problem.'

Sim took the empty seat beside the professor.

With a single gesture, Doctor Shika changed the image to that of a middle-aged man.

'This is Doctor Henry Knox. The Protectorate apprehended him in 1888 after he was found experimenting on prostitutes in London's East End. During a routine MRI scan we found that his brain stem had been compromised by a neurological parasite.' The ghostly image changed to show a three-dimensional scan of the worm wrapped around the spinal cord at the base of his skull.

'Using DNA methylation biomarkers, my team estimated the creature's biological age at approximately five thousand years. Hence the reason we named it Aeon.'

The image changed to Champollion.

'It seems to be able to survive between hosts, for a limited time at least. This man was also infected, although in his case the parasite was much younger, leading me to believe that you were close to the source when you discovered him.'

'There were others,' said Rufius, staring at the rotating image. 'The catacombs were filled with bodies.'

Kaori nodded. 'We think Knossos may be some kind of hive. The infected were trapped down there and went into a form of hibernation. Similar to that of Lepidoptera.'

'You think it's a butterfly?' asked Eddington.

The doctor shook her head. 'We have no idea what it is, or what it could become. The tests that we've run on the webbing from the cocoons exhibit all the chemical traits of a chrysalis.'

'It was going to transform?'

'Metamorphosis is a distinct possibility. Our main concern now should be tracking down anyone who may have been infected.'

'We know of one that may have escaped,' said Rufius. 'And there's a good chance he was one of us.'

'A member of the Order?' asked Eddington.

Rufius shook his head. 'A treasure hunter, one of Napoleon's *Savants Temporal*.'

Professor Eddington glared at Sim. 'We were not aware.'

'We'd only just discovered this —,' Sim tried to explain, but Rufius interrupted.

'Don't blame the boy. I was in charge of the mission. Bouchard was a rogue. We think he must have discovered a latent talent after unearthing the Rosetta Stone.'

Eddington ground his teeth. 'And you let him run rampant through history! Napoleon has already made significant deviations from the prime radiant. We are in serious danger of losing European unity in the twentieth century.'

'And we know how that turns out,' scoffed Rufius.

'History is a version of events that people have decided to agree upon.' Kelly quoted in a bad French accent, much to everyone's annoyance.

'This is yet another example of your reckless behaviour and general disregard for Copernican procedures.'

Sim saw the colour rising in Rufius's cheeks. 'I was about to shut him down when this happened.'

'More importantly,' interrupted Kaori. 'Is the fact that they could have infected any one of us. We need to begin testing for parasitical infestations amongst the Order immediately.'

'Why take a linguist to Knossos?' pondered Kelly, rocking back and forth in his chair.

'Because of the linear texts,' said Rufius. 'The ones that the Antiquarians tried to confiscate. They hold the answer to all of this.'

'What kind of test?' asked Eddington, ignoring their conversation and taking out a fountain pen from the spine of his ornately covered almanac.

'A deadly one,' suggested Kelly, with a mischievous twinkle in his eye.

Eddington made a note on the first page in crimson ink, the one reserved for the highest priority orders. Every Copernican in the guild would be reading the text the moment it was written. He paused, halfway through a sentence. 'Any latent signatures that we can use for pattern tracing?'

Kaori shrugged. 'They have a lifespan of five thousand years, which would disrupt the timelines of their host, so you could potentially use an auspice.'

Eddington sneered. 'I'm not about to resort to sideshow gimmickry.'

'We can test bloods for signs of raised cortisol, but to be honest the best defence we have right now are probably the seers.'

'Indeed we are,' said the Grand Seer, standing up and pointing at the image of Champollion. 'Where is this man now?'

Kaori looked a little surprised, as did most of the others. 'We have him in a stasis chamber in the secure unit.'

'I wish to read him.'

She scowled at the old seer, her eyes narrowing. 'You know what happened when Lyra tried to do that.'

Kelly nodded, took the quill from his cap and, mimicking Eddington, wrote something on the palm of his hand, 'I seem to remember being the one who saved her.'

There was a knock at the door.

A dark-haired man walked in. Kaori introduced him to the rest of the group as Benoir Cousineau, a student of Georges Cuvier.

'Lyra is awake,' he said. 'She wishes to speak to all of you.'

66

X-541

[Antiquarian HQ]

Konstantine placed the multi-bladed dagger into its cabinet and closed the door.

'You have done well X-541,' he said, turning back to face his guest.

Rothstein looked at the other exhibits lining the walls of the Antiquarian's most secret collection. 'Is that all of the relics?'

'Not quite, there is still the matter of the Ring of Solomon.'

The man checked a digital readout that shone through the skin on the palm of his hand. 'It is not within this continuum.'

The Grandmaster locked the glass case and slipped the key into his pocket. 'No, the mother carries it around her neck on a chain. The Paradox gave it to her before she left with his child.'

'Praise be to the timeless one.'

'Indeed,' said Konstantine. 'Where is the father now?'

Rothstein's eyes seemed to glaze over for a moment. 'Records show that he has been infected and is partially under the influence of the symbiote known as "Azazel". The engrams of another mind are protecting him from total synaptic integration, but not for much longer.'

'Another mind?'

Rothstein nodded. 'He carries the memories of another.'

'Then it is as we suspected,' said Konstantine, his lips twisting into a sardonic smile. 'The mother will be returning shortly. You must be ready to intercept the ring.'

'And the fugitive?'

'We shall know when we have Azazel. His knowledge will lead us to the future.'

'And heal the past,' the man recited mechanically.

'You'll need to assume a new persona. My spies tell me that the Xenobiologysts are aware of Rothstein's unusual lifespan.'

X-541's features began to distort. His skin became soft, it shifted and twisted like melting wax, the bone structure beneath it reforming to create a new face.

Konstantine nodded. 'An interesting choice,' he said. I wonder if the Paradox will remember.'

67

READING BOUCHARD

[Cryo Stasis, Xenobiology Secure Unit. Date: Present day]

The Grand Seer studied Champollion's rigid body floating inside the stasis field. Frozen in a single moment of time, he looked strangely peaceful, as if asleep.

'Fear no more the heat o' th' sun nor the furious winters' rages; Thou thy worldly task hast done,' he whispered to himself, removing one of his leather gloves and stroking the cold air with his fingers.

Taking a deep breath, Kelly gripped one of Champollion's hands and closed his eyes.

Chapter House. Date: 1880.

Lyra was propped up in bed on a mountain of soft white pillows. Their colour matched her skin, except for the dark shadows that lingered under her eyes. Her mother stood beside her, a smouldering fire in her cheeks warned them all that she wasn't happy about their visit.

'It's good to see you brother,' said Lyra with a weak smile. 'Come, give me your hand.' She held out an upturned palm.

Sim took it and watched his sister's eyes widen as she read his recent past.

'My, my, haven't you been busy.'

'No busier than you by all accounts,' replied Sim. He'd seen her like this before and each time it pained him.

She sighed and let go of his hand. 'I've something to tell you. All of you.'

Cryo Stasis

The history of the man had vanished.

Champollion's timeline appeared to be entirely empty.

Undeterred, Kelly dived deeper, followed the shadow of something that could once have been his life. It was nothing more than a faint echo, like an imprint of a fallen leaf on snow.

Surveying the void, his subconscious gradually sensed the traces of another. The barest threads of a life stretched so thinly over time as to be like strands of spider silk caught on an autumn wind.

It possessed a similar essence to the wraith that infected Lyra. A deathly, hollow feeling of a yawning grave, created by something so ancient that it couldn't be described as either dead or alive, like a comet that travelled too far from the sun.

'You will never age for me, nor fade, nor die,' he said to himself as he carefully plucked at the lines of its past.

Chapter House

'A few weeks ago I had a dream,' Lyra began, picking at the lacy edge of her sheet. 'It was more of a vision really, that Caitlin killed Josh.'

The others listened intently, they were all aware of how serious Lyra's dreams could be. Her prescience was one of the most reliable within the Seers Guild, and had been since she was three years old.

'She was convinced that he wasn't himself. That something had possessed him. She stabbed him with a strange knife. It looked something like this.'

Lyra held up the sketch of the multi-bladed dagger.

'We tried to find out what it was,' she said, looking at Benoir.

'It led us to the Rothsteins,' added Benoir.

'The bankers?' said Rufius, taking the picture. 'They supplied the gold that Napoleon stole from Wellington.'

'They may have been infected by the parasite,' said Kaori.

Benoir came to stand beside Lyra. 'Five generations, same man.'

'African?' asked Rufius, handing the sketch to Benoir.

'It's a talisman,' said Lyra. 'One that the Rothsteins bought on the black market.'

At the other end of the room, the Grand Seer stepped out of a long mirror, its surface rippling like water as he passed through it.

'Well?' asked Rufius impatiently, while Kelly brushed away invisible cobwebs.

His eyes were dark. *Like coal*, Rufius noted, a sure sign that he had been travelling through dangerous times.

'That one was different to that which infected you,' he

said, sitting on the end of Lyra's bed. 'Yours was quite possibly the oldest entity I've ever encountered.' Kelly turned to Lyra. 'What would you say? Ten thousand?'

Lyra nodded.

'By comparison, Champollion's was a mere pup, less than a millennium perhaps.'

'How can they survive so long?' asked Benior.

Kelly shrugged. 'Who knows? Their timeline is like a fine gossamer thread, stretched out through the Aeons. They're a species that witnessed the birth of our civilisation. In earlier times they might have been worshipped as gods.'

'But they are dying,' added Lyra.

'As all things do. They are the last of their race,' Kelly added solemnly. 'Unless they can find their queen.'

Kaori's eyes widened. 'Queen?'

'These are all males. Drones with no way to reproduce. They seek a mate.'

'Like bees?' said Lyra.

'Or ants,' noted Benoir.

Kaori shook her head. 'Bees are colony insects, eusocial, with three castes: queens, drones and workers. The workers are sterile.'

Kelly considered this for a moment. 'The thing inside Champollion was more like a worker.'

'And so where is their queen?' asked Rufius.

Kelly turned towards him. 'Somewhere they cannot reach without us.'

'In the past?'

The Grand Seer nodded. 'Bouchard has the ability to move back through time. Now we must find him before he finds his lost love.'

'First we need to inform the High Council,' said Kaori.

68

LETTER

Hello little one,

So, we've been on Tycho Station for nearly two months now and you're starting to move around. Which was a relief as for the first few weeks I thought I'd imagined you, except for the terrible nausea and the craving for Stilton and tinned fish — I'd felt nothing until now.

Your fluttering wakes me in the middle of the night like moth wings on a window. It's as if you've invented your own form of Morse code, tapping away inside me, trying to tell me something. In normal circumstances I would have an ultrasound image of you by now, instead I have a horoscope drawn up by your crazy grandmother. Which, by the way, I have no doubt she will bring out at every birthday until you're sixteen.

And the dreams you're giving me get stranger by the day. I guess it must be the hormones or the really dodgy cheese your grandfather rescued from the USS Helena. Whichever it is, they're quite the most unusual visions — Lyra told me once how she used to dream in her mother's womb. I'm beginning to seri-

ously wonder if you might be a seer, but that would be unlikely, it doesn't run in our family and I wouldn't wish that on you.

I've found myself starting to stroke the bump now, wondering what you look like. Mum says you're not much bigger than a prawn, which made me laugh. I said you're a baby dragon, not some random aquatic crustacean.

So anyway, today I made progress with the translation of Linear A, but in many ways I wish I hadn't. There's something wrong with it. It seems to be littered with the names of fallen angels. Not that I believe in all that stuff and, as far as I know, neither did the Minoans, they worshipped bulls. Don't ask me why. Each to their own.

Your grandfather intercepted a message on the wireless today. We learned that your other grandmother has passed away and your father has gone missing.

It made me sad that she'll never meet you, she was a good woman and didn't deserve that life. But sometimes there's nothing you can do, fate has a way of reclaiming its own, no matter how hard you try and avoid it.

I should have been there to support him, this isn't the first time he's disappeared. I know he's trying to find a way to deal with the grief, and part of me wants to go back right now.

I've sent a message to Uncle Rufius. If anyone can find your father, that man can. I can't wait for you to meet him. Rufius is like this force of nature, a hurricane in the shape of a man. Nothing seems to faze him. I'm going to ask him to be your godfather, even though I don't believe in the whole Christian ritual, I still like the idea that he would be there to watch over you and keep you safe, like he has for me.

69

THE RELUCTANT ENGINEER

[Nautilus]

Caitlin's mother swore like a sailor as the controls bucked in her hands.

'The rudder's not responding, we're going to have to slow down,' she said, her knuckles whitening as she strained to pull a lever towards her. The whine of the engines gradually changed pitch and the entire ship seemed to sigh with relief.

'Are you sure you want to do this?' her mother asked, tapping one of the many flashing lights on her control console.

'They're all in danger,' replied Caitlin, waving the half-finished translation of Linear A at her. 'The Minoans sealed themselves in that tomb on purpose, it was a terrible sacrifice.'

It took Caitlin and her father almost two weeks to decode enough to realise that the text was very different from

Linear B. It was an older, cruder language that spoke of demons and monsters.

Tycho Station had an eclectic library. The astronomer was an avid collector of rare treatises on occult subjects. One of which was the Book of Enoch, an ancient Hebrew apocalyptic text supposedly written by the great-grandfather of Noah.

The most interesting section was: 'The Book of Watchers'. The text described a species that stood apart from humans, super beings who came down to earth and joined with women, producing a race of giants that Enoch called the "Nephilim".

It was clear that the scripture was meant as a warning to those who turned away from God. But the names of those fallen angels matched those of the much earlier Minoan text, sending a cold shiver down Caitlin's spine. Linear A pre-dated the Book and its text told of how the Nephilim turned on mankind, drinking their blood and possessing their flesh. And how their king sacrificed his people, sealing them all beneath the maze.

She couldn't be sure what the Nephilim were exactly, but the warning was clear, no one should enter the tomb.

Leaving Tycho Station was not an easy decision to take. Caitlin felt safe in her little nest surrounded by some of the rarest books in history and her little bump. The baby was growing quickly, leading her mother to conclude that it must be a boy — Caitlin didn't care as long as it was healthy.

Going back into the continuum came with its own risks. Temporal dilation meant that leaving the Maelstrom would accelerate her pregnancy, she would be nearly full-term when they rejoined linear time. She was sacrificing months of maternity to stop them opening the tomb under Knossos.

'We're a couple of hours away,' said her mother, breaking her reverie. 'Go and tell your father to prepare the breaching field.'

Her father was a reluctant engineer. Her mother would always complain that he simply didn't have the knack, and in that way they were the same; Caitlin had always preferred books. She definitely hadn't inherited her mother's love of the mechanical.

Making her way down through the ship, Caitlin could hear her father singing away to the wireless as he worked. His deep, bass voice reverberating through the metal passageways.

'Farewell and adieu to you, Spanish ladies
Farewell and adieu to you, ladies of Spain...'

Caitlin stopped outside the engineering section, knowing the moment she walked in he would stop.

'For we have received orders,
For to sail to old England,
but we hope in a short time to see you again.'

It reminded her of the times they spent on their adventures when she was a child, teaching her to sail on the large clear lakes of Mesolithic Switzerland.

She wondered what it would be like to take her own child there, to spend weeks wandering through the pre-alpine ranges of Vercors.

'I know you're there KitKat. Come in and help me get this bloody breaching field aligned.'

70

HIGH COUNCIL

[Star Chamber]

K elly invoked an emergency session of the High Council that evening.

The Star Chamber was filled to capacity. Members of the Order returned from every corner of time to attend, as was their right. Though the High Council had the ultimate authority, the membership was given the right to sit in session.

In front of a hushed auditorium, Rufius and Doctor Shika presented the evidence. The lack of higher technology in the Chamber's time period meant that Kaori had to resort to a magic lantern show of glass slides.

Rufius spent most of his time trying to keep the Grand Seer from turning it into a farce. Benoir and Lyra watched stoically from the front row of the benches.

'You believe that these Aeons present a real danger to the Order?' asked Grandmaster Derado. As Head of the Draconian Guild, it would be his men who would be dispatched to find them.

'To the continuum. This is a colonising species,' Doctor Shika said, walking over to Professor Eddington. 'The Copernicans calculate that, should they find their queen, the entire human race could be lost within a century.'

'And yet you believe there are only three?' asked Konstantine dismissively.

Eddington got to his feet. 'Three that we have provisionally identified. Three who have survived for thousands of years, hiding among the rich and powerful. Once they're able to reproduce, their numbers would multiply exponentially like a virus — we would be facing the worst epidemic the earth has ever encountered.'

'And you're proposing that the Seers Guild commence testing the entire Order?' asked Konstantine, reading the report.

'Beginning with the High Council,' said Kelly with a wry smile.

A ripple of whispers rolled around the auditorium.

'This is a violation,' protested Konstantine. 'I cannot condone the invasion of privacy.'

Many of the crowd nodded in agreement.

'It's a simple procedure, lasting less than five minutes. We believe that testing is the only way to contain the threat. These creatures must be prevented from accessing the past.'

Konstantine laughed. 'But hasn't that already happened?'

'We believe so. One of Napoleon's officers, a Captain Bouchard,' replied Professor Eddington.

'And do we know where this Bouchard is now?' asked the Scriptorian Grandmaster.

Eddington shook his head. 'We do not.'

'He was last seen at Knossos. An area that you, Grandmaster,' said Rufius, looking at Konstantine. 'have declared a site of special interest.'

All eyes turned towards the Antiquarian.

He simply shrugged off the underlying accusation. 'The Minoan tablets have been classified as dangerous artefacts, the palace at Knossos is part of an ongoing investigation regarding out-of-place artefacts.'

'Talismans?' said Rufius.

There was a sharp intake of breath around the chamber.

Konstantine scoffed. 'We all know there are no such things as talismans. Only a child would believe that an object can have magical powers.'

'One that Hitler seemed very interested in.'

'I cannot answer for his motives. But I wasn't referring to Bouchard. I believe that the fugitive Joshua Jones has also been infected. Is that not correct Miss De Freis?'

The crowd fell silent.

The Chief Inquisitor stood and turned to Lyra. 'The council calls Lyra De Freis to the stand.'

Lyra reluctantly got to her feet.

The Raven led the questioning. 'Miss De Freis, can you tell us why you believe Master Jones has been possessed by this Aeon creature?'

She looked nervously around the vast chamber, her hands gripping the wooden rail to stop them from shaking.

'Miss De Freis?' insisted Mallaron.

'I dreamed that he died,' she said weakly.

'And how exactly did he die?'

'He was stabbed, in the back.'

The hushed silence of the audience was intense, each of them hanging off her every word.

'And who did this?'

Lyra bit her bottom lip, looking to Benoir for support. 'Caitlin Makepeace.'

'Master Westinghouse are you seriously suggesting we act on the testimony of this child?'

'She is no child,' Kelly's voice boomed through the chamber. 'She is one of my most talented seers I've had the honour to know, and her visions can be trusted implicitly.'

'It wasn't her fault, she was trying to save him,' pleaded Lyra. 'I think the weapon was supposed to cure him.'

'There is a cure?' asked Grandmaster Konstantine. 'Doctor Crooke, were you aware of this?'

'No sire,' replied the doctor.

'Because it hasn't happened yet!' snapped Lyra, turning to Benoir. 'We think the dagger was a talisman.'

Again there was a collective intake of breath at the mention of the word.

'There is no such thing!' screamed Konstantine, jumping to his feet.

Benoir went to protest, but the entire chamber erupted and his complaints were drowned out by the noise of the crowd.

It took the clerk nearly ten minutes to restore order.

Mallaron cleared his throat before he spoke.

'I think your vision may have been flawed Miss De Freis, as the Antiquarian Guild clearly refute the existence of such magical objects.' He turned to Doctor Shika and Rufius. 'For now, I propose that the Council adjourn to consider your proposal for testing. All in favour?'

The other members of the council raised their hands in agreement. Grandmaster Derado abstained.

'Motion passed by majority,' noted the clerk.

.　.　.

'They aren't taking us seriously,' said Kaori as they left the chamber.

'Konstantine is up to something,' replied Rufius. 'The man is more slippery than an eel.'

'We have to find Josh,' said Lyra.

'Yes, I think we do,' agreed Rufius.

71

COPERNICANS

[Copernican Hall]

Lyra had forgotten how impressive the Copernican headquarters could be for a first-time visitor.

Benoir stood open-mouthed in the central atrium, awestruck by the size of the complex, clockwork machine that whirred around them. Actuaries and statisticians swarmed past like shoals of abacus-wielding priests, their expressions a mixture of concentration and determination as if they were late for an important meeting with God.

Sim appeared from amongst the crowd and took his sister in his arms, giving her a long and tender hug.

'Mum said you were back on your feet,' he said, stepping back to get a good look at her.

Lyra tapped her temple and laughed. 'Takes more than a five-thousand-year-old parasite to take me down.'

'I heard the High Council weren't completely convinced.'

'Probably shouldn't have used the T-word.' Her smile twisted into a sneer.

Her brother nodded. 'Yeah, tends to send Antiquarians off the deep end. Better sticking to the statistics.'

'They put too much faith in numbers.'

Sim raised a finger. 'Careful that's my job you're criticising.'

'Have you started the sweep?' asked Benoir, trying to change the subject.

'We have. Which I assume is why you're here?'

Lyra's expression brightened and she took Benoir's hand. 'I promised him the grand tour.'

'Then let us begin,' Sim said, bowing gracefully and beckoned them to follow him.

Over the next hour, Benoir learned how the Hall of Copernicus was one enormous difference engine: a calculating machine capable of millions of simultaneous computations which were overseen by an army of engineers and analysts, commonly known as 'Clackers'. Their job was to ensure the smooth running of the cathedral sized computer, which had been intentionally located in an age before electromagnetic fields to ensure that the delicate quantum states of temporal calculus were not affected.

'Never mention anything about electricity in front of Eddington,' warned Sim as they climbed the brass staircase to the upper floor. 'He gets quite irate about such things.'

The higher floors of the building were home to the Division of Statistical Intervention, managed by the most senior members of the guild. Sim explained how this department was responsible for the modelling of potential adjustments, or 'refinements' as they preferred them to be called. The division was notoriously slow, Sim added in a low whisper as old, white-whiskered men pored over logarithmic tables, checking calculations on slide rules.

'Master Galarant has been working on the outcome of the Treaty of Versailles for most of his adult life,' said Sim, raising his voice as if the man was deaf.

Galarant looked up from his desk through thick-lensed glasses and smiled benevolently at Sim, then seemed to forget where he was in his work.

'The changes they propose have to be peer-reviewed by three separate actuaries before they are presented to Professor Eddington, and only then are they considered worthy of consideration.'

'Do they ever get it wrong?' asked Benoir.

Lyra laughed.

'What?'

'I've never heard a Copernican admit something was right or wrong. They always talk in probabilities. Nothing so simple as true or false.'

Sim stopped and turned back to them with a face like thunder.

'We have the hardest job of all. It's all right for you two, playing with your extinct species,' turning to his sister, 'or Lyra with her innate talents. Some of us have to slave over millions of data points and billions of incidental factors just to make a single approximation of the future.'

'I think the actual word he was looking for was "guess",' Lyra whispered in Benoir's ear as Sim stormed up to the door of the map room.

The interior of the chamber was shrouded in shadows. A dim light shone from the small brass sphere that hung in the centre of the space.

'The Infinity Engine,' whispered Benoir to Lyra.

'Master De Freis,' the professor's voice resonated around the chamber. 'I see you have brought guests.'

'My sister, sir, and Benoir Cousineau, a paleobiologyst.'

Eddington walked out of the darkness, his pale face lined with worry. 'Welcome to you both. I take it you have come to see the progress we are making on the search for your elusive Aeons?'

'Have you found them?' Lyra asked bluntly.

The professor moved a lever on one of the control desks and the Infinity Engine began to spin. He adjusted a dial and ribbons of light expanded into the space around them.

Sim went to another desk and began to manipulate the projection until a series of interconnecting timelines came into focus.

'These are the traces of the royal dynasties spanning the last thousand years,' explained Eddington.

The genealogies branched out across the space around them, creating a three-dimensional map of the most powerful families in European history.

Lyra recognised the symbols of Draconian squadrons marking various points along the timelines.

'So far we have isolated three potential candidates in the nineteenth century,' said Eddington, walking into the centre of the cluster and pointing to each of the symbols. 'King George III of Great Britain, Louis XVIII of France and Francis II of Prussia.'

'What about the Rothsteins?' asked Benoir.

Eddington nodded to Sim and the nexus of lines shifted, focusing into the detail of the Rothstein lineage. 'There are signs that they may have been complicit in the Aeon's plan, but no definitive evidence that they were infected.'

Benoir went to protest, but Lyra gripped his hand tightly, as if warning him not to interrupt.

'So what happens next?' she asked.

'Now that we have a temporal pattern, we can initiate the trace,' replied Sim. 'We follow them back through time, find out who they came into contact with, what impact they have had on the continuum. Try to estimate what effect their removal from history would have.'

'They have infiltrated the highest echelons of our society,' warned Eddington sombrely. 'Their interference in the affairs of state may make it impossible to correct without considerable consequences for European history.'

'It'll be a million times worse if they find their queen,' said Lyra. 'Have you located Bouchard?'

Eddington shook his head. 'He seems to have vanished. None of our watchmen have managed to locate him.'

'Rufius could find a fart in a hurricane,' said Lyra, studying the complex map as it slowly rotated around them. 'Where is he now?'

Sim made an adjustment to the controls and the perspective changed, homing in on a small shield-like symbol on the border of the Nineteenth Century.

'He appears to be in Paris, 1800.'

72

NAPOLEON

[Paris, France. Date: December 24, 1800]

From the Place du Carrousel, Rufius watched the entourage leave the Tuileries Palace for the third time. The two carriages were flanked by a mounted escort of Consular Guards riding proudly beside their General. Napoleon and Josephine were travelling separately with members of their family and senior staff.

After witnessing the explosion for the first time, Rufius knew exactly where the bomb was stationed on rue Saint-Nicaise, to the north of the palace. It was a *Machine Infernale*, a large wine cask filled with gunpowder and grapeshot attached to a cart with metal hoops. Still tethered to its horse, the conspirators paid a fourteen-year-old girl, Marianne Peusol, to hold the mare while they lit the fuse and ran away.

Marianne died instantly, as did the horse, twenty bystanders and the First Consul of France.

The second time, Rufius went back further and watched the men wheel the wagon into the street. He would learn later that they were Chouan royalists: Pierre Robinault de Saint-Régeant, Pierre Picot de Limoëlan and François-Joseph Carbon, following direct orders from General Cadoudal, but for now the names were irrelevant. Saint-Régeant and his accomplices arrived just after seven in the evening and Rufius watched while they paid Marianne to hold their horse and then walked off into the crowd.

He stayed at a safe distance to observe the detonation.

Someone must have given the signal to Saint-Régeant, who lit the long fuse at just the right moment so that the blast caught Napoleon's carriage squarely in the side when it passed. The wooden coach shattered into a thousand splinters, shredding the spectators who were blithely waving as he passed. Shop windows buckled and imploded under the pressure of the shockwave. Bodies were scattered across the cobbled street in front of Rufius.

Rufius knew that the consequences of this assassination would be meticulously calculated by the Copernicans. Professor Eddington's department would bring his considerable resources to bear on the outcome of the death of Bonaparte. But Rufius didn't need a chronograph to tell him that this was something to do with the Aeons.

Bonaparte's campaigns were responsible for the end of the *Ancien Regime*, the feudal system that ruled over Western Europe for a thousand years. Without his influence, the royal houses of Habsburgs and the Capetian dynasty would have continued to dominate for another two hundred years before their rivalry finally tore Europe apart in the worst series of wars that the world had ever witnessed.

And at least three of those houses were infected.

As a military man, Rufius had always been fascinated

by Napoleon's rise through the ranks. A Corsican by birth, the artillery officer excelled during the French Revolution, making General by twenty four. His brilliant strategic mind won him numerous battles and campaigns against Austria, Italy and Prussia. Inspired by Caesar and Alexander the Great, he tried to overturn the monarchies of Europe and create a new society, and he nearly succeeded.

Napoleon needed at least another fifteen years to establish a significant change, his empire and, more importantly, his legal system would have significant effect on the future of developing countries.

The probability that the Aeons had penetrated the House of Bourbon via one of Louis IX's descendants was high, and Napoleon posed a significant threat to their survival. There were a number of groups that had already attempted to assassinate him: Jacobins and Royalists both with good reasons to see him dead. One group in particular, the Choauns, led by a Breton politician called Georges Cadoudal seemed the most likely. A staunch Roman Catholic and supporter of Louis XVIII, Cadoudal openly opposed Bonaparte's dictatorship. The Copernican's extrapolations identified him as the most likely candidate to succeed in killing the First Consul.

Rufius went back again and moved opposite the Tuileries Palace, studying the crowd for the lookout, someone had to signal to light the fuse when Napoleon left the palace. A soldier lingered outside the Hôtel de Longueville watching the gates expectantly.

He was wearing the uniform of the Consular Guard and at first Rufius assumed he was posted there as part of increased security ordered by the Chief of Police, Joseph Fouché.

Then he recognised Josh.

The gates opened as the first of the mounted guard rode out onto the square.

Rufius strode quickly over to Josh, catching his arm before he could raise it.

'Monsieur,' he complained, turning towards Rufius.

'Josh?'

There was no sign of recognition. His eyes were cold and dead, like a shark.

Josh tried to pull his arm away, but Rufius held tight as the escort and carriages passed them and into Rue Saint-Nicaise.

The blast made everyone in the street cower and run, except for Rufius and Josh, they stood staring at each other, unmoved by the chaos around them.

Without the signal from the lookout, Saint-Régeant lost precious seconds and the cart had exploded too late, there were still many killed and injured by the bomb, but Napoleon survived and continued on to the Opera. There were rumours that he'd fallen asleep in the carriage, woken from a dream of an old battle by the explosion.

With his free hand, Josh reached for his bayonet.

Rufius's punch landed squarely on his jaw and his friend collapsed onto the floor.

73

CAITLIN HAS BABY

[Chapter House]

Alixia was tending to one of her prehistoric ferns when Caitlin stepped out of the shimmering portal.

Dropping her secateurs, she caught her before she hit the floor.

Lying in her arms, Caitlin groaned, rubbing her bloated stomach while her feet scrabbled to find purchase in the soft ericaceous soil of the palm house.

'It's coming,' she panted, gritting her teeth against the pain.

Seconds later, her mother and father stepped through the glowing oval, both carrying towels and medical supplies.

'She insisted on coming here,' her mother explained, upon seeing Alixia's look of concern.

'She wouldn't wait, but the time dilation — ' her father began.

'It doesn't matter,' screamed Caitlin.

'Let's get her downstairs,' said Alixia, calmly helping Caitlin to her feet.

. . .

They took her to one of the bedrooms in the Romanov wing. Alixia's husband, Methuselah, attached the Winter Palace to the main house when Caitlin was twelve and it was still one of her favourite places to stay whenever she came to visit.

Her screams echoed along the corridors of white marble as Doctor Crooke arrived with an entourage of nurses.

Caitlin's father was quickly ushered out into the Nicholas Hall by a stern-looking matron. It was an opulent ballroom hung with enormous crystal chandeliers. It had been the palace of Catherine the Great and the official residence of Russian Emperors until 1917. Methuselah had connected it to a period just after Catherine's death in 1796, when it was filled with vast collections of art and treasure that caused the palace to be extended twice.

He stood by the window watching the snow fall on St Petersburg and the frozen River Neva, wondering how many Tzars had looked upon it while waiting for the birth of their first grandchild.

Such a different environment from the one where Caitlin was born: in a terraced house in Wimbledon during the three-day week of the nineteen-seventies.

Two hours later the cries of a baby brought tears to his eyes.

'You can come in now,' his wife said, opening the grand doors to Catherine's bedchamber.

Caitlin was propped up in the large bed, the white embroidered sheets had been stripped away and bundled in a bloodstained pile in a corner. His daughter looked exhausted, but her eyes were smiling, holding the newborn baby to her breast, covered in an ermine cloak that had obviously been borrowed from the queen's wardrobe.

'It's a boy,' said Caitlin proudly, lowering the bundle so that her father could see.

The pink glowing face of his grandson turned up towards him and for a fleeting moment he saw the features of his own father. It was strange how old men and babies seemed to share some similarities.

'Isn't he beautiful?' cooed Caitlin's mother.

'Yes.' Was all he could think to say. 'What are you going to call him?'

'Ebenezer.'

'Really?' he said, trying not to sound disappointed. 'Isn't that a bit Dickensian?'

Caitlin sniggered. 'No, of course not! Who would call anybody that?' I think Thomas Joshua would be a fine name.'

'Tom Jones?' Her mother frowned.

'Has a certain ring to it,' her father agreed, stroking the boy's head.

Caitlin's mother wasn't convinced. 'Much as we appreciate the gesture. I think he should have his own name, you don't need to saddle him with a historical burden like that.'

'It was good enough for five generations of Makepieces,' her father protested.

'And that is quite enough Thomases, thank you. My grandson will be his own man, with his own name. I've never liked that tradition to be honest, all that Thomas Junior nonsense, just all too patriarchal for my liking.'

The baby snuffled and buried his head back into his mother's chest and Caitlin discreetly covered him with the ermine cloak. She stifled a yawn.

'You're tired. We should go.'

Caitlin took her father's hand. 'Find Josh. He needs to see his son.'

'We will,' her father promised, squeezing it tightly.

The nurses drew the curtains around the four-poster bed and lit the fire. Her parents kissed her and left.

Caitlin snuggled down into the mountain of pillows and fell asleep listening to the sounds of her son beside her.

74

GOSSY

[Xenobiology Department, Regent's Park, London. Date: Present Day]

'Where did you find him?' asked Doctor Shika, sealing the stasis chamber.

'Trying to assassinate Napoleon in 1800,' replied Rufius, taking off the thick gloves and unbuttoning the hood of his heated parka.

'How did he end up there?'

Rufius sighed and scratched at his beard. 'I lent him one of my old tachyons, which he somehow managed to lose in Prague 1620. One of the guards at Daliborka sold it to me. Seems he got in trouble with the local alchemists, ended up killing a Golem, or so the story goes. They talk about him like a fallen hero. I think he got infected by one of Rudolph II's physicians.'

Kaori went to the control panel and activated the screen. They watched through the thick glass window as a robotic sensor arm swept along Josh's body and images began to appear on the displays.

'Physically he's in good shape,' she noted, studying his vitals. 'There's no doubt he's been infected.' She tapped on the worm-like creature that was wrapped around his brain stem. 'But this is new.' Her finger traced along tail-like tendrils that were running down towards his heart.

'He didn't recognise me,' said Rufius, staring at the floating body of his friend.

'The parasite works on the neural pathways. It's wired itself directly into his frontal lobe. Josh would have no control of his actions.'

'Is he still in there? Does he know what's going on?'

Kaori frowned, her dark eyes narrowing. 'Hard to say. There are traces of a neurotoxin in his blood so the creature may be sedating his waking mind, which would be a small comfort. To be conscious in a body you're unable to control would be similar to total paralysis. He would literally be a prisoner in his own head.'

Josh could feel something alien waiting behind the door. Like the nightmarish monsters of his childhood, he could hear its steely claws scraping along the walls outside.

His mind had retreated into the safest place it knew, his bedroom. The faded Top Trumps of F1 cars were still pinned to the wall, holding up the peeling paper and he could feel the hard cover of his diary tucked away beneath the pillow.

As a kid, he would hide under the duvet to block out the world. Imagining that he was an astronaut being kept in cryostasis on his way to another universe or a crusader knight sleeping under canvas in the deserts outside of Acre. Anything to distract his imagination from conjuring up the demons that were waiting in the shadows.

His mother's MS kept her in bed for weeks at a time,

leaving an overactive nine-year-old to fend for himself. This was long before he discovered his talent for disabling car alarms. Back then he stayed up late and watched horror movies.

Josh could still remember the first time he watched 'The Thing'. Kurt Russell's exploration team trapped in Antarctica with an alien monster that could pass itself off as human. The way that creature came apart and grew legs gave him nightmares for weeks, but he managed to get a bootleg copy on video from Eddie and watch it over and over again, trying to recapture the fear that he'd felt the first time — but it was never quite the same.

The thing outside the bedroom door made him feel that way.

Where are you? Josh thought, searching his mind for the founder.

There was no reply. There hadn't been any sign of him since he left Prague.

Josh got out of bed and opened his wardrobe door, which led directly into the archives.

Wandering down the rows of empty shelves, he realised that a library without any books was a strange, soulless place. The founder's memories were gone and the structure was beginning to break down.

Ahead he saw the glow of a single reading lamp.

The founder was bent over a desk, surrounded by stacks of books. He looked old and wizened, the skin of his hands mottled with dark bruises, and his eyes shrouded by dark hooded eyelids.

'Joshua,' he said, his voice like dry leaves.

'What's wrong with you? Where are all your memories?'

The founder sighed, drawing back his cowl. 'Gone. Devoured by the creature.'

'I can feel it too, outside the walls. What is it? An alien?' asked Josh, unable to think of a better way to describe it.

The old man closed his eyes and tilted his head as if listening. A holographic map of their two minds appeared in the space between them, one wrapped inside the other.

A dark snake-like creature slithered over the surface of the three dimensional model. 'At first I thought it was a monad,' the founder explained, turning the pages of the book before him. 'But, this is a physical entity.' He tapped on an old woodblock print of a worm being removed from a man's skull. 'I have found a number of references to it. Medieval physicians believed it was the source of madness, Hippocrates called them "Ascaris", they were revered by Scythians for giving god-like powers.'

'Where did it come from?' asked Josh, staring at the malevolent shape.

'I have only been able to read some of its timeline, it's an ancient life form and it appears to have attached itself to your nervous system.'

'That thing is inside me?'

The founder nodded. 'From what I can deduce the entity seeks to control you and harvest your knowledge. My mental defences have held it back so far, but we may need to act soon before it finds a way to overcome them.'

'How? It feels like I'm trapped inside my own skull.'

'Yes. I probably should have mentioned that. It's using a chemical toxin to paralyse you. Quite impressive parasitical behaviour.'

'Can you kill it?'

'Perhaps, but it would need to be something just as ancient.' He closed the book and opened another, turning to an illustration of a temple carving. It showed a winged man holding a multi-bladed dagger over a sacrifice as the priest pulled a worm from the victim's back. 'This was copied from one of the temples in the Saqqara Necropolis in Egypt.'

Josh winced at the sight of the sharp blades. 'Looks a little brutal, are you sure I'll survive?'

'It's a talisman,' he said, pointing to the being holding the weapon. 'And that is Anunnaki. One of the elder gods.'

'The ones you used to defeat the Djinn?'

The founder nodded. 'They've obviously been called upon to deal with these parasites before. You need to find the dagger.'

'And how exactly am I going to do that?'

'I would begin with the Medici Collection.' The founder tapped his temple and the model shifted as their two minds separated. 'Of course, you will need to leave this body.'

'I can do that?'

The founder smiled. 'You do not require your physical form to travel through time. Seers often experience something similar when they are dreaming. Our minds are quite capable of traversing the continuum. Although you will need a host if you wish to have any effect on the past.'

Josh watched as the creature burrowed through the founder's defences, draining another section of his memory and behind them another stack of books disintegrated.

'I suggest you decide quickly. My mind cannot withstand this constant barrage for much longer.'

'So I have to move into someone else's body?' asked Josh, remembering the last time he'd lifejacked his way to Caitlin from the twelfth century. It took Lyra weeks to rid him of the multiple personalities he collected.

'Transference isn't a simple procedure. The host must be on the point of passing, so that you would occupy their body as their consciousness departs. You would need to know the exact moment they died.'

There was one death etched indelibly on his soul. One who he knew would give his life for him in a heartbeat — Gossy.

Steve Goss was always his best friend in every timeline, it was like a universal constant. In his original life, Gossy died in a car crash at the age of twelve. They were racing stolen cars along the A3 and Josh's car collided with him. The sight of his friend's car crumpling into a steel ball as it careered into oncoming traffic haunted Josh for five years, until he discovered he could travel through time. It seemed like a distant memory now, but his friend was never going to make old bones. No matter how hard he tried, some people were destined for a short life.

Gossy was like the brother Josh never had. Since the day they first met in primary school they had been virtually inseparable.

'Look inside your memories. Find the moment and focus on it. I will guide you,' said the founder, breaking his reverie.

Josh went back to the day he died.

In the current timeline, Gossy died a good death, as the colonel would say. His friend was a successful businessman, working in the city with a wife and kids. He'd even bought a house on Churchill Gardens, the same square where Josh first met the colonel.

That day was like any other Tuesday, except as Gossy walked home from the tube station he'd seen someone getting mugged and stepped in to stop it. That was just the kind of guy he was.

The man was no match for Gossy, but he had a knife, which shouldn't have proved much of a challenge, they'd grown up on an estate where knives were a necessity.

Gossy pulled the man off the woman and pinned him against the wall, not realising that the knife had nicked an artery in his leg. In all the versions of how he would die, Josh had always thought this was the most honourable, far better than the heart defect that would take him a few years later.

As Gossy started to lose consciousness, Josh could see his timeline unfurling. The founder's mind enveloped his, showing him the way into his rapidly diminishing timeline.

Josh could feel the weight of his body as he took it over. His mind trying to come to terms with the new shape that it found itself within.

Knowing that he was still losing blood, he turned to the woman for help. She was clearly terrified, her eyes wide and staring. His pulse was heavy, a dull thud in his ears told him he had less than a minute to find a way out of this.

'Juliana,' he said, he knew her name, he knew everything about her. The fact that he called her by her name seemed to bring her out of her trance. 'Call an ambulance, now!'

He took off his tie and wrapped it around the top of his thigh, twisting it into a tourniquet.

She nodded and took out her mobile.

His breathing shallowed and the world seemed to dim.

75

BRIEFING

[Xenobiology Lab, Regents Park Zoo. London. Date: Present Day]

The images of the Linear A manuscript flickered on a holographic display in the middle of the table.

Benoir was still having trouble coming to terms with the ghostly tablets hovering in mid-air, and twice Lyra had to stop him putting his hand out to touch them.

Caitlin stood at the head of the table. She looked tired but determined. Doctor Crooke had advised her to stay in bed, but Lyra had seen that look before; when she was in this kind of mood there was no changing her mind.

'From what I have been able to translate so far, this is a warning,' Caitlin began, enlarging a section of characters on the tablet. 'This text refers to them as "the fallen" or "watchers", it names seven of them but I think there were probably more. Somehow the Minoans managed to isolate them and entombed them under Knossos.'

'Until Bouchard came along,' added Rufius under his breath.

'Do we know what they were trying to do?' asked Benoir.

'They're a colony. What Rufius found under the labyrinth was a hive,' said Kaori, switching the visual to show an intricate network of connecting caves. 'We sent a drone in to map it. The lower levels contain over a thousand cocoons.'

'A sleeping army?' Rufius wondered aloud.

'The Antiquarians are refusing access to every other guild. Konstantine only allowed us into it because we had better tech than they did.'

Caitlin sat down in the chair and poured herself a large cup of tea. She felt exhausted, the baby was waking every two hours and the only thing keeping her going was caffeine and biscuits.

'Do we have any idea why Napoleon was interested in Knossos?'

Sim shrugged. 'We assumed it was treasure, like Egypt. He's certainly not an Aeon as far as I can tell. In fact, I would say he was going out of his way to destroy their dynasty.'

'How many have we managed to locate so far?'

'Six,' said Sim, proceeding to count them on his fingers. 'George III, Louis XVIII, Alexander I of Russia, Rudolf II, Bouchard.'

'And Josh,' added Caitlin.

'Plus we have the Ripper on ice downstairs,' said Doctor Shika, 'although he's completely insane.'

'George III was mad too,' added Lyra.

'It might be worth paying him a visit,' suggested Kaori. 'The madness maybe a sign of his mind trying to reject the parasite.'

'Though this be madness, yet there is method in't,' said Kelly, putting his hat on backwards.

'I'll go,' said Rufius, glaring at the Grand Seer. 'I'm used to working with crazy men.'

'And what about Josh?' asked Caitlin. 'I would like my son to have a father.'

'He's stable,' replied Kaori. 'We've put him into stasis while we work on a treatment.'

Caitlin's eyes seemed to harden. 'I want to see him.'

'We need to find the dagger,' insisted Lyra. 'It will release him.'

'How exactly will stabbing him with a five-bladed weapon do that?' snapped Caitlin.

Lyra shrugged. 'I don't know. I didn't see that.'

Rufius got up from his seat. 'We can't wait for the damned Council to realise how bad this could be. We need to find Bouchard!'

Sim took out his almanac and leafed through the pages.

'Our latest predictions have him heading towards Mesopotamia.'

'What's in Mesopotamia?' asked Lyra.

'Depends how far back he's going. Sumerian, Babylonian, Akkadian. It's basically the cradle of civilisation,' replied Sim.

'Hard period to reach, mostly stone artefacts,' complained Rufius.

Lyra glanced over at Benoir, who made the tiniest of shakes of his head.

'We need a tracker,' suggested Caitlin's father.

Rufius scowled and folded his arms. 'Oh no, not him.'

'Who?'

'Your Uncle Marcus.'

'Worst idea ever.'

76

BRITISH MUSEUM

[British Museum, London. Date: 1972]

A week later Josh left the hospital. He avoided looking at his reflection for the first few hours. The idea that he was inside the body of his best friend was hard enough to cope with, let alone actually seeing him staring back in a shop window. Moving around in another person's body was a strange sensation, like wearing a meat suit. Although Gossy was a similar physical height and weight, he was more muscular and physically stronger than Josh. It wasn't as if Gossy ever made an effort to go to the gym or keep fit. It was just genetics, his body was built differently. He could run for longer, lift heavier objects, even pee further.

All of which Josh found out on the first day.

Like learning to drive a different car, it took a while to get used to, but by the end of the day he had stopped walking into things and dropping stuff, and he felt ready for his first jump.

. . .

The British Museum was run by the Antiquarian Guild. Housed within its walls was the largest repository of ancient artefacts in history, collected over thousands of years by curators who scoured the past in search of relics from long lost civilisations.

The museum was the perfect place for the Antiquarian headquarters. While the general public spent their time wandering past exhibits collected from times when the sun never set on the British Empire, far below their feet an entirely separate collection held the remains of the long forgotten past. But the vaults were more than just a storage facility, they were a staging post, acting like an airport terminal for time travellers.

According to the founder, hidden within the labyrinthine archive was the Medici Collection, the rarest archive of ancient objects in the entire Antiquarian repository.

The Medicis were a fifteenth-century banking family who rose up to rule Florence as well as producing four popes and sponsoring numerous architects and artists of the Renaissance.

Behind the closed doors of their ducal palaces they hoarded more than just riches and art.

Cosimo Medici was an avid collector of books, sending his scouts all over Europe as well as Syria, Egypt and the Middle East. Grandmaster Konstantine had ordered the recovery of his vast collection before the Bonfire of the Vanities in 1497. The books went to the Scriptorians, but the Antiquarians secured the rights to the strange array of artefacts that came into their possession.

. . .

The founder advised Josh to go back to 1972. The museum would be busier than usual because of the 'Treasures of Tutankhamun' exhibition which would draw the largest crowds they'd ever seen.

It was also the year that the museum's manuscripts were moved into the British Library, so there were hundreds of Scriptorians already working alongside the Antiquarian curators. Everyone would be too busy to question another member wandering around the restricted section.

During the move, the Order had opened up the underground entrance. It was located in a disused tube station that had serviced the museum until 1933. Thanks to some subtle temporal shielding, it retained its original pre-war state, movie posters of King Kong and the Invisible Man were plastered alongside pamphlets warning of the rise of Socialism in Germany.

Three people were queuing in front of Josh, each one pulling back their sleeve to reveal the Ouroboros tattoo on their forearm before entering through a rotating metal gate.

Josh suddenly realised that Gossy's body didn't carry such a mark.

The attendant was an older, bespectacled gentleman with white hair that seemed to defy any attempt to be combed. The walls of his small wooden office were covered in postcards of old steam locomotives, and the badges on the lapels of his jacket carried the names of stations of which Josh had never heard.

Through the small window, he handed out thin cardboard tickets.

There would be another way, Josh thought, one for those

linears brought in to help move the books to the British Library — a password.

'Good morning sir,' the man greeted him as he reached the booth. 'This is a staff entrance. I think you may be lost?'

'Morning,' Josh replied, his words sounding strange coming out in Gossy's voice. 'I was told to report here by the Head Librarian, Caitlin Makepiece'

The attendant's eyes widened at the sound of her name and Josh realised how much he missed her.

'Ah well, yes. Let me see,' he said, picking up a clipboard of names.

'May I have your name?'

'Steve Goss.'

He ran his finger down the sheet. 'Goss, Goss, no, I'm not seeing a Goss sorry.'

'She said that you would ask me for a password?'

The attendant scratched his chin. 'Well, it's not standard practice, but can you tell me who was the grandmother of the last Tsarina of Russia?'

The man looked expectantly over the top of his half-moon glasses. His eyes blinking slowly as he waited for the answer to his question. His fingers toyed with the top of a small brass bell which Josh assumed would summon the guards.

For the first time in a long while, Josh regretted not having the benefit of the founder's memories or a tachyon. Jumping back two minutes would at least given him the benefit of knowing the question.

Then Josh heard the question in his head, being read by some TV quiz show host. Sitting with his mother watching University Challenge while she was shouting about the Russian Revolution and how the entire Romanov family was assassinated.

'Queen Victoria.'

The man nodded and pulled a lever, allowing the gate to rotate freely.

The vaults of the British Museum were massively extended by the Order during its redevelopment of 1827. The Antiquarian's temporal engineers connected a network of vast store rooms across time and geography to create the largest repository of historical objects ever known.

It was so immense that it required its own railway.

The Medici collection was housed in London along with the Elgin Marbles, the Rosetta Stone and other spoils of various British explorations. The Antiquarians kept their most valuable treasures close to hand.

Josh followed the others through the narrow passageways and into a central underground courtyard. It was beautiful, like the carved treasury temple of Petra, with monumental facades of classic columns and effigies of gods looking down on the plaza below.

He had never seen so many Antiquarians in one place. They were generally a solitary guild, preferring their own company, usually in museums or small antique shops. The square was swarming with gowned figures pushing hand carts filled with the treasures of ancient civilisations and porters moving huge stone statues on steam-driven carriages.

The Medici collection was stored in a restricted area, which meant finding a way to get past the security detail without raising suspicions.

Protectorate guards were standing on each side of the entrance to the secure vault. Both were wearing dark, temporal armour, the kind that light seemed to slide off, and holding fully armed gun-sabres.

He was going to need an old-fashioned diversion if he was going to stand any change of getting through there.

The steam cart chugged slowly across the atrium in front of Josh.

It ran on a series of tank tracks, connected to a drive system powered by a spinning belt from a miniature steam engine. It was possibly the clunkiest thing he'd ever seen; listing over on one side the porters were struggling to keep it level as they moved an enormous monolithic head in slow careful inches.

All it needed was a slight nudge.

The granite head toppled gracefully. Falling slowly enough for the crowd to move out of the way as it came crashing down onto the marble floor. Eighty-six tonnes of Polynesian god scattered across the courtyard, sending everyone for cover.

The guards left their posts and ran to assist the porters who were now having to deal with an unencumbered steam cart as it careered out of control around the square. An unintended bonus, as it created more chaos than the statue itself.

Unseen, Josh stepped through the stone arch and into the restricted area.

77

DINNER

Dinner at her parents' Chapter House was never a dull affair and Caitlin's baby had brought everyone to the party, including members that no one had seen in centuries.

Benoir looked overwhelmed by the gathering. Lyra found him fascinating to watch as he tried his best to mingle with the other guests. She knew he would rather be pulling a rotten tooth out of a mastodon, and was about to go over and rescue him when Caitlin caught her eye and waved her over.

'You look knackered,' said Lyra, sitting down beside her.

Caitlin laughed. 'Everyone else says I'm glowing.'

'Well, they're just being nice.'

The baby snuffled inside the swaddling and Caitlin adjusted the blankets. 'Do you want to have a hold?'

Lyra peered in at the tiny pink face and her nose wrinkled as she exclaimed: 'He's like an old man.'

Caitlin pouted and stroked his black hair. 'He's cute, he just hasn't grown into his skin yet.'

Lyra shook her head. 'No way am I ever having one of those. Wasn't it weird having it growing inside you?'

'It was lovely actually. It felt like I was connected to him. Although I had the weirdest dreams.'

'Welcome to my world.'

'They were so real, like previous lives. I thought it was the dodgy cheese dad found on one of the old warships, but they kept happening. Every night.'

Lyra's eyebrows arched and she leaned in a little closer to the baby.

'Did you do the test?'

Caitlin shook her head. 'There aren't any seers in our family. I didn't see the point.'

'I can do it now, if you like?'

Caitlin looked nervously down at her child. It was a simple test, but one with far-reaching consequences. All children born into the Order were supposed to be checked for seer latency. It was usually something the midwife would do after birth, but somehow no one had got around to doing it.

Lyra took off her necklace and slipped one of her rings on to it. She held it over the child's head and they both watched as it settled into a steady clockwise rotation.

'Looks normal,' said Caitlin with a sigh of relief.

'Give it a minute.'

The baby's hand reached up towards the shiny gold band. Its tiny little fingers waving at the gleaming ring.

Its orbit grew more erratic, others came over to watch the spectacle as the ring danced one way and then another. Whispering under their breath the words that every mother dreaded — Seer.

Lyra put down the necklace and touched the child's hand.

Her eyes narrowed as the contact was established between them and she began to read its timeline.

Suddenly, Lyra's nose began to bleed and her face went grey. She pulled her hand away as if she had been burned.

'What is it?' asked Caitlin.

'So powerful in one so young,' replied Lyra, wiping the blood from her nose and looking at it intensely. 'We need to tell the Grand Seer.'

'Not yet, he's too young,' pleaded Caitlin.

Lyra stood up and was pleased to find that Benoir was standing beside her. 'He's in great danger,' she warned. 'But I can't see what it is — I'm not strong enough.'

78

KING GEORGE

[Windsor Castle, England. Date: November, 1778]

George III sat half-naked on a gilded chair in the stable yard while servants threw ice-cold buckets of water over his pink, bloated body. Rufius, dressed as one of the King's guard, watched from under the eaves of the stables, as they doused the King of England, under the watchful eye of his physician, Francis Willis.

The King babbled constantly throughout the treatment. Words tumbled from his thick lips as he lamented on the poor quality of bread owing to the previous harvest, the American colonies and the state of the linen in his bedchamber. Random subjects blended seamlessly into a coherent stream of banal facts that none of the men around him seemed to pay any attention to.

The ice water appeared to be having little effect on his condition, but it was a damn sight easier to watch than the purging.

Rufius had observed this morning's ritual on three separate occasions and there was no doubt in his mind that the man was quite insane. His almanac still showed the monarch to be the third most likely candidate to play host to an Aeon, but Lyra's theory that the parasite may actually be responsible for his poor mental state was beginning to look unlikely.

Commonly known as Mad King George, his Highness was supposed to have once mistaken a tree for the King of Prussia. His sixty-year reign was as troubled as his health, dogged by revolution and conflict; both America and France shook off the mantle of their ruling classes during his time.

During his times of infirmity, the government, under the leadership of William Pitt, voted to invoke a Regency Bill authorising his eldest son George, Prince of Wales, to act in his stead.

Because of this, Eddington agreed he was a prime candidate for an intervention. The lack of direct influence on the running of the state meant that Rufius could intercede without a high probability of changing the future.

After his ablutions, the King would be dried and taken to his chambers for a simple breakfast. Rufius joined the others as they marched under the Norman Gateway and down through the Upper Ward to the Queen's lodge.

The doctor and his assistants oversaw his meal, before leaving him to recuperate in a simple room with nothing more than two chairs and views over the parkland that surrounded the castle.

Rufius stood guard outside the doors to His Majesty's apartment, listening to the sound of the man as he discussed affairs of state with his invisible courtiers.

. . .

'Your Majesty,' he said, entering the room after he was sure that the doctor's entourage had left.

'Falstaff? Is that you?'

'Aye lord,' Rufius said, thinking that he'd been called much worse.

'Come John, sit with me for a while and tell me stories of Prince Hal and his battles with Hotspur. Are you men naught but food for powder still?'

Rufius caught the mad stare in the King's eyes. A distant gaze that never stayed fixed on anything for more than a moment. He'd seen it before, in the lunatics of Bedlam, the seers who had witnessed too many alternate futures, their minds broken by the possible ways that a life could go.

Before he left, Doctor Crooke had given him something to calm the King. A potion of the usual noxious substances that he swore would temporarily alleviate the control that the parasite had over the man's mind.

'What say you to a drink my lord?' said Rufius, hastily stirring the mixture into a tumbler before offering it to the King.

George smiled. 'Why not John? What is it that Mistress Quickly would say? What, man, be o' good cheer!'

He downed the draught in one long swallow, handing back the empty glass and wiping his mouth with his sleeve like a peasant.

Crooke said the potion should take affect within minutes of entering his system.

'Chamberlain, have you seen my queen?' the King asked an imaginary person to Rufius's right. 'She promised me oranges today. Can you imagine such a thing so close to winter?'

'No sire.'

'Spanish no doubt. Willis will have them confiscated. I

swear the man grows fat on me!' He slapped his rotund stomach. 'I may die of starvation if not boredom.'

His eyes were losing their vacant glare. He looked at Rufius as if seeing him for the first time.

'You're not my usual man?'

The question was a sure sign that the storm in his mind was calming.

'No sire, I've been sent to ask something about your past.'

The monarch waved his hand, looking around at the empty room. 'Ask away, my other guests appear to have abandoned me.'

'Can you tell me what happened yesterday?'

Frowning, the King rubbed his chin, which had not seen a barber's razor for weeks; no knives or blades were allowed in his presence in case he tried to injure himself.

'Now let me see. I believe it would be that attack by the Nicholson woman. Such a strange lady, came up to me at St. James's and tried to stab me with a knife. Hardly left a scratch. Doctor Munro examined the poor creature and declared her insane.' He tapped his temple. 'Imagine that, a lunatic who thought they were a ruler.'

Rufius moved back to witness Margaret Nicholson's attack, which took place two years before. The fact that King George remembered it so clearly told him that it must have been the point of infection.

The woman approached the King as he stepped out of his carriage at St. James's Palace. She was holding a blank petition and claiming to have some right to the throne. The report said that she tried to stab him with an ivory handled dessert knife, but something else passed between them.

Rufius saw a dark shape crawl under George's silk waistcoat as they took her away.

She was certified insane and sent to Bedlam where she spent the next forty-two years.

Her rooms were on Wigmore Street in a small boarding house, squeezed into an already overcrowded mews of wooden buildings. Beneath her thin mattress Rufius found a bundle of letters, each one claiming her right to the throne, listing out an impressive lineage. To the "Board of the Green Cloth", the body that oversaw matters of the Royal Court, they would have appeared to be the work of a madwoman, but to Rufius they were clues, details of half-remembered lives of the Aeon that infected her. They had driven her quite mad, and it seems the parasite too.

She was a carrier, her half-hearted attempt to stab the King was nothing more than a diversion. The parasite used the attack to get close to George. It took a while for the madness to manifest in his majesty, but it was clear from the detail in the letters that the creature had moved through various members of the great houses to reach him.

Nicholson had been an unfortunate diversion in the Aeon's plan. A servant in the household of Lord Coventry, she'd been the only survivor of a house fire at her master's home, and the only escape route for the parasite that possessed him.

Rufius collected the letters, making careful note of how they were arranged and took out his tachyon. Eddington would have the first real evidence of these creatures and at least the beginnings of a trail to follow, one that might just save the sanity of a king.

79

STASIS

Kelly shook his head as he left. 'Sigh no more, ladies, sigh no more. Remember him as the prince he once was.'

Caitlin placed her hand on the cool glass of the stasis chamber, wiping away the condensation to reveal Josh's face. He looked serene, his hands folded over his chest as if he were lying in state.

'What was he doing in Paris?'

'Trying to kill Napoleon apparently.'

'Why?'

Kaori shrugged. 'Why not?'

She felt tears pricking the corners of her eyes and fought to hold them back.

'How long can you keep him in there?' she asked, as Doctor Shika checked the display on the side of the cabinet.

'Indefinitely,' Kaori replied. 'Although we're not sure

what the long-term effects would be. We mainly use these for our non-corporeal specimens or —'

'The dead?' Caitlin finished her sentence. 'Can he hear me?'

'No,' Doctor Shika shook her head. 'He's not experiencing time.' She studied one of the displays. 'We saw a spike in brain activity earlier, but it was less than a nanosecond.'

Caitlin bit her lip. 'Is he in pain?'

Kaori put her hand on Caitlin's arm. 'There's nothing to worry about. He's safe and we're working on a way to get that thing out of him.'

'How?'

The doctor swiped across the screen and selected one of the files. A three dimensional model of Josh's body appeared and alongside it a strange-looking device that looked like a many-bladed dagger.

'Lyra described it to me. She believes it's some kind of talisman.'

'Talisman, how is that going to help?'

Kaori rotated the model with her thumb and forefinger. 'The creature attaches itself to the neural cortex and its tendrils mesh with the dendrites of the subject's brain. Trying to extract it surgically would almost definitely kill the host, if not leave them brain dead. We think the device uses the outer blades to create a temporal field that interferes with the creature's nervous system, causing it to release the host, allowing us to extract it using the central blade.'

Caitlin studied the image. 'And you've tested it?'

'In simulations, hundreds of times.'

'In reality?'

Kaori's eyes dropped. 'We've been unable to find the

weapon. Lyra tracked it to a particular collector but it's vanished.'

Caitlin's mouth tightened and her eyes hardened. 'What was the collector's name?'

'Rothstein.'

80

MEDICI COLLECTION

[British Museum, London. Date: 1972]

W hen Josh reinstated the Order, he selected the various Grandmasters based on the founder's recommendations. Wherever possible he left them to run their guilds without any intervention, mainly because he didn't have the time or patience to micro-manage every part of the organisation, but mostly because he didn't really care.

The Oblivion Order had always been his father's brain child. If the founder's memories had died in Fermi's lab that day, there was a good chance Josh would have never tried to recreate it. Instead he'd carried him around like a monkey on his back.

There was no way to know what was going on behind the closed doors of their respective fiefdoms. The founder insisted that the dynamics of the five guilds would hold each other in check and if not there was always the Protectorate.

Konstantine had not been their first choice to lead the Antiquarians, but their preferred candidate, Galloway, had died and left them with no other option.

From the very beginning, they'd never been particularly fond of each other, resulting in a mutual dislike, which never really bothered Josh until Konstantine tried to have him excised.

Whatever the cantankerous old bugger was up to, he certainly liked to do it in style. The restricted section was modelled on the inside of a Great Pyramid. Its thick limestone walls sloped inwards, each massive block decorated with hieroglyphics and scenes from the temple at Luxor.

Oil lamps lit the corridors, filling the air with the rich aroma of incense and casting flickering shadows across the carved faces of the pharoahs.

After five minutes, Josh realised he had no idea where he was going. It seemed that one of the prerequisites for working in the restricted section was memorising the layout of the maze-like vault. Without a guide you could get lost for days, if not weeks.

At each junction, however, there was a symbol, allowing the curators to orientate themselves.

But without a map, he had no idea which direction to take.

'Are you lost?' came a voice from the shadows. One that Josh recognised immediately.

It was Caitlin.

She stepped out of the darkness, as beautiful and radiant as ever, but there was no smile, no sign of recognition and then he remembered she was looking at a stranger. He tried to control his emotions, but his voice was tight as he spoke: 'Yeah, I'm looking for the Medici Collection.'

'Me too,' she said, her eyes narrowing. 'Are you a curator?'

'No,' he lied, wanting all the time to pull her into his arms. 'I'm from the Scriptoria, I'm here for the Alkahest.'

'Ah, okay.' She didn't look convinced.

There was an awkward silence. He didn't know what to say, every part of him wanted to tell her who he was, but he knew how crazy it was going to sound.

'Do you know where it is?'

She nodded. 'Follow me, this place can be a little hard to read unless you have the key.'

The smell of her perfume drove him crazy as he followed her through the maze of passages.

'What's your name?'

'J...James,' corrected Josh, 'and you?'

'Caitlin. Caitlin Makepiece'

'Aren't you the Head Librarian?' he said, trying to sound like he wasn't quite sure.

She turned back to look at him. 'Yes. I'm on maternity leave.'

'Congratulations,' he said, trying hard not to cry. 'What did you have?'

'A boy.'

They reached a corner and Caitlin took out her almanac. 'It's just down here.'

Josh bit his lip, grateful for the bad lighting that hid the tears streaming down his face.

. . .

The door to the Medici Collection was protected by a complex lock, devised by someone with far too much time on their hands and a penchant for intricate clockwork.

'I don't suppose you have a key?' asked Caitlin, pulling a lensing helmet from her bag.

'No.'

She used the multiple views of the lenses to guide Josh while he tried various combinations. It felt good to be close to her, and he had to stop himself from moving the hair out of her face.

When they finally entered the correct combination, the door broke into eight parts and slid back away from them. Inside the vault the walls were lined with glass display cases containing some of the oldest human artefacts in existence.

Crudely forged figurines of lion-headed gods sat beside Aztec crowns and Incan death masks. Josh recognised some of them from the battle with the Djinn — it appeared to be an entire collection of talismans.

Caitlin went directly for the multi-bladed spear head.

'Don't see any books,' she said, taking the weapon out of the cabinet and levelling it at him. 'Want to tell me why you're really here?'

'I've come for the trident,' he said, nodding to the weapon. 'I need it to save someone.'

Her hands shifted on the shaft, it was obviously heavy. 'Me too, and technically it's called a quindent — since it has five blades.'

'Do you know how to use it?'

She shook her head. 'No, I was about to ask you the same question.'

'I assumed we could just read its past.'

Caitlin's eyes narrowed. 'Who are you?'

'You wouldn't believe me if I told you.'

'Try me,' she said, thrusting the blade closer so the prongs were less than an inch from his chest.

'You once told me that you got that scar on your arm from a sword fight with your Dad.' He pointed to the white line along her forearm. 'You drink pints of Guinness and when I first met you, you were working on your dissertation of The Art of War by Sun Tzu.'

'Josh?' Her eyes widened.

He bowed his head. 'I miss you Cat.'

She lowered the quindent and punched him so hard that he fell back on his arse.

'What was that for?' he said, rubbing his chin.

Caitlin thrust the blades towards his face, stopping just short of his nose. 'If that is you — you deserved it. If you're bullshitting me, then you definitely deserved it.'

'It's me.'

'What was the last thing I said to you before I left?'

He paused for a moment, feeling his teeth with his tongue. 'Everybody dies.'

She lowered the dagger. 'I don't understand. I left you in cryostasis, you've been infected by an Aeon.'

Josh got to his feet. 'Is that what it's called? The founder had another name for it.'

'Who's the founder?'

'Never mind. We need to get that back to wherever you're keeping my body. I don't have a lot of time.'

There were tears in her eyes and she dropped the blades and fell into his arms.

'I thought you were dying,' she said between sobs. 'How did you—'

'Transference, it's a kind of like a total intuit.'

'Kelly couldn't reach you. He said there was nothing left.'

'I'd probably left by then. God I've missed you. I'm so sorry.'

She buried her face in his chest. 'I'm sorry. About your Mum and what I said.'

'It doesn't matter now,' he whispered into her hair.

'How did you know about this?' asked Josh, picking up the weapon.

Caitlin smiled. 'Lyra had a dream that I killed you with it.'

Josh knew better than to question one of Lyra's dreams.

'Nice. I'm assuming you have a better plan.'

She paused, her lips pouting as though she were considering the options.

'Maybe we should go back and find out how it works,' he suggested.

'I don't know, this new body of yours looks pretty good.' A wicked smile broke out across her face. 'Maybe I'll keep this one.'

'Or maybe we should get on with saving the real me.'

'Yeah, probably should. We wouldn't want people wondering why Dougal doesn't look like his father.'

'Dougal? That's a name for a dog.'

She put her hand on the shaft of the quindent. 'See what happens when you leave me.'

81

ANNUNAKI

[Babylon, Mesopotamia. Date: 1750 BC]

The ziggurat rose from behind the stone walls. The golden sides of its upper tiers shimmered in the midday sun.

'When are we?' asked Caitlin, letting go of his hand.

Josh had no idea, the timeline of the weapon was unusual; it carried none of the usual temporal markers.

They stood shading their eyes from the glare, surrounded by a dune sea that stretched out towards the horizon. There were no trees, nor wildlife, and no sound except for the wind. It was a barren, empty world, devoid of life.

Except for the citadel that sat in the basin of the valley below. Its architecture was ancient and beautiful. The outer walls were decorated with tiled mosaics of a winged Pegasus, dragons and other mythical creatures.

'You could have got us a little closer?' she said, setting off down the slope.

'I'm playing it safe.'

She scoffed. 'That's a first.'

'So what's he like?' asked Josh as they walked down into the valley, their legs sinking into the sand.

'He's beautiful.' Caitlin turned to face him. 'He looks like a cross between my dad and your mother and he's got the most gorgeous eyes.'

Josh tried to imagine what that would look like but failed.

'Why didn't you stay in the Maelstrom until he was born?'

'You remember there was a tablet, from Knossos. One that couldn't be deciphered.'

He shrugged.

'Anyway, it turns out that it was a warning. The whole city was infected with Aeons and their king sealed them in a tomb under the palace. It was a terrible sacrifice.'

'And you came back to stop them opening it?'

She shook her head. 'I was too late. The Antiquarians had already been in. As had Rufius, Sim and a bunch of Dreadnoughts.'

'Are they okay?' asked Josh, thinking how long it had been since he'd seen the colonel.

'They are, but it turns out there are more of these Aeon things, and they've infected some of the most influential houses in Europe. Doctor Shika believes they are trying to find their queen.'

At the bottom of the valley was a dry river bed, winding like a path along the defile, leading indirectly to the city. Caitlin bent down and tapped the hard mud with the butt of the weapon.

'No water,' she said, getting to her feet. 'We need to get to the city before we die of thirst.'

Looking towards the shining ziggurat, Josh thought he saw something hovering above it. He was still too far away to make out any details, but there were shapes circling over the centre of the city.

They made better time on the hard pan of the river bed.

'How did you know where this was?' asked Josh, shouldering the weapon.

Caitlin laughed. 'You mean, how did I happen to save your arse in the restricted section.'

'I would have found it eventually.'

She ignored him. 'There was a collector, called Rothstein. Lyra thought he was another one of the infected, but he's actually an Antiquarian curator, he works for Special Acquisitions. Rufius told me about Konstantine's secret collection of talismans under the British Museum.'

Drawing closer to the citadel, Josh could make out the outline of wings in the sky above them. Huge birds were hovering like vultures over a dying buffalo.

A blue-tiled arch stood before them, set into the high walls, the studded wooden doors hanging open and unguarded.

'Ishtar?' Caitlin said to herself as they passed through the ornate arch.

The narrow streets were empty, although there were signs that someone had passed through recently. Their footprints still visible in the sand, not yet covered over by the winds.

High above, the birds squawked a warning.

'Martial eagles,' whispered Caitlin, grabbing Josh's arm and dragging him into the shelter of a doorway.

'What is this place?'

'I think it might be Babylon,' she said, inspecting the doorway behind them which looked as if it had been built for someone nearly twice her height.

Josh tried the door but it was stuck fast. The pitted surface of the wood and the surrounding walls seemed to be encrusted with layers of sand, as if it hadn't been touched for hundreds of years.

They kept to the shadows and made their way towards the heart of the citadel. It couldn't have been more than a mile wide, and the streets were like the spokes of a wheel, radiating out from the centre.

It took less than ten minutes to find the central meeting place.

The central plaza was dominated by the stepped pyramid whose square sides were decorated with stylised effigies of winged, lion-headed demons. Three hundred feet high and crowned by a golden temple, the ziggurat dominated the city.

The bones of the dead were bleaching in the sun, some of the bodies picked clean of flesh by the eagles. A dark cloud of flies scattered from the others as Josh and Caitlin approached.

What intact skeletons were left were well over six-feet tall, or would have been if they still had their skulls. Josh counted fifty bodies and every one of them had been beheaded.

There were no signs of a battle, and the way the bodies

were arranged looked more ceremonial, creating a ring around one central being who was even larger than the others.

The birds complained as Josh and Caitlin picked their way carefully through the carnage until they reached the central figure.

He would have been nearly seven feet tall standing up, Josh thought, kneeling down to examine the remains. Whoever these people were, they would have been giants.

'What happened here?' Caitlin said to herself.

Josh knelt down beside the body of the man and picked an amulet from what would once have been his neck.

'One way to find out,' he said, holding it up to her.

The interior of the temple was filled with tall, golden-skinned villagers. Rays of sunlight filtered through from the small windows set high in the walls, the beams focusing on a golden altar.

A body lay atop the table, his head slumped over the edge, his hands and feet tightly bound. A guard stood on both sides of the shaman, who was holding his hands up into the ray of light.

The shaman was reciting some kind of prayer in a language that Josh had never heard.

'Arkaddian,' whispered Caitlin before he could ask.

As the man repeated the litany, she translated: 'We who have lived though the dark terror of this — creature I guess, not sure what that word is. Have suffered long enough. We call on the Anunnaki to take this demon from us.'

They watched in stunned silence as the air around the dais began to distort. The crowd muttered protection spells under their breaths as the outlines of four figures shimmered into existence. Their faces were hidden beneath ornate helmets and their armour glowed in the semi-darkness, cloaked in rippling fields of light. Josh didn't recognise the design but it was clear they were from a highly advanced civilisation.

One of the four was carrying a quindent. He held the weapon above his head, gloved fingers moving along its shaft like a flute, pressing different markings. The outer blades retracted and the central point slid forward.

Caitlin's fingers subconsciously copied the gesture on her own device.

The shaman went to his knees as the other members of the Anunnaki surrounded the figure on the altar.

The first blade pierced the prone man's skin and he cried out, reminding Josh that there was no such thing as anaesthetic in these times.

Caitlin gripped his hand instinctively as the stranger deployed the other blades into the man's back. A blue flame washed over his skin, and his body went rigid.

'Electricity?' wondered Caitlin.

As the Anunnaki pulled the quindent free of the flesh, they could see a worm-like creature caught in a static field between the prongs.

The victim's body went limp, like a marionette whose strings had been cut.

One of the others held out a container and the Aeon was placed inside.

'Doesn't seem too bad,' whispered Josh.

'Wait.'

The third Anunnaki drew a long, curving blade from behind his back and sliced off the victim's head.

The others drew their weapons and the shaman was the next to go down.

Suddenly the crowd were screaming and running for the exit.

'Time to go,' whispered Josh, grabbing her arm.

Something detonated above their heads, sending a ring of blinding light across the chamber and everything went into slow motion.

Caitlin seemed mesmerised by the glowing figures that were moving slowly down the steps of the raised platform, carving through the bodies of the fleeing natives.

Josh reached for her quindent. It was glowing with the same field that surrounded the weapons of the four. As his fingers touched the handle, he felt what Caitlin was already experiencing. Its timeline was gone, replaced by something completely alien.

There was no way to use it to return home.

'Tachyon!' he shouted, breaking her out of her reverie.

She took out her tachyon and handed it to him like a child returning a stolen toy. Josh tried to set it for home, but the device seemed to come apart in his hands, crumbling from the inside as though it was being dissolved by acid.

The Anunnaki spread out through the crowd and they fell before them.

Josh pulled the necklace from her neck. 'You need to go now!' he screamed at her, forcing Solomon's ring onto her finger.

'What about you?'

'I'll return to my body, but you need to take this back and save me okay?'

She blinked, as if coming out of a dream, the effect of the talisman was counteracting the influence of the Anunnaki.

'But what if you don't?'

Josh held her face in his hands and looked deep into her eyes. 'Caitlin, you're my future, I know that now, please trust me. I love you.'

He kissed her and time seemed to slow. He felt the hairs raise on the back of his neck as she accessed the timeline of the ring, but knowing it was a one way ticket.

82

DEVICE

'She has the extractor,' said X-541, his eyes glowing.

'With no way to return,' replied Konstantine. 'Her tachyon was successfully destroyed.'

'He gave her the ring.' The light fading in his eyes. 'We have failed.'

'Not necessarily. There is still Azazel, assuming she removes it without causing too much damage.'

X-541 got to his feet. 'The memory must be preserved.'

'Then we should focus on its retrieval.'

'She will try and save the Paradox. It is her fate.'

'And Doctor Shika will preserve the parasite.'

'The laboratory is heavily shielded.'

Konstantine smiled. 'Then we need a suitable crisis to divert their attention.'

83

EXTRACTION

[Xenobiology Lab, Regents Park Zoo, London. Date: Present Day]

Caitlin appeared in the Xenobiology conference room still holding the quindent.

She looked around for Josh, but he was nowhere to be seen.

The others sat in stunned silence as she dropped the weapon onto the table.

'Josh is still alive.'

Doctor Shika picked up the device. 'Where did you find it?'

'I don't have time to explain. He's fighting for his life.'

Josh found himself inside the archives once more. The founder sat at his desk in an empty library, looking weak and old, clutching one last book of memories.

'Who are you?' he asked.

Josh realised there was hardly anything left of him. 'I'm Josh, the guy who's brain you've been hitching a ride in.'

The founder looked confused. 'I'm sorry, I don't remember. Have I been here long?'

'A while. It doesn't matter, it's nearly over.'

The founder blinked. 'What is?'

'They're going to fix us. We found the Anunnaki.'

'Ah, yes the ancient ones,' he said, his eyes lighting up. 'I know of them, it's all in this book.'

He held out the leather tome to Josh.

'No, you keep it,' said Josh, pushing it away.

'Thank you. I have nothing else left, the creature has devoured nearly everything.'

It had taken nearly an hour to bring him out of temporal stasis. He was naked, face down on an operating table, his arms and legs strapped down.

Monitoring alarms kicked in as their displays registered signs of distress on Josh's vitals.

Caitlin held the dagger the way the Anunnaki had done, pressing on the same symbols on the handle and the weapon began to glow. Kaori had wired the quindent to an electric current, and lines of static arced between the metal points as the blades re-configured themselves.

'It will kill him,' the creature warned through clenched teeth.

She ignored it, tears streaming down her face she raised the extraction tool above her head.

'Don't!' shouted Josh, but it was too late.

'It's not him. It's not him,' she screamed, plunging the weapon into his back.

The Aeon howled as the blades deployed, their electrical fields tattooing Josh's back with strange fractal burns as they worked into various points along his upper spine.

Inside the archives, Josh felt ghostly pinpricks on the back of his neck.

'It's started. I can feel something.'

As the blades moved deeper, he felt the dim echoes of pain and the founder seemed to gain strength.

'It's losing control of your nervous system.'

Caitlin looked to Kaori, who was studying the readings on the monitors, her face lined with concern.

Josh's body tensed, every muscle locked tight, she could see the cords in his neck straining against the pain. Caitlin went to pull the dagger out, but the doctor stayed her hand.

'Not yet,' she said, cancelling the alarms.

Josh could feel the knives plucking away the last of the creature's links with his mind.

'It's working, it's letting go,' he said to the founder, as the walls of the archive began to disintegrate.

He could feel his body once more, like a drowning man close to reaching the surface of the water.

Josh's body was shaking uncontrollably.

Another set of alarms were triggered, this time warning of impending heart failure.

'Now!' screamed Kaori.

Caitlin took a deep breath and wrapped her hands

around the shaft of the quindent. Carefully placing her fingers on the appropriate markings, she pulled it free. She felt the energy leeching from Josh's body, as the worm-like parasite was drawn wriggling from the wound.

Feeling her knees giving way, she handed the device to Doctor Shika and collapsed onto the floor.

A silent darkness swallowed Josh, a featureless void surrounded him like a night sky without any stars.

'Joshua?' he heard his mother's voice.

'Mum?'

'Joshua, this is not your time.'

She spoke to him like a naughty child in the way that only a mother could.

Josh scanned the emptiness. There were motes of light glimmering in the darkness like floating embers from a fire, but no physical sign of his mother. Yet he could sense her, just as he could when he was a child, falling asleep in her arms.

Unlike the time with the Golem, these were not simply the resurrected memories of his childhood. There was something of her essence unfurling around him.

'I miss you,' he whispered into the dark.

'I will always be with you,' she reassured him, 'but you must find your own path. Don't waste your life trying to fix the past. What's done cannot be undone.'

'But I have the power to change it!'

'Some things are best left to fate.'

'You deserved more than that.'

'I had you, what more could I ask for? There will come a time when you will understand that your children are the future.'

'We had a beautiful baby boy.'

'I know.'

'I wanted you to meet him.'

She smiled, or rather the embers seemed to glow a little brighter.

'Live your best life and be happy. Don't waste what time you have on things you can't change.'

The sparks of light gathered together into a pulsing star. Josh could feel her presence inside the glowing sphere, the warmth of her love growing brighter as it approached.

Like surfacing from a deep ocean, he felt the air once more in his lungs and the daylight burned his eyes.

84

LETTER

To my darling boy,

    I hope you never have to read this letter, but somehow as I wait to find out if your father will ever wake up, I feel it helps.

Doctor Shika has warned me that the Aeon we removed from him may have caused permanent brain damage. I wish I had another choice, but there weren't any other options.

The Antiquarians confiscated the device before Kaori had a chance to study it.

I cannot describe what I saw in Babylon, it was as if the Anunnaki were reclaiming their property and ensuring there were no witnesses, slaughtering everybody. I have no idea who they were, but they certainly weren't from our time. I couldn't even tell you if they were future or past.

All I know is that your father sacrificed himself to save me.

And now I have him back, or his body at least.

If there were a god, I would be praying to it, instead I rely on the memory of the man I love. He's strong, a survivor and if anyone can make it back from this, it will be your father.

85

WAKING

[Winter Palace, Saint Petersburg]

They transferred Josh to Caitlin's bedroom in the Winter Palace and she moved into the connecting room next door where Catherine the Great's lady-in-waiting used to sleep.

Josh slept fitfully, crying out in the night, his bedclothes soaked with sweat, pillows cast across the room. She did her best to console him, holding his head in her lap while the nightmares tormented him.

Doctor Crooke came to examine Josh every morning, bringing one noxious potion after another until he was sure that there was no trace of the parasite.

After a few days, the fever dreams abated and the doctor assured Caitlin that he expected Josh to make a full recovery.

On the fourth day he opened his eyes and smiled.

'Hi,' he croaked.

She stroked his face and kissed it. 'Welcome back stranger.'

'Are you okay?'

Caitlin laughed. 'I am now. You had me worried for a while.'

He pushed himself up onto the pillows. 'And the baby?'

She reached down and lifted a small Moses basket onto the bed. His son was wrapped tightly in soft white blankets. A pair of bright blue eyes staring up at him.

Josh's eyes were full of tears. 'He's so tiny.'

'Actually he's perfect. Any bigger and you can give birth to it.'

'Have you settled on a name yet?'

She shook her head. 'I was waiting for you. Did you want something to honour your father?'

They'd never really talked about his dad. Josh avoided the subject whenever Caitlin brought it up. 'I don't think we'll ever really know what his true name was, but I doubt it was John Dee.'

'What about your middle name?' she asked.

'Nigel is not something I would wish on my worst enemy.'

She giggled. 'Yeah, what was your mother thinking?'

Josh shifted his weight on the bed, grimacing as he tried to get comfortable. The wound on his back was healing quickly thanks to Doctor Crooke, but she could see he was still in a lot of pain.

'I think he should have his own name. Not live in the shadow of his grandfather.'

Caitlin looked down at their son. 'I've been through hundreds while you were lying in that chamber. It's a massive responsibility when you think about it, he's going to have this name for his entire life.'

'What about something like James, or Edward? They were good enough for the Kings of England.'

It was her turn to scowl. 'Jim or Eddy, no it has to be something that doesn't end up getting shortened.'

'You mean like Josh?'

'Or Cat.'

'I thought you like being called Cat.'

'I do, but that's not the point. I don't want our son to be a Jimmy.'

'You're not thinking of anything weird like Erasmus or Balthazar?'

'They're not weird, they just from a different time.'

Josh put his hand on his son's chest, feeling it rise and fall.

'Do you want to hold him.'

He nodded and she lifted the baby out of the basket and placed him in Josh's arms.

'Hey little mouse,' he whispered, touching his cheek.

As he studied the tiny pink face, a drop of blood fell onto the blanket. Josh's nose was bleeding.

'That happened to Lyra too,' Caitlin said, handing Josh a tissue.

'What is it?'

She sighed. 'I didn't want to tell you yet.'

'Did he just read me?' Josh looked surprised.

'Lyra thinks he's a seer, a very powerful one. Which explains the crazy dreams I was having when I was pregnant.'

'That's not bad is it?'

She shrugged, there were tears welling in the corners of her eyes. 'She wants the Grand Seer to check him. It's not the easiest of lives. Look at Lyra, she's tried to kill herself more than once. I don't want him to end up in Bedlam.'

'He won't. I promise.'

.   .   .

Josh slept for the rest of the day.

Caitlin sat and watched him while the baby snuggled against her chest. It was strange to think that less than a week ago she was travelling through the Maelstrom with no idea if she would ever see him again.

The palace was quiet. Snow fell past the window and the fire crackled and fizzed as snowflakes came down the chimney.

A warm feeling of contentment washed over her, as if in that moment, everything in the universe was perfectly aligned. There was nowhere else in time that she wanted to be, nothing she would rather be doing. It was a stillness, a beautiful calm.

Josh snorted loudly and woke himself up.

'Is there anything to eat? I'm starving.'

86

KELLY

[Winter Palace, Saint Petersburg]

The Grand Seer came the next morning with an entourage of black robed nurses.

'This won't take but a moment,' he assured Caitlin, sitting on the side of Josh's bed and taking out a set of tarot cards.

Caitlin gripped his hand tightly as one of the nurses took her baby from the basket. 'He's too young,' she murmured under her breath.

'The gift knows no age,' replied Kelly placing his hand gently on the baby's forehead.

He hummed something gently under his breath as he closed his eyes, the large deck of cards still gripped tightly in one hand.

Her baby wriggled in the nurse's arms and let out a small cry.

Kelly swore under his breath and his eyes snapped open, they were two dark pools. A small rivulet of blood ran from his nose.

'Either I mistake your shape and making quite,

Or else you are that shrewd and knavish sprite

Call'd Robin Goodfellow.'

The shadow passed from his face and he chuckled to himself. 'Little rascal has a powerful redactive ability, nearly forgot why I was here.'

He turned over a series of cards.

'Interesting,' he added, pulling out a small glass orb and squinting at the inverted image of the baby through it.

'What is it?' asked Josh, gripping Caitlin's hand tightly. 'Is something wrong with him.'

'No, he's a very healthy child. His timeline has been altered. There is the merest shadow of another, older soul, intertwined with his.'

'Is that bad?'

'Well, I couldn't rightly say, this being only the second time I've encountered it.'

'Who was the first?'

'You.'

Caitlin looked at Josh and then at her baby. 'You mean he's inherited something?'

The Grand Seer chuckled, slipping the scrying glass back into an inside pocket of his cloak. 'Oh no, this is something else. A valuable gift.'

'You're not making any sense.'

Kelly stood, removed his cap and bowed low. 'I have said too much. Your son is most welcome among the seers. I humbly invite him to join us on his seventh birthday.'

87

LYRA

[Chapter House]

L yra woke beside Benoir.
It was still dark outside and she slipped out of bed, careful not to disturb him.

Her bedroom was painted with the rays of moonlight that shone through the open window. A cool breeze parted the voile curtains and she stepped out onto the balcony.

Breathing in the night air, she watched the bats returning from the hunt. Gliding on silent wings, they formed a dark line across the silvery clouds as they made their way back to their roost. These small moments of normality gave her comfort. Knowing that the natural world continued on regardless of the work of men.

Her dream had left her feeling drained. The image of the circus was so real, so vivid that it was hard to believe there wasn't sawdust on the soles of her feet.

It was not the most complete vision, perhaps that was because of Benoir; she'd never slept so soundly before. Lyra couldn't shake the ominous sense of foreboding, that something bad was going to happen, but she had no idea when or whom it would affect.

'Are you okay?' he said, standing behind her.

'I had another dream.'

He wrapped his arms around her like a bear. 'You're freezing,'

'It helps me come back.' She shivered. 'Reminds me I'm alive.'

He nuzzled the back of her neck. 'I can help with that.'

She pushed back into his body, feel the warmth of him against her back.

'That's not helping. This is important, something bad is going to happen at the circus.'

He stopped kissing her. 'Like what?'

'That's the problem. I don't always get all the information. I saw a harlequin, you know the clowns in the chequered costumes. But he had no face.'

'They usually wear a mask.'

'I know that, silly. I meant beneath the mask.'

'Come back to bed,' he moaned softly into her ear.

She turned around to face him. 'If we're going to spend the rest of our lives together, we need to set some ground rules.'

His eyes widened in surprise. 'Okay.'

She took his hand and led him back inside.

'Rule number one. You are never to wake me when I'm dreaming, even if I call out.'

'Noted.'

She lay on the bed.

'Rule number two.' She pulled him down on top of her. 'Never, ever question what I see, it may not be entirely accurate, but every detail is important. Your job is to keep notes.'

'So now I'm your secretary?'

'Perhaps, if you're good. For now, let's just say you're an intern.'

88

JOSH

[Winter Palace, Saint Petersburg]

It took a few days for Josh to be sure that the memories of the founder were definitely gone. Free of that strange duality which nearly drove him mad, his mind was his own once more.

He told Caitlin about his father over breakfast, carefully skirting around the hundreds of adjustments they made to the timelines and totally left out the Nihil and how she had died.

'I think he sacrificed himself,' he said, staring out of the window at the snow.

'No one has ever managed to assimilate the memories of an entire mind,' she said, brushing a stray hair away from his face. 'No wonder I thought you were losing your marbles.'

'You thought I was going crazy?'

She pouted. 'Can you blame me? You tried to change the course of human evolution!'

He shrugged. 'Seemed like a good idea at the time.'

'You know Konstantine is still calling for you to be thrown back into Bedlam.'

'Probably best they keep thinking that, just until we sort this Aeon business out.'

'And how exactly are you planning to do that?'

Josh wasn't sure. For the first time in a long while, he didn't have the all-knowing voice of the founder in his head telling him what to do.

He picked up a slice of toast and added a generous layer of strawberry jam. 'I suppose we start by tracking down the other infected.'

Caitlin smiled. 'Already done, bar one.'

He looked impressed. 'I should have known you would have thought of that already.'

'They infiltrated the Royal Houses of Europe. Eddington and Sim have located three of them. Rufius persuaded Grandmaster Derado to keep them under surveillance.'

Josh remembered the conversation at the Jelgava palace.

'They're looking for their Queen,' he said, 'they called her the Hegemon.'

The baby stirred and Caitlin picked him up and rocked him gently. 'Rufius found an old hive beneath a palace in Knossos. The one where we found the tablets of Linear A.'

'The one you couldn't decrypt?'

It was Caitlin's turn to be impressed. 'I didn't think you were listening.'

'Did you manage to crack the code?'

She nodded. 'I had a lot of time on my hands while I was in the Maelstrom growing fat with this one.'

'What did it say?'

'It was a warning, something about the Nephilim, offspring of fallen angels.'

Josh looked puzzled. 'Angels?'

'Not men in white, I think they were trying to find terms for something they didn't understand. Religious references fit rather well when you're trying to describe something out of the ordinary.'

'Like temporal beings with glowing armour.'

'Like the Anunnaki,' Caitlin said, touching the ring on her necklace. 'It's a talisman isn't it?'

Josh nodded.

She took it off the chain and put it back on his finger.

'I don't want it,' he said.

'Neither do I. It's too powerful. Better you keep it, at least you know what it's capable of. I nearly ended up in the middle of the last ice age.'

He laughed. 'Yeah, it takes a bit of getting used to.'

'But it's connected to them, isn't it? The Anunnaki.'

He twisted the band around his finger. 'I think it's made from something of theirs, the metal is like nothing on the planet.'

'You've had it tested?'

'Yeah. Twice. No one can tell me what it is.'

She looked into his eyes, as if searching his soul. 'Promise me you'll protect him.'

'I will.'

'No matter what.'

He put his hand on his chest. 'Cross my heart.'

89

RANGER

[Chapter House]

Marcus Makepiece was a maverick. A wanderer who had travelled back further and wider in history than any other member of the Order.

Officially, he was a ranger, sent out to patrol the forgotten paths in search of lost pieces of the past. Off the record, he was notoriously unmanageable; a law unto himself who couldn't take orders and ignored any form of authority.

Her father told Caitlin that Marcus nearly died in an accident during a temporal breach; leaving his body fused with a cryptid, a creature of the Maelstrom. The incident was hushed up and Marcus was handed over to an experimental scientist called Belsarus who kept him like an animal in his own private zoo.

It took Doctor Shika's team five years to separate the chimeric genes of the cryptic and restore Marcus to something approaching normality, but what remained of his original being was still fundamentally chaotic, and once he recovered, Grandmaster Derado assigned him to the Rangers.

Rufius found him in Machu Picchu, studying the Intihuatana stone during the Winter Solstice. It took more than one attempt to persuade him to help them; the ranger eventually agreeing when Rufius mentioned that Caitlin had given birth to a son.

The tall, wiry man stood before them, looking more like a shaman than a member of the Draconians. His skin, darkened by the sun and hundreds of tattoos, was leathery and taut over hard muscles. He wore a patterned shawl, woven with intricate patterns in bright colours. Small metal charms were knotted into his long, unwashed hair and there were bones tied into his straggly beard. Around his neck were necklaces of opalescent shell, gifts from the Inca Emperor Pachacuti.

Caitlin knew that most rangers went native. Spending too long in the distant past, where life was simpler, was a welcome relief from the stresses of the later Industrial Ages and many never returned, preferring to disappear into obscurity.

But Marcus was different. His wanderings were in search of answers.

He wanted to understand where their temporal abilities originated. He was convinced there had been some kind of intervention in human evolution by another race. His research went beyond books and artefacts, exploring the myths and legends of ancient civilisations for clues, trying to piece together the parts of a jigsaw that had been scattered and buried by the sands of time.

'Brother,' he said, embracing Caitlin's father. 'It's been too long.'

'Indeed,' her father replied, patting him hard on the back.

They separated and Marcus took her mother's hand and kissed it lightly. 'Juliana.'

'Marcus, you look well.'

'Do I? I confess I've been avoiding mirrors of late. Too many bad memories.'

He turned to Caitlin, his bright blue eyes burning with an intensity that felt as if he were looking into her soul. 'Well now, KitKat, haven't you grown?'

Caitlin smiled, he'd given her that nickname when she was six.

'I've come to see the child,' he added with a smile, revealing a set of perfect white fangs. There were some things he chose to keep when the Xenos fixed him.

'He's sleeping,' she said, feeling suddenly protective.

Marcus shrugged. 'I can wait.'

He put down the large, club-ended staff and sat down at the table. 'Thomas, do you have any of that stew? I haven't eaten meat in three years and I quite fancy some of your special dumplings.'

Her father was two years younger than his brother, but to look at them now, Caitlin would have put it more like twenty. As her parents busied themselves with the dinner preparation, she watched Marcus closely. He had an aura about him, like a wolf, his eyes constantly in motion, catching every small movement.

'So Uncle, when have you been?' she asked, trying to fill the awkward silence.

He sighed. 'Staring down into the well of time. I was in Machu Picchu studying with the Inca when Westinghouse found me. Before that I rode with the Scythians from the Carpathian Mountains to the Ordos Plateau in search of an Enarei, a hermaphrodite shaman. But you didn't summon me to listen to my adventures did you?'

Caitlin shook her head and opened her almanac.

'Have you ever seen symbols like these?'

Marcus leaned forward and took the book from her. His eyes narrowing as he studied the ancient symbols of Linear A.

'Where did you find this?'

'In Crete, it was found by an archaeologist in 1900. We estimate it's over two thousand years old,' she added, not wanting to give too much away.

He shook his head. 'No, these are much older, they're the names of ancient gods — or demons depending on your point of view.'

'Like Nephilim? I found a cabbalic text that named them.'

Marcus closed the almanac. 'Nephilim, Anunnaki, Tuath Dé, they have had many names. Most older than the age of man. I've been chasing them for most of my life, they're nothing more than myth as far back as I have travelled, and I have travelled far.'

'I have seen them,' said Caitlin.

Her mother began to lay the table.

Marcus leaned forward and tore a chunk of bread from the loaf.

'Have you indeed? And did they look like fallen angels?'

'They were wearing some kind of charged armour, they were surrounded by shimmering fields of energy.'

He chuckled. 'What is it that someone said once? Any sufficiently advanced technology is indistinguishable from magic. From what I have discovered this group have appeared in the creation myths of hundreds of different cultures, from India to Ireland.'

'Who are they?'

Marcus leaned back in his chair, chewing while speaking through a mouthful of bread. 'No idea, ancient astronauts, beings from another time? Whatever they are, I found no physical traces of them. They became nothing but stories told around fires on dark nights, or cave art.'

Her father brought a large steaming bowl of stew from the kitchen and placed it in the centre of the table.

'Enough talk,' her mother said, ladling the stew into dishes. 'Time to eat.'

'They killed everyone,' Caitlin added bitterly. 'And took the Aeon.'

'Westinghouse told me about the parasite,' said Marcus, spooning an extra dumpling into his bowl. 'Said you need me to track one of them down.'

'His name is Bouchard and we think he's trying to reach their queen.'

'And you know where this queen is?'

'No, but he used a vestige from Knossos to escape.'

'He's a traveller?'

'Rufius thinks so. He was stealing gold for Napoleon when he discovered the abandoned hive.'

Marcus blew on the steaming stew, wafting the aroma towards his nose.

'Your mother's right, let's eat and then we can discuss how we find this Bouchard.'

. . .

Caitlin wasn't hungry, she left her parents and uncle to reminisce while she went to check on Josh and feed her baby.

Josh was dozing, propped up in the bed. She picked up the baby and lay down beside him.

90

HARVESTING

[Xenobiology laboratory, Hazardous Containment]

X-541 pressed his palm to the scanner and let the laser scan his retina.

'Good morning Doctor Shika,' the electronic voice chimed as the heavy steel door to the containment chamber slid open.

Ignoring the various warnings that were registering on his internal monitors, he walked into the freezing air of the chamber. It would only be a matter of minutes before his organic subsystems would start to fail.

The symbiote floated in a glass tube in the centre of the room. It was the most valuable specimen in the continuum.

Peeling back the skin on his forearm, an interface probe uncoiled like a metal snake and configured its head to connect with the port on the side of the computer terminal.

His mind entered the system, disabling the security systems in a nanosecond. The machine's memory architecture was archaic, no match for his quantum neural network.

It took less than a second to scan all of the files stored on the magnetic discs.

They had learned nothing of the symbiote's true nature, only seeing it as a threat, classifying it as a parasite — calling it: Aeon.

Higher functioning subroutines registered that there were thousands of other species within the database, an impressive bestiary of non-linear creatures from a realm called the Maelstrom. He stored the catalogue in his secondary memory substrate and tagged it for future processing.

Retracting the probe, X-541 went over to the symbiote. Twelve seconds had passed since entering the room. Somewhere in another part of the building, a security technician would register that. It would not matter, in forty-five seconds the virus that he deployed into the central processing unit would overcome all of the network devices in the building, the entire system would go offline. Containment fields would fail, releasing some of the deadliest species that ever existed.

Gas vented in jets as the glass walls of the tank retracted around the specimen. X-541 lifted the symbiote free of the holding clamps, cautious not to touch the fine filaments along its tentacles — even this body could be paralysed by its neurotoxins.

A metal needle extended from the end of his index finger and he carefully inserted it into the gap between the thorax and the head parts of the parasite. The organic interface into the creature's brain was located behind the armoured skull plate and gently manipulated the needle into position.

Thousands of years of data began streaming into his primary storage buffer; the memories and experiences of every host the creature had ever infected: Kings, Princes, Lords and Generals, a history of the rich and powerful — and more importantly the life of the infinite one.

The organic interface was excruciatingly slow compared to his own mental processes. It took almost an entire minute to download the data.

As the transfer came to an end he noticed that the final engrams were incomplete. The signature of the information was damaged, potentially by the crude extraction that the woman had performed. X-541 reviewed the structure of the data, realising that there was a missing piece and that the pattern of the last host was incomplete.

Some part of the one known as the founder had been left behind.

91

LEAVING

[Chapter House]

M arcus and her father were preparing to leave when Caitlin returned.

Her mother appeared from the pantry, wearing the travelling fatigues of the Nautonniers.

Caitlin could see from the expression on her face that there would be no changing her mind.

'We're going to take the *Nautilus* to the Minoan, just to make an initial reconnaissance sweep,' her father said, unrolling a temporal map across the kitchen table.

Marcus looked different, his hair was cropped short and the beard was gone. He also smelled a whole lot better. 'I think we should start here,' he said, tapping on a distant point on the timeline. 'If your man used something from the temple at Knossos.'

'I'm coming with you,' insisted Caitlin.

Her mother frowned. 'No, you're not, you have other responsibilities now.'

'We're just going to drop Uncle Marcus off and come

straight back,' her father assured her. 'Strictly a deployment mission.'

Rufius walked into the room, wearing the uniform of a Prussian officer.

'Are you going too?' exclaimed Caitlin.

He looked confused. 'Going where? I've just got back.' He sat down heavily and helped himself to some of the stew.

'When have you been?'

'Had some unfinished business with the Prussians at Waterloo. Couldn't leave Wellington with a weak left flank.' Rufius rubbed his face, he looked exhausted. 'Has Joshua made any improvement?'

'He's awake.'

The watchman's eyes lit up. 'And is he all there?' he said, tapping his temple with his finger.

Caitlin nodded. 'Back to his old self.'

'Good, good.' Then looking at Caitlin's parents. 'So where the hell are you lot going?'

'Knossos,' Caitlin's father said, rolling up the map. 'Dropping Marcus off at the last known location.'

Rufius pushed himself up from the table. 'There's something down there.'

'A Minotaur?' asked Marcus, baring his teeth once more.

'I've no idea, something was still alive. I was too busy saving men's lives to hang around to find out.'

Caitlin could feel the tension rising between the two men and tried to change the subject. 'But what about Konstantine's cordon?'

Her mother snorted. 'The *Nautilus* can breach it. I can land her within a millisecond and be out again before it registers on any of the Antiquarian monitoring stations.'

Rufius folded his arms. 'There's something about that

man, he's blocked my attempts to get onto that site on more than one occasion.'

'I've heard he's shut down the Infinity Engine research,' added Caitlin's father. 'Eddington is furious.'

'To the matter at hand,' interrupted Caitlin's mother. 'Marcus will pick up the search from Knossos. We will shadow him as he follows the trail.'

'I'm coming,' announced Rufius, unbuttoning his tunic. 'Don't suppose you have anything like that in a large?' He pointed towards Marcus's leather coat.

92

NAMING

[Chapter House]

J osh was on his feet when she returned, holding his son and staring out of the window. The baby seemed to give Josh a stillness that Caitlin had never seen before. It was as though he took away all of his pain, made him realise that there were still good things in the world, giving him something to hope for.

'They've gone?' he asked as she entered.

'Yes, Marcus is going to track Bouchard on foot.'

'I should have gone with them.'

'You're not strong enough, and my parents wouldn't take me either. Apparently we have more important things to do.' She stroked their son's head. 'Like coming up with a name.'

'Yeah, I was thinking about that. What about William?'

'Bill!' she exclaimed. 'Or worse still Billy! Are you mad?'

Josh looked taken aback by her outburst. 'Okay. I had another idea, but I'm not sure you're going to like it.'

Caitlin looked confused.

There was a light knock at the door, it was Lyra with Benoir in tow.

'Hi,' she said, peeking sheepishly around the tall door.

'Come in Lyra,' said Josh, handing the baby to Caitlin, who frowned slightly. She hadn't seen Lyra since the incident at dinner and was still not sure if she'd forgiven her for telling the Grand Seer.

Lyra came straight over to her and kissed her. 'I'm sorry,' she said, 'it was a shock for me too. I hope you don't hate me for it.'

Her honesty was so intense that any bad feelings that Caitlin was harbouring simply melted away.

'No,' she replied. 'You did the right thing. It was just, I don't know. Hard to imagine, but it kind of makes sense now.'

They sat beside the fire. The palace was not the easiest place to heat and Lyra knelt on the fur rug with Caitlin, playing with the baby, while Josh and Benoir took the rather stately chairs.

'We wanted your help,' began Josh, 'with the name.'

Caitlin looked up, but he continued before she had time to protest. 'We can't agree, and it's driving us crazy. So, I wondered if maybe, you could just look ahead a little and see what we finally came up with?'

Lyra's expression grew serious. 'You want me to read his timeline just to find out what you're going to call him?'

'Basically, yes.'

'No,' said Caitlin.

Lyra looked to her step-sister. 'You didn't know he was going to ask?'

Caitlin glared at Josh. 'Maybe he's not completely back to his old self after all.'

'We don't generally read children, and especially not

babies,' Lyra said, sitting back on her heels. 'Their lives are so unformed, so fluid, that our intervention can have dire consequences.'

'But you read him at dinner, Caitlin told me, that's how we discovered he's a seer.'

'No, I did not. HE read ME!' Lyra insisted. 'There's a difference.'

'Sorry. I thought — '

'Well don't!' Lyra snapped. 'I feel bad enough that I had to be the one to tell you. I know how hard it is to be one, let alone raise a seer.'

Benoir put a gentle hand on her shoulder and Lyra immediately relaxed.

'Sorry,' she whispered. 'I should also mention that most seers already know their names. It's an unfortunate consequence of the gift. If he could speak you could ask him.'

'Will you ask him?' Caitlin said softly, taking Lyra's hand.

Her step-sister smiled. 'Of course, silly.'

Everyone was quiet while Lyra took the baby in her arms and stroked its head. She made small cooing noises and the baby's fingers tangled in her hair.

'Hello Zachary.'

Josh smiled. 'Zachary Jones. I like it. Sounds like a space pirate.'

Caitlin nodded too. 'I wouldn't have chosen it, but it's not terrible.'

'Zack,' said Josh.

'Zachary,' insisted Caitlin.

'We'll see.'

'There's something else,' added Lyra. 'He has memories, I thought at first they were yours,' she said, looking at

Josh. 'But they're older, from a man called the — the founder?'

'What?' said Josh, sitting forward in his chair. 'How?'

Caitlin's face flushed and she turned to Josh, her eyes blazing. 'You said he'd gone.'

'I thought he'd died. After the Aeon, there was hardly anything left.'

Lyra chuckled, rubbing noses with the baby. 'He says he took them from you. That you were in pain. It's okay, they seem to be getting on rather well.'

'Can't we get him out?' asked Josh.

Zachary began to cry and Lyra held him close, whispering: 'I don't think that's a good idea. He seems very content. This founder's memories are helping him to understand who he is, to come to terms with his abilities — I would leave it be.'

Caitlin was close to tears. Josh looked from one to the other trying to work out what to do. He felt the ring of Solomon on his finger. The metal warm on his skin, the urge to reset the timeline was tempting, but he remembered his promise to Caitlin. Even though he'd lost his mother, the baby had given him something new, something he never thought he would ever feel, a sense of completeness.

'What did Kelly say?' asked Lyra, handing Zachary back to Caitlin.

'He said it was a valuable gift.'

93

KNOSSOS

[Knossos. Crete. Date: 1100 BC]

The conning tower rose out of the stone floor, shaking loose slabs that were laid down over a thousand years before.

Marcus and Rufius stepped out through the hatch, each shouldering a different kind of weapon. While the ranger favoured a blade, the watchman carried a gun-sabre, the preferred heavy assault weapon of the Dreadnoughts. He had to admit that one of the benefits of travelling through the Maelstrom on the *Nautilus* was that temporal limitations regarding technology didn't apply.

The Antiquarian monitoring stations were posted at regular intervals along the palace's timeline on high alert for any disturbances in the continuum. If Juliana's calculations were correct they would have approximately thirty minutes before the closest one would be alerted to their presence.

. . .

The two men watched the stones carefully reverse back into place as the tower of the *Nautilus* disappeared beneath the floor.

'Interesting way to travel,' said Marcus, lighting a torch with a flint and squatting down beside the broken clay tablets.

Rufius grunted. 'Beats trying to find something to weave with.'

'Oh, there are ways,' said Marcus, brushing the dust from the indentations. 'Something has changed here recently,' he added, tapping on one of the symbols. This text is not quite the same one that Caitlin showed me. It's been altered.'

'This is where I found Champollion, the translator.'

Marcus sniffed the air like a wolf, his eyes narrowing as he caught a scent of the past.

'Bouchard was here,' he said, placing his feet in a series of dusty footprints. 'And he went this way.'

They moved off into the dark retracing the path of the Frenchman.

'Lead the way old man,' said Rufius.

'Less of the old man,' Marcus muttered.

Rufius followed the ranger through the corridors of mummified remains. Wrapped tightly in papery bundles so fragile that one touch would turn them to a cloud of dust.

'They've been storing their dead down here for hundreds of generations,' said Marcus, pausing next to one body and wiping the dust from the inscription above it. 'This is King Asterion, last of his line.'

'We're close,' noted the colonel, looking ahead to where

the tunnel widened. 'There are more ahead, but they're cocooned, like moths.'

Entering the chamber, Rufius smelled the familiar acrid taint in the air. A musty scent, like the inside of a termite mound.

Marcus moved stealthily from one alcove to another, each body now wrapped in a silk-like cocoon, nothing like the mummified remains they'd seen earlier.

Rufius heard the skittering of claws once more and turned to see a tide of large rats pour out of one of the side tunnels.

Handing him his torch, the ranger picked up two of the nearest corpses and threw them into the path of the rats. Realising what he was attempting to do, Rufius lit each one in turn. The binding caught easily and their desiccated bodies burst into flaming torches. Marcus threw more onto the pyre.

'We need to find where he left,' shouted Rufius over the roar of the fire.

Marcus pointed to a sarcophagus in the centre of the chamber. 'There. The tomb of Minos himself.'

The rats, repelled by the fire, turned their attention to the mouldering corpses on the far side of the temple, giving the two men a brief moment to make for the ornately carved stone coffin.

The fire spread from corpse to corpse, filling the chamber with thick, acrid smoke that tasted of charred bone.

'I'm definitely too old for this shit,' wheezed Rufius as they ran.

'Now who's the old man?' asked Marcus, leaping over a fallen statue.

They reached the sarcophagus and jumped inside, pulling the lid over them.

Rufius took out his tachyon and switched on the torch.

'So, where now?'

Marcus's eyes were black, his face twisted into a demonic expression, suddenly looking more Maelstrom than human.

'I'm looking,' he whispered, fingers moving through the air.

The bones of the previous occupant cracked beneath him as Rufius tried to get more comfortable.

'Maybe we should hail the Nautilus.'

Marcus held up one finger to silence him and picked up the skeletal hand of the King.

'Uruk,' he said, taking a ring from its bony finger and placing it on his own. 'Sumer. Around two and a half thousand back from here.'

With that Marcus disappeared.

The heat inside the sarcophagus was rising and Rufius could feel the sweat running down his neck.

'Enough of this.'

He pressed a button on his tachyon. 'Juliana, are you receiving me?'

Nothing came out of the tiny speaker but static.

'Never should have got rid of the Mark IV,' he said as the Mark VI fell to pieces and he took out a battered older model.

94

NAUTILUS

[Nautilus]

'Damned fool,' grumbled Rufius, holding up a small hand mirror and trimming the singed hair from his beard.

'So he just left you?' asked Juliana.

Rufius nodded. 'Said something about Uruk and jumped back two thousand years. Left me in the middle of an inferno.'

'Uruk,' repeated Caitlin's father, walking over to a small collection of books.

'That's typical of your brother,' said Juliana, scowling at her husband, 'never did play well with others.'

Thomas ignored his wife, pulling various leather bound tomes off the shelf until he found the one he was looking for.

'The man's not right in the head, not since the accident,' Rufius agreed. 'Got some kind of death wish. Nearly set the whole damn place on fire. Hardly what you'd call a stealth mission.'

'Uruk's in Sumer,' said Thomas, consulting *Kennett's Guide to Mesopotamia*. 'East of the Euphrates, rose to prominence in around three thousand BC.'

Rufius put down the scissors and the hand mirror. 'Yes, I know. Home to the legendary king, Gilgamesh and apparently the Queen of the Aeons.'

A light began to flash on one of the bulkheads and Juliana checked the paper tape streaming from one of the brass slots.

'It's from Sim. Konstantine's monitoring stations have responded. He's mobilised the Dreadnoughts, they're ordering us to return immediately.'

'Is there any way to contact Marcus?'

Thomas shrugged. 'He's not a great one for almanacs or tachyons.'

'Neither am I after that last incident. The Mark VI literally fell apart in my hands. Lucky I always carry my trusty old Mark IV.' He fished the components out of his pocket and dropped them onto the table.

Juliana picked the internal gearing up and examined it.

'This didn't fall apart,' she said, turning the brass mechanism over to show Rufius the scorching. 'This is a gunpowder burn.'

Rufius took the part and sniffed it. 'It blew up?'

She nodded. 'Just enough charge to render it useless.'

'Someone wanted to strand you there,' added Thomas.

Rufius slammed his hand down on the table. 'Konstantine.'

'Caitlin said the same thing happened to her, when they were trying to escape from Babylon.'

Another message issued from the slot, this time it was from Caitlin.

DON'T COME HOME. MEET AT THE CIRCUS.

95

MEETING

[Exposition Universelle, Paris. Date: 1889]

Lyra, Caitlin, Josh and the baby were waiting by Cuvier's caravan when the Nautilus surfaced through the floor of the main ring.

Benoir had taken the sabre-tooth cats back to their own time for safety. Uncle George reluctantly agreed that all the animals should return to their own eras. He was busy overseeing the handlers as they moved the lumbering beasts out of their cages in a kind of organised chaos.

'What's happened?' asked Caitlin's mother, stepping down from the hatch, followed by Rufius and her husband.

'There's been some kind of major malfunction with the tachyons. They're all broken, people are trapped all over the continuum,' explained Caitlin. 'Grandmaster Konstantine is petitioning the High Council to commandeer the *Nautilus* to assist in the rescue mission.'

'Emperor Konstantine,' said Rufius under his breath.

Lyra opened her watch, the mechanism fell out onto the floor. 'Every Mark VI in the Order has failed.'

'They didn't fail, they self-destructed,' said Rufius.

'How?' asked Caitlin.

'We found evidence of a small explosive charge behind the temporal correction mechanism.' Her mother took the casing from her daughter. 'This residue is gunpowder,' she added, scratching the dark scorching on the inside.

'You're saying that the Antiquarians built them with a self-destruct mechanism?'

'A remote destruct mechanism,' corrected Rufius. 'Which seems to have gone off exactly when we were close to finding the Aeon base.'

'You think Konstantine's infected?' asked Josh.

Rufius nodded. 'Makes sense to me. He's blocked every investigation I've tried to make into the site at Knossos. Requisitioned any artefact related to the Aeons. To be honest, I'm surprised he let the Xenos keep the specimen they pulled out of Josh.'

Caitlin's expression darkened. 'It's been stolen.'

'What?'

'Someone managed to break into the Xeno's secure unit and steal the specimen. Their entire system is down, including the one managing the containment fields, every creature they've captured was released.'

'This is serious,' said Caitlin's father turning towards the *Nautilus*. 'We should start emptying the forward compartments, make more room.'

Her mother nodded and followed him back to their ship.

Rufius scratched his beard, his fingers still finding singed ends. 'Where are the Draconians?'

'Most of them are stuck in their garrisons,' said Sim, stepping out of Cuvier's caravan with a large tray of tea cups.

'And the Dreadnoughts?'

'Dealing with a breach in 1526.'

Rufius picked up a delicate china cup and a handful of chocolate bourbons. 'Looks like we're on our own. I suggest everyone get some rest and food. We're in for one hell of a night.'

'So what's the plan?' said Josh, sitting down opposite the colonel and Cuvier who were mulling over a map and smoking a Turkish hookah.

Caitlin was changing Zachary and the others were helping empty the inside of the Nautilus, which seemed to include a wide array of the most random objects Josh had ever seen.

Rufius blew out the smoke from the pipe and handed it to Georges.

'We've boiled it down to two options,' he began. 'I'm favouring the one where we storm the Antiquarian HQ and chop the emperor's fat head off. Whereas Georges here thinks we should find Derado and rescue the Dreadnoughts, let them sort it out.'

'They're better equipped for this sort of thing,' explained Cuvier through a mouthful of smoke.

Josh felt the weight of Solomon's ring on his finger. 'I may have a third way.'

'By all means,' said the colonel waving his hand. 'Give us the benefit of your years of experience.'

Ignoring the remark, Josh continued. 'Marcus is already in Uruk. Which means he found Bouchard and —'

'Failed to change the outcome,' Rufius finished his sentence.

'And I might be able to reach him.'

'Assuming he stayed around long enough. You can't trust

399

rangers you know, especially ones that have been touched by the Maelstrom.'

'We might be the only ones who can stop this.'

'How exactly? Assuming of course that you could persuade Juliana to postpone her mission of mercy and drop us off in Sumer.'

Josh held up his ring hand. 'Because I still have this. It's a talisman and I've experienced their timeline up close. I know how to reach them, I can get us to the Queen.'

'And then what?'

'Well, that's where your years of experience kick in.'

96

GOODBYES

[Exposition Universelle, Paris. Date: 1889]

Caitlin was feeding the baby when Josh climbed into the caravan.

'Hey,' she whispered.

Josh smiled, there were a million things he needed to say to her and no time to do it.

'I've got to go,' he said, sitting down beside her. 'I have to try and fix this.'

She took his hand in hers. 'I know. You wouldn't be you if you didn't.'

They'd nearly had this conversation a hundred times in as many lives. He always avoided it, knowing that the revelation might end any chances of happiness.

'This is not the only life we've had,' he began.

'I know,' she said, 'Zachary showed me when I was pregnant. It took me a while to work it out, but those dreams, they were like other versions of my life. The only constant in them was you. It didn't make any sense until they told me he was a seer. Alixia said she had similar experiences when she was carrying Lyra.'

Josh felt the emotions swelling up like a wave. 'I've tried to make the best life for us, to put it back the way it was, but somehow it always went wrong. Somebody died, or never existed. There were too many variables. I couldn't save everybody.'

'That's not up to you. You just need to live the best life you can. Look what we made,' she looked down at the now sleeping baby. 'You've spent too long in the past, you've forgotten to think about what the future could be. Zachary changed that. I've seen how you are with him. It's like he calms the storm in you. I've never seen you so relaxed as when you're holding him.'

'Mum told me that my life would change when I had a child. I thought she meant for the worse, nappies and sleepless nights, but it's not that at all.'

Caitlin laughed. 'Speaking as someone who's had to deal with most of that so far I'd be careful what you say next!'

Josh took the baby from her and looked into his face. 'He's like an anchor, holding me to one place. I've spent so long wandering through time that I'd lost my bearings. I nearly lost you. He's like a vestige of us, through him I can always find home, always find you.'

There were tears in her eyes now.

'So, now I have to fix this final thing, and then we can get on with living.'

She leaned forward and kissed him. 'Right answer.'

97

QUEEN

Marcus's body was trapped inside a half-finished cocoon. His eyes were glazed, staring off into the distance just like Shags after he smoked too much weed.

Checking his neck, Josh's fingers found a weak pulse. There was a wound below his ear where he assumed the parasite had entered.

Beside Marcus, sealed inside another alcove was Bouchard. His chest had been ripped open, the ribcage spread apart like butterfly wings. Whoever removed his parasite hadn't been as delicate as Caitlin, or cared very little about the host.

He was somewhere deep within a ziggurat. Above him, millions of fine threads interlaced to create a silky canopy strung across the stepped inner walls. Suspended within the web, Josh could make out the ridged shell of an enormous keratin coffin and surrounding it were hundreds of smaller objects, the husks of long dead corpses.

'Incoming,' hissed Marcus.

Something moved out of the corner of Josh's eye. Turning towards it, he saw the creatures coming down the walls.

'Get out of here,' said Marcus, straining against the bindings.

'No,' Josh shook his head and began to cut the cocoon with his dagger.

'Step back,' Marcus warned him, the bones of his jaw beginning to lengthen. 'I don't want to hurt you.'

Josh did as he was told, unsure of what the man was becoming. His body was changing, muscle and bone fusing into something nightmarishly familiar.

With a roar he broke free of the fraying bonds and shook off the last of the web. He stood nearly ten feet tall, a mass of chaotic energy made flesh. His skull distorted, becoming more like that of a wolf, and his skin hardened until it looked more like armour. There was a hint in his dark eyes of familiarity, he nodded to Josh and ran towards the tide of skittering creatures, ripping them apart with long talons and sharp teeth.

The parasite that infected Marcus lay squirming on the floor, and Josh ground it into the stone with the heel of his boot.

Sheathing his sword, he took out the beacon. It was a simple temporal transmitter, something that Caitlin's mother had cobbled together from the spare parts of one of the broken tachyons. Josh looked up to the chrysalis and pressed the button.

If everything went to plan they should be here in seconds — one of the benefits of a temporal rescue team.

Before he made it half way across the chamber, something dropped from the webbing above him. Josh drew his sword and instinctively assumed a low fighting stance, grateful for the combat memories the founder had gifted him over the last few years.

The glow of the armour was similar to the Anunnaki in Babylon. It crouched as if ready to spring, gripping a deadly curved blade in each of its gauntlets.

Josh tensed, confused as to where it had come from. Looking up, he saw the rent in the fabric of the web above him and the long cut along the underside of the chrysalis.

As the shimmering warrior prepared to strike, the conning tower of the Nautilus erupted through the stone floor between them. Its temporal fields knocking them both to the ground.

When Josh got to his feet the Anunnaki was gone.

Dreadnoughts poured out of the hatch, each wearing full battle armour and carrying heavy-calibre gun-sabres. They moved into a defensive position, forming a square around Josh and opened fire on the creatures that descended, lighting up the darker reaches of the webbing and revealing a horde of insect-like terrors moving towards them en-masse.

Bodies piled up around the Dreadnoughts who made every shot count as they fought to keep the onslaught back.

Josh watched as a second wave moved through the thick strands that were still holding the giant chrysalis in place. At first he thought they were going to join the attack, but soon realised they were using their mandibles to widen the rent that the Anunnaki had made in the carapace.

They were freeing their queen.

. . .

'Sorry we're late,' said the colonel with his usual understated sense of humour. 'Took Cuvier's advice and got some reinforcements.'

'We'll be running low on ammunition soon,' the Dreadnought Commander observed. 'We're going to need to retreat in good order.'

The colonel pulled the clip out of his own rifle and checked the magazine. His expression was one that Josh had seen a thousand times before, it was a sign that the situation was getting desperate.

The blind, spider-like creatures sensed the change in the Dreadnought formation and increased their attack. The colonel's weapon ran out of bullets and he threw it aside. From inside his coat he pulled a Scottish Claymore, skewering the terrible jaws of a leaping beast before it could reach him.

They were a strange hybrid of ant, spider and beetle. Covered in a hard spiny carapace, with large vicious mandibles and sharp spiny legs. Nothing like the parasites, these were obviously soldiers bred to defend the nest.

Marcus appeared from the shadows, tearing through the creatures like a fox through a chicken coop. He took the Dreadnoughts completely by surprise, who were unsure whether to shoot him or protect him.

'That makes sense,' said the colonel, watching Marcus.

'They're trying to release the queen,' shouted Josh, pointing towards the chrysalis.

'Fall back and switch to incendiaries,' Rufius ordered the Commander. 'Light it up.'

. . .

The first of the fire bombs exploded overhead and the detonation sent the soldier drones into a frenzy. The dry webbing caught quickly, fiery lines of orange threaded through the nest like fuse wires igniting pockets of dead material as they went.

The Dreadnoughts focused the next round on the ground, creating a firewall between them and the things that were falling from the ceiling.

Josh could feel the heat rising as strands of burning web floated down onto them. The supporting threads gave way, unable to hold the weight of the chrysalis and it tilted, slipping from its bonds, and fell towards the ground.

Sensing the threat to their queen, the drone soldiers retreated back from the wall of fire, gathering around the hard shell of the coffin, which had cracked along its entire length.

'We're running out of options,' said the Commander while his men regrouped.

They looked exhausted, the heat and the relentless attacks had taken their toll. Everyone kept one watchful eye on the chrysalis as they checked and reloaded their weapons, wondering if whatever came out of it would be worse than the things they'd already faced.

'We need to contain it before they release whatever it is in there,' the colonel voiced what everyone else was thinking.

Josh saw one of the cocoons twitch in the alcoves behind them.

'I think the others are waking,' he said, going over to the nearest body.

The colonel opened the bindings with one stroke of his sword.

Inside was the emaciated corpse of a man; an old priest, still wearing the chains of high office, his skin taught and blackened with age. His body was nothing more than a bone sack, but something lived within it. A shape moving under the skin. They watched while it snaked over his chest and into his neck.

His jaw seemed to slacken, the sides of his mouth cracking and peeling apart like the petals of a flower as the creature burst from his throat.

Josh saw multiple rows of sharp teeth just before the colonel brought the sword down on the man's head, slicing cleanly through it, and the body of the parasitic creature fell to the floor in two neat longitudinal halves.

The other corpses were waking.

'We need a new plan,' said Josh, turning back to the others.

'You sure do,' said Doctor Shika, appearing beside him.

She wore a kind of ghostly armour and was carrying the most lethal looking sword he'd ever seen.

'Where's Marcus?' she asked.

The re-animated corpses were no match for the pair of them. Marcus and Kaori were like berserkers, slicing through the zombies as if they were rag dolls.

Josh watched in awe as the Xeno doctor's armour seemed to take on a life of its own, as though she had harnessed the power of one of her non-corporeal monsters and wore it like a suit.

Marcus was far more visceral, his entire being was chan-nelling the destructive power of the Maelstrom.

The Dreadnoughts left the two changelings to it and went to inspect the chrysalis.

Cracks ran along the length of the thirty-foot pod, and a sticky, viscous liquid was leaking out over the floor.

Josh examined the outer shell, careful not to tread in the spreading pool.

'It's a pupa,' said the colonel, tapping on the exterior with the end of his sword. 'Like a moth. Whatever made this has gone through some kind of metamorphosis.'

Holding torches close to the hardened shell, they could see that the material was semi-opaque and inside the amber case something shifted and the cracks extended further along its carapace.

'We need to secure this now!' shouted the colonel, waving to the rest of the squad.

But it was too late, as they watched, the carapace split, its segmented sections falling away as the legs of the creature within flexed.

'Fall back!' shouted the Commander.

The chrysalis exploded.

Josh and the Colonel were thrown sideways by the force of the blast.

Standing amongst the debris covered in slime and internal organs was Caitlin, wearing temporal armour and carrying the largest gun-sabre Josh had ever seen.

'I knew you'd mess it up,' she said, wiping something green out of her eye.

'How?' he stuttered.

'Zachary showed me.'

98

ORDER

Grandmaster Konstantine had disappeared.

The High Council voted unanimously for Georges Cuvier to take his place and the tachyon Mark VI was removed from service, replaced by the modified version that no longer carried the self-destruct mechanism.

The *Nautilus* was commandeered by the Draconians and spent the next few weeks distributing supplies and replacement tachyons to those who were still stranded in time.

The Xenobiology department tracked down most of their missing specimens, although it was rumoured that some had escaped into the wild. There were a number of incidents in which members of the public had reported seeing a ghostly shark in various parts of Regent's Park.

Marcus came to the Chapter House to say goodbye. His body had returned to normal, but Josh couldn't quite look at the man the same way, especially when he was holding his son.

The colonel made several more trips into the Napoleonic before Professor Eddington was completely satisfied that the outcome was optimal. Waterloo was seen as the final defeat for Napoleon who, after a hundred days, abdicated in June and was eventually imprisoned on St Helena. Louis XVIII was returned to the throne once Doctor Shika had successfully removed the Aeon.

An investigation into how the Aeons had managed to infiltrate the Order concluded that all members in senior positions would have to be regularly tested for physical and mental fitness, a procedure that Professor Eddington took an extreme dislike to and it was rumoured that he had struck one of the doctors during his examination.

Caitlin resumed her role as head of the Great Library while Josh took care of Zach, life for the most part returning to some kind of normal.

Lyra and Benoir got married. It was a grand affair, Benoir, as it turned out, was distantly related to Grandmaster Denon who insisted they have the ceremony at Notre Dame. The cathedral was filled with flowers and the bride entered on the back of a giant woolly mammoth.

99

JOSH AND CAITLIN

[Exposition Universelle, Paris. Date: 1889]

It was a month after the wedding before they heard from
Lyra. Everyone assumed she and Benoir were doing
what all newlyweds do, taking a prolonged honeymoon
through the Mesolithic and early Cretaceous.

The invitations were for front row seats at the grand re-
opening of the *Cirque d'Histoire.*

Benoir stood in the centre of the three rings, dressed in the
formal red coat of the ringmaster.

The colonel sat next to Caitlin, holding the baby, who
loved his bushy red beard and pulled at it with no mercy.
Josh came back with popcorn and took the seat beside her,
nodding to Sim and the rest of the De Freis family who had
taken the rest of the row.

The tent was a vast canopied space which could have
comfortably housed half of the guild, and as it neared the
time, the stacked rows began to fill up quickly. Men and

women in all manner of dress appeared from thin air, thanks to an ingenious piece of ticketing by Uncle Georges that could put them directly into their seats.

The band started to play *La Marseillaise,* and a procession of ancient beasts appeared through a curtain draped at one end of the tent. There were mammoths and mastodons, sabre-tooth cats and giant flightless birds. At the head of the caravan of megalithic monsters was Lyra, wearing a shimmering silver dress and a plume of white ostrich feathers.

The audience rose to their feet as one, applauding the magnificent beasts as they paraded around the outer ring of the circus.

She looked magnificent and happy and Caitlin felt tears streaking down her face as she clapped and cheered with the others.

The audience settled down to watch the show, which began with Benoir and his incredibly fierce looking cats.

At the end of the first act, Caitlin noticed that Josh was distracted by something in the crowd. She followed his gaze, finding one of the harlequin costumed clowns walking between the stepped benches towards the ring.

He was a tall, dark-headed man, smiling and handing out small candies to the crowd. She had never seen him before, but Josh seemed to be disturbed by him.

'Are you okay?' she whispered in his ear.

His expression was dark, she could feel the muscles tensing in his legs as he went to get up. 'Stay here.'

Watching him disappear into the mass of amazed faces she felt a sudden pang of anguish and turned to find Zachary staring at her with an intensity that looked strange on such a young face.

'I need to check on Josh,' she said to Rufius getting out of her seat.

Josh moved through the crowds that were milling around trying to buy toffee apples and bags of spiced fruits from the candy-striped confectioners. He kept his eye on the harlequin costume, which seemed to glide between the jostling people with ease, his colours blending with the gaudy dress robes of the Order.

He kept telling himself that he'd been mistaken, that his eyes were playing tricks on him. That he hadn't just seen Dalton Eckhart handing candy to kids.

The harlequin turned, catching the rays of a stray spotlight and there he was, just as Josh remembered him in Highgate Cemetery, before he became consumed by ambition and power. He waved at Josh and then disappeared into the masses.

Benoir was back in the centre of the ring, calling for everyone to return to their seats.

'Hey,' said Caitlin from behind him. 'You okay?'

Josh turned and smiled. 'Fine. Just thought I saw a ghost.'

'Really, who?'

'No one special. Do you want some more popcorn?' he said, pointing to a seller who was counting the change out on his tray.

She nodded and they took the last two cones.

When they go back to their seats, Rufius was looking at them strangely.

'Where's Zack?' asked Caitlin, looking along the row.

'You took him to the bathroom,' said Rufius, his confusion increasing.

'No, I didn't. I've been with Josh.'

The old man got to his feet. 'No, I gave him to you.'

Caitlin dropped the popcorn and looked around the stand.

'Where is he?' she shouted over the roar of the crowd as the next act came on stage.

To be continued...

TESSERACT

The story continues in Tesseract...

Other books in the Infinity Engines universe.

The Infinity Engines

1. Anachronist

2. Maelstrom

3. Eschaton

4. Aeons

5. Tesseract

Infinity Engines Origins

Chimæra

Changeling

Infinity Engines Missions

1776

1888

You can download 1776 for FREE plus get updates and news by subscribing to my mailing list (simply scan the QR code below).

ACKNOWLEDGEMENTS

Thanks to Karen for the late nights and the grumpy conversations about plot. To my girls for putting up with a dad who is permanently wittering on about random historical facts.

I would also like to thank the editorial team: Simon for the grammatical and fact checking, Karen and the advanced readers (Dee, Simon, Nick, Sarah, Daniel and Sean) plus all members of the Infinity Engines readers group that continue to support my crazy stories.

Most of all, thank you for reading my work, without you it would never have seen the light of day.

If you would be so kind as to leave a review that would be most appreciated.

Cheers,
Andy x

ABOUT THE AUTHOR

For more information about The Infinity Engines series and other Here Be Dragons books please visit: www. infinityengines.com

Made in the USA
Monee, IL
23 April 2023

32292888R00249